PRAISE

A total delight. If Anthony Trollope wrote a soap opera about a modern royal family, what you'd get is *The Spare.*

— CAT SEBASTIAN, AUTHOR OF *HITHER, PAGE*

Miranda Dubner has created a beautiful intergenerational royal family drama, flawlessly weaving together the various dramas and romances of each character without shying away from difficult topics. You'll fall into the story on the first page—and you'll never want to leave.

— BRINA STARLER, AUTHOR OF *ANNE OF MANHATTAN*

The Spare wrings you out, then fills you up again. It doesn't tug at your heartstrings, it punches. And the scorchingly beautiful queer romance at the center of it all makes it one of my all-time favorites.

— JAIDA JONES, CO-AUTHOR OF THE *HAVEMERCY* SERIES AND *MASTER OF ONE*

THE SPARE

A NOVEL

MIRANDA DUBNER

Copyright © 2020 by Miranda Dubner

ISBN (ebook): 978-1-7348006-8-5

ISBN (print): 978-1-7348006-1-6

First ebook edition: April 14th, 2020

First print edition: July 2020

Cover by Crowglass Design

To my mother and father.

The ravens are now treated almost like royalty. Like the Royals, the ravens live in a palace and are waited on by servants. They are kept at public expense, but in return they must show themselves to the public in settings of great splendour. So long as they abide by certain basic rules, neither Royals nor ravens have to do anything extraordinary. If the power in question is political and diplomatic, the Royals now have hardly more than the ravens.

—Boria Sax, *City of Ravens*

Quoth the raven, "Nevermore."
    —Edgar Allan Poe

1

A string quartet played Vivaldi. His Royal Highness Prince Edward Nicholas William Desmond, second son of Her Majesty Queen Victoria II of England and the Commonwealth, steadied himself against a marble counter. The afterimages of a hundred flashbulbs burned neon in his vision. Those were a fact of life. He could blink them away with the lazy affect he had learned as a child. But the questions shouted by the reporters outside rattled like pinballs in his skull.

"Talk to any old boyfriends lately?"

"D'you know who leaked the photos?"

"Who's the mystery man?"

"Over here, Eddie! How'd Mum take the news you're into boys?"

"Top or bottom, Eddie? The world wants to know!"

The royal family walked red carpets alone, or in pairs, for security reasons. He had arrived separately from the rest of the circus tonight, which left no cover for him. Nothing to do except pretend he didn't hear, even knowing the photographs in tomorrow's papers would broadcast the tension in his body and the lie in his smile all over the world. They were probably being posted online at this very moment, while he hid in a public toilet at the Royal Opera House guarded by two seething close protection officers, with no choice but to carry on.

"All right." He swung around, fully expecting to be addressing himself in the mirror when he opened his eyes. Instead, he was talking to a large arrangement of delphinium and calla lilies. A sudden memory of his grandmother pointing flowers out to him in the botanical gardens jolted painfully in his chest. Mary would have been incensed by this. "She would tell you to pull yourself together. You aren't a disgrace. Your privacy was invaded. You haven't done anything wrong. You will go out there and be a prince. You know how to do that. This doesn't change anything." He turned the doorknob with a harsh, quick flourish.

The wealthiest and best-connected of London society were packed into the opera house like jewel-encrusted sardines, in anticipation of the Royal Ballet's gala premiere of *A Midsummer Night's Dream*. The Queen's attendance ensured a glamorous turnout, especially now that she had a freshly outed son. Every glance carried an edge, from sympathetic and curious to cold and appraising. Royal protocol demanded that no one speak to him unless he initiated conversation, but whispers always carried.

"Surprised he's here—"
"Ladies' man, isn't he?"
"Both at once, probably."
"Should have guessed…"

The cocktail hour crowd parted as he strolled through the lobby and up the stairs, hands thrust casually into the pockets of his bespoke tuxedo. Its clean, modern lines set off his great-grandfather's lacy, silver and gold shirt studs and cuff links, much like his attempt at nonchalant sartorial excellence provided contrast to his desire to smash every wineglass in sight and then run. Tossing back the untamed curls brushing his jacket collar was a meager distraction from hostile, pitying, disappointed stares. *This does not make me shameful,* he wanted to snarl at the disapproving society matrons and their scandalized husbands. *And I am not yours to judge.*

Eddie headed for the champagne bar in the center of Paul Hamlyn Hall as if he didn't have a care in the world, though he felt like a castaway swimming for a life raft. On any other night, he would have been enchanted by the setting. The hall, its vaulted glass ceiling three stories high, had been turned into fairyland for the gala. Live ivy wound with strings of twinkling lights climbed the balcony supports. Each small high-top table and seating arrangement had an arch of flower-laden branches. The walls were covered in fine cloth screened with vines and forest scenes, giving the impression of unending depth.

He was barely managing his usual studied bonhomie. Royals did not worry. They were not anxious. They never had anywhere else they were supposed to be. They were relaxed and attentive at all times. Some amount of self-deprecating discomfort might be written off as humility, but too much of that and they risked tacitly admitting modern royalty was at best extremely silly, and at worst an utter fraud.

Eddie had walked that line with adroit precision for years—there was a reason the press nicknamed him "Prince Charming." But tonight, he had no idea where to put himself. Being in the United States when the story broke, and for the two weeks thereafter, had given him a buffer and room to think. Royalty was a curiosity there, and his appearances were more tightly controlled. In London, drifting among the people who made up his family's social, charitable, and political lives? His panic tasted like a mouthful of coins. He signaled for a glass of champagne at the bar.

Eddie glanced at the perimeter of the room as he took a

sip. Here and there, prowling like wolves at the edges of deep woods, were expressionless men and women in sober black suits. Seeking them out was a coping mechanism of his since childhood. Eddie had grown up with a team of armed minders at the periphery of his awareness. Several barely foiled kidnapping attempts had seen to that. The updates and code names, itineraries and check-ins that bounded his life were a comfort rather than an imposition.

Too old to hide behind his detail, Eddie imagined the radio chatter instead. In the mix would be the voice of the man at his back nearly every day for eight years. Even the dread of his first public social appearance in England since the story broke had been tempered by anticipation. Isaac Cole was somewhere in the building. Eddie hadn't seen him in weeks. Other members of his team had told him that the head of the entire royal protection detail forced his bodyguard to take a holiday while Eddie was in the States. But now they were in the same place again. Eddie long ago stopped trying to convince himself he wasn't thrilled to know that.

"Eddie!" One of only three people here allowed to call his name crashed into his side in a skid of blush silk and fluttering cutouts designed to give the impression of butterflies. He steadied his younger sister with an arm around her waist. They hadn't seen each other since before the pictures came out. She held on to his wrist. He wasn't sure if she meant it as supportive or needed support to stay upright. With Alex, it could be both.

"Sorry, it's these fucking shoes." Princess Alexandra of Wales smiled at him. "I didn't break them in."

"Why not?"

"No time, and I hate scratching up Louboutins."

"Is a pristine red sole worth cracking your head open?"

"Depends on the day. Are you all right?"

"Why wouldn't I be? Questions about my sexual history and orientation yelled at top volume are an extremely pleasant way to begin an evening out." He spoke low enough that only Alex and the hovering bartender heard. He froze, wondering if she'd sell the comment for a few hundred pounds. Or a few thousand, this week. But he caught sight of the tiny rainbow stud in her right ear, and the woman, in her pristine white shirt and black brocade vest, only winced in solidarity as she passed him another flute of champagne. The recognition and the anonymous sympathy were easier to accept than he thought. *Not your fault*, he reminded himself.

"I'll kill them." The force in Alex's voice both buoyed and worried him.

"Please don't. I'd rather not talk about it here."

Alex nodded, hitched herself onto a bar stool. She kept hold of his arm, ostensibly for balance, but he knew better. She wanted to protect him, keep him near her. He pressed his cheek to the portion of her elaborate hairstyle that looked like it might survive the affection, and handed her a glass of her own.

"Then what a pleasure it is to see you, Your Royal Highness. And how are things in our favorite ex-colonies?" She sparkled, violence turned to vivacity in a blink of the eye.

"I think we should take them back. At this point, they'd probably greet us as liberators. Tell Mum, she listens to you."

Alex laughed. It carried, inviting onlookers to enjoy their usual, carefree double act. But she didn't let go of him. They had been close since they were children, despite a five-year age difference. With family, Alex was unwilling to compromise or leave anyone behind. Physically, she took after their mother, with effortlessly creamy skin Eddie only pretended to and an oval face made for stamps and currency. Honey-blonde hair, thick and straight, a hairdresser's dream. Only their unsettling, pale blue-green eyes gave away that they were sister and brother. Their father's eyes. They made her look like a painting. They made him look like a ghost.

Eddie bore an uncanny resemblance to Malcolm Varre, his infamous father. It was one of the many things he wished to ignore tonight. When his parents divorced, he spent a lot of time wishing away his high cheekbones, angular jaw, and widow's peak. Not to mention his indecently pink lips, curling hair, and out of place, clotheshorse body. All hell on a boy trying to live through secondary school, prince or not.

"Mum doesn't listen to anyone but Mum," Alex said. "Sometimes Arthur, probably."

"Well, he is the heir. Where is the daring young man in his flying machine, anyway? Too busy being a hero to attend the ballet?"

"Didn't you get the memo yesterday morning?" Their private secretaries circulated memos among the family whenever something of note occurred, instead of troubling many busy and over-scheduled people with talking to one another. Their grandmother used to call it *Coronation Bleat*.

"Jenny's had her hands full trying to *keep* me from reading my mail. Come on," he said. "What about Arthur?"

A commotion at the hall's entrance interrupted them. Sophia, Duchess of York, the Queen's sister, stalked in wearing a tuxedo of her very own, short hair slicked back, crimson velvet scarf with a deep fringe looped around her neck. A stir went through the assembled as she shunned them all in favor of heading straight for her niece and nephew, kissing them each firmly on both cheeks.

"Children." She took the seat next to Alex and leaned back, one elbow propped on the bar. Her stare was hard as she looked past them, over Eddie's shoulder. "How are we tonight?"

"Been worse." Eddie's lopsided smile was in danger of slipping off his face and crashing to the floor.

"I heard what went on out there. It's disgraceful." She hissed the final word.

"We're trying not to dwell," Alex said.

"Why would we dwell?" Sophie's voice was flat. "Who could have predicted that the press would respond in such an appalling fashion? Why should we mind?"

"Is that why you're dressed like Julie Andrews' understudy in the national tour of *Victor/Victoria*? Don't look at me that way. I'm publicly bisexual now, I'll make all the musical theatre references I please. I'll belt Cole Porter songs prancing on top of this bar if I want to."

Sophie snorted into her champagne flute. "Do that, Edward. But let me get my phone out first. I'll sell the footage to the Daily Mail for fifty thousand pounds and leave this tawdry life behind. Now cheer up. The pictures were hardly your idea. What were you talking about?"

"Alex was about to tell me why Arthur isn't here tonight."

"Oh, that will lighten the mood." She snagged an hors d'oeuvre off the tray of a passing waiter, gesturing in a magnanimous fashion for them to carry on. Sophie's role as public ringleader was one she took seriously.

"His Group Captain's died," Alex said, in an undertone. "The funeral is tomorrow, but he's gone up today to be with his unit."

"God. Was he sick? Did anyone know?"

"It was quite a shock." Alex accepted Sophie's offer of a second glass of champagne; Eddie waved her off.

"Dreadful business," Sophie said. "Arthur won't have long now. There's been pressure to ground him for years. Every time your mother gets a cold they all start braying about how irresponsible it is for Arthur to be in active service. If word ever got out—"

She cut herself off. They might have insulated themselves in a cone of protocol at the end of the bar, but the Prince of

Wales flying combat missions in the Middle East was a state secret. It only went on because of the Queen's approval, and the refusal of Group Captain Willoughby Miles to give anyone under his command preferential treatment. Arthur was an exceptional pilot, so he had his missions like all the rest, and promotion on merit to Squadron Leader when he qualified for it. Eddie remembered how proud his normally reticent brother had been to earn that extra stripe.

"It's past time for him to hang up his flight harness," Sophie went on. "He's thirty-one years old. The RAF was never supposed to be his career."

"He loves it." Alex had an edge in her voice, and Eddie touched her elbow. She leaned against him for a second, only the hint of a flounce in the motion. Message received, then. "He can't sit around the palace his whole life, waiting for The Inevitable." Most children probably didn't learn inflected euphemisms for their mother's death and the line of succession from birth, but the Kensingtons couldn't afford to ignore the ramifications. Ever.

"Of course not," Sophie said, in her impatient way. "But there are activities better suited to a future king in this day and age, and he should acquaint himself with them."

"Come on." Eddie became aware of the growing number of people, as they waited for the true main event of the evening to occur. "We can't do anything for or about Arthur right now."

Sophie finally got around to giving him a once-over.

"We're practically twins, Eddie."

"Oh, nearly. And the red scarf is symbolic of…?"

Sophie fiddled with the heavy, fringed velvet. "Rob will be here tonight."

"Your ancient mating rituals mean nothing to me, thank god," he said. Sophie wagged a finger at him.

"Do you think it'll work?" she asked, ironic smile only

imperfectly masking an insecurity she never seemed to shake about Admiral Robert Helmsley. "We've hardly spoken in months." The solid, quiet Navy man was Sophie's opposite, dedicated and somber. Eddie had never known him to laugh without Sophie there. Their decades-long, on again-off again relationship would be a running joke in the family as well as the tabloids if the two of them weren't so serious about it.

"It's unfair of you to bait him with a tuxedo. He'll be a hopeless case."

"Maleficent at twelve o'clock," Alex whispered, with real pain. Her hand tightened on his forearm.

"And she's dressing the part." Sophie's expression soured. Eddie shifted so that his back was no longer to the room.

Helena Wallace wore a black silk gown, tight on top, with an undulating hem, calling to mind any number of animated villainesses. But Eddie knew the comparison was faulty. She couldn't be defeated by a trident or a sword. If only.

As always, a dull ache spread through Eddie at the sight of her. Helena had been his mother's best friend, their welcome guest on family holidays, often found at their weekend breakfasts, back when that was something they did. She was ever up for a chat or a horseback ride. She was in the inner circle—*was* the inner circle. Her career in society journalism had been assured from the very beginning, with her unparalleled, informal access to the royal family. But that hadn't been enough for her. Investigative work was her real passion, uncovering scandal and punishing corruption. Capable of pretending legendary sympathy, she got movie stars and politicians to admit things in front of BBC cameras that they would never tell their mothers.

And as for the Kensingtons? They all relied on her. Loved her. She took Alex shopping. Made Eddie smile. Listened to Arthur. Glamorous, polished, and still up for stretching out on the rug in front of the fireplace and playing a board game,

Helena filled the gaps Victoria's schedule left in her children's lives. And, as it turned out, in Victoria's marriage as well.

Eddie caught Sophie's eye and tilted his head at Alex, whose knuckles were now white on the sleeve of his tuxedo. Sophie linked her arm through Alex's. "I think I see Rob, dearest. Come along. He's sure to have brought some likely lieutenants with him for seasoning, you can scare the wits out of them."

Alex hung on to Eddie for the briefest moment, then went with Sophie and didn't look back. Alex took Helena and Malcolm's twin betrayals hard. She had been only ten years old when both of them disappeared from Buckingham Palace.

Helena's relationship with the disgraced former husband of the Queen of England might have tarnished her household name, but in London's rarefied social and professional worlds, the power players were far too afraid of what she might know about them to blackball her. If any of them cared in the first place.

Her chandelier earrings and matching bracelets caught the light. Eddie wondered bitterly if his father had picked them out for her himself, or merely paid for them. Royal observers speculated—not loudly, but loudly enough—that perhaps Malcolm had been allowed to keep the title and holdings of the Duke of Edinburgh as long as he never made Helena the Duchess. But in the twelve years since the Queen's former husband and former confidante were photographed arriving at the opera together in public, Malcolm's hand at the small of Helena's back, neither one of them seemed inclined to get married.

Eddie didn't put it past his mother's lawyers to slide something like that into the innumerable agreements, both official and not, that governed the dissolution of his parents' marriage. It had been the first divorce of a reigning monarch since Henry VIII and Anne of Cleves. The world was riveted, then frustrated, by how amicable it appeared to be. Eddie sometimes thought they would have been better off to break the shell and leave nothing to the imagination. It had been unthinkable then, and impossible now. Nothing to gain by causing a scene.

Tonight, with camera flashes still burning the insides of his eyelids, all Eddie wanted was a scene.

Rage followed Eddie's sorrow when he saw her. It broadened his shoulders, put steel in his spine. At least with Helena he knew where he stood—on quicksand. Especially with the suspicions he couldn't shake clamoring for attention in his head.

She drew up alongside him and motioned to the bartender. The tilt of her head, the way she leaned that slight bit towards him, she was baiting him into conversation. Eddie knew he should walk away, that this was reckless, and stupid, and probably futile. But he had to *know*.

"Here for a quote, then?" Such a foolish opening gambit with a player like Helena. She gave him a pitying smile, as if to say *Why would you try something so clumsy?*

"Good evening, Your Royal Highness. Cozy this evening, isn't it?"

"Us and two thousand of our closest friends."

"And how is Britain's favorite prince?"

"Arthur is quite well. And you? Still doing a dishonest day's work, raking in the muck?"

"I prefer to think of myself as providing a valuable public service." Her diamonds shimmered as she accepted a glass of champagne over the polished gold and black bar. "Unlike those bottom feeders who invaded your privacy so disgustingly."

He didn't move, didn't even narrow his eyes. "I didn't know you cared."

"The situation is abominable. I've said so in print." The calculating glitter in her eyes matched her earrings.

"A few column inches reminding people how you used to

be part of the family, combined with the vague implication that my sexuality was 'obvious' from childhood, heaped with a healthy dose of disapproval for my mother's parenting techniques. You've been quite generous." Eddie's personal assistant had not been wholly successful in shielding him from the news.

"You should be thanking me."

"As if I ever would."

"Any port in a storm, Edward."

"I'd rather drown."

"Then you're getting your wish. Lucky little Prince. But I could help you, if you were to sit down with me. Give you an out."

The sensation of helplessness didn't ease, but now he felt raw and white-hot inside. "I think you've done more than enough outing of me."

Helena's veneer cracked as soon as the words were out of his mouth. He saw the surprise, the admiration bending into approval in her expression. With a sickening lurch in his gut, he knew his suspicions were right. She'd done it. She had been the one to dig out and release the photos of him cuddled up tight to a university boyfriend, adoration plain on his face. To expose a vulnerable moment in a way that invited criticism and the worst kind of public speculation when she knew how much harm it would do.

"I will never, ever understand you. It wasn't enough that you were family? We loved you, and you capitalized on anguish you helped cause to sell newspapers, at the expense of children. And you're still doing it."

"You're not a child now. And you should thank me," she repeated. "You don't have to hide any more."

"That was my decision." Eddie could hardly breathe through the haze of shame and his own stupidity. Desperate for safety he could never have and hardly believed in. As if, by wishing, he could make the past a terrible dream.

A tall shadow appeared at his elbow. "Your presence is required upstairs, sir." Rafael Harris regarded Helena with a barely professional chill in his eyes.

"Mummy's calling?" Helena's voice was purposefully light, but it had thorns in it. "And you, surrounded by all these beautiful men. How have you managed without compromising yourself?" Her tone was too knowing. Eddie went hot all over except for the icicle of fear inserting itself between his ribs. *She doesn't know anything about your feelings*, he reminded himself. *She's fishing, that's all.* He lurched back into the moment, the chatter and the perfume reasserting themselves. He was a prince. He was a Kensington. He had to believe that mattered more than his own pain.

"I don't know, Helena. Compromising oneself is more your style. Enjoy the ballet."

Eddie turned to go, and saw his father. Malcolm wasn't supposed to be here tonight. But there he stood, in conversation with an acquaintance, glancing at Eddie. Malcolm's pleasant expression sharpened into a grin when their eyes met, and for half a second Eddie wanted to return it. But something about insults and injuries stopped him. Harris spoke quietly into his wrist mic and interposed his body between Eddie and the crowd.

"We'll go up Victoria's Stairs," Harris said. Eddie let the hand on his back guide him to the private staircase built for his great-great-great-great-grandmother, so that none of her subjects would see her laboring in all her finery on her way to the royal box. Friezes of operatic scenes decorated the walls, and a succession of crystal chandeliers hung from the high ceilings.

Eddie stopped on the first landing, gripping one of the velvet-covered banisters.

"You need to tell Mother he's here," he said. "I don't want her to be surprised, or, god, Alex."

"It's been done, sir."

Eddie swallowed, trying to breathe calmly. "May I ask a question?"

"Of course."

"Have I ever made you feel uncomfortable?" He forced himself to meet Harris's gaze. Attractive yet forgettable, Harris often took point at these gatherings. He looked like James Bond's kid brother in a tux, more like a social secretary than a trained killer with his open face and easy, quiet manner. Harris specialized in knives. Now he looked like he wanted to use them.

"Not for a single minute." Harris glanced left and right, then held his hand out, as if they were going to shake on it. Eddie tentatively fit his long, knobbly fingers around Harris's palm. Harris pressed them, hard. "I've been on your team for the last two years. You have never done or said anything that made me feel the least bit uneasy for any reason. You are a joy to protect. Never try to duck us, never cause trouble. I think if anyone fired on us you would probably try to jump in front of *me*."

"She leaked the photos," Eddie whispered. "I'm not sure how, or if it even matters. But she had it done."

"It's not your fault." Harris let go of his hand. "If there were anything to do, we would do it. Unfortunately, we're only allowed to kill for you under very specific circumstances."

"Thank you." Eddie tried to smile. "Everything feels utterly pointless at this moment. And I know I should be going up those stairs, but…"

"Please don't let that woman poison you against yourself." Harris clasped Eddie's shoulder. "Would you like me to get Cole off the roof?"

Eddie rubbed his forehead. He wanted Isaac more than anything. But he also didn't want to need him. "No. Thank you."

Harris waited a beat, then raised his wrist to his mouth. "Harris here, coming up with Curly."

Eddie winced, wrinkled his nose, getting himself back to normal with a well-worn complaint.

"Can't I have a code name that sounds even halfway interesting? Like Viper. Or Sex Bomb." Harris blew air through his nose in his on-duty laugh. Eddie preferred his off-duty laugh, which sounded like a barking seal.

"That might prove confusing in a tactical situation." Harris kept his fingertips in the small of Eddie's back as they climbed the second flight of stairs. Two close protection officers from Victoria's detail guarded the entrance to the Royal Box and its adjoining suite, where a cocktail party was going on. Eddie nodded to them. Gunny Jones, the head of Victoria's security detail, poked her head out of the suite to confirm his presence with her own eyes.

"Good to see you at last, sir," she said. There was deep sympathy in her eyes, the same as he'd been getting from most people who worked for his family since his return home. It made him feel wildly ill at ease. Usually they ignored everything that went on, and the Kensingtons relied on that veneer of normality to remind themselves of their responsibilities. But there were situations, Sir Anthony Pritchard—his mother's Private Secretary and one of the most powerful men in England—once told him during the divorce, that transcended discretion, and must be acknowledged with grace. *Not your fault, not your fault, not your fault.* "Will you be joining us? Princess Alex and the Duchess of York are already here."

Eddie wrapped himself in the thickest, strongest, most impenetrable layer of *Prince of the Realm* he could conjure. Two dozen or so luminaries of society and the theatre world, basking in the reflected glow of their sovereign's—his mother's —approval were hardly going to be his most difficult room.

Gunny ushered him through the door, into the flow of ever-so-polite conversation.

The looks he received from men and women were more openly flirtatious and appraising than usual, which set him back nearly as much as scorn would have. Alex tucked her hand into his elbow and stayed glued to his side, clearly feeling guilty for abandoning him earlier. Eddie was nervous for a different reason now.

Victoria, deep in conversation with the directors of the Royal Opera and the Royal Ballet, was resplendent in a pale blue column of a gown that delicately brushed her figure. The neckline, while not too low, still left plenty of room for her sparkling teardrop diamond-and-sapphire jewelry. Her hair was pulled off her face into a gentle style around a matching tiara. She was the most elegant woman in the room without ever seeking to dazzle. He had the oddest urge to run up and ask for a hug. When their eyes met, she didn't react at all. It gutted him, but he knew his insides were made of gaps where his mother was concerned. He tried to wear it lightly, especially now that he knew for a fact that he had been compromised by her former best friend. It would cut her to the core if she knew. He resolved that she wouldn't find out from him.

The house lights dimmed. The Queen's guests went to find their seats, giving the family time to collect themselves before their official appearance in the royal box.

Usually Victoria liked to center herself silently, no matter how much fuss Sophie and Alex created between them before an entrance, but tonight she reached out and took Eddie's hand. "It's good to see you."

"Dad's here," he blurted out. In case she didn't know. In case there hadn't been time to inform her. A flicker in her smooth expression, and she inclined her head.

"I know, dear. Gunny told me. It's all right. You're looking very well." The last statement, almost a question, carried the weight of a command.

"As well as can be expected."

"You'll come through it," she said, and he didn't know which of them she was trying to convince. The rumble of the audience subsided, reminding the royal family that they had a job to do. Victoria only let go of his hand when the orchestra struck up "God Save the Queen."

"They're playing my song," she murmured. It might have been his own frazzled mental state, but he thought he heard an apology buried in the words. The door to the box was opened for her by an attendant. Victoria faced the roaring applause of over two thousand people alone.

Eddie looked around at his family, taking in Alex's determination, Sophie's impatience. Arthur's absence. His own nauseated terror of disappointing everyone gave way in the face of knowing there was no escape. The thought of Isaac somewhere nearby made it easier to breathe. He took his sister's arm and they went together into the spotlight and the storm of noise.

2

By the time Isaac Cole stepped into the Royal Opera House, the lobby was almost deserted. Three weeks of enforced holiday behind him, a pile of books and a personal best in a half-marathon later, he was back where he belonged. "Cole here." He spoke into his wrist mic. "Outer perimeter check complete." A few latecomers hurried by, made nervous by the overture coming from inside the theatre and the armed men and women guarding its doors. He catalogued and dismissed them.

"Harris here. Take Victoria's Stairs." Harris sounded tense, a far cry from his usual ironic lightness. He had the polish Cole lacked, the love child of F. Scott Fitzgerald and Hugh Grant, born with the skill to move in crowds like these without shouldering through them, chip first.

Cole told himself it was a trick of the night that he thought he could smell Eddie's cologne on the staircase. Harris met him on the landing, pointed at his earpiece and drew a finger over his throat. Cole turned off his mic. Harris caught him up on the last few weeks, capping the recitation with Helena Wallace practically telling Eddie outright that she had leaked the photos.

"Fuck. I should have flown out when the story broke."

"Even before Wallace got her claws into him, he wasn't doing well." The two men stood in silence, while the muffled sound of the orchestra bled through the walls. "He'll go to pieces if he sees you."

"I'll make myself scarce, then. I have the tuck-in shift, anyway. Better this way."

Harris watched him more carefully than Cole was comfortable with. They were close, or what passed for close between men like them. They understood each other. Both had killed for their country and lived to never tell the tale. "This is one hell of a job," was all Harris said. "We're with them nearly every waking minute, and for what? So we can refrain from punishing the people who hurt them, in the name of civilization."

"We're not civilized," Cole said. "That's why we have the job."

"Speak for yourself. I know which fork to use."

"So do I. It's the salad fork for maiming, the meat fork if you want to put someone down."

Their quiet joking blunted the edge of being essentially powerless against most threats their protectee had to face in the world. They were for the easy problems. The deadly ones. Not the slow drip of misery. They went up to the corridor outside the royal box together, meeting up with Shannon Kimsey and Michael Taggart, the head of Princess Alexandra's detail. Kimsey had been on Eddie's detail for less than a year.

"Crawling around in the vents, were you?" she asked.

"Up in the flies," he said. "Can't be too careful in opera houses, you know. There might be phantoms."

"Not until the Paris trip next month," she said. "I'll let you know if my dreams are troubled by falling chandeliers and musical geniuses in masks."

"Please don't remind me. If Curly watches that movie one more time I'll have to be committed."

"How did anyone ever think he *wasn't*—" Kimsey shut up when she saw Cole's glare.

"Were you going to say something about stereotypical pastimes of queer men as it pertains to your principal?"

"No." Her voice was very small.

"Good." He refused to look away until she did. "No sleeping on the job tonight," Cole said, line open to the whole team. "We're working the ballet, not watching it."

For him that meant patrolling inside the opera house, every short burst of conversation from all three teams a routine cacophony in his ear. "Watch out for those phantoms," Kimsey murmured as he left in an apology he appreciated for Eddie more than himself. Some of the dancers gave him speculative looks as he slipped through the wings, his white shirt a beacon in the backstage dark. One blew him a kiss. Cole shook his head and grinned, moving on.

Making his silent way along a catwalk over the stage, he could just see into the royal box. And in it—Eddie. Illuminated by the spill of golden light off the stage, face rapt as he watched the performance, refusing to acknowledge that more of the audience was looking at him than the ballet.

Cole had joined his detail eight years ago, a former SAS operative turned undercover agent for MI5 with enough blackout tape in his file to satisfy the most nervous Whitehall bureaucrat. Pulled off the street one afternoon by New Scotland Yard while working undercover—standard procedure when MI5 needed to speak to one of their agents—he was put in a conference room with the Queen's Private Secretary and offered a job as bodyguard to Prince Edward, who needed someone who could blend in with him at university. Cole hardly qualified for that, but Sir Anthony was almost persuasive enough. The lure of living under his own name did the rest.

The first time Cole met his protectee, in a drawing room at Buckingham Palace, the hope radiating from the young prince made him feel lightheaded. The posh teenager with the messy hair and the perfectly tailored clothes lit up with a wondering, enthusiastic smile when he saw his new bodyguard. He practically bounced on his toes as he crossed the room, holding his hand out, already trusting that this complete stranger would never let him be hurt. Would, in fact, keep his secrets and go with him anywhere. A partner in crime and a protector, all in one.

I can't do this, Cole remembered thinking. *Not a chance.*

"Isaac Cole?" The prince's voice was breathy, deeper than Cole expected. A voice made for playing the leads on 1930s radio shows. He sounded like The Shadow should have. He was still holding out his hand, waiting for Cole to catch up.

"Your Royal Highness." They shook. There was some kind of jolt through Cole's midsection. Nerves, probably.

"Please, call me Eddie." The prince beamed. Actually beamed, as if he were a lighthouse. Cole hadn't been aware he lived in a storm until that moment.

He told himself he could walk away at any time, go back to undercover work. But on that warm afternoon, Eddie charted a course through the rocks, and Cole had followed him without question ever since.

Eddie's hard shell of self-possession was firmly in place now, but Cole knew where he kept his tension so that no one else could see it. The prince's shoulders would hurt him tonight. It was a fact of life for Cole, like knowing the fingers of his own right hand would ache before a rainstorm. But no matter how familiar Eddie's moods and body language were, that jolt of impossible, baseless recognition whenever Cole saw him had never gone away.

Cole forced himself into motion again, nodding to a theatre tech holding a giant bag of confetti for the finale. The second half passed without incident.

As the final notes from the orchestra died away, and the applause rose, Cole kept to the plan. It wasn't easy to walk away from the royal box. Not when Cole knew how raw Eddie must be, with those pictures out in the world. Cole had been outside the room when they were taken. He remembered how happy Eddie had been, rosy-cheeked from blushing, untroubled for once by what he wanted or who he liked. To have it turned on him in this particular way was more than an insult. It had been meant to wound, and wound deeply. Cole stopped his fingers from clenching into fists.

Harris inclined his head as Cole passed him, going for the back stairs. "I have Curly," he said.

Cole nodded. His steps slowed when he heard the bustle of a dozen people coming into the hallway, laughing and chattering away. Everyone orbited Her Majesty as she left the royal box on the arm of the Royal Opera Director. Victoria had an aura about her, some magic that scandal and time didn't tarnish.

"I am so greatly looking forward to meeting the principals," she said to her companion. "Edward and Alexandra have quite upset the old order of things. I remember when they had an earlier bedtime than I did. Now it's later, and for much the same reason—so I have time to put my feet up." The genteel humor, the Queen laughing at herself, allowed for an answering smile and immediate demurring from the dapper man in the red bow tie. Victoria left no room for any response except the one she wanted.

"Oh, Mother," Alexandra said, in that offhand, loving tone she took with her mother in public. But Cole's attention was caught by a familiar laugh, a genuine one. *He must be talking to Sophie,* he thought, the only person in that crowd Eddie felt comfortable with besides his sister. The sound jumped for an instant above the hum of the crowd retreating down the hall. Cole's face remained impassive as he kept walking away, as the longing hit, as the needle fell into the worn groove Eddie occupied in his heart.

THEIR ROYAL HIGHNESSES left the gala reception a quarter of an hour before the festivities officially ended. The late Queen Mother had been fond of shooing her grandchildren out in front of her while proclaiming "Kensingtons don't straggle," in carrying tones. Not for them to close down the bar, to emerge into the cool night with bow ties hanging open and shoes dangling from their fingers. No, they strolled the paparazzi gauntlet to their cars, all smiles. Victoria got into the first car, heading back to Buckingham Palace. Once she was gone, the lightning storm of camera flashes and questions shouted to Eddie picked up. A few of the reporters found time to direct attention at Alex, as well, about her supposed relationship with a pop star. Eddie wasn't sure which one she was supposed to be dating at the moment, but it hardly mattered. Alex didn't date anyone. Rob Helmsley walked out with them, which was unusual. Eddie never blamed him for avoiding being seen with the royal family, but he clearly had other things on his mind tonight than protecting his reputation. His arm went around Sophie as soon as the car door was shut. Must have been the tux, Eddie thought.

Alex let out an exhausted groan. "I envy Arthur his fighter planes." She turned sideways in her seat, taking advantage of the tinted glass to throw her ankles over Eddie's legs. She didn't have to bother with a pleading look. As she and Rob began discussing the performances, Eddie released her feet from her strappy heels. Sophie checked her watch and pressed the button to roll down the partition.

"Yes, ma'am?" A light, quiet voice, more familiar to Eddie than his own, spoke right next to his ear. He snapped to attention. *Isaac.*

"Is there a reason we're still sitting here?" Sophie asked.

"Too many shows getting out in the West End. An alternate route to Kensington Palace is being cleared." Eddie felt like such a cliché, because he really was happy to listen to Isaac deliver the traffic report.

"And this couldn't have been foreseen? With clocks? And maths?"

"We could just take the Tube," Eddie said. "No one would notice, right?"

"I'm not putting those shoes on again," Alex said. The town car pulled out.

Eddie, from his position in the rear-facing seat, leaned closer to Isaac. "Heard a rumor you were skulking about," he said. The corner of Isaac's mouth lifted. "How was Paris?"

Isaac lowered his voice. "It was Paris. You know. Beautiful...for lovers...always a good idea."

"Did you eat some *pain au chocolat*?"

"Never without you." Isaac had no idea what his favorite food was when he joined Eddie's detail. Eddie inveigled him into trying all sorts of different things. When Isaac took a bite of his first chocolate-filled croissant, the expression on his face was all Eddie needed to see.

"You could have made an exception."

The driver murmured a question Eddie didn't catch before Isaac could reply, and the partition slid up. Eddie settled back, and found Sophie observing him.

Sophie had lived all over the world, in a succession of warm and expensive places, for most of Eddie's childhood. She hadn't made a secret of her belief that royal duties were roaring wastes of time and did not apologize for avoiding them, and consequently her family, at all costs. When she did come back—infrequently and never for long—she was an excellent playmate. Eddie had loved her vitality and the freedom she embodied, a far cry from his own careful, buttoned-up persona, even as a child.

But during the bleakest part of his parents' separation, when Eddie and Alex went back and forth to school in a cordon of protection officers to fend off the tabloid photographers—Malcolm gone, Victoria withdrawn so far into herself that she barely spoke except for government business, Alex refusing to leave her side when she wasn't marched off to school, Arthur away at Eton, Helena inexplicably vanished, Grandmother doing her best to keep up appearances—they arrived home one afternoon to a commotion in the private entrance to Buckingham Palace. Sophie was in the front hall, wearing a sarong and a bikini top under the uniform jacket of a British Airways pilot. A light dusting of sand still clung to her legs. She barked orders at the shocked footmen and harried butler. When she saw her niece and nephew, she flung out her arms and dared Alex not to hug her. Smelling like sun and tanning oil, she drew Eddie in too. He still remembered the consuming relief of seeing her.

Sophie had told them to "Go eat a snack or whatever it is you do," and strode up the stairs to find Victoria. A few minutes later, the noise of his aunt, mother, and grandmother all arguing together echoed through the family apartments. It was the first hopeful sound Eddie had heard in months. Sophie's presence immediately changed things. She dragged them out of the house, arranging movie screenings and museum visits. She became their rock, and no one seemed more surprised than her that she managed it. Eddie and Alex's bond with her was forever cemented.

Which meant Eddie would not hide whatever Sophie saw in him at this moment, even if she did seem uneasy, appraising. He lifted his chin and looked out the window at the passing city lights for the rest of the ride.

Upon arrival at Kensington Palace, Isaac headed across the courtyard to the security office. Eddie certainly did not watch him go: a trim, muscled figure in a suit that blended too well into the night. Alex leaned on Eddie as she walked to the door without shoes on. He envied her. His oxfords pinched. They left Sophie and Rob in the foyer, sparring about the artistic merit of the Mendelssohn Wedding March. Alex slid along the black-and-white checked marble floor in her stockinged feet. She was staying the night in one of Sophie's guest bedrooms.

"Bet you lunch at the tearoom Rob's still here in the morning," Alex said. Sophie and Rob doing their best impression of a pair of fractious teenagers didn't sway her from firm belief in their love.

"I'm not taking that bet," Eddie said. "She's got that look."

"As if you noticed anything in the car but every time Cole turned his head."

Eddie usually enjoyed Alex's teasing about his connection with Isaac. It felt like proof his feelings existed. But tonight he felt sick. Somehow, he'd managed to come through a forcible outing with more to hide, not less.

"Damn it, Alex," he said, dropping his head back. The carved plaster ceilings had no comfort to give. "I'll have to be even more circumspect in public now. Let me talk to him in the car, will you?"

"What's changed?"

"Oh, come on. Before, I was just unusually dependent on him. Now, if it seems like I have some sort of crush? They'll all pick up on it."

"But you—" Alex didn't finish the sentence when she saw the look on his face.

"Leave it, all right?"

Alex nodded slowly, looking as lost as he felt. She hugged him tightly. "Don't have to worry about creasing your suit now," she said. He put his arms around her and kissed her still perfect hair.

"Never."

"Lunch tomorrow?" she asked, trying to lighten the mood.

"I think I'm going north, see if I can't crash a funeral."

Alex raised her eyebrows, but didn't comment on his travel plans. "Day after next, then. I am going to collect."

"I wouldn't expect anything else."

Eddie put his hands in his pockets, watching her disappear down the hall in a last flutter of silk. He smiled wanly at Harris as they headed down the corridor.

"Thank you for extracting me earlier," he told Harris. "You fought a dragon for me."

"I wouldn't give Ms. Wallace the advantage of flight, sir," he said. "But it is an honor to serve in any way." His blue eyes were steady and warm. Comforting, in their way, if not the eyes Eddie wanted. They were the best he expected to get tonight.

"Will you tell the team to coordinate with Arthur's for the trip? I don't want to cause trouble."

"No trouble at all. I believe Finnery and Jones are on the roster for tomorrow, they like a long car ride. Cole and I are on in the evening."

"Thanks. I hope you have a good day. What would you like from the tea room? Alex will insist on insisting."

"I'm partial to the lemon meringue tartlets," Harris said.

Eddie's smile brightened. "Your bowing to the inevitable is appreciated."

"Long experience, sir."

"Good night, Harris," he said.

"Good night," Harris murmured. He closed the door, and

Eddie was alone. Alone always happened so suddenly. One minute a carousel of fuss and protocol, then walk through a door and it was just him and his flat.

While Eddie was at university, some pipes burst in the old carriage houses attached to Kensington Palace. In the ensuing remodel, several modern flats were created, intended for long-term staff. Eddie surprised his mother and Sir Anthony by asking if he might commandeer one after he graduated. The request had been granted, and he fitted the place out with the help of an architect and interior designer who respected his taste. They created a sleek penthouse with a decidedly untraditional open plan layout. He could cook for himself when he had the time, a film or football game on the television in the lounge area. A soft, charcoal gray sectional couch, a deep brown leather club chair, and open shelving along two walls, filled with books, completed the look. The original beamed ceilings remained. It felt like a home for a normal sort of person instead of a museum. If that normal sort of person happened to have a Rothko hanging on the wall over the electric fireplace, of course. A Rothko his father had given him for his eighteenth birthday.

Home. Three weeks of buzzing, raw anger coupled with exhaustion overwhelmed him. He wasn't even startled by the sight of a man in a tuxedo standing at the foot of the stairs. Not alone, after all.

"Eddie."

"Hi."

Isaac's face was in shadow, but Eddie could read the concern, the offer in his eyes. And all for him. That this experienced, highly trained, and often tested former soldier was so willing to be affectionate with him—and no one else—had been a heady, dangerous reality since the beginning. A bodyguard shouldn't rouse so many feelings in his protectee. Especially now. But when Isaac held his hand out, Eddie went without hesitation. Isaac met him halfway, and they came together in an embrace that shut out the rest of the world.

They hadn't done this in years, not since he was barely out of his teens, and much more fragile. But Eddie remembered what to do, how they worked it out. Eddie slid his arms under Isaac's jacket, hands finding the straps of Isaac's underarm holster and gripping tight. The strangest things became comforting. Like the fact of someone prepared to die for him, to do damage on his behalf when he could only smile, absorb the lies and half-truths, the statements out of context, any unguarded word or gesture magnified beyond belief. In the secret history of attempts on his safety, of stalkers, of former servants and false friends ready to expose anything about the royals they could find out, Isaac Cole was an instrument of vengeance. Seldom used, but unwavering.

"I'm sorry," Isaac said. "I should have been there."

"You were on holiday," Eddie whispered.

"No. The night the pictures were taken. Should have wiped his phone. I didn't know."

Eddie remembered that night, his first year at Cambridge, with a boy he *liked*, a boy he maybe could *have*, after a life of pretending he wasn't interested, jealously watching his school friends disappear into broom closets or disused stairwells, emerging with reddened lips and shifty expressions, but he couldn't even do *that* because he was a fucking *prince*. He'd told Isaac to wait outside the door so he could be normal for five minutes, and look what happened.

"You don't have anything to apologize for. It's me—I told you to stay outside, didn't I? I fucked it up, I did this—"

"It wasn't your fault." Isaac said it, and Eddie finally believed it. Wrapped in Isaac's attention, held in his arms, he could finally admit that this was what he'd been wanting, needing, for the last few weeks. He felt sick, like he was betraying everything Isaac stood for by being so greedy. Taking advan-

tage. Eddie was no longer a traumatized nineteen-year-old,
and he couldn't stand so close. He pulled away, practically
making a run for the stairs.

"I'm going to take a shower," he called.

"I'll be here when you get out."

Eddie took the stairs two at a time.

"YOU'RE AN IRRESPONSIBLE FOOL," Cole told himself. He went
to the windows overlooking the garden, leaning his forehead on
the frame. The chatter through his earpiece was calm. He took
a deep breath, and then another, trying to let go of the strong
urge to leave and find the fucker who not only took those
pictures but sold them, and hang him up by his thumbs. But
Cole could no more stalk into the night to commit mayhem on
behalf of a Prince of England than he could go upstairs, get
into the shower, and wash Eddie's hair.

The water hissed on. Eddie would have undressed by now,
laid his tuxedo out on the table in his dressing room for his
valet to take care of in the morning. Cole imagined steam
rising from the state-of-the-art rain shower as Eddie stepped in,
getting soaked immediately, turning his face up to the spray. He
showered whenever he got home from a public appearance, no
matter when that was. Reaching for the fruity, lush scents he
preferred at the end of the night, and the sea sponges he liked.
They were too rough for Isaac's taste, but he knew discomfort
was sometimes Eddie's only way of reminding himself he was
real.

All the things he knew after so many years. The way Eddie
fixed his tea (piping hot, sweet and milky), his favorite way to
work off frustration (the heavy bag in the security team's
weight room), what he looked like when he was sad, angry,
overjoyed, and so much more. Most of what Isaac knew went

beyond description. Feelings and impressions, the result of years of smiles, abrupt conversations, and endless watching.

Cole had turned down multiple promotions, which Eddie knew nothing about. When convenient to Eddie's schedule, he left for the day to train new protection officers, running through hand-to-hand combat drills and takedown scenarios in a castle or an airplane, but that was all. He had no desire to move up. He would rather stand guard in the rain outside a new restaurant owned by an up-and-coming protégé of Gordon Ramsay's, man the wall during yet another benefit gala for yet another charity, be stationed at the back of the royal box at a West End opening. Or fly out to New York City or Paris for their Fashion Weeks, wading through designers and publicists and models as Eddie and Alex cut their usual, super-fashionable swath. Protect a subtly different Eddie in each of those situations, some other facet of his charming, beautiful, public face brought to the fore. He would watch any Eddie as long as he could. But his preference was to be on the tuck-in shift, which endeared him greatly to the rest of his team. They had families, significant others, lives. Isaac had this.

A clock in the foyer chimed the hour, and he straightened, double-checking his watch. One in the morning. He heard the shower go off, the faint sound of drawers opening and closing. Eddie closed cabinet doors, never left clothes strewn about unless he was ill. Every Eddie he knew was considerate of the people around him, especially if they couldn't speak up for themselves.

Eddie clattered down the stairs in pajama bottoms so old and faded the gray and blue plaid looked more like a suggestion than a pattern. The hot pink t-shirt from his sister's birthday party last year, "ALEX 21" emblazoned on the back, stretched over his shoulders and the slight curve of a belly that he had long since stopped trying to get rid of. His wet hair curled wildly around his face, dripping on his shoulders.

Cole saw it all in the hazy, dim reflection in the window. Of every version of himself Eddie had tried on and kept, refined, or discarded over the years, this one was the most precious to him. This was his Eddie, the one only he got to see. Eddie maintained a professional distance with most of his detail. Cole was different. That thought pleased him. Because he was an irresponsible fool.

Eddie padded barefoot into the kitchen and turned the kettle on. He relaxed that final, precious bit. Then their eyes met in the window. Eddie grinned, and Cole saw all the reasons he should have been off this detail, out of this job, years ago. No matter what he wanted. Or maybe because of what he wanted. Three weeks without contact should have no effect whatsoever on either of them. You maintained your distance or you died. Or worse, your protectee died. That's what had been drummed into him since his first day of training. What he drummed into new officers on training missions. Hypocrite that he was.

"I have to go."

Eddie shoved his hands into his pockets. The familiar gesture of buried disappointment dragged down the waistband of his trousers, revealing the slight dark trail of hair on his stomach. Isaac couldn't breathe. "Have a good night, then," Eddie offered. No petulance. No trying to get him to stay. And Isaac would have. Had, in the past. Put up his feet on Eddie's extremely comfortable couch, watch the footie, talk quietly into the night like friends might do. Eddie might get closer, press into his side, fall asleep against him. But they'd gotten too old for all that.

Isaac left Eddie standing alone in the kitchen, reaching for a mug. He walked into the night through the garden doors, resisting the urge to look back.

"Curly's in. Cole out. Goodnight, all. Overnight shift, you have him now."

3

Buckingham Palace—impossible to heat, expensive to maintain, wired by countless electricians fueled by hope alone—bore drafty, silent witness to the heartbreaks of several hundred years of British royalty. Victoria stared at her mother's collection of photographs, set out on the wide Chippendale sideboard in Mary's bedroom. Mary never went anywhere without her rogue's gallery, as she called them. During her final illness at Windsor Castle, they had been at her bedside. Now they were back home, as if Mary's baggage had arrived back from a trip before her.

There was only one official portrait in the rogue's gallery, of Mary and Alexander at their dual coronation, grave and determined. Alexander ascended the throne at twenty-eight. He hadn't wanted to leave Victoria with the job so soon, but in the end, he hadn't been able to avoid it. Victoria had been twenty-six when he died. She understood why Mary preferred snapshots taken on holiday or at Christmas. Victoria, still wearing her opera gloves, traced the outlines of the dead—her aunts and uncles, her own grandparents. Her brother.

He did not appear much in the forest of faces. Mary had

refused to make a shrine to him anywhere. No monuments. No memorials. Just a few snapshots on a dresser. There was one of all her children, taken at Balmoral: two little girls on a horse with a teenaged boy holding its bridle. Only one of him by himself. Victoria studied the photo of her long-departed older brother, namesake to her second son. Edward, Prince of Wales.

He was on the family yacht, *Lyonesse*, leaning against the railing near the stern, laughing at her as she took his picture. His white bell-bottom trousers fixed him cruelly in the late seventies. A blue chambray shirt with deep collar points was plastered against him by the same wind that swiped his honey-brown hair back from his forehead. She remembered that trip with desperate fondness, even though she had been seventeen and sulking, plagued with anxiety over starting university that autumn and the photo spread she'd done in *Life*, obsessed with her own concerns. Edward jollied her along, a little sister too self-absorbed and stupid to appreciate his effort, or to try understanding him in return. That was the last summer they all had together. A few months later, he was gone.

A wave of longing, of sadness, hit Victoria head-on. Edward had been so bright. The golden boy, the best of brothers. Distant affection would have been expected, even preferable, because he was so much older, and away at school. But instead of being annoyed by the presence of not one, but two much littler sisters, he treated it as a joy. At the age when most boys would be scoffing at children's games, he sat for tea parties and seriously discussed the merits of being the princess as opposed to the dragon in a fairy tale. He went riding and swimming with them, he played hide and seek, he made up stories. And in return, they were the knights of his Round Table, his staunchest defenders.

Edward needed more defending than they knew. He smiled, he laughed, he danced, and the first time Victoria caught him breathlessly snogging one of the grooms during

Christmas at Sandringham, she was six years old. But she was his knight, and she never told anyone. Not that, in retrospect, it had actually been her secret to keep. Once she got to school, once she understood the reputation her adored brother had, the injustice of it made her want to scream and smash things. Rumors surrounded him and his set, fast men and women with more wealth than they knew what to do with. "I'm only an embarrassment with the best," was his joke to their parents. Alexander and Mary didn't rein him in. They trusted maturity would come with age. But age never came.

It was almost forty years since his plane went down in a storm off the Scottish coast. He had been at the controls, flying solo. He used to say he loved it up in the air, relishing the sense that his life, if only for a few hours, belonged solely to him.

There had been an outpouring of public grief too loud to bear, and an avalanche of speculation wrapped in the thinnest, wettest tissue of sympathy. Had he been drunk? High? On his way to an illicit meeting with a lover? Was it suicide? Had his plane been sabotaged by his parents so that he wouldn't continue tarnishing the family name?

Victoria, suddenly the heir, thrust into the spotlight, reeling from her own loss, withered a little inside with every question, every insinuation. Helpless, wretched shock engulfed her. Warped her, if she were honest. And later, made her determined to hold on tighter to her own children, to keep them safe. Because in the internet age, where every rumor lasted forever, she wouldn't have the opportunities her parents had: to buy off greedy former lovers, to bury photographs, to muzzle the press. The value of exposing royal flaws, as measured in page clicks, was simply too high.

Looking back, it explained her behavior towards her second son, her other Edward. But in trying to protect him, she had organized the circumstances that led him to this horrible point.

Mary never approved of the secrecy, not once her grandson was out of university. *Let him date a man if he wants*, she had said, waving her hand. *It's not the Dark Ages. It isn't even fifty years ago. What are they going to do, write letters?* Victoria never asked Mary outright if she wished she could have handled things differently fifty years ago. It all had to come out sideways, under the table. Passing information back and forth like spies.

Now, she couldn't even do that. Victoria's silk evening gown rustled as she sat down on the edge of the bed. She pretended her mother was there, propped against pillows with the entwined "AM" designed for Alexander and Mary's coronation embroidered on their cases. They were the only personal touch Mary had allowed in her "dreadful" hospital bed at Windsor, and now they were back on her double bed where they belonged. Mary, however, was not. Victoria stroked the counterpane.

"It was all chaos and foolishness tonight, Mum. Eddie did so well, under the circumstances. Held it together beautifully. I'm not a very good mother, am I? You'd tell me I courted this particular disaster, and you'd be right.

"Malcolm was there. Helena, too, with no advance notice, might I add. I'll have to put Anthony on the scent, put the fear of God and Royal Displeasure into the opera house directors. I should have sent Alex and Eddie home for the reception, made up some excuse for them." She rubbed her forehead. "I should have left orders for him to be shot on sight. They probably wouldn't do it. Probably. What a mess."

She wasn't only referring to the situation at the opera house. How many times had she come in here to do exactly this? To sort out a heart that refused to stop hurting over people she'd stopped loving years ago. Malcolm and Helena inspired many feelings, indifference not among them. Though she had more pity for Malcolm. Thinking about Helena still filled her with rage. And now no answering sympathetic homicidal response from the space to her right, no hand patting hers. No vicious, airy dismissal that invariably took the sting out of the hurt.

She fell backwards onto the mattress. "Oh, Mum."

You can have a bit of a cry, she told herself. She needed her mother more than a grown woman ought to. Too old for this nonsense. But all the same.

There was a soft tap at the door.

"Your Majesty?" Victoria's assistant on the night shift appeared as if by magic.

"Ainsley." Victoria sat up, wiping her eyes with the backs of her hands. "Come in. What are you doing here?" They both knew it was a silly question. Once alerted to her presence in the building by one of the equerries on duty, Ainsley wouldn't let her dwell too long in Mary's bedroom. It was one of the many unspoken agreements between Victoria and her staff. They took care of her, and she permitted it. But the niceties must be observed.

"Your dispatch boxes are in the study, and your tea. Will you need anything else?"

"I'm all right. Do you have the schedule for tomorrow?" Her smile was watery, but genuine. She liked Ainsley Harper, a sharp-eyed woman in her early thirties who came on board a year ago, recommended out of the Admiralty offices by Rob Helmsley. Victoria looked for a particular quality in her assistants. A ruthless, efficient sort of kindness to match her own.

"It's on your desk."

"Thank you. You may go."

Ainsley inclined her head to the correct angle and withdrew. She couldn't keep herself from looking back, and Victoria felt uncharacteristically impatient with the theatre of it all. *Of course I'm not all right,* she wanted to say. *It's obvious to everyone. But try and admit it, in my position. How can I still be caught unawares by pain that never seems to go away?*

Unable to resist prodding at it, like her grief was a full-body, wildly colorful bruise, Victoria stepped into her mother's study instead of carrying on to her own. It hadn't been touched since Mary fell ill. If the state of her bedroom since her death resembled a lovingly maintained museum exhibit, her study was an archeological dig, headed by enthusiastic graduate students and overseen by distracted experts.

Mary had moved into Buckingham Palace during World War II, and for over seventy years, this room had been solely her domain. It was not messy, precisely. It was, however, full. The correspondence, articles clipped and, later, printed out from newspapers, memoranda, notes, and general ephemera of a life requiring a great deal of organization and management had long since overgrown the five ancient wooden filing cabinets lined up between the large windows like soldiers on parade.

The manila files spread long ago over to the large Tudor dining table in the center of the room. It had survived since the sixteenth century, but now, under the weight of numbered bankers boxes liberated from the royal archives, seemed to be regretting its longevity. Mary's desk blotter was clear, but there were precarious stacks of papers that could be anything at all on either side. Mary occasionally spoke about her responsibility to history, with a seriousness Victoria envied. Now Victoria wondered if her mother's plan all along had been to crush history entirely under her contributions to it.

Although she knew she had a full night's work ahead of her in her own office, Victoria could not resist sitting at her mother's desk and leafing through the nearest handful of papers. Jumbled together were travel itineraries, wads of receipts, notes to Mary's dressmaker. A menu from Mary's 40th wedding anniversary dinner stuck out of a birthday card from Alex, drawn when the princess was still in her crayon-and-stick-figure period. There was a sheaf of the light green steno pad sheets

Mary preferred, each dated, each holding a few cryptic thoughts. Victoria loved her mother's spidery handwriting, her caustic descriptions, her unintelligible notes from years past. One page from 1960, one from 1987, one from last year. The page from 1960 noted that her son had brought her roses that day.

"Mother, what were you *doing*?" Victoria sighed, leaning her cheek on her hand. She could decode no overarching scheme, no order, no method to what she was beginning to fear was her mother's madness as she approached the end of her life. Victoria grabbed another stack of paper, copies of notes Mary had littered her family's life with, keeping the footmen busy. Even after she got an iPhone and discovered texting, she still favored handwritten messages. "V – wearing peach for hospital opening – green suit again for you?" "S – don't slouch." "A, A, E, come for tea, my darlings." Each signed with her flowing, ornate *M*.

At the bottom of the pile, as if conjured by Victoria's current bemusement: *V – utter mess, I know. Find that clever young man, the one from Cambridge. Look in 2008, it was in the spring. Love you— Mother*

Victoria blotted her eyes with a tissue. Her makeup must be absolutely ruined. "What on earth are you talking about?" she asked the piece of paper, but she was laughing a little, too. *Look in 2008.* She went to the mantel. All her mother's datebooks were lined up there, mismatched until 1947, but made specially for her thereafter at her husband's order. One for each year, bound in smart, dark red leather by Smythson of Bond Street. There were sixty-seven volumes, stamped with her mother's seal, aging each in their turn. Victoria pulled out the one for 2008 and started paging through. Appointments, bits of reminiscence, every word sounding in Victoria's head as if Mary were speaking directly to her. And then—

April 12th: Journalism student requested quote for his school assignment. Cheek! Have decided to do it for spite.

April 25th: Met with Daniel Black. Quick, respectful. Lovely. Gave him a quote. Mischief incarnate. Follow him.

It appeared that she had followed him, too. A file of articles by a Daniel Black popped out at Victoria from the uppermost layers of papers, now that she knew what to look for. He did war reporting for the *London Journal*. At least, he had done. The last clipping was dated almost a year ago, with an article by another reporter attached—*Journal Reporter Injured in Roadside Blast*. She took a fresh sheet of Mary's stationary from her desk and scrawled *Daniel Black for QM's papers* on it. She had more work for Ainsley, after all.

THE PHONE RANG IN A DUSTY, gloomy, Whitechapel flat. It was an old rotary desktop behemoth, with a jangle to set a person's teeth on edge, demanding answering on pain of complaint from the neighbors.

First an elbow, then a hand poked its way out from under the duvet. The laundry pile on the unmade bed shifted, heaved, resolved into a figure sitting shakily on the edge of the mattress in the dim light. Hunched over his knees, he groped for his glasses on the nightstand and crammed them onto his face. His hip ached. It would have done less, if he'd been stretching like he was supposed to. The lines in the old hardwood floors in the hall blurred together before his eyes. His elbows dug into his thighs, hands clasped behind his neck. He tugged at the curls there, listening to the baleful caroling. Very few people used his home number. It was an anachronism at this point, especially in his former line of work. Anyone who wanted to get in touch with him had known to use his mobile, but he had turned that off and thrown it in the back of a drawer over six months ago. He didn't even remember which drawer.

Five rings. Six rings. He was less interested in whoever might be on the other end of the line than he was in shutting the damn thing up. So he heaved himself up and aimed for the doorframe, a few steps away. He avoided looking at his reflection in the mirror hanging over the hall table.

Shivering in boxers and a thin, old t-shirt, he squared off against the phone. It had once been connected to an ancient cassette answering machine, but he had ripped that out and smashed it against the wall sometime in the last year. He imagined the phone puffing up and turning red with rage at being ignored, vibrating its way along the table and finally falling into the wastebasket, like in a cartoon. No such luck. It continued to shriek at him.

The molded plastic handset hummed under his palm. Nine rings. Ten. Most people gave up after ten rings. Even his mother gave up after ten. But at fifteen, he jerked the handset out of its cradle, ready to bludgeon himself into unconsciousness with it, because he sure as hell wasn't ready to talk.

"Daniel Black," he said. Modulated speech wasn't beyond him quite yet. What a pity.

"*Daniel Black.*" His editor's voice came down the wires at such high quality it felt like the infuriated woman was right there in the room. "Are you still alive?"

He made a noncommittal noise.

"Progress. Put some clothes on, I'm taking you out."

Daniel went to the window, trailing the phone cord behind him, and moved the curtains aside with a single finger. The editor-in-chief of the *London Journal* leaned against the side of her town car across the road, ankles and arms crossed. Her silver-white hair was brushed back from her face in a soft bob, her lipstick was dark purple, and her gaze as she eyed him was determined.

"If you aren't down in fifteen minutes I'll have you institutionalized."

"Why so long?"

"Because I can see from here how long it's been since you've showered. Get on with it." He watched her tap the screen, heard the click of the disconnect half a second later. He hung up, too. She pointed to her watch, glowering at him as she got into the car. Gilda Trafford ran one of the world's last independently owned newspapers. The London Journal was internationally respected due to her leadership. "Driven" didn't begin to describe her. Her commitment to her job was total, which did nothing to explain why she was here, in the middle of the afternoon. He squinted at the clock. Morning. He stopped, rocking back on his heels, realizing he had no idea what day it was, and nothing was plugged in to tell him. He didn't remember the last time he *had* known the day.

The phone rang in his hand, startling him into cursing and nearly dropping the thing on his foot, which would be the very last thing he needed. He put it to his ear.

"Fourteen minutes." She hung up again.

He stood there for another couple of seconds, until inevitability crowded his limbs and got them moving. It was more like twenty minutes by the time he got himself sluiced down and dressed in a pair of jeans from university days—the only trousers that even halfway fit him now—and a shirt gone stale in a dry cleaning bag. He had to fasten his belt two holes tighter. Could have gone for three, probably. He meant to trim his beard, but shaved the whole thing off with long rakes of his electric razor because his hands were trembling so badly at the thought of going outside.

Daniel found his dead cell phone so that he could feel its weight in the pocket of his corduroy blazer. He gripped his keys so tightly, he thought they might draw blood. He went back to the phone, dialing her number. He still knew it by heart.

"You're late."

"Could you—" He leaned his forehead against the open door. He could see the light in the entryway downstairs.

"Spit it out, Daniel."

"Tell me to leave my flat," he whispered, hitting his fist with the keys in it against his thigh.

"Oh, Danny."

Gilda refrained from displaying what she called a *stereotypically maternal attitude*. She gave all her reporters, no matter their age, the same speech on their first day working for her. "I am not your mum and I am not your friend," he remembered her saying. "I will throw you under the nearest bus if you deserve it or it becomes expedient. I have no time to like you. Now get out there and find a story to convince me I shouldn't give your desk to someone else." The only praise one could expect from her was being published, and it had to be enough.

Years later, hers was the first face he saw when he woke up in an American military hospital in Germany. She was the one to get him a post-traumatic event specialist and physical therapy. She didn't fire him, not even when it became clear he was no longer capable of doing his job. She hadn't given his desk to someone else.

But now it sounded like she was at a loss. It only lasted a single breath, and then she was all business again.

"Out. Now. I'll come upstairs," she warned. That spurred him into action. If she saw the state of his flat, she would have him carted off.

"You're a fright," she told him, as he slowly levered himself into the car.

He grimaced. "It's good to see you, too."

"And you're a liar." She settled back with her phone in her hand. On average, she received five hundred e-mails an hour.

He remembered the days of the buzz, wondering if the next message, the next call, text, radio wave, carrier pigeon had the big story hidden inside. The anticipation and the fear, all wrapped up together. The point at which he knew a story was going to work or not. All those sensations echoing through him all the time. Gone now, buried under anxiety and terror.

At one time, he had been one of the best. The way Gilda looked at him now, over the top of her bifocals, he could tell she remembered that, too. She hadn't so much as glanced at her phone since he got in the car, which was its own kind of terrifying.

"How are you, Daniel?" she asked, dark eyes examining his face. The weight of seven years of mentoring settled onto his shoulders. She had made sure he got the chance to prove himself from the start, giving him assignments much bigger and more difficult than a rookie reporter ever should have had. He had a facility with language, he remembered her saying. He hated disappointing her. He hated that it was all over.

"I don't even know what the options for answering that question are any more," he said.

She raised an eyebrow. "That's unnecessarily melodramatic."

"You had to bully me into going out the door."

"So you've abandoned any pretense at living?"

Anger welled up like blood in a paper cut. "What do you want to hear? I have no idea what day it is, my flat is disgusting, my leg hurts, I hadn't shaved in weeks, I don't remember the last time I had a full meal, and I'm incapable of writing anything because whenever I try, I hear bombs go off. But I'm great, Gilda. I'm fine." He closed his eyes.

"Well, that's better," she said, after a moment. "Daniel, you are a phenomenal writer. You get to the heart of things. Facts without flourish. You let them speak for themselves. It's been long enough. To lock yourself away is indulgence. It's selfish.

You have to pull yourself together. Even your therapist thinks you should."

"Doesn't doctor-patient confidentiality mean anything?" he asked, peevish. She smirked.

"Bad form, Danny boy, I haven't talked to your therapist."

He groaned. "I can hardly leave the house," he countered. "I can't go back to the sandbox, I can't cover anything with a pulse. It's not going to work. You might as well get on with firing me. I don't know why you couldn't have done it over the phone," he said. He knew he sounded bitter. Ungrateful, even.

"I'm not here to fire you," Gilda said. "I have an assignment for you."

"What could you possibly have for a washed-up war reporter with a bum leg and a horror of loud noises and chaos?"

"Nothing with a pulse."

4

The mourners at Group Captain Willoughby Miles' funeral could, if the need arose, command a large war and personally wage a small one. The church was a sea of blue, medals, and gold braid, as hundreds of officers in the Royal Air Force gathered to pay their respects to the family and memory of a man they had loved. The Marines and the Navy were widely represented from his days commanding air wings during the first and second Gulf Wars. And, of course, the most well-known officer ever to serve under his command was there, standing at the front of the church, having been asked by the family to say a few words.

Squadron Leader Arthur Wales spread out his prepared notes on the lectern, smoothing the deep creases in the paper. The words ran together in a jumble as the old panic at having to speak publicly overtook him. He turned the paper over so that the stilted, appropriate, now useless expressions of grief he'd wrung out of himself at one in the morning wouldn't distract him.

"I spent all night writing, and I still don't know what to

say." He held his gloved fist to his mouth. There was a rustle in the assembled, but not a disapproving one.

"Group Captain Miles served his country with distinction for over forty years," Arthur said, thinking through his notes from the night before. "He was a strong presence even in an occupation not known for creating retiring personalities." That got a communal laugh. "You're remembering the cigars, aren't you?" he said. The laugh got louder.

"We've heard so many stories about him today. About his joy in service and in keeping us all on our toes. He didn't seem to think those were different things. He threatened to defect whenever there was talk of promoting him. That the Soviet Union had fallen made no difference, did it? He once demanded of Air Marshall Vickers, in my hearing, that the second Gulf War be ended early so that he could be home in time for his thirty-fifth wedding anniversary." He looked to Audra Miles, bracketed by the eldest of her grown children in the front row. Her eyes were red, but her smile was genuine. "But if you knew him, as we all did, you know that duty was his calling.

"All of the people who spoke today have more right to it than I do, and I hope I won't go on too long, but I do have a story of my own to share. When I first made Flight Lieutenant, there was understandable reluctance to put me in the air. I found myself grounded, banging down my Squadron Leader's door every other day begging for a flight assignment. I was frustrated. I had no idea what the future held. All I wanted was to fly. I'm sure I caused more than a few headaches for people in this very room." Another rumble of laughter from the pews towards the front.

"After months of this, I was called to the office of one Group Captain Miles. I knew his reputation. He pointed me into a chair and told me I was being transferred to his unit. He strode up and down, chewing on one of his cigars, and told me no one wanted the responsibility of putting the future King of England into the air strapped to a jet engine and a couple of missiles, and who could blame them? He said it was damned selfish of me, but he was willing to take me on. In return, I would do everything by the book at all times. I'd fly like my granny was sitting behind me. And if anyone in the squadron had a baby to go home and see, or a flu, or a hangover, I would be the one to take their assignments on, and never complain. Not once, or he'd ground me for life.

"I agreed. Of course I did. He ordered me to take mechanical engineering rotations as well. I had to know how the thing worked from the inside out, get my hands dirty, so that I could trust it. If he could have sent me back to school to be a mechanic, I think he would have.

"But even in that, there was no preferential treatment. He gave us all his advice, his time, his attention. Even the most junior pilot cadets under his command got to know him. He made us mentor each other. He did not inspire loyalty as much as he seemed to bear it, with heavy grace. May we all be as humble, and as sure, in the execution of our duties.

"I learned so much from him, both as a man, and as someone who will one day bear a great burden of responsibility. After that first day, it was never explicitly acknowledged between us, but he never let me forget. Under his command it was an honor, a privilege to serve as Squadron Leader Arthur Wales, who was never allowed to shirk a flight rotation and learned to maintain his own bird. Who is most grateful to his Group Captain for giving him the sky. Thank you."

He saluted the coffin and made it back to his seat without weeping.

As one of the pallbearers, he exited the church first, his share of the coffin an anchor chain around his waist, tethering him to the earth. Lost in the effort of putting one foot ahead of the other, he noticed a slender man in the black and gold of a

Royal Navy lieutenant at the end of the last pew. The face was familiar, but he struggled to place it until, shocked, he realized it was his brother's. He acknowledged Eddie's presence with one sharp nod, and then set his jaw. When the coffin passed out of the church, Eddie saluted with the rest, his own eyes fixed on the middle distance, as correctly aligned and still as any soldier.

As the hearse drove away for the short trip to graveside, Arthur felt as though the ground was solid under his polished shoes only because he believed in it. Audra Miles came up and took his hands without ceremony, as if he were any other officer under her husband's wing. It comforted him.

"He was so proud of you," she said. "Talked of you all the time, said you were coming along. He said," she paused, weighing what to say next, whether she should, but something in his eyes must have convinced her. "He said that if you learned to be as careful with people as you were with planes, you would make a very fine king." Arthur swallowed hard, and found, when he opened his mouth, that he had no words left to tell her how much hers meant. He managed to get out a "So grateful—will be very much missed—" before he stepped back. It wasn't adequate. He didn't know what could be. She was immediately swallowed up by other mourners, her children and her sisters surrounding her like a flotilla.

Arthur felt a hand on his back, and turned to see Eddie at his side. There was no time to ask him what the hell he was doing here. Eddie stayed near him as Arthur was surrounded with officers of all ranks looking for a word. Arthur realized his brother was acting as attaché, greeting people, funneling them into and out of Arthur's field of attention, leaving him more time to talk to the people he knew and liked, taking on conversation with those who clearly only wanted to say that they'd had a word with a prince. It grounded him, much to his surprise. Eddie was *good* at it. It was easy to forget that Eddie had spent four years working at the Naval Intelligence offices in London before he left the service to join what the Kensingtons called, amongst themselves, the "circus." At the time, Arthur was scornful of that decision. Now, listening to him speak with other Navy officers, saluting superiors with precise bearing and attention, looking more comfortable than Arthur could remember seeing him for a long time, Arthur wondered what Eddie's true feelings on giving up his commission had been.

"You came in uniform," he murmured, as they fell in beside each other on the way to the gravesite.

"Incognito," Eddie told him, with a quick smile. "I put my hair up. That's a disguise, right?"

"You look like pictures of Grandfather during the second World War," Arthur said. Eddie looked quite pleased with himself. "I appreciate it. Given everything, especially this week."

"Heard from Sophie and Alex that you might be a little low, what with one thing and another." So Eddie didn't want to talk about his current problems right now. Arthur felt relieved about that—he knew when he was out of his depth—but with a sting of guilt, he resolved to try again later.

"What, the end of my professional career?" They drew apart from the slow parade of mourners, the corresponding black-suited shadows of their protection details rearranging to give them privacy.

"A little thing like that."

"It's official at the end of the week," Arthur said, the words ringing in his ears, the aftermath of his life exploding. "Group Captain Miles and I had discussed it, but I wanted to wait a few more months. No point now. They'll have me in a desk job before you can say my full name, and I want the last posting in my jacket to be combat. Foolish, I know. No one is ever going to see it."

Eddie shook his head, but didn't say anything.

"I'm moving back to London," Arthur went on. "Probably to KP, eventually, unless you have some very strong objections to my invading your bachelor pad." He had been tongue-tied a few minutes ago, but now he couldn't seem to stop laying out the rest of his life in measured tones.

"It's a palace," Eddie said. "I think we'll manage not to step on each other's toes." There was a pause, and then, more tentatively, "You're welcome to come over for breakfast, if you'd like."

Arthur glanced at him disbelievingly, but Eddie was watching where he planted his feet along the gravel path. They hadn't had the opportunity to be all that close when they were children. Arthur was sent away to boarding school while Eddie stayed in London, attending an excellent day school. Arthur supposed his own education had been a way of signaling the old guard that tradition still mattered, while Eddie's was a sign that change was possible. Children, Arthur thought, should never be raised as proofs of concept. And it had all backfired. Aside from a handful of friends, Arthur grew up insulated and withdrawn, preferring computers and machines to his fellows. Eddie learned to be good at being a prince around everyone. Arthur didn't know how to handle that, even now.

Their divergent upbringings had driven distance between them, bridged only by traumas they never quite managed to acknowledge. They hardly seemed to speak the same language. Arthur felt generations older than his glamorous sibling. Eddie's ability to manage the spotlight, all that attention, made Arthur bitterly envious at various points in his life. But not today. Today he was grateful that Eddie had decided to come, unprompted and uninvited. It gave his grief cover. It might even comfort, if anything could.

~

AFTER THE GRAVESIDE SERVICE, their details got them neatly away for the long drive back to London. Eddie had his own car ready, but Arthur asked him to ride along, feeling vulnerable as he did, and ridiculous for feeling vulnerable. A quick grin flashed in return, Eddie clearly surprised to be asked, and pleased to accept. It felt brotherly. Or something.

In the car, they waited until they couldn't be seen by anyone connected with the funeral before leaning forward at the exact same moment and angle to shrug out of their uniform jackets. They caught eyes, and the recognition was palpable. As was the loss. They had learned that move from their father.

"Heard from him lately?" Arthur asked. Eddie shook his hair out, ruffling it with his fingers. He made a face.

"No. He wouldn't call me unless the world were collapsing. You?"

Arthur shook his head. They went silent, each looking out the window.

"So have you thought about what you're going to do next?"

"Jesus Christ, Eddie, it's been a half-hour since they put his coffin in the ground. Should I have a ten-point plan already, like a good Kensington? I suppose you did." As soon as the words were out, burning resentfully between them, he was appalled. "I'm sorry," he said. "I'm so sorry." He pinched the bridge of his nose as if to staunch bleeding, digging into the collar of his undershirt with his other hand. He pulled out a heavy gold ring on a chain and held it tightly in his hand.

"Perhaps my timing was thoughtless," Eddie said, and for a second, Arthur thought he would leave it, but then he carried on, reasonable and inexorable. "But it's either me now, or Mother and Sir Anthony and all the rest of them later, complete with lists of patronages ordered by size, impact, and public approval, and look-books for your new wardrobe."

Arthur stared at him in mild horror. Eddie shrugged a

shoulder. "We have a few hours. I mean no disrespect to Group Captain Miles, but here we are. And you need to find a life direction if you want to choose it for yourself. Space has been reserved for you, lo these many years." Despite the lack of resentment in his tone, Arthur couldn't help but think he knew who that space had been taken from. Eddie was a fierce champion of several organizations and causes, but he had to do it quietly. Arthur knew about the equine rescue and Eddie's work with LGBTQIA youth and domestic abuse victims. But all of that was kept away from the news.

As the heir, he was expected to have the greatest reach, championing public, forward-looking projects with a wide scope. While he had been involved in some initiatives over the years, his military service had come first. In his absence, what the others could do was limited. It wouldn't do for the heir to the throne to be overshadowed by a more publicly available and politically savvy brother. Joint appearances had been limited since their twenties, once Eddie's greater skill at working a crowd became a liability for Arthur in the press. But then Eddie's image took a turn for the party boy, the infamous Prince Charming, and Arthur's quiet, serious enthusiasm for various charities had been praised almost universally as a balm to the "frivolous" behavior of their second prince. The injustice of it had vaguely bothered Arthur for years, but now it hurt like jamming his thumb in a door.

"I can't avoid this, can I?" he asked, not quite rhetorically.

"Bills to pay," Eddie told him gently. "And Windsor Castle needs a new roof put on." That edged a grim laugh out of Arthur. He thudded his head against the back of the seat a few times, longing for the thrust and pull of a fighter jet beneath him, the intimate claustrophobia of the cockpit and face mask. At one of their last meetings, Group Captain Miles talked about the promotion list. There was a careful pause before Miles said, *"Your name won't be appearing, Wales. You know why."*

Arthur hadn't done anything other than nod. *"You've got other jobs to do. And don't let me hear that you've been wasting time once you're out."* So that was it, then.

Arthur said a final good-bye in his head. The thrumming under him was only a partitioned town car blazing through the North Country on its way back to London. Stolen time. That's all the last nine years had been.

"Tech sector, I think," Arthur said. "It'll have to be tech. I don't know anything about anything else."

"Military?"

"No, domestic. Start small. Information accessibility. Some kind of program. Subsidized laptops for all children. Like the National Health Service for technological literacy."

"If that's your idea of small, they'll be begging you to go back to a combat zone."

"You think?" Arthur let himself smile.

"The Tories will hate it, Everingham has them on a tight leash. The Liberals don't want new ideas, they've closed ranks around what's already there from terror of Everingham's 'financial responsibility' nitwittery. He probably has a shrine to Thatcher in his study. Labour's toothless right now, except for Seaton, he makes a splash no matter what he says."

"Seaton? I have to start paying attention."

"Terrible fate, happens to all of us. Benedict Seaton, Parliament's classically named rouser of rabble and Petrifier of Tories. His parents are from Jamaica. He's glamorous. Amazing suits."

"You sound jealous."

"Impressed," Eddie corrected. "He's very popular. Since Labour has no clout at the moment, he can say whatever he wants. And he does."

"So I need the Conservatives," Arthur said. *Work the problem,* he heard in his head, from hundreds of tactical exercises over the years. "Well, all right. To hell with small. To get them, I make it about business. I throw the laptops in as a pilot program in concert with some kind of... innovation leadership initiative? Bring more tech companies to London, something like that. Get some giant sponsors. Apolitically, since we're royal and all."

"You're getting the hang of this. They won't be able to say no," Eddie said, gleeful. "It's a great idea. And fitting for your reentry into the public eye. Bringing together business and government, without losing sight of the needs of common folk, the press releases write themselves. Catch yourself a bunch of famous guest speakers and you're golden. You could get a full week out of it, especially if you bring in some high-level military development people."

"What do you think about doing it with me?" Arthur asked. "Now that we've essentially taken a desire to do some good for schoolchildren and turned it into an international three-ring circus."

"Welcome to the family business," Eddie told him. "You'd want my help? I'm not exactly known for doing this kind of thing."

"As long as we're going about this like we're the bloody Medici. You can talk to Seaton without it being scandalous, make it look like you're chatting about suits or something. I can't. No one would believe it. And... look, I'm not good at this yet. Not the way you are." A shadow ran over Eddie's face, but it was too quick to catch on to before his face smoothed out again, so Arthur went on. "I'd like your help getting everyone together. Behind the scenes, if you'd prefer, but all the same. And who knows, if the public gets to the point where they can accept one openly involved and intelligent prince, what about two?"

Eddie nodded uncertainly, almost like he didn't know what to do with himself. "It would... it would be a pleasure. All right. Let's." They shook on it. The rest of the car ride passed

in a flood of ideas and texts fired off to their private secretaries. When they were closer to the city, Arthur covered his
mouth for a jaw-popping yawn.

"Sorry, damn. Long couple of days."

"Of course. I don't have much else to do today. Cleared the
decks when I heard about the funeral."

"Why did you come up, anyway?"

"Thought you might appreciate someone waving the flag.
Your flying career hasn't been the most popular with the family
over the years, but I know what it's like to give it up."

"How did you cope with it?" Arthur asked.

"I went to a lot of parties, dated around. You know. The
usual, for the likes of us." Eddie tried to smile, but he couldn't
quite.

"Hard to adjust?" Arthur hazarded.

Eddie looked thoughtful. "I think it's like people who end
large projects and sink into depression. Being in Intelligence
gave me a purpose. I didn't have to pretend. As much," he
said. "Have to keep up the front, don't we?"

Arthur didn't miss the weariness on his brother's face.

"No, er, other…?"

Eddie sighed loudly. "No, Arthur, I'm not sneaking into gay
bars on the weekends. Cole would have my head. He says one
of the most recognizable men in the country makes for a
terrible wingman."

"He would," Arthur said, happy for a change of subject.
"How is he?"

"The best, as usual." Eddie's smile always looked genuine
until he actually meant it, at which point whoever was on the
other end of it realized there was no comparison. "You'll see
him if you move into Kensington Palace after all. When we get
back, want to scout the open apartments? See what might suit
His Royal Highness, Arthur Alexander Richard Henry, Prince
of Wales, Earl of Chester, Duke of Cornwall, Duke of Rothe-

say, Earl of Carrick, Baron of Renfrew, Lord of the Isles, and Prince and Great High Steward of Scotland?"

"How in God's name do you get all that out in order?"

"Forging your signature, obviously."

"We'll burn the place down."

5

D espite his brave words to Arthur about controlling one's own destiny in the car the day before, the prospect of meeting with the Royal Communications Team left Eddie jittery and on edge. The first time he'd been summoned, at sixteen, it was suggested that he dress in a more "mature" style, leave aside his beloved woven thread bracelets and a crystal pendant Alex got him while they were on holiday in the Caribbean, and focus on sport instead of drama club at school. "You wouldn't want to give people the wrong idea, I'm sure," the head of the communications team told him. Sick to his stomach, he emerged from the meeting—which he had gone to himself—and met Sir Anthony in the hall. "Everything settled?" his mother's private secretary asked, clearly encouraging. Eddie nodded, fighting back tears, hand clapped over the bracelets on his other wrist. "Your mother will be delighted to hear it." Those words struck terror and shame into Eddie's heart. Had she minded? Had he been doing something wrong? But he couldn't ask Sir Anthony, or his mother, and no one ever told him.

He acquiesced immediately, shoving his accessories to the

back of a drawer and joining the football team the next week. Much later, he realized that in the near-wartime atmosphere of the royal divorce, he became an easy target for the public relations office. Photographers camped out on the route Eddie took to and from his day school in London. If he looked pulled together, it might give the impression that Buckingham Palace was running smoothly, and the palace machine needed all the help it could get. In retrospect, he knew it was an unacceptable weight for a miserable sixteen-year-old to carry.

During university, a deal was struck with the press. An official photo-shoot at the beginning of each semester, a couple of interviews during the term, and the photographers stayed away. Freed from the constant scrutiny, Eddie went back to his old ways. Brought back the cheap jewelry he got at street fairs around the world, wore all the slouchy shirts he wanted, and adopted skinny jeans as a uniform.

In Naval Intelligence, it was easy to keep his head down, off the radar of his own personal sharks. But as soon as he resigned his commission, the communications team re-entered his life. "You have to stop going to the theatre so much by yourself," had been the first directive. "Don't go to any more Formula One races, the fan magazines are starting to talk about you and Garrett," after his friendship with England's most famous driver became public. When he and Alex wangled their way into attending the Winter Olympics, he was given a list of which events he could and could not attend, based on their level of presumed manliness. (Skiing and snowboarding, fine. Pairs figure skating only accompanied by Alex. Men's figure skating, not a chance in hell. So he had snuck into those events smothered in a parka, sunglasses, and a truly foolish novelty hat.)

They encouraged him to be seen with models and actresses, to compete in charity football and polo matches, anything to make him look "strong." They suggested, frequently, that he cut his hair. He responded by taking Cole along when he had his hair styled. Once or twice he'd gotten him to wear his gun on the front of his belt in case the stylist had been paid to "slip" and cut a whole chunk of it off. He wouldn't fall for that trick a second time in his life, thank you.

A succession of Royal Communications Directors each avoided open bigotry in their own delicate ways, but the message was consistent: left to his own devices, the ways Eddie spoke and dressed, his interests and his behavior, all projected a certain image. One that might give the wide world *the wrong idea*. Whether the idea was accurate never seemed to concern them.

People would see what they wanted to see. What they were told to see. Self-determination mattered much less than a compelling narrative, a confirmation of basic assumptions. His self-loathing eased when he learned how to move within all of that, turn it to his own advantage. But by the time he did, the damage was already done.

And now, bets were all the way off. The communications team hadn't intercepted the photos ripping the cheap veneer from Eddie's life. They had failed him. He tried to armor himself in that knowledge.

He lingered in his closet, picking out one of his treasured pairs of ripped skinny jeans, festooning his wrists with bracelets and his fingers with rings. Every one of them had some significance—even though he couldn't wear them, he still collected charms on holidays, and Alex brought them back for him. A white t-shirt beneath an unbuttoned, collared shirt and blazer would have to do. He barely thought twice before twirling his hair into a tiny bun at the back of his head, teasing the wisps falling out of it into soft curls at the nape of his neck. For good measure, he folded a tie into the breast pocket of his school-boy-style blazer. Catching sight of his reflection in the mirror, he nearly lost his nerve. A sharp rap at the door distracted him from the nervous flutter in his belly at how much he liked how he looked.

"Time, sir," Allan Finnery said, in his utterly correct way. If Eddie hadn't made a point of taking every new member of his detail out to a particular pub in Wales at least once, he would never have known that Allan was a master at darts and could sing every verse of "The Rocky Road to Dublin" in order. And that would have been a shame.

"I know—is Cole out there?"

"Give us a minute." A lower murmur through the door, and the sound of footsteps on the stairs, one set up, then one set down.

Eddie slid his closet door all the way open and stood there, arms out to his sides, heart pounding as Isaac looked him over. "What do you think?"

"Give them heart failure by walking into the room, why don't you?"

"I'd release a swarm of bees if it ended the meeting faster." Eddie crossed his ankles and tipped his chin for full effect. "Do I look all right? Not too...? Never mind. Worrying about *that* is pointless today. You're allowed to have a cigarette on the way to the firing squad, right? Let's go."

Isaac didn't call him on his babbling. Truly, Isaac was the best. Allan met them at the car, and Eddie flopped into the back seat. He didn't miss the look Isaac and Allan shared, and he closed his eyes, hoping for a rogue black hole to swallow the town car.

THE OFFICE of the Royal Communications Director was at the heart of Buckingham Palace's administrative facilities. The impeccably decorated suite contained an early 19th century dining table and ten chairs used for conferences, a rosewood partners desk, and four wing chairs artfully arranged for this occasion around a silver cart loaded with cakes and an 18th century tea set. Isaac preceded Eddie into the room, doing an expressionless once-over of the assembled before melting out the door. The presence of the Queen's Private Secretary made Eddie feel incalculably foolish for his outfit.

Sir Anthony Pritchard lingered over their handshake, cataloging Eddie with a once-over of his own. A fixture in Eddie's life since birth, he was a distant, strictly correct presence by Victoria's side. Preparing her speeches, keeping her schedules and itineraries, playing goalie with the unending responsibilities and demands on her time. This included her children. Eddie couldn't count the number of times as a child he'd been gently and politely rebuffed at his mother's office door by the seemingly ageless, gray-haired man in front of him now. He gave a stronger impression of being above reproach than anyone Eddie ever met, and was capable of felling a grown man with a disapproving stare. But today, Sir Anthony did not *seem* disapproving. In fact, the corner of his mouth twitched in what could have been a smirk. To Eddie's shock, he murmured, "Lovely tie, your royal highness."

Sir Anthony might as well have *Do not antagonize the Communications Director* tattooed on his forehead, and yet.

Sir Thomas "Call-me-Tom-but-really-never-call-me-Tom" Foster-Hume's normally avuncular expression seemed strained today. Generations of careful out-breeding from the mid-1800s on had returned a chin to the attractive, symmetrical facial features characteristic of his family going back to the Restoration. His sparkling cufflinks caught the light as they shook hands. Though Sir Thomas wasn't the worst of the Communications Directors in the past decade, Eddie found the man's bright red power tie and flashy jewelry off-putting. After five years on the job, it indicated a level of insecurity that could only be soothed—and temporarily, at best—by the exercise of authority over the people Sir Thomas felt were his betters. Which boded ill for this meeting.

Eddie reminded himself that he was in no position to throw stones on the subject of anyone else's accessorizing, arrayed as he was in what felt now like an entire booth in the Covent Garden Market. Deputy Communications Director Portia Searle offered him a brief handclasp. She wore a narrow silver cuff bracelet and an Elsa Perretti *P* pendant, a black pencil skirt and hunter green blouse completing her no-nonsense picture. Eddie took a seat.

Sir Thomas moved to his own desk, shifting folders around as if searching for something. Portia's fingers twitched on the leather-bound portfolio in her lap. Impatience with her superior, perhaps? Eddie couldn't say he blamed her. No one enjoyed having their time wasted. Finally, prop in hand, Sir Thomas sat down heavily. He opened the manila folder. Eddie suddenly couldn't breathe. Sir Anthony sighed beside him.

The pictures had been taken with an early cell phone camera at a bad angle. Most of them were only Eddie at twenty, all gawky limbs and a startled hedgehog's worth of brown hair, grinning drunk and unrepentant at a party. But a few showed him flopped all over some less visible figure, on a couch that had seen many better days. Stretching for a kiss, body language focused solely on the object of his affection, clearly in love. It took a second or two to realize that the recipient of his affection wore a Cambridge men's rowing team jersey and sported several days of facial hair. Seeing the evidence of a night that had been so important to him tossed around like it was nothing, like it was *worse* than nothing, brought his nausea screaming back.

"Is there anything you want to tell us, Your Royal Highness?"

Before he could speak, help came from an unprecedented quarter.

"Tom." Sir Anthony twitched the photos into a pile, returning them to the folder with a sharp snap. "This isn't an interrogation. No one is demanding explanations, for God's sake."

"I simply wished to give Prince Edward the opportunity to contextualize, as it may prove useful in shaping the message going forward."

"You've done a bang-up job so far." Sir Anthony leaned back and crossed one ankle over the opposite knee. "He knows exactly what those pictures indicate, and so do you, and so does everyone. It's offensive to brandish them as if it were a crime scene."

"I can't do my job without all the relevant information."

"The pictures were taken. The pictures were sold. You made no efforts to intercept them or run interference. This office simply cowered while Prince Edward was left to shift for himself in America, at the mercy of every reporter and buffoon with a smartphone. Her Majesty is displeased, and sent me to this meeting for one reason and one reason only: to ensure that at no time anything leaves this office with even the hint of a suggestion that Prince Edward is at fault. Is that information relevant enough for you?"

Sir Thomas's bottom lip pursed and spread like an accordion burdened with an amateur player. Sir Anthony remained very still.

"We were trying to track down who sold the photographs." Sir Thomas was all bluster and clearly knew it, which only made him redder in the face. "It was imperative to make sure that this was not the first foray in a coordinated media attack. To get ahead of the response."

"The pictures were taken by Simon Etheridge. He was one year below me at Cambridge. I suspect he was cleaning out an old hard drive and decided to make some money." Everyone seemed surprised when Eddie spoke. "I do, of course, regret that the pictures have become public. It was a private moment, supposed to remain that way. But that has a funny habit of not happening when we're involved." He thought of Helena's bright, diamond-chip eyes, and was proud of how level his voice stayed.

Portia leaned forward and placed her portfolio over the manila folder. "Do we have anything to worry about from the man you were involved with in the photographs? Do you think he'll give an interview?"

"No." Eddie remembered the conversation with Travis on the night the pictures were released. *I'm so sorry, Eddie. You know I'd never—never in a million years...* "He doesn't want the notoriety. He's married, has a few children. He wouldn't want the scandal in his own life. Or his husband's."

"You can hardly tell who it is, anyway." Portia said. "I think we're safe from that angle. The real question is, with all due respect, what do you want to do?"

"What are my options?"

"I strongly suggest you put out a statement," Sir Thomas broke in. "Through this office, asking for your privacy to be respected." Eddie didn't imagine the subtle, exasperated flutter of Portia's eyelashes. He sympathized with it.

Sir Anthony spoke with uncharacteristic impatience. "The horses are gone, Tom. They are sipping rum cocktails from hollowed-out pineapples on a beach in Jamaica. Slamming the barn door seems anti-climactic. And it won't work. By implication he has been asking for privacy about this part of his life right along, and look where that's got us. The minute we say a word that acknowledges it, positively or negatively, it's open season on him. We don't dignify these sorts of things with responses for a reason."

We do, Eddie thought. *We do all the time*. But passively. Gently. In response to trends, not scandals. Too many pieces about a lack of engagement with the environment? Sophie made an appearance at a few wildlife sanctuaries. Stories about Alex being spoiled? She magically appeared spearheading a charity dresses event for underprivileged schoolgirls. Driving the national conversation was as easy as finding a likely Kensington and castigating them for an invented shortcoming. But this was different. It was explosive. And worse than being untrue, it had been hidden.

Sir Thomas blotted his forehead with a handkerchief. "Then you think we should do nothing? You've been castigating me for doing nothing for the past five minutes."

"There is a difference between strategic action and a lack of imagination."

"Then why weren't you in here three weeks ago?"

"Why weren't you doing your job?"

"Gentlemen—" Eddie put up a hand, trying to inject some authority into his tone. They both startled. Eddie hadn't realized before this moment how much these two pillars of Buckingham Palace's organization disliked each other. "I believe Portia has something she wants to add."

Portia smiled tightly and nodded to him, acknowledging the patent absurdity of requiring intercession from a member of the royal family before she could speak in her own meeting. "Thank you, your royal highness. Sir Thomas, Sir Anthony, we ought to examine the big picture." She opened her portfolio and took out a crib sheet. "The overall response is not a complete disaster. There is negative coverage from the more fringe websites, and of course some of the papers are making it their business to be as inflammatory as possible, with predictably awful results. Most of the respectable major outlets have taken the line we might have wished, with varying degrees of discomfort—decrying the invasion of privacy and so on. They seem to feel it's the no-lose tack. As, might I remind you, do we. There are the usual jokes, of course. Photographs are circling with annotations 'proving' your sexual orientation. The tabloids are having a field day, but so far they haven't gone anywhere too ridiculous. The usual 'sources close to,' love nests, heartbreak from former girlfriends, and so on. No secret babies in this story, though there wouldn't be. One report about you secretly having AIDS received so much public backlash the Sun actually took it down. Most of the think pieces from the under-35s are supportive as well, although many of them are unhappy you didn't come out yourself. The response on social media has been delighted in some quarters. You have been romantically linked with several athletes and actors so far, and fair play to you."

Eddie listened to her through the ringing in his ears. "I —that is—"

"The worst of it is a few ancient MPs trying to put a bill in Parliament that would remove you from the line of succession."

"Being the spare isn't what it used to be." *Unfit*, Eddie thought. *That's what they think of me.*

"Sir, while it sounds bad, that effort won't go anywhere. The real problem is the perception that you've been lying all this time. The public doesn't like feeling out of the loop."

"I haven't *been* lying," Eddie said. "I'm bisexual. And there are plenty of things we all choose not to disclose."

"Of course," Sir Thomas said, recovering his officiousness in a dismissive wave of his hand. "Reality isn't our first priority. We're speaking of perception. You're the most socially visible of your siblings, and you buy a tremendous amount of goodwill. Especially, with respect, as the Prince of Wales hasn't been seen in public with a woman in over five years. Your own romantic exploits are of great interest because that's all the royal-watchers have to go on. The harmless fantasy of the playboy Prince who might at any moment walk into a chocolate shop and sweep a woman off her feet." The condescension was all-consuming. As if Eddie didn't know.

"No fantasy is harmless. Haven't they learned not to look to us for happiness?"

It wasn't his fault that his parents' divorce had been the first of its kind in the public imagination in nearly five hundred years. It had nothing to do with him. But the shame of it never left his head. The questions, the innuendos, the way their teams tried so valiantly to keep the teenagers insulated from the media circus surrounding their upheaval. Arthur, already away at school, had been shielded from the worst of it. For Eddie and Alex, there was no way to ignore their father's sudden absence and their mother's all-encompassing withdrawal. They were utterly lost, and Eddie wasn't sure, even over a decade later, that either of them had found a way back.

Portia took over again, with a frustrated glance at her boss.

"We usually expect approval of a public figure to go down while they're casually dating. Yours never did. This regrettable situation—the invasion of your privacy, I wish to be clear—threatens the image we've built for you over the years. But it also gives us an opportunity." *My image*, he thought. *Looking cheerful enough for the paparazzi? Hiding everything I feel because so much of it is unacceptable?* "If these pictures hadn't leaked, we would have asked you in for a meeting anyway, to discuss a change in the direction of your arranged socializing."

"Why?"

"One long-term bachelor prince is acceptable, even amusing. But two seems like a trend. Frankly, the Prince of Wales' lack of attention to his romantic life will become much more noticeable when he moves back to London. It was really only a matter of time before there was a gay scandal, one way or another."

"Do you all sit around and come up with ways of reducing a person to the most base stereotypes you can find as part of your work, or is it a hobby?"

Portia didn't take the bait.

Stalemate. Tom's lower lip was playing "Lady of Spain." Portia regarded Eddie coolly. He could feel Sir Anthony preparing to join the fray. He thought of Arthur, fingers clenched around a glass of whiskey the night he told Catriona it was over for good, one of the few times he ended up on Eddie's couch. The real panic in Arthur's eyes whenever the press cornered him about his personal life. The way his brother was so reserved around women, because of the hell it became for them if it got out they were friends. How could Eddie refuse to protect him? He wondered why he should be grateful for the percentage of the population willing to tolerate his "scandalous" identity, and why he should apologize for keeping something from complete strangers who felt entitled to him for reasons no one could ever adequately explain. Was he supposed to emerge, butterfly-like, from the chrysalis of the closet, when most people didn't have the first idea of what bisexuality meant? They would dismiss it as thoroughly and automatically as Sir Thomas had.

"What do you have in mind?" he asked, deep voice grating. Tom's lip stopped mid-stanza. Portia raised an eyebrow. She slid another sheet of paper across the table to him.

"We've prepared a selection of suitable candidates for a longer-term connection. The usual roster of socialites, both aristocratic and not. All of them have been thoroughly vetted and approved."

Eddie scanned the list. "I haven't been on a date with a single one of these women."

"All part of the point, sir," Sir Thomas said, smirking in an overenthusiastic, between-us-lads way. "Essential to draw a line between before and after. Those girls you take out aren't what you'd call 'marriage material,' are they?"

"You utter—" Eddie was cut off by Sir Anthony making a tiny noise in his throat, no more than the slightest press on an intake of air. Eddie composed himself. "Is it expected that one of these connections will end at the altar?"

Portia looked as if she very much wanted to shrug, but couldn't get away with it. "Past a certain point it's up to you, obviously. But there's less room for shopping around in this portfolio, so to speak. These options wouldn't be mediated through PR firms and non-disclosure agreements. The point is that you appear to be considering the idea of marriage."

"Her Majesty is keen to see her children settled with supportive partners, but at their own pace," Sir Anthony put in. Eddie's jaw ached from clenching. He believed his mother wanted him to be happy. But in a way that would cause the least fuss. He didn't blame her.

"The timing is a problem," Sir Thomas said. "In the wake of the photographs, you understand. Makes it look more like a beard than usual."

They weren't beards, Eddie wanted to snap. But he found he didn't have the energy even for that much self-defense. His spine felt like it might snap. He didn't owe this stuffed shirt an explanation for his life, for his public—and private—dating. He didn't owe it to anyone. But there was pressure from all sides, and the narrowest line to walk.

"I don't see why I should change my behavior because of something that happened seven years ago," he said finally. "If I do that, I'm admitting there was something wrong with what went on before. I'll decide how to handle any disclosure of my sexual orientation. It is, after all, mine. I would have agreed to this... ramping-up scheme a month ago, so I'll agree to it now. As you said, it's a matter of perception. People will draw their own conclusions. So when do we start?"

"Excuse me, your highness?" Sir Thomas faltered under the weight of Eddie's sudden acquiescence.

"When do we phase in the chosen ones?" he asked. He was suddenly impatient with them, with this meeting. With himself most of all. "You must have a timeline for this. You're an image team, not a matchmaking agency. You don't have my best interests at heart. You think it's *time*. And since Arthur refuses to play this little game, you're coming after me. Which is fine. He has to choose a future queen. I simply have to swan around with a light meter for the paparazzi helpfully grasped in my hand. I've been doing that for years. So I'm asking you, in your professional capacity, when should we start?"

Sir Thomas blinked at him, clearly unprepared for this level of buy-in. Portia cleared her throat.

"You have not dated marriageable prospects publicly before. You were seen on a few double dates with the Prince of Wales, Catriona Mellors, and her friend Lily Wentworth while you were still at university, and that got some positive attention —and remarks that you were a bit too inexperienced to be settling down, but that's not a problem any more. The timeline is good, what with Royal Ascot coming up. And it has to be someone you like. Chemistry is so important."

Eddie thought about his extended family and silently disagreed. But Portia was still talking.

"You're something of an easy target where romance is concerned. Generally speaking, the public is much fonder of a fairy tale than something that belongs in a gossip rag, but they've been cheerfully giving you the benefit of the doubt all this time."

"Funny, the fairy tales so often end up in the gossip rags anyway."

"It's the nature of the game," Portia said. He decided he liked her better than Tom. Perhaps if the opportunity ever presented itself, he would refrain from dancing on her grave.

"So you want me to be doing something with 'romantic potential.'"

"Eventually. Be seen with women in your own social stratum, is the main thing, to start. Make sure whoever it is has her eyes open. Most of the women in that file would need to be introduced to the nation at large, and that invests people. You can't start something up with one of them and then drop her. That would make you look like the villain."

And I already look too much like the kingdom's most notorious modern adulterer for that, Eddie thought. He suspected Portia and Tom were also thinking it.

Eddie nodded numbly, hands clenched into fists under the table. "Are we done here?"

"Have someone get in touch with our office when you've selected a few names, and we'll make sure they're invited to the Royal Enclosure at Ascot. It's been a pleasure, sir," Sir Thomas said. He looked as though he meant it. Well, he ought to, given how he'd won every point he wanted. Portia had something like pity on her face.

Sir Anthony stood up, effectively ending the meeting. He didn't check his watch. But then, he didn't have to. There were enough timepieces in this pile to keep a team of clock restorers busy year-round. Eddie shook hands with Sir Thomas and Portia once more, resisting the urge to wipe his hand on his trousers until he got out the door.

"Edward?" Sir Anthony hadn't called him by his first name in years. Hearing it yelled by crowds didn't phase him, but in a hallway at Buckingham Palace, spoken quietly, it jarred. "Are you truly comfortable with this?"

Eddie rubbed the back of his neck. A few strands of hair caught in a bracelet. He winced. "I used to think—I wanted it to be my own idea. Some grand, outrageous gesture. My choice. Too late for that now."

"I am… I harbor no small amount of regret for my role in persuading you that it would be better to let things take their course naturally, rather than force the issue with a public decla-ration. I thought you remained protected enough for that. I was mistaken. I apologize. Your privacy should never have been invaded in such a way, and your wishes should have been respected when you first expressed them, these many years ago."

Of all the things that had happened in the past few weeks, an apology from the man referred to in the media as "the Queen's sword" was the most unbelievable. He said the first thing that came to mind, and as usual, it was a mistake. "You're serious?"

Sir Anthony flinched. It was subtle, but still managed to strike guilt into Eddie's heart. "I get to go home to my husband at the end of the day. So does Thomas Foster-Hume, though I have always been perplexed about who *would* marry him. Clearly Jeremy Foster-Hume felt differently. We did things a certain way for certain reasons at a certain time. I believed that mold would suit you and your position. Again, I was wrong. Please accept my apology, and know that if I may be of any assistance in furthering your desires—whatever, and whomever, they might be—I will do what it is in my power to do." He gave an abbreviated bow, and walked away.

Eddie gaped at his retreating figure until Isaac cleared his throat.

"Ready, sir?"

"I... yes."

He didn't meet Isaac's eyes, striding down the hallway as fast as he could without breaking into a run. He had somewhere else he desperately wanted to be.

At twenty-two, Eddie had become the official Patron of a tiny, unknown organization operating out of an East London storefront, dedicated to helping LGBTQIA teens and adults, many of whom were rape and abuse survivors. He never said much about it, though at the time he gave an impassioned quote to a friendly journalist about how too many people were made to believe they were worthless, helpless to get out of terrible situations, and no one should have to feel that way. As far as the public knew, his work for the London Crisis and Counseling Centre was limited to fundraising. Even now it was still considered more questionable in some circles than his patronage of an organization dedicated to boarding and caring for retired racehorses, but that was why he hated those circles.

"Eddie!" Tonya McIntyre, the Centre's director and one of his closest friends, reached for his hands as soon as he got inside the front doors. She was the recovery specialist brought in seven years ago when a traumatized nineteen-year-old prince refused to let go of his bodyguard. They agreed very early on in his therapy to ignore royal protocol. Her twist-out contained every color of the rainbow, curls a fluffy waterfall around her round, brown face. The LC3 was her baby. She looked him up and down. "I heard a rumor you might be about this afternoon."

"Thought I'd drop by, see if there was anything I could do."

"We have a mailer going out about alcoholism, you could stuff envelopes."

"All I need is a wet sponge, a table that doesn't rock, and a dream."

"Far too good for you, your highness." Tonya led him back to her office. He smiled at the potted vine trailing fat green leaves all around the room. The plant had been much smaller when he began seeing her.

"How are you?" she asked.

"You're not technically my therapist anymore."

"Still technically your friend."

"You don't sound like my friend. You sound like my therapist."

She took a sip from a plain mug, watching him over the rim. "I'm moonlighting. Take your time." One of the first things they worked on initially was his reluctance to accept help at all, on the grounds that he didn't honestly deserve it. The more things change. He tugged at a bracelet.

"Rough couple weeks," he said. "Brought up some things."

"You could have called me."

He rubbed the back of his neck. "There was the time difference. And I didn't know how to talk about it. How to feel, I suppose."

"Do you now?"

"No. I've been presented with enough options, I'm sure I can work something out. Apparently I should be outraged at the invasion of my privacy."

"It seems like a lot of people are outraged about that."

"Is it terrible to say that I'm not even sure I noticed that part of it, at first? My privacy has been under constant bombardment since I was born. When I was a teenager, a footman sold pictures of my breakfast for thousands of pounds. But *now* I'm supposed to wring my hands? I don't want people to think this time is different, or somehow worse. I'm not a victim of my sexuality. I resent the implication that I should behave like one." He stared out her office window at the brightly colored playground equipment the Centre could afford because someone, a long time ago, had done something horrible to him and put him on the path to this place. "I thought about coming out when Stephen and I were together. Being able to act like I loved him would have been an unimaginable luxury. But look what happened with Arthur and Catriona. The press practically sent him into hiding after the breakup. As bad as it is with a woman, with anyone else it would be infinitely worse. And it's not like I have someone in mind with whom to remind the world that at least one Kensington is capable of actual human connection. Sorry. I didn't mean to go on."

Tonya handed him a mug of tea. "I did ask. Not much to unpack at all, is there?"

Eddie threw her a jaunty salute with two fingers, leaning a hip against her desk. "I came here right from a meeting about it. Roped into a public relations campaign teasing the idea that I might 'settle down' with a suitable woman—of course—to banish the specter of queerness, as if that's all it takes. Maybe I should walk around in a t-shirt emblazoned with the definitions of bi- and pansexual." He allowed himself an eye roll. "That would help, I'm sure. It's what the world needs, a prince associated with ungrounded and phobic stereotypes about people with nonbinary sexualities. I already have an infamously and tragically gay dead uncle and an infamously and tragically unfaithful father. Why shouldn't I fulfill their expectations?"

"Eddie." Tonya cut him off before he could apologize again. "Tell me some true things."

"I'm not your patien—"

"Three. True. Things."

He swallowed. "I like the color purple. My favorite book when I was a child was about two children running away to live in an art museum in New York. My e-reader broke two days ago and I haven't had time to ask anyone to order a new one."

"Good," she said. "My turn, right? You're not expendable to the people who love you. You aren't defined by public perception. You control your story."

He hunched as she spoke. "Doesn't feel much like I'm in control of anything," he whispered.

"Of course it doesn't. How could it?" Her voice was warm. She touched the back of his hand, and he met her steady gaze. "Do you mind the course you've chosen? The public relations stunt, I mean."

"I would have done it anyway, to give Arthur cover while he settles in. The spare, you know. Multi-talented. Good for parts. And now? It seems... easiest. Find someone I like, be seen here and there. Then we break it off, and it's splashed all over forever, but what do I care? Everyone gets to conjecture themselves into a stupor at all stages."

"While grim, that's hardly a grand commitment. Why accept the fictional premise of what you're going to do? You might have a good time, as long as it lasts. You're allowed that. They don't get to define you. Only you get to do that." The sympathy in her eyes felt like scraping his knuckles on concrete.

"Come on, there has to be someone who needs more help than I do," he said. "Please, Tonya. I can't spend all day crying in your office. Let me be of service to someone. Brighten a day." She stared at him for a long moment, then looked at the clock.

Eddie's role when he volunteered at the Centre was mostly

to talk, one on one. Or he played video games in the common room with whoever wanted to. No cameras, no feel-good spreads about his good works. He was a presence, whenever he could be, for people who didn't believe anyone was on their side.

"If you're up for it, I think Mikhail could use a chat," Tonya said. "He's from York. He's here because of an abusive partner, an older man who convinced him to leave university and move in with him. Controlling with money, isolated him from his friends. Apparently things came to a head when Mikhail denied him sex and the piece of shit beat him outright. He blames himself for the whole thing. He's skittish, standoff-ish. But he says he's done, wants to figure out something else. He doesn't have any money, a job, nothing. His family kicked him out when he came out." She shook her head. "No matter how many times I see it, I'll never understand. Says he can't talk to any of his friends. He's talked about his best friend back home, and I think you might be able to convince him to get in touch."

Eddie nodded, and took a few deep breaths, consciously dropping his public guard. Royal was fine, he couldn't get away from that, even if he wanted to. But fake was not.

Once they got to the right door in the Centre's shelter, Tonya knocked softly. "Mikhail, there's someone here today who wants to see you. Are you up for a conversation, love?"

The door opened, revealing a sickly oval face on top of a scarecrow body, a shock of dyed purple hair sticking out under a ragged knit beanie. He startled at the sight of Eddie. Tonya looked between them, smiled when Mikhail nodded and stepped back.

Eddie walked in and folded up on the linoleum floor, back to the wall opposite the metal bunk bed. He found it best to make himself small and low. It helped convince people to relax, jar their expectations. Mikhail sat down gingerly on his bed, favoring his right side.

"Why d'you want to talk to me, anyway?" Mikhail asked, crossing his arms, head ducked to hide the angry multicolored bruising around his left eye.

"Tonya told me you might use a chat."

"And you've got nothing better to do?"

"I help out around here. I'm Patron." Eddie shrugged.

"Saw your name on the wall, didn't I? Doesn't usually translate into house calls."

"Wouldn't take it personally if you hadn't been paying much attention. Most people aren't on their way in here."

"Too right. You're famous here this week, though. Everyone's talking. Are you going to deny it?" Mikhail watched Eddie expectantly, like the next thing he said might make or break this entire thing, like he was hungry to discuss trouble not his own.

Eddie let out a breath he had been holding for over half his life. "No. I'm massively queer."

Mikhail grinned, sudden and sharp. "Knew it. You looked too happy in those pictures. We all remember being that happy." Shadows crowded in to his eyes. "So what you want with me?"

"To talk. See if you need anything in particular."

"Me boyfriend not to break my face. It'd be fine if he…" Mikhail trailed off. "Shit. I don't want to go back there."

"I don't want you to," Eddie said. "No one can stop you, but I don't want you back there with someone who hurts you."

"You don't even know me."

"I don't need to know you for that." They sat there for a few minutes in silence. Mikhail was fidgety at first, wincing when his shifting pulled at obviously bruised ribs.

"I liked it in the beginning, being his…his boy, you know? Being special." He spat the words like they had a bad taste.

Eddie nodded, waiting.

"It's easy, right? Being what someone wants. Not like being wanted much was ever in the cards for me. But that doesn't mean he could tell me not to see my friends, or tell me I was stupid and couldn't make it at university, right?"

"Right. And it doesn't say anything bad about you if you listened to him for a while."

Mikhail hugged his own knees, red-rimmed eyes getting teary. "I don't have anywhere to go. Aunt and uncle don't want me, tossed me out when I said I liked boys. Bible thumpers, couldn't bear the thought. Been a shit mate for the last couple years to anyone who knew me before. Nobody's going to take me in. And I've got nothing, I had to sneak out, he's got it all locked up. There's some stuff I really want. I know that's shit, I know I shouldn't care so much, but it's just... He's got my whole life, what's left of it. What I kept for myself."

Eddie swallowed against the rush of empathetic terror. "Who was your best friend before this?"

"Galen. He held on longer'n most, I guess."

"Give him a call," Eddie said. "I promise, the people who love you will be so happy you're trying to do something else with your life now."

"You think?"

"I think he'll at least go shopping for some new clothes with you," Eddie said. "That's what friends are for sometimes, right?" He pushed his cell phone across the floor. Mikhail stared at it like it might grow teeth and start jumping. "I'll dial," Eddie offered. "And I'll talk to him, if you can't. Or if he says anything that upsets you."

Mikhail pushed his hair back off his face, ignoring when the purple bit flopped right back over. His voice shook when he rattled off the numbers by heart. Eddie dialed and put the phone on speaker.

A cheerful voice answered. "Whoever's calling me from a

blocked number better be offering drugs, gainful employment, or a fine arse."

"Galen?" Mikhail's voice was a squeak.

"Who's this?" Less levity, more curiosity coming through the speaker.

"S'Mikhail." Silence. "I left the fucker."

"Shit, Mikey, where are you? Can you get someplace safe enough, I can get on the next train and come down, just don't go back there before I get to ye, don't let him—"

"No, shut it, I'm gone already, right? I left two days and four hours ago," Mikhail said, rocking back and forth. "Been staying at this place in London, they let you stay a few days and figure things out. I'm good. Thinking. About what to do next, y'know?"

"Shit. Right. Okay, how can I get the money to you for a train ticket? You're coming to mine." Galen sounded so fierce, Eddie could practically hear his grip on the phone. "Got a couch or you can bunk in with me, or maybe not if that's—if that reminds you—"

Mikhail cut him off again, bright red flush spreading across his cheekbones. "Don't be stupid. M'fine."

Galen started up talking again, and Eddie scooted toward the door. He poked his head out, and Harris turned automatically, raising an eyebrow as he had to look down at Eddie. Eddie motioned to him. Harris crouched.

"I want to go on a fear-of-god," he said, voice shaking a little bit despite how firm he tried to make it. "Can you ask Isaac to meet us?"

"Your highness," Harris said. He didn't have to keep speaking for the bleak reprimand to be effective. Eddie appreciated that.

"I'll stay in the car. I promise. He's so alone, hasn't talked to his best friend in over a year. They're on the phone now, his friend is already talking about taking him in, and—he doesn't have bodyguards if he goes back there to get what belongs to him."

Harris nodded. "I'll make the call." The sigh was implied.

Eddie went back in the room in time to hear Mikhail, looking shocked and more vulnerable than ever, saying good-bye to Galen.

"He's… he's coming down to get me. To *get* me, and to try and get my stuff. It's Friday, innit? He's in a band, he's gonna miss a show for me, a standing gig. He said it like it was no big thing, but I know it's hard, it's chancy, they might lose the job 'cause of me, and—"

"It'll be all right."

"It won't. It won't, John's going to be home and he's going to be mad, and Galen's not… he's not a big guy. He talks a big show, but John's gonna hurt him, I know it." He was trying not to cry openly. Eddie put his hand on the floor between them.

"He's not going to, because you and me are going to take a ride over there right now and get your stuff, and have it back here so when Galen comes the two of you can stay a night in the city, go see an act he likes if you want. I can get you in anywhere you want to go."

Mikhail blinked. "And who'm I gonna have to blow to get *that?*" He was trying for a joke, but there was a serious under-current that turned Eddie's stomach. He decided to fall back on honesty.

"There's so much in the world I can't do anything about. I want to do this. You've been through a hard time, right? You deserve some fun with your best mate. Although I'd appreciate if you didn't tell Tonya about us going to get your stuff."

"We're going to *get* it?"

Eddie's smile was grim. "Yes."

Mikhail's eyes were wide. "You, me, and what army?"

Eddie got to his feet and held out his hand. "Mine."

THE NEIGHBORHOOD MIKHAIL had run from was a solidly upper middle-class suburb, nearly abandoned in the middle of the day. Plastic bikes and trucks stood abandoned in a few neatly manicured front lawns. Mikhail sat next to Kimsey, leaning on her. Eddie was convinced she gave off "big sister" pheromones. Or perhaps Mikhail felt safest around women just now.

Mikhail watched Harris and Isaac, both dressed in street clothes, like he needed to know exactly where they were at all times. Cole got out his black leather jacket for occasions like this and had slid into the car looking ready to overthrow a small country for MI6. Eddie loved that jacket. Harris was in a long trench coat, looking a bit too much like a model no matter what he wore. Knitted Victorian bathing trousers would probably suit him. Harris turned around from the passenger seat and looked Mikhail right in the eye.

"Here's how this is going to be. We make sure the coast is clear, you come in and point to your stuff, and we take it away."

"His stuff, too," Cole said. "We'll set it on fire in the yard, if you want. And if anyone gets nosy, we'll tell them you're having some friends over."

"I never do that," Mikhail whispered. He was shaking.

"First time for everything, right?" Cole grinned, but his eyes were hard. "Nobody's gonna do a thing to you, even if the fucker is home."

When Mikhail didn't look convinced, Cole shrugged out of his jacket and skinned his shirt off. No one was more shocked by this than Eddie. Never mind the scars from a bullet and shrapnel, the dark dagger stretching across his pecs and down the center of his chest commanded attention. Cole twisted so they could see the elaborate angel wings painted permanently onto most of his back.

"I was SAS," Cole said, and smiled as he tugged his black t-shirt back on. "Let me at him. Got your key?"

Mikhail shook his head, eyes still devouring Cole. Eddie knew how he felt. "Never had a key."

Cole and Harris shared a look, then gave the trio in the back seat identical short nods and exited the car. They walked casually up to the house, leaping over the fence into the back-yard without breaking stride.

"Please God," Mikhail said, staring after them and crossing himself.

"You're religious?" Eddie asked, mostly to make conversation.

"Raised Eastern Orthodox. Didn't really believe any more until I… until I needed the help. You think God understands?"

"Probably appreciates the honesty," Eddie said, shrugging. "I like being in churches, but that's about all."

Mikhail nodded, eyes still fastened on the house. "If I go back in there I feel like I might not ever come out."

"You will. You have us with you." After two minutes, the light behind the front door flicked on and off twice.

"All clear," Kimsey said. "Let's go. Sir, as much as it pains me, I would be more comfortable if you went into the house instead of waiting by the car. It makes playing lookout easier."

"Whatever you say," Eddie said, pulling his knit hat far down over his head and tucking his curls up into it. "You ready? We'll get you out. I promise."

Mikhail's face was so tight. Eddie used a trick Isaac taught him a long time ago for getting someone's attention. "I need to hear your voice, Mikhail."

"Okay," he whispered.

"Okay," Eddie repeated. "You've got to go in, because Galen's coming and he's going to love this story, right?"

"Yeah." Some of the color came back into his face when Eddie mentioned Galen. "Yeah, this story is going to be sick. He's going to be so upset he missed it."

"So we better do it. You'll win bets in bars for the rest of your life. The time you, Prince Edward, and his security detail broke into your shithead ex's house and stole all your stuff."

Mikhail's bravado didn't last, and apparently Eddie had morphed into person-he-trusted, because by the time they made it up the front walk, Eddie had him clinging to his side like a koala. Eddie wrapped his arm around Mikhail's back. "You're having a mate over, that's it."

"To a place I don't legally live."

"And the mate's a prince."

"You must really get off on saying that," Mikhail said, any remaining awe at Eddie's presence gone.

"I find it grounding at times like this," Eddie said primly.

They went into the house, and Mikhail shuddered, catching sight of a spot on the floor in the front hall where the carpet was slightly discolored. Eddie didn't want to think about why.

The worst part was how normal the house seemed, a classic garden home layout that someone kept up with, decorated like something out of a magazine. No evidence a punk kid lived there at all.

"All my stuff's up in the back bedroom," he said. "It's locked up."

"Not anymore," Cole said, standing in the doorway leading to the kitchen. Even though he was a few inches shorter than Eddie, he made the place seem smaller, one hand braced on each side of the frame.

"I don't have anything—I should get some bin bags," Mikhail said, but Cole stopped him with a shake of his head.

"We brought, come on. I'll show you."

Eddie's heart broke as he followed the scared, sad boy up

the stairs. The way Mikhail's hand trailed over the banister, the almost dreamy look on his face. Eddie recognized it. Even bad memories could be precious, when you didn't have anything else.

Harris was already inside the small bedroom at the far end of the hall. A laptop covered with scratched off stickers lay carelessly tossed in the middle of the bed. Otherwise, the room looked uninhabited, except for the locks on the dresser drawers and closet. There was a broken-open padlock on the door. Mikhail gritted his teeth.

"He made me sleep in here when he was unhappy with me," he whispered. "Locked me in. For a couple days, once. I only had water from the en suite. I was delirious when he found me. He never did that again."

The snap of unfurling fabric jarred Mikhail out of his trance and Eddie from his desire to throw up. A duffel bag had appeared on the ground by Mikhail's feet. A second wad of black fabric was removed from one of Cole's trouser pockets and snapped into a duffel shape as well.

"Repurposed parachute fabric," Harris explained, smiling tightly at the looks on Eddie and Mikhail's faces. "Mostly we use the smaller ones down the shops. But these come in handy."

Cole jimmied the lock on the closet with a vicious-looking folded bit of metal and went to work on the dresser. Mikhail stared uncomprehendingly at the contents. "I don't want to take most of this stuff," he said. "I know that makes me ungrateful, I know it, but…"

"No. You don't have to be grateful to him. For anything. It's okay," Eddie said. He held out his hand, waiting for Mikhail's nod before he rested it on his shoulder. "Take what you want."

"I'm not going to have anything, m'gonna be a burden, Galen's going to—"

"What kind of fairy godmother would I be if I let that happen? Only take what you want."

Mikhail looked at the clock and swore, eyes going wide with fear. He nodded to himself, and then got to work. He sorted out the older stuff, liberating the punk clothes from the backs of the drawers. A box covered with band stickers. A few very well-thumbed paperbacks from under the bed, held together with binder clips. A tangle of tarnished silver chains and charms taped behind the nightstand. The laptop. Socks and underwear, old band t-shirts, a pair of ripped skinny jeans. He shuddered when he touched some decorative leather cuffs. Eddie didn't want to think about what he might be remembering. Mikhail took them. He left the thin black collar that matched them.

"I'll get a new one," he said, like he'd forgotten they were there. "Maybe Galen'll help me pick it out."

Finally, he looked around. "I think I'm ready," he said, voice trembling. "There's one thing, though, it's not in here." He looked wildly around at the ransacked drawers and open closet. "He took it, he had it, I don't know where—"

"What is it?" Harris asked. "We can look."

"S'a picture of me an' Galen at Glastonbury Festival. I tried to hide it all over, but he'd find it an' then…"

Cole looked at his watch. It was going on 2:30, around when John usually started for home for lunch, according to Mikhail. "We're running out of time, sir," he murmured.

"I can't leave it, I can't leave him here," Mikhail said, getting frantic. "He'll burn it again or tear it, he'll hurt him!"

"He can't hurt Galen," Eddie said, cupping Mikhail's bony elbows in his hands and holding his gaze. "He can't get to him. It's a picture. You're getting the real thing. I promise, Galen's on his way, remember?"

Mikhail collapsed into Eddie's embrace with one broken, terrified sound.

"No time," Cole said, voice hard. "Kimsey says the neighbors are starting to get home from picking up their kids. Got to go, sir."

Harris reappeared, shaking his head. "No joy," he said. "It's not anywhere people usually keep things like that." There was a hardness to his face, his body more rigid than Eddie had ever seen him. Whatever he had found in the search, it wasn't good.

"There'll be new pictures of you," Eddie told the shaking boy in his arms. "I promise."

"That was the last happy day of my life," Mikhail said, face pressed into Eddie's chest.

"So far," Eddie told him. Harris and Cole each hoisted a duffel. Mikhail took one look around the wreck of a bedroom and went. He looked into the master bedroom, with its navy blue accent wall and matching duvet cover, and went pale around the edges, eyes burning with rage.

"It's a *room*," he said. Then he spat on the ground and walked down the stairs, clutching his laptop like a child in his arms.

They made it back into the car without incident. Kimsey shoved Eddie into the car after Mikhail. Harris and Cole were having a conversation in the front seat. Mikhail went rigid as they passed a car at the entrance to the cul-de-sac.

"That's John," he said, flinging himself down.

"The windows are tinted," Kimsey told him, rubbing his back. "He can't see you." Mikhail still couldn't stop hyperventilating. At the end of the next block, Harris caught Cole's eye and they shared a nod. Cole pulled the car to a halt and Harris ducked out after grabbing something from the glove compartment.

"What's going on?" Eddie said, watching Harris shove his hands into his pockets and walk back the way they'd come, whistling, like he didn't have a care in the world.

"Harris thought of a place he didn't look for the picture," Cole said. Eddie opened his mouth to say something, but Cole shook his head, jerking his head at Mikhail.

By the time they got Mikhail back to the Centre, through traffic, it was almost four o'clock and he was vibrating with adrenaline, shock, and terrified anticipation. He kept asking where Galen was, checking if he knew where to come. All Eddie could do was reassure him, and make a few unobtrusive calls.

"Where did you whisk him off to?" Tonya asked, raising an eyebrow at the duffel bags.

"We went shopping," Eddie said. "I think you should retain as much plausible deniability as possible."

"What, again?"

"As many times as I can."

"You can't save them all, Eddie."

Eddie looked down the hall. Cole stood guard in his customary undercover stance, slouching against the wall. He straightened when a woman in hijab holding two little boys by the hand came down the hall. He murmured something in Urdu, and the woman sized him up before she responded. In a couple of beats, Cole was on one knee, touching fingertips with the braver boy and talking to them quietly.

"I can try."

They convinced Mikhail to try taking a nap. With Cole standing guard outside the door, he managed. Galen arrived, all inexpertly frosted tips and frantic, obstinate expression, a tornado of pent-up energy and volume. He was tripped up by Eddie's presence, doing the most profound double-take Eddie had ever seen outside of an animated cartoon.

"What the fuck?"

"That's 'What the fuck, Your Royal Highness?' to you," Cole murmured. Galen snapped to what approximated attention.

"Your Royal Highness?" It came out on a thin sigh.

"I met Mikhail earlier today and took an interest. He's sleeping right now. I thought perhaps you and I could talk for a few minutes with Director McIntyre before you go in and see him. He's had a rough few days."

"He's had a rough few years," Galen said. His defiance crumpled. "I have to see him. I promised. Won't wake him. But I have to see him."

Eddie couldn't do other than agree. Galen disappeared without another word, coming back out with suspiciously bright eyes. "He's well out, you're right. So what do you want to talk about?"

About forty-five minutes later, after a meeting Galen called "the most awkward 'so what are your intentions towards my son' conversation I've ever had," he went inside to wake Mikhail. They kept the door open so Mikhail wouldn't feel trapped. They needn't have worried. Eddie could hear the sleepy murmur and then the shout. He poked his head in to find Mikhail wrapped around Galen, arms and legs locked in place like he would never let go, face nudged into his neck. Galen rocked him back and forth, one knee on the bed, other foot on the floor. Eddie couldn't hear what he was saying, but the fierce, helplessly devoted look on Galen's face told him a story, and he left them alone.

They emerged a few minutes later, hip to hip, fingers in each other's belt loops like they were ready to fight being separated at any moment. Cole and Kimsey escorted them to the car.

"Time to shop," Eddie said. They went to Topman first. Two hours later, Eddie dropped them off at a fancy hotel laden with parcels from various shops as well as a couple of sacks of greasy fish and chips takeaway. They exchanged phone numbers and email addresses so Eddie could send Mikhail and Galen pictures he had taken of them together. At the last minute, Mikhail gave Eddie a careful one-armed hug, not meeting his eyes. Eddie let out a breath as the two young men piled into the elevator. They waved as the doors shut.

"Quite a day's work, sir," Cole said, coming to stand behind him. "Harris reported back. He's got the picture." His voice was chill with satisfaction, letting Eddie know that the fucker had tried to put up a fight with a determined, trained killer.

"I'll mail it on," Eddie said. "Don't want to remind him now." He tried to hide a yawn, before deciding it didn't matter.

"Saving souls takes effort."

"I didn't," Eddie protested.

"Don't give me any of that. You got that boy's world turning again. Both of them. That's worth something."

"Take me home," Eddie said, shifting his weight so that he leaned against Cole. "I've got that damned reception tonight. Maybe some fish and chips for me on the way?"

"Yes, sir."

"Will you watch some football with me tonight?" A pause, during which Eddie couldn't remember how to breathe.

"'Course, Eddie."

7

D aniel hefted his computer bag higher on his shoulder. The stiffness of his new clothes reminded him to stand up straight. It had only taken a week for Gilda to force him back to the land of the living, although he wasn't sure Buckingham Palace could be called living as he customarily thought of it. He kept thinking each successive experience was the strangest one: having the hired car sent through the gates round the side of the Palace by armed guards, getting out at the Privy Purse Door, seeing the tourists clustered outside the tall black metal gates from the inside, being greeted by a footman in full livery, red coat, well-turned ankle and all. It took significant effort, but he refrained from asking if life had improved since Belle and the Beast fell in love.

Knowing in an abstract way that the palace was a working office building hadn't prepared him for the sight of chest-high copy machines and rolling desk chairs in converted Georgian receiving rooms. The footman led him through a few of these —rooms of older computers on open plan desks pushed together in groups of four, phones ringing, muted conversations, laughter. The wiring for the computers ran over the carpets in insulated sleeves. The *office* of it all felt impermanent when he looked at the moldings and fine plasterwork ceilings, the landscapes on the walls.

Until this walk-through, he hadn't considered how much administration went in to being the royal family. There were the ceremonial duties and the major public appearances to plan for and coordinate. Then there were the hundreds of organizations and charities to which each Kensington was connected. Someone had to keep track of schedules, plan events, keep everything moving, while overseeing the legal and political ramifications of it all, shaping the message from the palace, dealing with the press, and the inevitable scandals and missteps. Many someones. And the sheer effort it must take to keep this pile going, never mind all the other royal residences. The briefing book given to him by the palace a week before had also mentioned something about tracking and maintaining the royal art collections—including jewelry and wardrobes— and keeping up with finances going back to the time of William the Conqueror. The people who did all that had to work somewhere. Most of them worked here, although the bulk of the art and royal collection administration was done out of Windsor Castle.

It sounded like the bullpen at the *Journal*, but here, no high heels were kicked off under desks, no jackets draped across the backs of chairs. The entire place was on best behavior, as though at any moment the Queen might walk through. It made sense. She might.

He was passed off to a black woman about his age with an intricate sweep of thick braids who introduced herself as Matilda. She took him to a honeycomb of smaller offices where Legal and the Research Unit did their work, and then to a row of large, finely appointed offices. This was where the private secretaries worked, a rotating staff with round-the-clock access to members of the royal family and their lives. At Matilda's desk, there was a mound of paperwork four inches high for him to sign. Injury release forms, non-disclosures about anything he might see or hear outside the scope of his assignment while in the palace. The legal team at the *Journal* had gone over it all in detail already, he understood from Gilda, and his mandate was laughably broad—a circumstance that did not escape the woman sitting across from him. Her eyes reminded him of dentists' drills.

Matilda led him away from the last vestiges of the world as he understood it. The residence was as much a museum as the rest of the place, though of a different time period. Daniel's mother was an interior designer. He'd grown up with enough decorating books and magazines around to know what he was looking at. Austere early 1950s décor clashed with the crown moldings and high ceilings. Whoever had redone the residence would not have wanted to seem showy in the postwar era, when rationing was still a reality for the whole country, and so many lives had been lost. The furniture was all antiques, but these were worn, used pieces, like the ones legions of grandmothers had. A few updates to upholstery and wallpaper had been done in the 1980s, judging from the stripe and floral prints, but that was all. Seventy years of careful housekeeping by professionals meant that there wasn't an extension cord, stray book left on an end table, or cell phone charger to be seen.

"Do people actually live here?" He aimed for conspiratorial amusement, but the sound echoed and died.

"Did you expect a three-bedroom bungalow with a back garden on? This is a palace."

His leg was already screaming. Palaces were overrated.

"We thought about moving everything to an office in a different part of the building, but Her Majesty wanted you to see everything *in situ*, as it were. The Queen Mother's filing system was…"

"Eccentric?" he offered, firing a smile across the enemy's bow.

"Individual," she said. Quellingly.

Daniel paused, positioning his body weight over his right side in the way his physical therapist had expressly forbidden. "Were you close with her?"

"I was her private secretary for the last four years. It's been a great shock to the whole system around here."

"I'm not here to cause trouble," he said, as gently as he could given the way the nerves in his hip were throbbing down his leg. "Not interested in digging anything up. I'm here to get the job started. Today I am an archivist."

"I've read your contract," Matilda said. "You have first option to publish stories taken from her notes. And to do interviews, look for corroboration from people who knew her and so on."

"Well, you could hardly expect my editor to lend me out for free," he said, with more confidence than he felt. When her flat, unamused expression didn't change, he decided to try something else.

"I met her once, you know."

Matilda nodded. "It's why Her Majesty asked for you. Apparently you made an impression."

Daniel shrugged—an old, bad habit Gilda was always after him for—not disliking the implicit praise. "It was for an assignment in a journalism course. We were told to take news pieces from the first half of the 20th century and research them again. I chose a puff piece from World War II about what the royal family was doing during the Blitz. I called Queen Mary's office to see if she would comment, since at the time none of the press would have been able to get access and all that. I never expected a response, but then I got one."

"That would have been about ten years ago?" she guessed,

looking him up and down. "They weren't much for press around that time."

"Understandably. So I get a couple of vigorous phone screenings and then they drag me in for a meeting. Right here, actually. Convinced I was going to throw up on my shoes, or hers, maybe. But she was incredible. Answered all my questions and then some. She dragged me down to the basement so I could see where they spent the nights. I wasn't expecting her to have an extra power pack."

"Nobody does, about the Kensingtons," Matilda said, voice laced with bitter affection. "Their energy is mind-boggling."

"It must take a lot to keep up with them."

"Believe me, it does," she said. "But it's worth it for the chance to be on the inside of such a wild old ride. I'm out now, of course."

"Pardon?"

"It's my last week here. I'll be available for interviews, but they don't like to keep us around too long. New blood needed, you know? I can't stay on indefinitely, looking after a batty old lady's papers. It wouldn't look good on the rolls." She was wounded and frustrated and blithe all at once.

"I don't want to make her look foolish," Daniel told her. "She wasn't a batty old lady. And even if she was, I'd be dragged up and down Hyde Park by my ankles if I said so."

Matilda's expression became marginally less shuttered. "Well," she said briskly, "don't say I didn't warn you about the state of things."

She led him without comment or fanfare down a corridor littered with various coats of arms of the current House of Kensington. She opened a door, and he nearly turned and ran. The Queen Mother, among her other fine qualities, clearly had a great deal of respect for the mental fortitude and organizational ability of her future biographers.

"She said she was putting her papers in order," Matilda

said, fondness mixing with now understandable exasperation. "She neglected to leave any clues as to what that order might one day have become. I'll have sandwiches sent up at lunch." He was about to tell her not to bother, and then remembered this job would take more energy than lying in his bed all day, and thanked her instead.

"If you need anything, pick up the phone. I mean that quite literally, an operator is on duty on that line at all times."

"I don't have to press a button?"

"No," she said, smiling for the first time. "Welcome to Royal life, Mr. Black. If you need me, let the operator know."

THE CLOCK on the corner of the Queen Mother's desk chimed. Daniel looked up from a stack of papers, uncomprehending. He did a double-take when he saw the time. It had gone four o'clock in the afternoon while he wandered the room, dipping in and out of diaries, paging through files at random. Getting a feel for her. He hadn't expected the day to go so fast, and to have so little to show for it. The endeavor had him feeling uncomfortably voyeuristic. These were her thoughts, some meant for others to see, some not. Maybe it would have been easier if he hadn't met her, if she hadn't been kind to him. The note she'd left saying *Find that clever young man*, had been propped up on the mantelpiece, obviously so that he would find it and understand both the tacit approval and the crushing responsibility. The dead woman was on his side. A ringing endorsement if ever he heard one. She had wanted him specifically to put her life in some kind of order. Looking around at the filing cabinets and the overflowing banker's boxes, he wondered if she'd known what she was asking.

He was going to need an assistant. Or three. Or to accept this being his life's work.

He shied away from that thought. Gilda had presented this as a way of getting back in the game, avoiding talking to him about ramifications or future plans. Probably didn't want to overwhelm him. Everything was on a trial basis, as if he weren't an utter mess lucky to get a foot in the door. Not that this was a door he had ever considered going through before.

Gilda and the queen were friendly. Queen Victoria once told an interviewer that she read the *Journal* first thing every day. It did not escape most people that the *Journal* was the one paper that rarely provided coverage on the royal family's activities outside the Queen's duties as head of state. But the possibility of a royal scoop was almost as good as a royal scoop. Part of Daniel's job here was to pull out enough papers and extracts to publish a retrospective in the Queen Mother's own words for a feature in the *Journal*, with the royal family's approval.

"So you're the grave robber."

The world came back into focus on a slender blonde standing in the doorway, wearing a black bikini, lemon yellow flip-flops, and a Union Jack beach towel hanging around her neck. Daniel thought for a second he might be hallucinating. Training and the notion that he should recognize this person kept him from spitting out something unfortunate. He thought he should probably stand, but his leg wouldn't play.

"Pardon?"

"The grave robber. The memory thief. The *biographer*." From her wide mouth, that was the most damning epithet of all. He examined her face. For the last year he'd lived under a rock, but the rock of the National Health Service had a lot of glossy magazines in its waiting rooms.

"Your Royal Highness," he said, using his arms to lift himself out of the chair far enough to bow, very awkwardly, from the waist up. She lifted her chin.

"Call me Alex."

"No, I don't think I will," he said.

"You're refusing to honor a request for familiarity from a member of the Royal Family?" she asked, arching a well-shaped eyebrow.

"When it's the opening salvo at a declaration of hostilities, absolutely."

Her eyes widened in exaggerated shock. "What gave you that idea?"

He smirked. He'd been told his smirk was irritating. Her reaction didn't disabuse him of the notion.

She sauntered farther into the room, flip-flops clapping between the thick carpets and her feet. "You're only here to paw over my grandmother's life looking for scraps."

"She did invite me," he pointed out, ignoring the sharp pinch of guilt in his stomach. Princess Alexandra had hit on what bothered him most about this project. Usually subjects could consent to be interviewed. But he didn't know which of the Queen Mother's papers had been intended by her for public consumption. It looked to him that she'd been sorting things into two broad categories, fair game and a burn bag. But she had clearly lost too much time during her last bout of pneumonia. Was his role to finish the job for her, or to put that failure on display? At one time, there wouldn't have been a question in his mind.

The memory thief, the princess called him. Of her grandmother's memories, or her own?

"There's no accounting for taste," she said, blinking lazily at him. "She invited a great many peculiar people in." Her voice was downright coquettish, but she squared off like they were MMA fighters in the octagon. In her expensive, revealing swimsuit. (And he still didn't know why *that* was.) It made him feel exposed. Like she expected something of him he might not have to give.

"I'm not at liberty to publish anything all that exciting, even if I do find it."

"What's to stop you?"

"Contracts. The fear of God, my editor, and your mother, in that order. Honor."

"That's a big concept for a man in the news media."

"Well, I've been sick." Despite the likely career suicide of going up against a Kensington—although Daniel knew he didn't have much of a career to destroy—Princess Alexandra's glower was an arm slamming down on the keys in his dusty piano of a brain. Waking him up.

"What other conditions are there on what you can publish?" she asked, suddenly all business. He now understood firsthand what a colleague once said over after-work drinks about talking to the Kensingtons. *"It's like being in a very polite wind tunnel that keeps changing direction. No question they can't sidestep, no implication they can't shatter with a single comment. It's maddening."*

He leaned back in the Queen Mother's gunmetal gray, rolling office chair, like a thousand others he'd sat in over the years. A hard plastic rug protector was tucked underneath the desk, spreading out behind it, so he could actually roll. He wondered if he could get up enough steam to go crashing out the nearest window. It seemed simpler than remaining a target for Princess Alexandra's—Alex's?—eye lasers.

"I can't publish any 'intimate details,' so if your gran was in the habit of documenting her amatory adventures, her secrets are safe. I'm prevented from using anything someone tells me as an excuse to go poking around."

"How can they possibly enforce that?" Alexandra asked, brow furrowing.

"They're counting on the frankly obscene amount of available material to dissuade me, I'm sure. I can't go trawling exhaustively after every little scrap of gossip, I'll be here the rest of my natural life." They both shuddered at once, and then, taken aback, watched one another warily. "I'm not allowed to make anything up. You'd think that would go without saying, but I'm told the royal beat is something else. My scope for interpretation is somewhat limited. I need corroboration from a reputable source for anything that upsets the apple cart, so to speak. Murder, infidelity, criminal behavior. I get to decide what reputable is, unless the palace doesn't like something, in which case they're free to attempt discrediting me any way they see fit. If I were them I'd be building a compelling case that I abuse prescription pain medication, but I'm not doing their jobs for them. And, I can't write about anything that I hear or see in the course of my employment here. Which I'm assuming you knew, or else you wouldn't be in here looking like Gidget Goes Buckingham."

"Do you?"

"Do I what?" He'd lost track of his own rant.

"Abuse prescription pain medication."

"No. Why? Do you want some?"

Alexandra examined her nails, flipping the switch to insouciance. "We all have to amuse ourselves somehow."

"I'm sure you have better things to do."

"Of course I do. I'm going for a swim."

"A what?"

"A swim. You go to an available body of water and submerge yourself. And in your case, if I'm lucky, you drown. Too much to hope for, but so pleasant to imagine." Her smile reminded him of a wistful shark. He had to admire how thoroughly she was taking advantage of his contractual obligation not to print anything she said.

"So you're off for a swim in your family's pool in the middle of the day? I don't know why anyone would think you're a drain on public resources."

"If you think we're all so bloody useless, why are you doing this? Surely a heroic war reporter such as yourself must have all sorts of important assignments to cover."

A hit. A very palpable hit. And someone had been doing

some research of her own. Not enough to find that he hadn't put up a byline in a year. Or maybe she was saving it. She seemed the type to hoard advantages and let them out inch by little inch.

"You think I don't understand my subject?" Daniel wanted to see her boil over again. Instead, she simmered. Damned Kensingtons.

"You don't understand the job. You can't possibly understand Mary if you don't understand the job."

"So what's the job?" Daniel realized he was half out of his chair, hands braced on the desk. Her weight was forward, on her toes. He relaxed, with an effort. He couldn't outrun her, even if he wanted to try. She settled back, fingers straying to the hem of her towel. As if she wanted to pull it across her in the still, cool air. But she didn't. A shred of vulnerability from the warrior in front of him.

"There's a leadership dinner here tonight. A bunch of politicians who think I'm an idiot are going to not-very-surreptitiously stare at my arse while I'm forced to be polite to them. I thought I would go for a swim to relax after visiting the cancer ward at Children's Hospital this morning." She looked judgmental when his eyebrows rose. "What, didn't think I was good for much?"

"Your highness, please believe me when I say I have no way of knowing what you're good for at all."

"I'm good at entertaining children. Children with cancer. They're all very brave. I came back here for a swim and a cry. I got the cry out of the way early, so I thought I'd come see you."

"I'm honored."

"You should be. I'm very important." The moment held. Her jaw remained clenched.

"The Children's Hospital—that's one of your grandmother's charities, isn't it?"

"She went in person. Took me with her sometimes."

"Is it difficult?"

"What do you think? It's like we don't have feelings, to you."

"It's a job, you said."

"A job and our lives." Her voice was flat. "If you don't understand the connection between the two, you'll never be able to write about Mary, or any of us."

"Why do you call her Mary?"

Alexandra clouded over, taken aback by the question. Daniel prepared for scorn so withering he would never even think about regaining a sense of self-worth. He saw the split-second change in her expression as she decided to answer him honestly.

"After my grandfather died—that's the King, to you—she said she missed hearing her name. He was one of the few people who used it. That's the thing. Even if you're a professor or a doctor or something, you can leave your house incognito. Here, everyone always knows, and they *can't* call you anything else and still be respectful. So it's really only your family who can even speak to you, and once people in your generation go, you're sort of lost in a sea of your titles, not your self." She cut herself off. "Look, what I'm saying is if you think it's all waving from carriages and eating truffles, you are an incurious ass who should have his pencils taken away."

"I already don't think that. But you can't deny that you live an outrageously privileged existence."

"Do a ride-along with me on my next full day of appearances, and then we'll talk about it." She reached up and redid her ponytail, watching him while her hands worked. Then she crossed her arms. "In exchange, you can use me as a confirming source."

His eyebrows flew to his hairline. "You're serious?"

"Yes. I can't stop you. I can make sure you're accurate. But I want something else."

"Yes, your highness?"

"All right, two things. First: I get to veto a story if I think it will do grievous emotional harm. I have one in mind. I'm not going to tell you what it is. But if you run across it, I'm going to stop you. By asking nicely or by demanding not nicely. There are factors in our lives you cannot possibly understand, priorities that you don't care about."

"As a journalist, I'm not supposed to."

She waved her hand impatiently. "Fine. Right. Duty to the country and all that, except we're supposed to be the face of it and none of you care about *that* when it's time to file. Second: call me Alex."

"Is that a condition?"

"Ironclad. Do you agree?" She stuck her hand out across the desk. Daniel looked from the manicured nails and slender fingers to her intense, pale green eyes. He didn't trust her. But she only wanted to veto one story, and it wasn't actionable, he told himself. He knew about himself that he wouldn't go back on it, even if he came across something truly shocking. He was too curious. An agreement was an agreement. So he took her hand. They shook, but she held on to his hand too long. He realized she was staring at the ropy scar winding across the back of it. He hardly noticed it any more.

"What happened?" she asked, thumb brushing over it very gently.

"Roadside bomb," he said. Her mouth tightened, but she didn't pursue it.

"I'll have my private secretary get in touch. Call it research."

"What else would I call it?"

Her smirk was a flawless mirror of his. It was a very

annoying smirk, after all. As he watched her go, a single thought pounded through his brain.

Daniel, what are you doing?

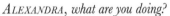

ALEXANDRA, what are you doing?

Alex sliced through the water, swimming harder than usual. Eloise, one of the kids she visited often, was doing poorly. She put on a brave face for the Princess, they all did, but she'd been tired today, the purplish smears around her eyes dark and menacing. Her mother had been itching to run Alex out of the room so Eloise could sleep. But Eloise hadn't wanted to sleep. She wanted to spend time with her very own princess. Alex felt like she was about six years old and unbearably selfish for staying so long. Eloise looked sad when they waved goodbye. She was too immunocompromised for a hug.

Alex broke the surface and ripped off her goggles, flinging them into the deep end. She pressed her palms against her eyes. They stung with chlorine and tears. Eloise was going to die. All three of them knew it, none of them wanted to say it out loud, and her heart was breaking as if it had the right.

She hadn't been thinking clearly, which obviously was why she went out on a limb for that nosy, unbelievable journalist with the sloe eyes. Prying into corners where he didn't belong, between the covers of Mary's life, when Alex hadn't been allowed to look at her diaries. Mary told her stories, so many of them. They all blended together into the version of her life Mary wanted her granddaughter to know.

Alex wanted a little control over something. Anything. Even if it was a tenuous fantasy. Sometimes people needed those. After so many years living with the humiliation of journalists speculating over every expression on her face, every adolescent mistake, every outfit, it felt viciously satisfying to hold it over that man's head that she knew more than he did, that she could stop him talking if she wanted. She knew she didn't have any real standing, but he looked like the kind of person who would keep a promise. She caught sight of her reflection in the water, and wondered if she looked like the kind of person who could tell.

She trailed her fingertips through the face she saw in the water. The pool room was designed to keep the light in, greedy for any sun it could catch. Even in the late afternoon on a cloudy day, it glowed. Like she was already underwater. Already drowning. She paddled out into the deep end, bobbing around like she was a kid again. Buoyancy was a part of life back then. It hadn't been buoyancy she felt while sparring with that reporter. That *biographer*. It was the pressure of a champagne cork after the bottle had been shaken. Giving him access to deny him a scoop. Turning power, and powerlessness, to her advantage. Not a bad day's work. Even though the day wasn't over yet. Just what she needed—a dinner with a herd of stuffed shirts all ready to write her off as a frivolity. Her very existence had been remarked on in the critical press as "an unnecessary expense" when her mother had gotten pregnant for the third time. A second child might be a necessary evil for the succession, but a third was blatant showing off.

In another century, Alex and Eddie's loyalties would have been endlessly questioned. Plots swirling around them, their very lives in danger. This was better. All they had to deal with was a press establishment with the instincts of piranha, political leadership who sneered at them, a public that longed for them. Oh, and they were both estranged from their father, had stilted relationships with their mother and brother, and had to walk around with armed guards all the time.

It wasn't much better. At least the medical care no longer involved leeches and bleeding.

A quiet cough interrupted her. "Time to get ready, Alex." Lydia, her private secretary, stood in the doorway. "Sorry."

"No trouble, of course." She clambered out of the water and grabbed her towel. It had been ridiculous to go in there wearing her yacht bathing suit. She had thought to put him off his game. She hadn't expected a man with a drawn face, scarred hand, and no game at all.

THE PAIN in his hip started sharp, and got duller and broader as the day went on. Daniel hadn't sat in a desk chair for any length of time in over a year, and his body wasn't used to being in one position. He had actually done his stretches this morning, cursing and sweating through a half set of each before showering, but he hadn't stretched throughout the day as he was supposed to. By the time the sun went down, he could barely bend at the waist, much less stand. He leaned on one elbow, Mary's handwriting blurring in front of him.

"You're still here?"

For the second time, Princess Alexandra appeared in front of him. Now she wore an understated green dress with a narrow patent leather belt, hair falling around her face in soft curls. A modern porcelain doll, she took up not an extra square inch of room. It chilled him.

"Does it ever feel strange to carry a purse to an event in your house?"

"It's a half-hour round trip to my bedroom if I forget my lip gloss."

"Surely you have people to fetch for you."

Alexandra tilted her head to one side. "Why would I ask them to do that instead of carrying a purse?"

Daniel couldn't come up with a single good reason. He was

also having trouble thinking through the agony radiating down his side and into his back.

ALEX FLEXED her feet in her high heels. She could already taste taking them off, like a horse getting a last wind in sight of the barn.

She had about a dozen comebacks ready whenever he got around to responding, but they all died an ignoble death when she saw his face, white and lined as he levered himself up. She made to grab for him, steady him somehow, but he shook her off. His whole left side seemed tensed, and there was a look of the wounded animal about him. She forced herself to behave normally, and not yell for one of the footmen.

Daniel sank back into the office chair with an agonized grunt he didn't even try to hide. She tossed her purse on the desk and went to the bottom drawer of Mary's desk, where the bottle of gin was kept. She heard her grandmother's voice, suddenly. "*Only a screw top will do in a pinch, Alexandra. Nothing else concentrates the frustrations quite like wrenching open the bottle you intend to drink straight from.*"

She opened it with, as it happened, quite a satisfying wrench. "You're not on some sort of epic painkiller right now, are you? This isn't going to kill you?"

"Couldn't have. They make me woozy. Had to focus today."

Alex thrust the bottle at him, feeling distressed and embarrassed. He'd been busily damaging himself in pursuit of something she insulted him for, and she hadn't even noticed. Daniel tipped it into his mouth and winced. "She didn't go for the good stuff, did she?"

"She said a person wasn't supposed to enjoy emergency spirits, otherwise everything would start to look like an emergency. You're absolutely wrecked, aren't you?" She was unsure what to do with her body while his slumped and winced away from itself.

"That paint thinner didn't help. I'll be fine," he told her, putting the bottle on the desk. "Eventually. I need to sit for a little while and then I'll be out of your hair."

"I thought sitting caused the problem in the first place."

"Different sitting."

"You think you're getting home like this?"

"I think I'm doing anything I have to do 'like this,' your incredibly highness."

She bit her lip. "What happened?"

"The same thing that happened to my hand," he said shortly. "I don't want to go through it, if you don't mind."

She nodded. Alex had looked him up on the *Journal* website while getting her hair blown out after her swim. Whatever else was true of him, Daniel Black clearly never aspired to getting his name on an article about the circus of her family life. She hadn't fully considered until this moment that he might not want to be here. "What makes it better? The pain, I mean."

"My physio highly recommends getting into a bath if I can stand it. Or the pool in my block of flats. Water helps, lets me stretch it while taking the weight off."

"What about those epic painkillers?"

"I have some in my bag, but I'd rather not, especially not now that you've liquored me up." Alex felt all the weight of her strident animosity settle on her like it was made of iron bars.

"Well, look, if a pool makes it better, come swim with me."

"Pardon?"

"I was going in again anyway. It's heated, even." The horror in his eyes was fading to banked longing. Some faraway, soon-to-be-berated part of her considered that if such a look were turned on the prospect of a person instead of a dip in warm water, Daniel Black might be formidably charming.

"While that does sound lovely, I'm afraid I don't have anything to swim in," he said, with some relief, as if that settled it.

"You can borrow some of my brother's," she said, enjoying the way he gaped. Finally, something about where he was cracked his calm veneer.

"You're going to lend me the Prince of Wales' swim trunks?"

"Of course," Alex said, mouth curving in the first honest, if still not nice, smile she'd directed at him yet. "Eddie's won't fit you."

In the water, Daniel was a man discovering the existence of a deity. He looked around, capable of paying attention to other things now that the pressure was off his lower body. He did not look at the princess. Alex was wearing a dark red performance two-piece this time, all economical lines and full coverage. It confirmed that earlier she was trying to rattle him with the string bikini. No-nonsense was an aesthetic he appreciated far more, despite this not being the time, the place, or the woman.

She finished pulling her dark blond hair into a pony tail and dunked. She had insisted on helping him into the pool. Alex had a swimmer's body held in check. He could see the sketch of stretch marks where her arm and shoulder muscles had been bigger at one time. It made him feel less self-conscious about the mess his lower body was. His t-shirt didn't stay tucked into the trunks, and her arm supporting him around the waist was about to be up against the more impressively disturbing of his two large scars. So he struggled out of the half-wet shirt and watched her face stutter as she stared at his midsection. He saved her the trouble of asking again.

"I nearly died. Should have died. My insides were… not

inside," he said. "They pumped eighteen units of blood into me during the first surgery at the mobile hospital, another twelve during the second round in Germany." He couldn't meet her eyes, instead searching out a point at the far side of the deep end. One scar looped over his stomach like an illustration of an inchworm in a children's book. The other pinched and rippled over his left hip and down his thigh. And credit where it was due, her astonishment veered into horror and right back again.

"I don't remember much of it. I remember thinking *the inside of my body smells really bad* and *I hope Bram Gervais doesn't write my obit, that fucker,* and then I woke up in an American military hospital outside Berlin with my editor yelling at me that she couldn't run the paper from her fucking Blackberry, so I'd better get on my feet. I have flashes of other memories, but they mostly involve significant amounts of pain and hushed conversation. You never want to hear hushed conversation. It isn't comforting."

"That sounds terrifying," she said. She couldn't tear her eyes away from the hip scar, where the bunched skin was pressing the waistband of the swim trunks out. "How badly does it hurt?"

Daniel blinked at her. "I'm not sure I understand the question. I suppose it's like asking you how much you're a princess. Degree stops mattering when it's a fact of you."

Alex nodded, biting her lower lip. It was the second time he'd seen her do such a normal, vulnerable thing. Then her eyes fastened on him in a look that was almost a glare. Before he knew it, she'd grabbed for his good leg and hauled it around her waist.

"What—" he sputtered, as she walked toward the deeper end of the pool, hands on his hips.

"Relax. I have you."

"I'm twice your size."

"I used to be a champion swimmer. I can take it."

Daniel settled more of his weight on her by degrees. She didn't flinch, putting her hand out to grip the side, and he followed suit. They floated like that, their faces a few inches away from one another.

"Why did you stop competing? Don't look so suspicious. I need a distraction, and you're the only one here."

Alex avoided his eyes. Hard to do at this distance, but she managed it somehow. "It became inconvenient. Practices were kept locked down, but meets were public. They tried banning anyone but school photographers from events, but parents took pictures and sold them to the papers. You could hardly tell it was me, with the goggles and the swim cap on, but they were still published. There was national interest in my times, and all kinds of speculation about my performance, that the other members of the team were told to hang back. And once I hit puberty…" she trailed off. The water danced shadows over her face.

"It was frightening. Too many pictures of me in swimsuits all over. I know the cyber-security detail found them in some very bad places. With other girls in the background. Security at meets had to be increased because of stalkers. Two of them were arrested and institutionalized. I held on as long as I could, but it got to be too much. I still love it, though. They couldn't take that from me. I wouldn't let them." She looked back at him, the bottom of the pool reflected in her eyes. "Nothing matters when you're in the water," she said. "Nothing except what you can do, and what you can't."

Her story broke over him in waves, each one pulling him under a little more. Even buried as he'd been in endless drafts of stories and *World of Warcraft* raids back then, the royal divorce had penetrated his consciousness. "Right around the time your parents split?"

Her flat affect was all the confirmation he needed. Or deserved.

"Honestly," she said, dragging the mood up much the way she'd done to his good leg, "I was too good at it. Most people don't think it's sporting for us to excel in public, what with all our natural advantages. Hell, since we stopped marrying our cousins we even have chins now."

He was about to make a joke about the Hapsburgs when one of Alex's security guards (an older man named Taggart, Daniel had been introduced to him earlier) came in, radiating concern. Daniel almost pulled away, but realized that the man wasn't focused on him, or his proximity to Alex.

"There's been an incident, ma'am. You need to get out of the pool."

8

SIX HOURS EARLIER...

Despite Sir Anthony's dire predictions at his job interview, Cole frequently made it home for Friday night dinners. He walked from the Tube station in the gathering dusk, a shadow among shadows. He didn't put on the tough-guy swagger perfected before the age of thirteen, when he realized his feelings for some of the older lads hanging out on the corner by the off-license were more than friendly. In this neighborhood, people still knew each other, still brought a cake over to recent arrivals on the street, still stood outside on a summer evening and talked. Here he was Sandra's and Yossi's boy, the one who gave their sons black and blue reasons to leave him alone before disappearing into the service at eighteen. The one who came back without stories to tell, shrouded in the respect the SAS lent a man.

The lads on the corner by the off-license were still there, the next generation's versions of the ones he'd been friends with, had been himself. Not their sons yet, for which he was grateful. He hadn't lost that much time. Though he knew at least two of the boys he'd figured things out with were married with kids now.

This section of the East End was his first home. He could name the businesses and families who lived on this block by heart. The light was on in Yossi's garage on the corner, and Cole could see him, standing around looking at an engine with four or five of his friends. The mechanics who worked for Yossi and the men who spent time there were Cole's adoptive uncles, watching him grow up, teaching him the languages of their own youths because he wanted to learn more than their own sons did. They never reproached him when he turned out to be something different than they thought. His gayness was one more wildness in a long string of them.

He vaulted the low garden gate when he reached the house at the end of the street, an echo of his childhood. It took years before he would go in the front door, even after he left undercover work, convinced his presence made the house a target. Isaac slid into the house, kicking a football out of the way. Toys and backpacks were scattered around, the unmistakable noise of a bunch of children rattling upstairs.

Isaac made his way along the dim hallway without making a sound. The kitchen was a warm place, remodeled over the years by Yossi and his fellow tinkerers to be open plan with a breakfast bar, small sitting area, and an attached sunroom. Sandra was checking on the roast. Long blonde hair streaked with gray fell to her waist, standing out against her dark jeans and black t-shirt. No matter how quiet he was, she always knew when he came into the kitchen. "Hello, my favorite," she said.

He kissed Sandra on the cheek. She smiled at him with that little half-turn of the corner of her mouth only he got. He put an arm around her waist. She had been his only constant for thirty years. They understood each other. Had made each other.

The rest of the family arrived, invading the kitchen by degrees until it became clear why Sandra had wanted it remodeled. She needed a place to put them all. But she took pride in cramming them all around a table once a week. It meant she succeeded in holding a family together. Yossi had six children with his first wife, Karen. Lovely Karen, smile beaming in the few photographs Isaac had ever seen of her, died in a car crash when her children were little. When he married Sandra, a lawyer raising her eight-year-old nephew on her own, they all moved into this house, a few blocks away from the Orthodox enclave Yossi and Karen had lived in. It had been a scandal. Sandra kept kosher for Yossi, kept Shabbat, but that was all. She wouldn't cover her hair, and the only long skirts she wore were bright, patchwork things more at home at a music festival than temple.

Four of Yossi's six children with his first wife were older than Isaac. They married early and started having babies at once. His step-siblings and their spouses were a communal blur to Isaac, a wall of noise and questions and tentative affection that he crept around. Still, he'd left undercover work because of them. He never wanted to duck away from his own family on the street in case they saw him and broke his cover. Never wanted to endanger them, even if he also didn't really want to talk to them. With certain exceptions.

"How's the prince?" Rivvie asked, running into his legs. He picked up his seven-year-old niece, brushing the hair out of her eyes. She spent a lot of time with Sandra, as both her parents worked full-time, and spent the most time with him as a result. The rest of the kids and most of the adults viewed this the same way they might if Rivvie came home one day with a pet tiger. He was her partner in crime, as far as she was concerned, good for trips to the candy store and piggy-back rides no matter how big she got, for playing board games and watching movies. He liked that part of his life, wandering around with a kid on his shoulders, collecting approving (and occasionally amorous) looks from strangers instead of the usual kind he got. It made him feel real.

"He's good. We went to the ballet a few weeks ago. I'll take you to the Nutcracker this December."

"Will he be there?"

"I don't think so," Isaac said. Her face fell. "But maybe I'll ask." She immediately brightened. Being a child was uncomplicated for her, and he intended to make sure it stayed that way.

"Oi, dickhead, you made it," Omer called out from the back door, jerking his chin at Isaac. Isaac nodded back. Sandra's yelling at Omer to stop that was as familiar and ineffective as it had ever been. They were closest in age, thrown together from the beginning. Outside the house, Omer and Isaac were ready to fight bloody for each other. Inside, their truce had its limits.

"That's a bad name," Rivvie said, tucking her chin over his shoulder. He rubbed her back.

"It is. But you shouldn't take him seriously when he says things like that to me," he said. She gave him a hug, tight around his neck, in that semi-strangling gesture of affection peculiar to happy kids.

"I never do," she told him solemnly.

Omer bellowed that he was going to the park, and Rivvie leapt out of Isaac's arms like a cat offered a laser pointer. All the kids ran outside, Omer their very own Pied Piper.

"It surprises me how good he is with all of them," Isaac murmured. "I can barely deal with one at a time."

"He's a terrible brother to you," Sandra said, shaking her head.

"I'm thirty-three years old. I think I can take a little bit of teasing."

"It's nonsense. You give each other such a hard time." Sandra said, drying a pot. "I tried, you know."

"We're all adults now," he said. "He wants to feel all tough because he knows I could fold him in half backwards without breathing hard."

Sandra pursed her lips. "Some of you are more adult than others," she said. "And you didn't hear me say it."

"Never."

Yossi, barrel-chested and graying, disappeared into the downstairs bathroom when he got home. From the beginning, he had taken Isaac along to the garage, and taught him how things work. He was the one who discovered the quiet, combative child's facility for languages when he heard Isaac cursing fluently under his breath in words he could only have learned from some of Yossi's men. After that, Yossi and the other mechanics spoke to him solely in Hebrew, Urdu, and Pashto until Isaac understood everything and had no British accent left when he spoke to them. He took Isaac to the Orthodox synagogue with him and Omer, and made sure he went to Hebrew school so that Isaac had *something*.

They shared a nod when Yossi emerged, drying his hands on a towel. There hadn't been distance between them until Isaac joined the military. Yossi, a strident pacifist, moved to the UK from Israel when he was a teenager instead of going into the army. He wanted a life without violence, and he never wanted to be part of oppressing another person. Isaac knew Yossi saw his enlistment as a betrayal. They never talked about the tension. Isaac didn't see the point.

Sandra watched Yossi come and go with the smile reserved only for her husband. Sandra was like that. She parceled herself out and everyone lucky enough to have their own little piece of her held on tight.

"I heard from Lilli today," she said, taking the challah out of the oven.

Contact from his mother frequently made him wish for the days when his location was classified. "What's her status?"

"What is ever that woman's status? She's in the south of France at a chateau. Her latest conquest broke her heart before she had a chance to break his. She's carrying on, talking about how old she must be, how she ought to come home, except that some 'dear diplomat' keeps begging her to stay." Sandra regarded a wax trail down the side of the candlesticks with a critical eye, scraping at it with a thumbnail. "I suppose even boredom is glamorous when you're wearing a zebra print bikini. Although I have to say her going on to her decrepit sister about how she's become a sexless, undesirable crone is somewhat wearing."

"You aren't decrepit. Go ahead, wear a bikini. Yossi would faint."

Her purely youthful grin as she poured wine into the Kiddush cup held its own secrets, even from him.

"I think I'm going out tonight," he said.

She raised an eyebrow. Some nights he couldn't manage dinner, even though he wanted to. She didn't push him these days. Enough for her that he showed his face. "Now your glamorous life is making me jealous. You'll be safe?"

Isaac barely suppressed a snort.

"Yes, I know, you're a fierce commando. That won't stop someone from spiking your drink."

Being worried about at close range still felt unusual, even after all this time. In his flat above the garage, he changed into black skinnies, Vans, and a tight red t-shirt cut low enough to show his collarbones and sheer enough to tease the shadow of his tattoos. He styled his hair down, feathery along his cheeks, so it turned his narrow jawline vulnerable instead of sharp. It made him seem softer, more approachable. Isaac could break down and reassemble an assault rifle in no time at all under heavy fire and had extensive training in resisting torture. He needed all the help he could get.

Shrugging into his black leather jacket, he shot out the door into the night. The pieces of his life fanned out behind him and vanished as he made his way back to the tube station. Now he swaggered. Put on the tough until he got to the center of London. No one to guard, nothing to guard against more than the usual for a gay man out for a night on the town. He lengthened his stride and rolled his head on his neck to loosen up. Shook his arms out, put his hands in his pockets. Made himself walk slower, actually look at the billboards in Piccadilly Circus, head off to Leicester Square on a direct route without scanning every rooftop. Every other rooftop would have to do. It didn't help his central problem, the reason he was out here.

The protection detail job came with nightmares of spectacular failure. Of kidnappers ripping the principal away, assassins' bullets getting through, confusion and horror and realizing one couldn't do anything. There were approved ways of dealing with those fears. But there was no sanctioned method of handling the desire to see Eddie's chin tipped up as he took in the city.

There had been times, years ago, when Eddie was more playful, when he'd looked at Isaac with mischievous, daring eyes. Isaac would change into street clothes so Eddie could wander in the world with no fanfare, no plan. On those nights, Eddie was quick to nudge Isaac, grab his wrist, drag him into street parties in Barcelona, underground clubs in Prague, late-night open mics in New York. Sometimes people clearly thought they were lovers. Isaac enjoyed that, damning as it felt. So did Eddie, if the occasional conspiratorial smile at being someone else for a little bit was anything to go by. It had been a long time since Eddie had pressed up close to him at a crowded bar, since Isaac left his hand heavy in the small of Eddie's back to make a point to a stranger about who belonged to whom.

Isaac cursed at himself. This weekend was supposed to be about regaining his balance so he could continue to do his job. Other people, other bodies gave him a buffer against the way Eddie spoke, the light in his eyes when something pleased him, the way he moved and smelled and looked longingly at every soft surface like he wanted to throw himself onto it in complete abandon. Isaac wanted to grip the sides of his head and yell in frustration. This had to pass. He had buried it before, and he would do it again.

His destination was one of London's most fashionable clubs catering to a largely gay clientele. Safe enough for what Isaac had in mind. A dance, a few drinks, too loud for a conversation and no need for one anyway. The bouncer let him in without so much as a twitch of his eyebrow when Isaac flashed his badge. Isaac was permanently "on the list" at any number of exclusive locations around the world, but he still thought—for a fleeting second—about checking in with Harris about Eddie's plans for the night. No. He told himself to stop. He was off. Off. Not on. The other thing. The opposite. On his own. Free. Adrift. Alone.

Isaac took the last bits of his outfit out of his pocket. He ran a gold glitter stick over his cheekbones, then tucked a pair of glasses with thin black frames over his ears, making him look proper hipster. The pixie professor look did pretty well for him. The woman at the coat check gave him a cheery once-over as she handed him his ticket. He grinned back.

Parlance looked like a spaceship inside, multiple levels vibrating with noise and filled with people on a Friday night. He sank into the anonymity of the crowd. The usual mix of finance cads on the prowl, overindulging uni students thrilled to be let in at all, the occasional pop star. He recognized heirs and heiresses of various fortunes, displaying very different behavior than they did around, for example, the queen. He remembered a few of them from the crowd Eddie ran with when he dated Lord Stephen Everingham. None of them knew him. Yet more advantages to being part of the wallpaper.

Don't think about that, he told himself. Drink and a dance. That was all he needed, all he was here for. Tonight was about a lack of Eddie, and what that meant for his life and his chances at actually having one. He slid onto the floor, black hair brushing his cheekbones. He knew it looked stark against his cool, pale amber skin.

Isaac had company almost instantly, a blond with big blue eyes looking down through his lashes. "Hi," the angel said, voice so breathy and feathery it gave the single syllable a full dramatic arc. Isaac raised an eyebrow, fit himself to the music and the body in front of him, wondering idly if he was supposed to be feeling anything at all. He slipped into his role as Puck in a court of Oberons, men and women coming and going in his arms. His dancing went dirty as the night wore on him, as he lost patience with coyness. Damp shirt sticking to his back, hair falling even further out of place. Another beat, another body, moving how the other person wanted so they'd wish for things to last forever or four minutes, whichever came first. And they all moved on, because he could fake a lot of things, but only a specific kind of person wanted to press against a body that used to run around Afghanistan with a knife in its teeth. A person might tell themselves danger's what they were after, but it was the *idea* of peril that they wanted, and Isaac contained the real thing.

And then someone came up behind him instead of slotting in front. Someone tall and slender, putting their hands on him with a teasing brush of knuckles on his sides, tapping fingers on his hip bones like they were playing along to the DJ. A little hello, a little invitation. He leaned back into it. The smell of very expensive cologne and something forbidden and intimately recognizable wrapped around him. Isaac stretched out, tilting his head to the side. Offering. Lips, licked very recently, brushed his bared skin. Dragged along it, sucking soft kisses under his jaw. He heard a deep inhale, a cut-off moan, answered it by tipping his head the other way.

He got nipped for his trouble. A soft laugh rumbled in his chest—and was laughing softly something he did? He pressed back harder, losing himself, losing the self-consciousness of being too old for this place, of being too deadly and too poisoned by unrequited love. *Unrequited love.* It turned his stomach, and he lost the beat, all the air knocked out of him. The friendly lips up against his neck pressed harder, then teeth worried at his earlobe.

"You left." The hazy, rough whisper floated into his ear. "Come back."

A hand trailed over his belly where his shirt rode up, making him shiver. He loved being touched there, and most people never figured it out unless he told them. He wanted to melt backwards. Those long arms felt big enough to fold around him, to keep him.

So he let them. He wrapped his hand around the forearm pressing into his belly, threading their fingers together. This was exactly what he needed, what he was looking for all this time.

It started to unravel when he looked down and saw the rings on his mysterious dancer's fingers. One ring had a piece of rough jade in it, another had silver vines chasing each other in a geometric pattern. The thumb ring had cut-outs of playing card suits. Eddie had one like that.

"You a gambling man?" His last word died without enough air to hold it up as he looked into Eddie's flushed face. The bass pounded into his heartbeat until he couldn't tell the two apart.

Eddie's hair wasn't combed back, falling down past his chin in loose, messy curls. His lips were bitten like he was already having the best sex of his life, already had to keep quiet. He did the closest double-take Isaac had ever seen, heavy eyes widening in shock and a hint of outraged jealousy. Isaac was submerged in liquid, wondering panic.

It explained why the bouncer let him in, thinking he was part of Eddie's team. And it was funny, wasn't it, that they both ended up here. Isaac, needing to forget. Eddie, wanting to pretend. Eddie dancing with men like he'd always wanted, unheard of until this week. Eddie coming up on a man the same size and shape as *Isaac.*

The song changed. The lights went even lower, purple and blue strobes making Eddie pulse in the darkness, the beating heart at the center of Isaac's universe. They didn't move, hidden in the center of the dance floor. Eddie leaned in, pressed their foreheads together so they could hear each other. Isaac taught him that. "I thought you were off tonight," he said.

"I am."

"I'm sorry." Eddie dropped his mouth to Isaac's ear, wrecking him with one sad, desperate syllable after another. "I'm so sorry I want you so much. Have no right."

Isaac might have been trying to keep himself under control, but his body dimly remembered what to do with the information that he was wanted in return. The urge to give this man in particular whatever he wanted, whatever he needed to feel good, overwhelmed him, and as they stood together, Isaac had the strangest feeling that Eddie was about to start dancing again. With *him.*

The building rippled and groaned in a way Isaac's body knew on a deep, visceral level. He folded Eddie under him in a protective crouch before he was consciously aware a bomb had gone off.

ALEX'S FINGERS tensed on Daniel's hip, like she suddenly realized how close they were. Daniel wanted to move away purely by reflex, even though they weren't doing anything. It felt like being caught by someone's parents, except it occurred to him that he would rather be caught by an armed bodyguard than this woman's mother. Taggart didn't even seem to register his presence, which put him on edge immediately. He recognized a man in an emergency situation without enough information.

"Your highness, there has been an incident in the city center," Taggart repeated, "and I'm afraid I need to ask you and Mr. Black to get out of the pool."

The change that came over Alex was extraordinary. She froze up for a second, maybe two, but then began cutting through the water towards the nearest ladder before Taggart finished speaking.

"Is Mum all right? Where is everyone?"

"Her Majesty and the Prince of Wales are safe in Paris and the Duchess is in Rome," he said, handing her a towel. Daniel got back to the stairs and stepped out, taking his own towel from a pool attendant—and wasn't *that* bizarre, under the circumstances.

"What about Eddie?" she asked, as Daniel walked up, limp out in the open.

"We need to get you somewhere less exposed."

Her face went white. She pulled the Union Jack beach towel around her.

Everything seemed hushed as they made their way up to the family apartments. Daniel thanked the hot water gods for working well enough on his hip so that he could walk. Alex got her hands on her phone and started scrolling as soon as Taggart shut them in her bedroom suite.

He only hesitated for a minute before he put his arm around her. His skin was clammy, sticky from the chlorine, but she leaned into him anyway. "This is my nightmare," she told him quietly.

"Take heart," he said. "It's killing me that I'll never be able to write about this." A wan smile flickered on her mouth, and he counted it as a win. "Look, let me stay with you. Until you know. You shouldn't—no one wants to be alone right now."

She nodded. They huddled up in a blanket on the couch in

her suite. She insisted they turn the television on. They waited. Daniel watched the reporters on the screen talk about theories and counter-terrorism tactics being deployed minute by minute. He remembered when he would have given anything to be one of them. Right now, holding Alex as she waited for news, he didn't want to be anywhere else.

The world tilted. The world hurt. Screams, smashing glass. A crash above his head—Isaac—*Isaac*—jolted hard into him, something hit his shoulder where it met his neck. Arms too tight, forcing him down. More hands, different—"Cole?"—*IsaacIsaacIsaac*—and there the world went again, dipping the other way, and he couldn't hear anything over the ringing in his ears.

Yanked up, hauled into a bent-over run, a body on either side and one behind, pushing him. Training since childhood taking over, since that first very serious conversation when he was a very little boy—Eddie released himself into their care, knowing there was nothing else he could do, despite the frantic, terrified voices pressing in through a fog all around them. He wanted to stop, he wanted to *help*. His job was to get out. His body was not to be on the line. It had been drummed into him since childhood, and he listened now. He was given no other choice.

He tried to look back, but his officers wouldn't let him deviate. The floor was covered in broken glass, spilled alcohol, pieces of wall. Heat spread through him, heat all around him. Fire, but he was out already, out, and there was no going back, no helping except by getting out of the way. That was his job, to get out of the way. Get his team out of the way.

His hearing came back in time to catch Harris yelling at Kimsey for emergency clearance as they shot into the alley behind Parlance, as she brought the car to a halt. She must have given it correctly. Eddie reached behind him to keep hold of Isaac's wrist—*isn't supposed to be there, isn't isn't no yes stay*—to keep him close. There was no time, so Isaac leapt into the car after shoving Eddie into the back seat. The car took off through the night. Kimsey and Harris calling in the update —*Curly secure, repeat, we have Curly*—

Eddie shook, alcohol overlaid with adrenaline and terror. He clung to Isaac, practically straddling him, folded in half on the seat. Isaac kept Eddie down, below the level of the windows, crouched over him.

"I have to check you out, Eddie," he heard. Harris. He shook his head.

"I'll do it," he heard. Isaac. *Yes.*

"You're not supposed to be here." Harris. Another pair of hands on him, and Eddie whimpered, pulling away with nowhere to go. Isaac's body felt like a furnace, the heat of him what drew Eddie on the dance floor, a minute and another life ago.

"Let him." Isaac. After a pause that didn't quite happen, that Eddie felt rather than saw, Harris began checking him for injury. He got fistfuls of Isaac's shirt in his fingers as he was felt all over for blood and broken bones. Some breaking couldn't be found by touching.

"Do you hurt anywhere?"

"Shoulder," Eddie managed. Harris probed at him with his fingers. Another curse. Eddie had no idea if it came from him or not.

"A chandelier came down on me," Isaac said. "Must have clipped him."

"Injuries?" Harris.

"I'll live." Isaac.

"Is Mum all right? Those people—"

"Stay down, sir," Harris ordered. "We're finding out."

"*Are they alive?*"

"Yes," Harris said, after too long spent listening to someone yelling in his earpiece. "Everyone is secure except us. Lockdown conditions."

Eddie went limp, smoke and terror all he could smell when he inhaled. His stomach kicked, and he closed his eyes against the nausea as the car took another turn, clutching his phone in his hand.

Gravel crunched and spat under the tires as they pulled into the courtyard at Kensington Palace. He left the car after Harris, resisting the urge to reach back for Isaac. The KP security team met them in the courtyard and half carried, half dragged him through the palace, only stopping when he was in his own flat, surrounded by protection officers, more guarding the doors. It felt like he hadn't stopped moving since the moment after he realized the body in his arms was Isaac's. When he gave in to the wild desire to keep dancing with him, an instant before his selfishness was repaid with destruction.

Eddie gripped the edge of the kitchen counter. Isaac was behind him, lurking near the refrigerator. He felt ridiculous in his club clothes, surrounded by his security team. Harris, Finnery, and Jones were all covered in soot and dust. He knew he must be, too, but he couldn't look at himself. His shirt had daisies on it, for fuck's sake. Ten minutes ago, he had been dancing. The thought of all those people in the club who didn't have bodyguards, the ones who might be lost—the ones who might have been saved by the trained professionals tasked instead with saving *him*—

But they had saved him, and now they were waiting for him. Waiting for him to be a prince, or a scared boy, or whoever he was going to be when he lifted his head. He had a responsibility, and he clung to it.

Eddie rubbed his forehead. "Is there any word yet on what… on why? Is anyone… did everyone at the club get out all right?"

Kimsey cleared her throat. "The police have one suspect in custody already, and are looking for two others. It's still an emerging situation."

He nodded, straightened, looking them each in the eye. "My sincerest thanks. Truly, I… I don't deserve any of you. If there's anything you can do, with the emergency responders, or the police, I would be very grateful. Anything you saw, if there's any chance my presence there was part of it—"

"We're already coordinating with New Scotland Yard," Kimsey assured him. "It's very unlikely you had anything to do with it, one way or another."

"I want to be sure," he whispered. "I want to help." Those little words sounded so foolish in his ears, but everyone else in the room seemed to understand. Harris made eye contact with Isaac and nodded, as if something was settled now.

"We understand, sir," Harris said. "You should get some rest. We're going to clear out, give you some peace." No one moved.

"I'll be all right," Eddie told them. "Thank you. Truly." The reassurance worked, because a few smiles were sent his way as Kimsey, Finnery, and Jones filed out.

Harris and Isaac shared a look and stepped out of sight. Eddie's fingers tightened on the marble slab, rings biting into his flesh. Any second now Harris was going to tell Isaac to get out of here, tell him *we need to talk about this* in some kind of ominous way, and Eddie would probably fall to his knees, sobbing, begging for Isaac to be allowed to stay with him, only for a few hours—

He stared blankly at the dimmed lights, at the television set. He wanted to turn on the news, but he couldn't. The ground crumbled under his feet every step he took.

He made his way, from chair back to banister, up to his bedroom, sinking down at the foot of his bed because it felt safest to be somewhere he couldn't fall off. Eddie texted his siblings with shaking fingers, telling them he was okay. He even texted his mother, after an agonized moment wondering whether he should bother her. He got immediate responses, but couldn't read them. He flung his phone across the carpet. Wrapped his arms around his knees.

And when he looked up, Isaac stood in the doorway, watching him. His heart leapt.

"Harris and I agreed I'm staying to sort you out. Couldn't leave you like this." Every word sounded like a wall coming down, pried out of him in the lilting burr that had driven Eddie mad since he was nineteen years old. He felt a strange tickling sensation on his cheek, and only realized he was crying when his hand came away glistening.

"Bombs went off," he said.

Isaac came closer, moving slowly, like Eddie was a feral cat he didn't want to scare. "Remember that camping trip we took in Scotland, when you were done with university? You, Arthur, your friends, all up in the Highlands?"

Eddie nodded, clinging to the idea that there were times other than this night.

"You woke me up early one morning, and we talked. About compartmentalizing. Doing what you have to, so that you can go on."

"You held my hand." It seemed essential to point this out. Eddie couldn't stop turning the events of the last—had it only been an hour?—over in his mind, every second since he'd seen a slender, lethal-looking man dancing with abandon in the middle of a dance floor and couldn't help himself. "Bombs went off. Where we were. Something was going to fall on me and you stopped it, and—and then you got out with me, because we were dancing."

"Eddie—"

"If I hadn't been dancing with you, you would have been trapped there." The terror must have translated to his voice, because Isaac went down on one knee, reaching for him. Their fingers tangled for the second time that night.

"I'm all right. Look." Isaac pressed their hands to his own chest. "Even if you hadn't been there." They stayed that way as, outside, emergency response household cavalry units pulled in. The noise of efficient men and women taking up positions outside the palace sounded very far away. "Come on. You need to get all this off."

Eddie let himself be pulled up. Isaac kept the lights low in the dark gray bathroom, turned the shower on, helped him undress while he waited for it to heat up. Eddie caught glimpses in the mirror—two awkward shapes moving in the rising steam. The points of contact as he held on to Isaac's bicep as he kicked off his skinnies smudged their outlines together. Eddie knew he was naked, but the information didn't belong to this moment. He had more important things to do than worry about whatever bodies had been meant for an hour ago.

"You too," he said. "You need to clean off." He leaned too heavily on the shower door handle, knees already threatening to buckle. "Please."

They were eye to eye with Eddie slumped down. Eddie thought he would have to beg for a second, before Isaac tugged off his sweat-soaked, filthy t-shirt. Isaac's hands weren't large, but they could kill. They could help him, save him. Arouse him, an hour ago, when the world didn't hurt. Isaac paused with his skintight jeans hanging down his hips to take his socks off, and Eddie felt their impending mutual nakedness as a physical weight. He had to avoid it for another minute. The water hitting the tiles as he got into the shower almost drowned out Isaac's exhale.

The pucker of a gunshot wound, the ragged scars from shrapnel and the neater ones from knives, the dagger inked in the center of his chest. In the mirror, Eddie could see the folded wings on his back. He imagined the two pieces combining if Isaac spun fast enough, turning him into a human optical illusion, a chimera, the smoke when a magician decides to disappear. Isaac split himself down the middle over and over, and Eddie just wanted to hold him together.

"Nobody checked you," he said, looking at the bloody scratches on Isaac's neck, his shoulder, down his back where something sharp and heavy crashed into him. The bruises already forming. A chandelier, he thought he remembered. "In the car."

"Eddie." Isaac took his hands again, but Eddie pulled away.

"Let me," he choked out. "Let me make sure."

Even though Isaac's eyes were endless darkness and tension sang through every inch of him, he stepped under the water and raised his arms at his sides. Waited for Eddie to touch him.

Eddie began at the top of his head, pushed all that black hair off his face. Soot and horror washed off them both and swirled down the drain as Eddie stroked his hands down, tilting Isaac's head to the side and dabbing at the scratches with a washcloth. Then he went over Isaac's arms, his hands, his torso, sweeping up his back and down his sides, skin so warm it felt like it could burn him. He wanted to kneel, but Isaac stopped him before they could go that far. They cleaned themselves off. It was the sharp smell of lemons for Eddie tonight, a bottle down to the dregs anyway, which was good, because

Eddie knew that he would associate the scent of lemons with burning forever, now. Lemons and burning, lemons and terror, lemons and Isaac under the water. They stared at one another as their excuses washed away. Eddie could hear the bass line from the club under his heartbeat again. There was no hiding any longer. He felt shattered into a hundred pieces that he could kick in front of himself like pebbles if he wanted. With desperate certainty he had never felt in his life, he reached out.

ISAAC BARELY HAD time to register Eddie's set expression before Eddie kissed him like their lives depended on it. Maybe they did.

The first touch was like this: melting into a new mold, a fistful of wet hair before he was conscious of the action, other arm clamped around Eddie's back. Eddie's fingers digging into his back and his waist, near-pained little noises disappearing down Isaac's throat. He thought there must be a collection of those sounds gathering inside him, piling up like coins in a dragon's hoard. Ill-gotten, rightfully belonging to someone else, but he didn't care. They kissed until they were out of the suggestion of breath. Eddie clung to him, ducking his head to rub his cheek against Isaac's shoulder. He needed so much, and Isaac had it to give. He relaxed his frantic grip, but Eddie wasn't done with it, jostled closer.

This wasn't one of his Eddies. This was someone else, midnight darkness howling in his usually kind green eyes. His heart began pounding, felt like maybe the shock catching up with him. He knew he should push back, but some kind of Eddie-specific instinct kept him rooted to one spot. He should be moving, should be fighting this, should be trying to change the outcome like a man with more on his mind than getting what he wanted and was so very afraid of. Through the fear, and the bewildering shock, and the crushing pressure of not being exactly here for so long, all he could hear was Eddie murmuring "Yes," again and again. The heartbeat under his hand was quick and strong, and *I did that* sang in his veins.

So Isaac held him tight and clutched at the wet skin riding over the muscles in his back, and kissed him until Eddie cried from it, until they were both crying. He tried to give it like he had while working undercover, fall back on detachment and deny any suggestion of satisfying his own need. It didn't work. Eddie was too far inside him, he saw that now. Eddie was safe. Eddie was safety. The unlikeliest, worst place for Isaac to find something that made him feel fully human. He would kill to see his prince with that thrilled, frantic light in his eyes for what Isaac gave him. Murder in cold blood, and he knew how. All the affection he never had for anyone, the flip side of all the death he dealt out at the end of a gun or whispered words over campfires and in alleyways. It hadn't burned the capacity for tenderness out of him, though it should have. Though he didn't deserve this, he took it with both hands.

For Eddie's glazed eyes and that smile on his face, trembling and relieved and somehow, even in the aftermath, happy. With Isaac. The answering pulse in his own chest, his groin, his entire body thrumming with how easy it was to give in to the devils he'd been dancing with since the day they met, a suicide run if he ever saw one. The curve of Eddie's waist under his hands was inevitable. Too many times Eddie looked for him in a crowd to avoid hearing his prince moan into his ear as Isaac used his nails on the small of his back. His loyalty unquestioned. His devotion beyond reproach, beyond reason.

Isaac knew, when he didn't wrench himself away in the first second—with sinking, rising, horrified joy—he wasn't going to. He didn't *want* to. Somehow, under his nose, Eddie developed the feelings he'd been warned about. Transference. Improper emotional investment. Overdeveloped sense of indebtedness.

No punishment could ever be enough for taking advantage of it. Isaac knew he was a dead man. His soul was forfeit. He had to say something as his resolve blunted like ice against a hot glass.

"This is a stress response, Eddie, *sir*, we have to stop."

"It is *not*. From the first minute, the first second I saw you…" The mutiny drained from Eddie's face, along with all the color. "Unless—unless you didn't want—Oh, god, Isaac, I'm sorry, I wasn't thinking—"

Isaac knew Eddie's fear of forcing himself on someone, and he shook his head. He didn't have the words to explain the problem, and as he replayed what Eddie said first, the idea that they had both been on this ride the whole time overwhelmed him. He reached for Eddie, not to take him in his arms, but to hold on as if Eddie was the only one who could drag him to safety.

Eddie dragged him in, licked into his mouth as Isaac's hands came up, one in his hair again, the other over his lower back. Moaned. Eddie *moaned*, and what was he supposed to do with that? He inhaled it, felt Eddie shifting and shoving at him like he wanted to climb. Isaac pulled one of Eddie's legs up around his waist, and the hand pulling his hair wasn't a threat. It was a promise, as sharp teeth settled into his unmarred shoulder.

He shut the water off, pulled Eddie out of the shower. Isaac got them into Eddie's bedroom in a confusion of limbs and intention. Eddie's erection was obvious and insistent, pressed against his own.

"They almost took me away from you," Eddie whispered, clinging to him. "Stay with me."

"I can't," he said, and the words were ripped from inside him. "I can't. You're—Eddie, you've got to understand that."

"Bombs went off," he repeated, like that was the most important piece of this puzzle, like Isaac was *missing something*.

The warm metal of his rings pressed in to Isaac's cheeks, surprisingly gentle when his legs were so tight. He'd forgotten his own arousal. Faced with it now, his head swam. He leaned their foreheads together.

"You could have died," Eddie said, fingers flexing against Isaac's cheekbones, ghosting his lips over Isaac's jaw, inhaling under his ear again. "You could've, there was a *bomb* inside with us, if we hadn't been dancing I never would have known. You could have been killed, right there, and I would've learned it from the news or someone. Would have been a few feet away from you, and I wouldn't be able to say goodbye, tell you... I'm seeing it, can't stop it, can't stop being taken away from you because I'm supposed to be more important, except I'm not, I'm really not. Please. Please, Isaac."

Isaac's hands slid up Eddie's back before he could tell himself to stop again. He cradled Eddie while he kissed him. The gentler he was, the more Eddie crowded closer and held tighter, and part of Isaac soared with a terrible sensation of relief. The flood of images conjured by Eddie's words was a horror movie in slow motion. He'd come so close to losing him, so close to being alone in his flat or in the wrong part of town while bombs went off and sirens wailed and him knowing nothing. If the worst had happened, he would have been destroyed. A terse phone call in the night, abandoning him to guilt that would last as long as he did.

"You left," Eddie said. Time and reality compressed until they were back in the club, in that instant before they recognized each other and the world tilted and caught fire. "Come back."

He would have spent the night slumped against Eddie's bedroom door if there were no other option.

Isaac pushed Eddie down until he sat on the mattress, grateful for how dark it was. He wanted to be a random hookup in the club, what Eddie had been after. Wanted to give

Eddie the fantasy he could bring anybody home. His fingers dug in harder as he imagined Eddie getting it from anyone else, already high on Eddie's suggestion that he had wanted Isaac longer than Isaac wanted him. They had never touched like this before. They could be strangers in a darkened hallway.

So let him offer that. Let him be that. He went to his knees on the floor in front of Eddie, hearing Eddie's breath catch. Those long fingertips reached out, stroking along his cheekbones and coming away covered in gold glitter. His breath caught at that, and at the look of utter bliss on Eddie's face when he dared raise his eyes again. Eddie's chest rose and fell in quick little jerks as he panted, gripped by adrenaline. They both were. There could be no slowing down.

Isaac reached up and tangled his left hand in Eddie's right, feeling the edges of the rings between his fingers. He mouthed the skin above a hip bone in a soft kiss, brushing his lips over the swell of Eddie's belly, feeling the muscles of his abdomen clench and jerk the wet tip of his cock under Isaac's chin. The smooth, hot skin of his dick caught on Isaac's stubble, making Eddie curse, keeping him in the moment. The hand Isaac wasn't holding made its way into his hair, pleading instead of demanding. Isaac more than perhaps any other person in the world knew how much it cost him for that gesture of trust.

He finally let himself sink down on Eddie, feeling the weight and the pressure of him, the taste salty and smooth, the smell of sweat, want, and abating fear hitting the back of his nose. He thought, for one dizzying second, that he would never get the memory of it out of his head. He went down fast, like he could dislodge the fear from his throat with Eddie's cock and leave no room for it to return. He shifted lower to rub his stubble on Eddie's stomach, the delicate skin over his hips, his thighs. He risked looking up. There was no hesitance in Eddie's eyes, only a stare with so much heat inside it that Isaac could barely breathe. He knew in that moment exactly what he had to do, what he wanted more than anything.

Isaac climbed up on the bed, helping Eddie further up so that his head was against the bottom edge of the pillows monogrammed with the family crest. Isaac flung them off the side of the bed, making more room for his prince to stretch out. Eddie pulled his knees up, eyes fastened to Isaac's face. Isaac bent over him and kissed him until his lips were wet and dark pink, only leaving him long enough to retrieve a lube packet from the pocket of his discarded jeans.

Eddie made a sound, a sharp whine, when he heard Isaac slicking his fingers. He struggled onto his elbows, stomach rippling. Isaac smiled up at him, sparks firing in his eyes. Eddie's mouth hung open a little, it was the most endearing thing Isaac had ever seen. His head fell backwards when Isaac's fingers dipped behind his balls, as Isaac settled down between his legs. Eddie fumbled for a pillow, folding it in half and shoving it behind his head so he could sink back and still watch.

Time lost all meaning as Isaac teased him, stroking home with specific, clever fingers that twisted and probed without stretching. Eddie gave it up with helpless, squirming abandon. Unreasonable, uncontrollable possessiveness welled up in Isaac, and he pressed deeper, wanting Eddie to give him everything, wanting to take it all so he could show Eddie what it really meant for someone to take care of him. What he wished he'd done six years ago, to erase an unwanted touch with something good. Something for him. That task, that gift, had gone to another, and Isaac made his peace with it at the time. He'd had no choice. Now, here, he felt like he'd been given a second chance. A first chance for a second time.

He bent his head and licked up Eddie's cock, sucking it down again. He worked him, got him to the edge, kept him there until Eddie started to thrust and then backed off, over and over, until Eddie cried, reaching for him and holding back every time. Until finally he couldn't wait to see it any longer and got the head of Eddie's cock wedged in the back of his throat and swallowed, pressing his fingers deep inside him at the same time.

Eddie choked off a yell, coming down Isaac's throat with unintentional pulses of his hips and clenching around his fingers, all that brilliant tightness and burning heat. Isaac pulled off, sucking at him, tasting him. Sticky-salt on his tongue, impossible to ignore, sweetness all through him. He felt Eddie's body holding tight to his fingers and moved them in slow circles, milking his orgasm out of him before slipping them out.

Isaac brought Eddie's shaking legs down to the bed, ignoring the way Eddie reached for him, pleading with exhausted fucked-out noises. Isaac settled him, taking the pillow out from behind his head and shoving it under the small of his back to save it from aching in the morning. Tugging the free half of the duvet over him. He stroked Eddie's stomach, his chest, his face with his clean hand, soothing him to sleep. Eddie smiled as he went, like he had nothing to concern himself with, like he hadn't been in an explosion. Like he hadn't been fingered and sucked to an orgasm that, at least from this angle, had to be one of the best Isaac had ever given. Soft and slow and overwhelming. Like his prince. His prince.

EDDIE WOKE up alone a few hours later, only gold glitter in the whorls of his fingers to prove it happened at all.

10

The security office in Kensington Palace was packed. Harris looked up as soon as Isaac came in, only doing a slight double-take when he saw Isaac's wet hair and fresh outfit. Isaac had rummaged in Eddie's closet on his way out, grabbing track trousers and an old Henley to wear home. It reminded him of being a teenager, stealing clothes and disappearing quietly into the night while the posh boys he'd fucked slept on in their pristine beds. There had been less shame then.

"Special treatment," Harris said, the ghost of a normal smile on his face as he looked up from his laptop. "Typical."

Isaac cringed inside, hoping his glazed eyes, jittery hands, and a flushed face would be filed under adrenaline comedown rather than sex. "You know how he is," was all he said. Even that felt disloyal to Eddie.

"He uses you to feel better. Always has." Harris shrugged. "We scrubs will have to make do, won't we?"

"Terrifying when you try to be relatable." Their banter rang hollow, but they did it anyway, for the benefit of everyone else in the room. Isaac was horrified at how scratchy his voice sounded. *Smoke inhalation,* he thought. *Instant alibi.*

"What about you?" Asked much more tentatively. Isaac bristled and stood down in half a breath. He and Harris were on the same team. Victims of the same attack their protectee had been caught in. Well-qualified victims, but that never mattered.

"Not my first explosion in an enclosed space." He gave the impression of a shrug. "It was loud and scary. I survived." Some of the greener agents in the room looked at him with equal parts disbelief and admiration. He knew he had a repu- tation. Didn't even mind it, most of the time. Harris's expres- sion was inscrutable as only a well-born British man's could be, when he knew how to cut a man to pieces without breaking a sweat. He was looking for something, and Isaac had no idea if he found it or not when Harris finally gave him a curt nod.

"You should go home and get some sleep."

"No arguments from me," Isaac said, rolling his sore shoul- der. Soft cotton tugged over scratches and reminded him of the man he'd left upstairs. The guilt waited for him. "Not what I signed up for on my night off."

"Thought you'd be fighting like a weasel to get back on the detail," Harris said. "Which is locked down, if you'd like to know. No changes to the roster. Procedure."

Half of him wanted to stay, insist on it, force them to march him out. Half of him wanted to run. "Sure," Isaac said. "Me being at the club at all is going to cause some headaches down New Scotland Yard. He's a big boy, though, doesn't need me holding his hand forever."

Harris didn't quite take his unexpected acquiescence in stride, but he let it go. Small mercy, and the only one Isaac was likely to get for a while.

A few members of the emergency rapid response unit gave

him an extremely dirty look as Isaac walked by them, head down, on his way through the courtyard. Isaac was confused for half a second, before he realized he still looked more like a one night stand than a protection agent. Did they think the Prince would drag home a bit of rough while people were bloody and dying in the street? They probably did. He might have slouched as he flashed his badge at them, might have swung his hips in a manner highly unbecoming to a senior officer.

It honestly wasn't the most unprofessional thing he'd done in the last couple of hours.

A helicopter thudded overhead. Sirens whined miles away. The fighter jets tasked to do fly-overs of the city were too far above him to see, but he knew they were there. That's how this worked. Emergency workers pulled victims from the wreckage while in nondescript buildings all over the world, intelligence analysts switched gears, changing focus instantly to sort through the missed hints for their bread crumbs. Counter-strikes were being discussed and discarded even now. Without enough information, assets were mobilized in dozens of countries in response to one outrageous act. That world of action and reaction, missions, the constantly shifting ground—Isaac had traded it in for one absolute. Eddie.

The dark windows of Kensington Palace stared at his back like a judgmental dowager. A week ago, hell, two hours ago he would have fought to get back on Eddie's detail, procedures and duty rosters be damned. More than that, if he'd suggested that he stay on, or get some sleep in the break room, or even if he went back upstairs into Eddie's flat none of them would challenge it. That was where he belonged, the space he made for himself.

The space Eddie made for him. From the minute he joined the prince's detail, Eddie came after him with question after question, like he had to make the quiet dark-eyed stranger his own. Isaac went for it like a man in the desert who thought he saw an oasis. He hadn't realized what was happening.

His hands shook in his pockets. He couldn't outrun the sensations of Eddie's body, Eddie's breath and pleasure and tears, Eddie holding on like he would shatter if they stopped touching.

It wasn't the first time Isaac fucked his way through the aftermath of something horrible. Soldiers crashing adrenaline-fueled bodies together when their minds couldn't get over what they'd seen, done, proving they were alive. Isaac lost himself in that a time or two. But not Eddie. Eddie was careful with himself, kind to himself in ways Isaac didn't understand—and kind to Isaac in ways he never wanted to examine. When he thought of what Eddie asked—begged—to do. The spread of his hands over Isaac's body. *"Nobody checked you. Let me."* He wanted to walk until he got to the ocean and keep going until the water closed over his head.

What was that, Cole? He asked himself, in the voice of long ago gunnery sergeants tasked with turning him into someone who took orders, understood boundaries. *What possessed you? Touching what doesn't belong to you.* He imagined dropping to the ground and doing push-ups, hundreds of them, thousands of them to burn the memory of Eddie's sharp fingernails out of his back. Isaac used to know how to run until he fell forward into the dirt and sharp rocks, switch to crawling until he achieved the objective set out for him. He used to love that about his life, knowing he could take any amount of pain without breaking.

He couldn't take this. Even if in the moment it felt like the only thing to do, in the uncompromising darkness he knew the way Eddie reached for him didn't matter. Nothing mattered but the mission, and Isaac had failed his spec-tacularly.

No one died, he told his racing heart. *You got him out, you got him safe. You got him to sleep.*

Isaac had been an instrument for so much of his life. At such and such a time he would be in such and such a place, and someone might die, or a building might be blown up. A message sent, and received, while the messenger remained a slice of shadow, a man with no name and no face, who had never been there at all.

Media outlets were forbidden from publishing photos with close protection officers in the foreground, for security reasons. He would get between Eddie and the cameras whenever he saw that shadow around Eddie's eyes, the one that told Cole his protectee needed a moment to fend off the breaking in his head. It was the same look that drew Isaac to take Eddie in his arms, the same knowing.

He knew, with raw, vicious satisfaction, bordering on delight, that tonight he had been everything Eddie needed.

It terrified him. What it meant. What it could do to both their lives. He couldn't avoid loving Eddie. Knew he would die for him. Eddie could point at anyone on the street, say he wanted them taken down, and Isaac might ask a few questions, but his hand would be on its way to the knife in his pocket all the same.

But it was more than that. Violence wasn't Isaac's first language, but he spoke it most fluently. He was conversant in loyalty, and halting at love, although he recognized key phrases. He and Eddie had grown up together, in a way. They were two extremes, but the six years he had on Eddie were spent interrupting the power of men dangerous enough that the world wasn't allowed to know their names. Time out of time, so when he landed on the prince's detail, he knew he had a lot to learn about a life that didn't involve ducking truant officers, slitting throats, or pretending to be a pretty bit of rough to get in with the son of a crime boss who liked that sort of thing.

Dressing like a university student to blend in and accompanying the man second in line to the throne to his literature classes made about as much sense as anything else Isaac had ever been sent to do.

Isaac sketched the outline of a person around himself for Eddie. A person who had a favorite beer, who followed a football team, who occasionally went for a night out. While Eddie was at Cambridge, Isaac did all the reading along with him. Might as well, he thought then, he had to sit through the lectures either way. Books he'd only ever heard of in passing made their way into him, and he found he liked having them there, tucked under his breastbone. With Eddie, he went cliff-diving in Spain, yachting in the Caribbean, got doused in Prosecco in the front row of an EDM show in Sweden at dawn. Eddie relied on him. Trusted him. Understood the part of him that could never stop looking for the threat, but got him to laugh anyway. Eddie made his life brighter.

How could he not eventually fuck that up? If they were caught, it was the kind of tawdry, illicit scandal the public loved, because it gave them carte blanche to criticize. It might somehow be acceptable if it were Alex and a member of her detail. But the prince and another man? He might as well paint a target on both their backs.

For a second, he had to tell himself the truth. He wanted to be caught with Eddie. To be caught, over and over, and have it not matter. To have it be a known quantity. To survive red carpets, Eddie's hand cradled in his. Press close to him on a couch, in a way Isaac barely ever had, with anyone. Allow himself a looseness in his limbs that might be second nature to some, but for Isaac felt like the worst kind of weakness. He didn't know how.

There was confusion in the streets, lots of people on cell phones looking for signal, hugging each other, crying. He could feel the harsh, uneasy stares, the edging away, the quick, frightened glares from the people who saw a man walking around alone the night bombs went off, who imagined he was too lean and dark to be acceptable tonight. He tried to stand as if he had nothing to hide, but of course he did, more than most people who were harassed on the street for looking too Middle Eastern for the likes of some.

He knew there was going to be trouble when a trio of Viking descendants in Union Jack t-shirts started following him. The kick of anxiety in his belly was dulled, channeled by a lifetime of training into heightened awareness, but he still didn't like this. He went the opposite direction from home by reflex. It had been drummed into them all in counter-ops training, but he hadn't needed to be told. He heard Yossi's voice in his head, echoing through weekend afternoons while they worked on replacing the broken window on Mo Adwallah's van yet again after someone threw a rock through it, when Isaac was a teenager. *Don't take it to your own front door. Don't give them a way to find you again.* He knew as soon as he left the main road they'd be on him. He wished he had backup. Plausible deniability if the cops came. But there wouldn't be any cops tonight. These neighborhoods weren't a high priority to begin with, and right now?

Cole went down a side street lined with shops, all closed up. Good. No witnesses. He could feel his victims at his back. So he turned. He wanted the trouble. Wanted to forget Eddie's skin gently sliding beneath his knuckles by driving them into something. Hard.

"Can I help you gents with anything?"

He was met with some unimaginative comments about his ancestry and suicide vests.

Isaac remembered sitting on the stoop with Omer, both holding plastic bags of ice to their black eyes. They'd been about eleven. They thought they were going to get a dressing-down from Yossi for fighting in the schoolyard, taking down some little fucker who knocked Omer's yarmulke off and ran around with it, taunting him, until he ran right into Isaac's fists. *"I'm proud of you boys,"* Yossi told them instead. *"Your battles are his battles,"* Yossi told Omer. Then he turned to Isaac. *"Your battles are his battles."* His eyes were fierce. Probably with tears, Isaac thought now. *"Never forget that. You will never forget that."* Neither one of them ever had, no matter how much they fought inside the house. Over the years they extended the dictum to their motley crowd of friends. All their battles were the same.

"All that's original, that is. Never got it before," he said now. His East End accent reasserted itself before a fight. Any fight, from the schoolyard to the sandbox. Pumping adrenaline turned him back into the scrappy, fire-eyed kid ready to have a go at anyone who wanted one. "Look, boys, s'been a long day, can't you leave it? It's my city got messed up too, innit?"

They got redder as a unit, although he could see the smallest of them hanging back slightly as Cole didn't do what they were expecting.

"Maybe we should—"

"Shut it, fuckin' hell," the middle one said, squaring up. "Don't be such a pansy about it, Christ. It's what they all deserve."

"Oh, right," Cole said. "You're checking all the boxes, aren't you? Any phobias you don't have? I'll make this easy," he said, pushing up his sleeves. "I was born here. I grew up here. I served this country proud in ways you must have washed out of, given that Her Majesty's military usually prefers its soldiers have brains. So if you still think you can take me, you big strong men, then come on. But I've killed better men than you for less, so think about it. M'beggin', here."

"You'll be begging when we're through," the middle one said.

"You seem a bit too excited about that, mate. Maybe watch

out. You might play for my team after all." He knew he shouldn't have provoked them. He should have tried harder to lose them, and this wasn't a fair fight. There could have been eight of them and it wouldn't have been a fair fight. He was filled with regret and remorse, as they advanced on him. But, as he drove the heel of his hand into the big talker's nose, he remembered his year ten school counselor remarking on his "limited set of coping mechanisms." Surely the best way to cope with xenophobic, homophobic shitwagons when they outnumbered you three to one and were set on beating you to a pulp was to punch them in their smug fucking faces.

He wanted to take them out of commission, not kill them. The biggest one went down hardest, the middle one fought longest, clearly falling back on his kiddie karate lessons. The smallest one waited until the very end and tried to clip him across the temple with a bottle, and Cole broke his wrist. Not badly, he didn't think. He called them in as assault victims, and waited until he saw the flashing blue lights before he slunk away.

When he got home there was a hulking lump on his doorstep, illuminated by a phone light. Cole went into a defensive stance instantly, before the lump stretched and stood and resolved itself into Omer.

"Thank God," he said, only a little sarcastically. "You're alive. Sandra's got me waiting up for you. Yossi's at the garage in the dead of night. If you're alive, you're in trouble."

"I'm alive."

"You're in trouble." Omer stomped ahead of him into the house. "Found him," he called out. "Told you he'd be all right."

Sandra flew out of her chair. The television was on.

"You were there, weren't you?"

The news was on, showing flashing lights and people with blood at their temples, covered in shock blankets, sitting on the kerb. He nodded, gazing numbly at the screen like it had any answers for him. She held him at arm's length, taking in his change of clothes, his wild hair, the blood on his knuckles. She spat out a stream of profanity in Hebrew that took Cole aback, because he didn't realize his blond, English-speaking, High Tea-serving aunt knew how to suggest that whomever Cole got in a fight with had taken time out of his busy schedule having relations with goats.

"Have to go tell Dad you're alive." Omer left through the kitchen door. He ruffled Isaac's hair on the way out. Isaac supposed this was what having a family felt like.

Sandra made him tea. She sat with him while he drank it, one hand gripping his wrist so hard it hurt. He didn't try to move it. He apologized for not telling her he was all right. Sandra shook her head, hardly able to speak.

"All those years, I knew I wouldn't know," she finally said. "I was ready for you to die without my knowing, because that's what you wanted, that's what you chose. But now…"

His jaw ached from a lucky shot. "I know. I'm sorry. I should have called, but then I was with the prince, and—"

"You were what? You were off! Did they bring you in?"

"Not really."

"Tell me what happened."

"What's to tell? Bombs went off. It wasn't the first time. I didn't think I would hear them again, ever. And not here." He told her he'd been there when the explosions happened and helped get Eddie to safety. He left out the sex and the way Eddie had smiled at him, so trusting, eyes filled with desire and adrenaline. He left all that out. Another nail in a very tightly shut coffin.

"I'm so sorry."

"What was it all for, if bombs are going to go off here anyway? I went over there to stop that happening, didn't I? I drove this wedge between me and Yossi, I don't know what it did to your marriage—"

"Be honest, now, you weren't so naive as all that when you joined up. And what it did to my marriage is none of your business," she told him sharply. "My marriage is mine, and you are mine, and that is as close as those two things will ever get."

"I left," he said. "He and I fought so much over it, and then I left without resolving anything."

"Oh, come on," she said, dragging him out of his chair as she stood. She took him upstairs, to her and Yossi's bedroom. It was painted a soft, pale orange. The walls glowed when she turned the bedside lamp on. She pulled him down on the bed with her, like he was a little boy instead of a killer. He curled up, awkwardly. Even though he wasn't that tall, he was still bigger than she was. "Stop worrying for five minutes. You're home."

He settled into the bed, mashing one of the pillows under his cheek. They lay there in silence for so long he thought she might have fallen asleep. It was the only reason he could bring himself to start talking.

"Yossi was so upset when I wanted to join the army. He said I was betraying my people. I told him I didn't have any people. It took years for me to figure out he meant him, and Omer. And you."

"He was afraid for you. For what might happen to you."

"He said I betrayed him."

"Maybe you did. Choosing the ways of a father you never met over the man who did his best to raise you."

"Did you think that?"

Sandra's fingers tugged on a bit of his hair. "Did I ever say that? I don't remember being shy about my feelings."

"You never fought me so much." He traced one of the swirls in her skirt. The last time they'd been here like this, like a parent and her child, was the night before he left for basic training.

"Remember my favorite Austen novel?"

"*Persuasion*, right?"

"Yes. The hero is a man who came from nothing. A loving family, but no prospects. The only way he has of making his fortune is to try his luck in the navy. He believed natural talent, his intelligence, his courage, were everything he needed to succeed. So. He goes. He comes back a rich man. I thought you needed a chance to make your fortune."

"Life isn't a Jane Austen novel."

"I would have preferred almost anything but the military for you. But you wanted to fight until you were bloody. Until you made whoever else pay. There was rage inside you, and I couldn't keep you away from it. So better you do something with it that wouldn't land you in prison. I couldn't make you be something other than what you were. And I didn't want to try, because I didn't want to be like my parents."

"You hardly ever talk about them."

"There is hardly anything to talk about. We were raised in a house where all the furniture and carpets were white. I was to do very well in school, and Lilli was to be beautiful. We succeeded at our chosen paths in life. And then I saw you." She rested her hand on the back of his neck and stopped talking. He knew it was his turn. Finally, after a long quiet, he took it.

"I almost didn't realize it was a bomb until the second one went off. It's normal in my head, that noise, that feeling. Part of my landscape. So I didn't get scared until I realized that the prince was right there, that it was happening at home. I don't know why it didn't scare me until then. But I'm scared now. We don't know who did it yet."

"You're all right, little boy," she said, leaning over and pressing her lips into his hair. "You are."

"Does Yossi still feel like I betrayed him?"

"You'd have to ask him yourself."

Isaac shut his eyes tightly, and tried to block out the world. Some time later, he heard the door open, heard Yossi say—

"I knew one day I would find you in our bed with a younger man."

"What's this 'our,' old man? You're behind on the rent."

"Twenty-five years behind," Yossi said, walking into the room. Isaac could feel them communicating over his head, without words. He felt the bed dip under Yossi's weight, a solid hand settling on his hair. He curled in tighter to Sandra and pressed back at the same time.

"I'm sorry," he whispered. There was a pause.

"For what?" It was Yossi's voice, gruff and comfortable.

"For leaving. For coming back but never actually coming back."

"What do you mean?" Sandra, this time.

"I hurt people. I killed people. And I spied on people. And I lied." He could feel himself shaking. "I know what you meant now, Yossi. I know you didn't want me putting myself through all that. I know now."

Yossi's hand tightened. "The things you did…They were bad people. They were disgraces. I'm sure they deserved it."

"Mostly they did," Isaac murmured. "Sometimes they didn't deserve exactly what they got, and sometimes they didn't get exactly what they deserved."

"You deserved to come home," Yossi said. "And even if you didn't, *we* deserved you coming home."

Isaac felt something cold, wrapped in an old tea towel, pressing against his swelling knuckles. He rolled onto his back, cramming himself between his aunt and uncle. He kept his eyes closed, although he knew they could see the tears leaking from them.

"You're safe now," Sandra said. He nodded fast, even if he

didn't believe her. Even if he never believed that. She blotted his cheeks with her shirt sleeve.

"I don't think I can talk anymore."

"You don't have to," Yossi told him. A minute later the television went on. He stayed there until he could feel something other than the floor shaking beneath him, hear something other than Eddie's voice gasping his name.

11

E ddie woke to rain clattering against the windows. He reached for the telephone without opening his eyes. The voice on the other end of the line spoke immediately.

"Good morning, sir."

"Good morning, Siobhan. Would you mind sending someone with an update on last night for me in about twenty minutes? And some breakfast."

"Of course." She didn't hang up. "I'm very glad you're all right."

"Thank you," he said. "Truly. I'll drop by later if I have a minute."

"Oh, no, you don't have to—"

"We've all had a shock."

There was a slight pause. "I'm sure everyone here will be pleased to see you if you can manage it. I'll have everything sent up right away."

"Thank you again. See you soon." He hung up. Lay there, contemplating the near future. Twenty minutes to pull himself together. A week wouldn't be long enough. A peal of thunder

startled him out of bed. It reminded him of last night. Everything reminded him of some part of last night. *That's what
trauma does*, he heard Tonya in his head. *Trauma makes everything
happen all at once.*

He turned the shower on as hot as he could stand. He
couldn't step in without seeing Isaac in front of him, his
focused eyes, his sure touch. He wanted it to be that part of the
night again. Wanted to feel Isaac's hands, scarred and callused
in places he never expected, that little hitch whenever Isaac
drew his left index finger back, the crooked fingertips on his
right hand. He loved those fingers, macabre as it was to trea-
sure evidence of Isaac's hand having been stamped on during
his second tour of duty. Eddie didn't know the whole story. But
the fact of Isaac's survival made his heart race. The crinkles
around his eyes made Eddie ache, because Isaac had survived,
and found his way to him.

Whatever Eddie needed, Isaac gave him. Eddie felt small
and unworthy of that kind of devotion, but last night he
believed it in how Isaac treated him. Meeting his eyes, tugging
on his hand, moving over him with a will, digging his thumbs
in everywhere so Eddie had something to push against, a place
to put the helplessness and the fear. And the desire.

He could tell himself his crush on his bodyguard developed
after the Incident happened, that his feelings were the result of
pathological, psychological transference and the worst white
knight complex known to humankind. He remembered the
frustration and the sick shame as Tonya gently described how
this was something that happened all the time to people with
security teams or people who were rescued from similar situations, that it was completely normal and would pass with time.

It didn't. The truth was, he had been drawn to Isaac since
the day they met, wanting to know him inside and out, to be
trusted and adored in return. His feelings ran too deep, too
quickly. By the time he knew what they were, there was

nothing to do but endure. Until now. He stomped on the rising tide of shame. He had no time for thinking about this. His head was a mess of concern for Isaac, for everyone who'd been at the club, and at this point Isaac was the distraction. He had things to do. Maybe later, he'd have a chance to… to what?

When he got downstairs, Harris was already at the breakfast bar. The circles under Harris's eyes looked as if they had always been there, but he wore a fresh suit.

"Did you get any sleep?"

"A few hours. Sent Cole on his way last night. The protection details are locked down because of the emergency, or else he would be here. He's at his flat right now."

Harris automatically assuming he needed to know where Isaac was at all times had been standard operating procedure for years. It seemed downright sinister now.

"Were there any casualties?"

"No. It seems one of the bombers lost his nerve when constructing the devices. Several people are in critical condition, and there is no shortage of serious injuries, but the explosives used weren't designed for maximum mortality." The matter-of-fact way Harris spoke was comforting and chilling all at once.

"Will you make sure Jenny knows where the victims are being treated?"

"Of course. Two of the perpetrators were in custody before midnight, and a third is being tracked down as we speak. They are members of a group called 'Britain First,' which itself has ties to a number of known nationalist organizations. The Queen is receiving frequent updates." Harris reached out and touched Eddie's wrist. "They had no idea you were at that club. They were trying to make a statement about what they consider to be degenerate behavior, not the monarchy."

Eddie released an extra bit of breath. "I have to thank you—"

"You don't." Harris spoke quietly but firmly. "This is what we all signed up for. It is a privilege. If Cole were here, he'd tell you the same thing."

Eddie couldn't help his cheeks getting hot. "He, er, stayed with me for a while last night. I hope he didn't break too many rules."

Harris gave him one of those hard-as-ice inscrutable looks he was so very good at. "There aren't many rules in emergencies."

ANDREA, the head chef at KP, brought his breakfast herself. He gave her a hug, and went over to the administrative offices afterwards, to say hello to Siobhan and the rest of the staff who kept his life running. He tried to give them what he imagined they expected: a stiff upper lip, affected by the tragic events, but not too much. A little tired under the eyes, a little haggard was fine, but only for a bit. In case they talked. Not to the press, but to their friends. In case one of those friends told a different friend, who might tweet about it or get in touch with someone from the Sun, and that's why he was slightly paranoid.

Eddie turned the news on when he got back, blanching when he saw his own face on the screen. Somehow the press had it that he'd been in the club. It must have been the bartender, she was the only one who got a good look at his face. So now the coverage wasn't about the investigation or the victims or the search for anyone involved in planning the attack, or anything other than that Eddie had been there, and what did *that* say about the media's priorities?

He finally went upstairs and checked his cell phone. There

were the texts from his siblings he hadn't answered last night—another stab of guilt, although someone would have told them he was safe at home—and a few from friends. One nervous message from Mikhail and Galen. They were all more or less frantic. He fired off messages in return.

Portia answered when he rang the image team's office.

"Your Royal Highness, I am so glad you're all right." She genuinely did sound relieved, he thought. Death announcements wouldn't be his favorite part of the job, either.

"I am as well, thank you. I got your call. Is there something I can help you with?"

"If you're feeling up to it, a public appearance. We've already prepared an interview with the BBC later on today, a quick little thing to air in prime time, to assure everyone you're all right. It would go a long way, especially to defusing the rumors that you're dead and being replaced by a bionic clone."

His voice was very hard when he responded. "Portia, people were seriously injured last night. I wouldn't want to draw attention from a very real tragedy with my spot of good luck. Pictures, but no interview."

"Sir—"

"I won't do it. I won't sit there and smile without so much as a bandage on my forehead while there are people sitting in hospital wondering if their loved ones will ever open their eyes again. It's unseemly. You're already clearly worried about my being associated with the club, or else someone would have woken me to go down there with Mum. Set up a photo op, I'll go on it. Doing something sufficiently respectable? Getting out of the car at 10 Downing for a security briefing, perhaps? Something to let them know I'm not being replaced with a bionic clone, as you put it, that it's still business as usual. You can put Arthur in the shot, too, remind the nationalist wankers that the line of succession is secure with a couple of strapping men in it."

Portia was reserved but impressed when she responded.

"Are you after my job, sir?"

"It would be a conflict of interest," he said, and hung up the phone.

He immediately rang Alex, who picked up almost before the call connected. They talked for a few minutes, and it was easy enough to tell her the story of last night without mentioning that he and Isaac had made love in his very own bed in Kensington Palace. He did say that Isaac was with him at the club, because it would get out eventually, but didn't mention that Isaac hadn't started out the night with him. Alex didn't think anything of it. For her, Isaac was a constant in Eddie's life, like his having brown hair and preferring toasted cheese sandwiches to almost anything else a person could have for lunch. She expected Isaac to be at Eddie's side. It dawned on him—what if Isaac decided he couldn't stay there after last night? He forced himself to focus on Alex.

"I was trapped all night with that journalist who's come to work on Mary's boxes."

"What, not raining verbal abuse down on him?"

"He's not actually that bad. Gwen Shelton texted me, too," she said, striving for some normal conversation. "This morning, as soon as she saw you on the news. We're going for tea next week." Mention of his childhood best friend made him feel a little better. A nice surprise. What a concept.

Victoria got on the phone afterwards, warmly businesslike. "Doing all right, Eddie? I heard from Sir Thomas a few moments ago. You were a bit forceful with Portia."

"Wanting me to smile for the cameras while they're shoveling rubble out of Leicester Square? We're lucky I didn't drive to her house and yell up at her window." His voice shook as he spoke to her. She was his mother, after all, he supposed that was all right.

"Now that would have been a photo opportunity." There

was muted, genuine laughter in her voice. "I don't want you to do anything you aren't comfortable with."

"I sense a 'however' hoving into view off the starboard side."

"We'll discuss it after the security briefing," she said, in her I-am-your-mother-and-also-your-sovereign voice, but there was a depth to it that concerned him. They weren't close the way she and Alex were, didn't have the bond of shared burden that she had with Arthur, when Arthur could be pried out of his fighter planes. He could, however, tell her moods apart from quarter tone shifts in the sound of her voice, even if he didn't understand them the way his siblings did. He was still her son, after all, even though from the way they talked sometimes it felt more like they were colleagues who had never really gotten to know each other. They said their good-byes, and he threw his phone down on the bed.

He spent some time looking through the early reports Harris left for him. He tried to watch the news, but footage from the night before sent him stumbling to the toilet, throwing up his breakfast as the world tilted away again. He shuddered, pressing the heels of his palms against his eyes. *You're safe. Isaac is safe.* Eddie wished he'd held on tighter in the night, that even in his sleep he could have convinced Isaac to stay. To wake up with Isaac defied imagination. *Rules multiply after an emergency.* He was curled up on his bed when his cell rang again. Expecting it to be Arthur, he swiped to connect and brought it to his ear without looking at the display.

"H'lo?"

"Eddie, I saw the news. How are you?"

The sound of that particular voice was so shocking, he didn't know what to say. He checked the clock. It was already nine-thirty. He didn't know what time he thought it would be, but it made sense that the contributor of half his genetic material wouldn't have gotten up and allowed the world to intrude until a civilized hour, even if there had been a national emergency the night before. Only with great effort was he able to control his desire to hurl the phone out the window.

"I wasn't hurt, but I'm sure the news told you that." A hurriedly released statement from the image team said that Eddie had been at the club for a friend's birthday, and that no one in the prince's party had been injured, as they were all in a private room. For once, he appreciated the effort on his behalf.

"I wanted to hear it from you." Malcolm sounded sincere, but then, he always did. Eddie could picture the scene. His father in the sun-drenched enclosed terrace at the back of his townhouse in Belgravia, monogrammed navy dressing gown hanging open over coordinating pajamas, the way he dressed of a morning in Eddie's memory. Ironically old-fashioned, never stodgy. Dark hair brushed back, the lines in his face barely noticeable. Phone held to his ear in a finely proportioned hand, expression of concern wafting over his features.

"Now you have. Is there anything else?"

"Edward…" A thread of hurt in Malcolm's voice garroted Eddie's heart. "I also wanted to offer my support, with everything that has gone on for you recently."

"That's rich, when it's your girlfriend brokering the pictures to the tabloids."

"*What?*"

Satisfaction at setting Malcolm back mixed with relief so palpable Eddie felt lightheaded. Malcolm hadn't known. *Malcolm hadn't known.* "Oh, yes. She told me at the gala the other night. You remember, the one you showed up to without notifying anyone beforehand. So forgive me if your approval, or not, means very little to me, when you don't have the courtesy to let any of us prepare for managing your presence."

A pause. And then, low, as if it were an admission Malcolm was not proud of: "I don't want there to be this distance between us."

Eddie pulled his knees up, wrapping one arm around them, hunching into himself. This was positively the last thing he could deal with today. The absolute last. "I don't think what you want matters all that much."

"I'm your *father*."

"Some things you lose your right to say. Consequences, Malcolm. Look the word up if you have trouble with it. I know it's not a natural part of your vocabulary."

Eddie stabbed viciously at the end call button and flung the phone away. He stood up and walked to his closet, regarding himself in its mirrored inside wall. He lifted his chin, turned it this way and that, looking for an angle that didn't betray him with his resemblance to a man he wished he didn't miss. The phone buzzed twice and then went silent. Coward couldn't even be arsed to leave a message.

Malcolm Varre, Duke of Edinburgh, ex-husband to the Queen of England and father of her three children. Not a father *to* them. Eddie had exacting specifications for what counted towards being someone's father. A dad, even, laughably naïve as that sounded. And they didn't include insider trading, indirectly supporting cruelty to animals, and infidelity. Or abandonment, betrayal, and a complete unwillingness to acknowledge he might have done something wrong in any of the forgoing situations. Malcolm seemed to think it was reasonable that he should do what he pleased and get away with it. Everyone should love him, and there should be no repercussions if he behaved unlovably. Everyone should "be an adult about it," even when those people were children. And of course, being an adult about it meant seeing things Malcolm's way and not demanding more from him than he was willing to give.

That had been fine, or at least it had gone unnoticed, back when he was the beloved husband of the Queen of England. Then he could do no wrong, especially in the eyes of his children. He took them yachting, to the horse races, to EuroDisney. He brought his sons to his own tailor for miniature versions of his wardrobe. He accompanied his daughter to her swim meets. He got seats for them all in the stands at football matches, and spent long afternoons reading with them on picnic blankets. Even state outings became fun when Malcolm was involved. He gave a shine to everything he touched. He could kick a football, climb a tree, ride a horse, and then he'd change into his tux and be every inch the underestimated aristocrat at a dinner party or cocktail hour.

There were pictures of Malcolm holding eight-year-old Eddie on his lap during a state dinner at Buckingham Palace. Eddie had given his nanny the slip and run downstairs in his Spider-Man pajamas. He stopped short as soon as he was fully visible, aware that his master plan to sneak under the tables and steal all the napkins wasn't going to work with everyone staring at him. Victoria had been appalled, but Malcolm jumped into action. He swept Eddie into his lap, turning an unthinkable faux pas into the talk of the night. Eddie remembered the First Lady of the United States being absolutely charming to him. On his other side, Victoria radiated tension, even though the President was telling her stories about what his own children got up to, years ago, in the New York State governor's mansion.

For a full week afterward, the papers berated her, either for not managing the nursery better or, worse, for perpetrating a cheap stunt, while casting Malcolm's behavior as adorable and the very sweetest. She must have known how it would play in the press: she was his mother, and the Queen, *she* should have had more control. Malcolm was a father making the best of it.

"He looks so much like you," he remembered the First Lady saying.

"Oh, yes, we're all very proud. We don't know who the mother is," Malcolm answered, bouncing Eddie on his knee.

The fact that he used to enjoy it when his father lay total claim to him made him feel miserably guilty, even now, over ten years after the divorce. It used to make him feel physically ill, so that was progress. Eddie had thought his father was every inch a prince from a storybook. Malcolm excused himself to bring Eddie up to bed that night. And then, according to gossip he heard much later, on his way back from tucking in his son, Malcolm found time to duck into a guest bedroom with Lady Lydia Thorby, Countess of Heath, and spend a half hour improving royal relations in the West Country.

While the children were in the nursery, infidelity was Malcolm's only vice. The alcohol abuse and relapse into drug addiction came later. The royal children were meant to be insulated from their parents through barriers of household and nursery staff, but Eddie had memories of Malcolm staggering in, barely supported by his protection officers. Shirt half open, eyes glazed, muttering or yelling, depending on whether he was drunk or rolling. It terrified Eddie, even more so because no one outside the family knew what was going on. That part of the story had never been told to the public. It was hardly mentioned in private. He and his siblings never talked about it. Aside from a few scattered comments over the years from Victoria and Sophie, it went unacknowledged. Malcolm disappeared one night, sending word that he was in an exclusive, in-depth rehabilitation program in Scotland. There might have been a chance—but when he came back, he took up with Helena Wallace, and that was the end.

"*We don't know who the mother is*" haunted Eddie. Malcolm infamously repeated it during the divorce, when a reporter asked him a question about custody of the children. Looking back on it now, Eddie thought he understood. Malcolm was a proud, unhappy man, trying to make sense of what he'd done, of losing his entire family all at once. There could hardly be a joint custody arrangement that took the Queen's children away from her. He took refuge in sarcasm to prove that he still had power. But back then it made Eddie feel like he betrayed his family simply for existing, his hair and face a constant reminder of everything they lost. His father's little ghost.

Eddie blew out a long breath and went after his phone. He saved the number Malcolm called from as "Do Not Answer - MV" and then called Tonya. No shame in needing help, he told himself. None at all.

MALCOLM PLACED the portable handset back in its cradle. Modern telephones were such ugly conveniences, he thought, distracting himself out of necessity, holding on by his fingernails to the cliff face of his ability to cope. All black and gray plastic, hunching in their charging stations. The white and gold receivers of his youth, with wheels that one truly dialed, remained his mother's preference to this day. She had people to navigate touch-tone menus for her. The old telephone in his father's study had buttons with edges sharp enough to catch under a fingernail and a handset heavy enough to kill.

He retied the tasseled sash on his dressing gown as he returned to the breakfast table. The muted news report was still showing images from the bombing, a recent photo of Eddie superimposed on one corner of the screen. Malcolm forced his hands to unclench. Eddie was fine. Shaken, but all right. Fussing from a distance would do no good, and Malcolm wasn't a candidate for father of the year for calling to check up on him.

Did you really think it would be any different? A muscle twitched in his jaw in response to the voice in his head. It was the same voice that used to send him to pills, to other women, to whatever he could get his hands on. The voice wasn't irrational, or even unkind. Just clear that he was a tremendous disappointment. And him, nearly sixty, far too old for all this. Father long dead, mother living in the country in luxurious, self-imposed rustication, claiming she simply couldn't bear London any longer. Easy to understand why, given how steep the comedown from "Queen's mother-in-law" to "disgraced ex-consort's mother" had been.

Finally ran up against someone you couldn't charm your way around? Now the voice was his father's. Sir Ranulf Varre, a horse breeder and an archaeologist, regarded his son with deep suspicion that verged on outright contempt. Malcolm didn't excel at sports or show any pride in his exclusive schools, would rather disappear into seedy clubs with the flashy set than go fox hunting. Sir Ranulf found his son's popularity in the upper echelons of society inexplicable, and with enough liquor in him, would wonder aloud if Malcolm enjoyed the company of other men. He did not put it nicely. The only thing Malcolm ever did that his father took pride in was marry Victoria. Thank god the old man died before he could watch him screw that up, too.

It was fitting that Malcolm's sons were his primary source of rejection now that his father was gone. He long ago gave up hope of real reconciliation, telling himself the Kensington machine drove the wedge between them, Victoria's resentment and Sophie's vitriol fueling the fires. Reading between the lines of gossip columns was sufficient to assure himself that his children were alive and well, but having to find out from the news that Eddie had been in the midst of a domestic terror attack?

For the first time in his life as an estranged father, Malcolm thought that perhaps his son was right to reject him. Especially if what Eddie said about Helena was true.

He heard the muffled click of high-heeled slippers on the carpet before Helena walked in wearing a mint green silk robe, last night's eye makeup looking smoky and a hint wild now. She made him feel shabby and rumpled, a sensation that once held a certain amount of appeal. Today, he resented the assessing glance and infinitesimal eye roll at his expense. It was supposed to be fond. He was supposed to share it. And yet.

"I heard the news," she said, gesturing at the television as she went to the sideboard for toast and coffee. "Bloody awful. This is going to disrupt programming all day. I already got a call from the office. The PM is giving an address later and then there's a Q&A I have first crack at."

"They can't have known he would be there. The bombers," Malcolm murmured. "It couldn't have been an attack on him specifically."

"Of course not," she said. She dropped a second lump of sugar into her cup with a satisfied flick of her wrist, and picked up the coffee pot. "Don't be absurd. He's not important enough to blow up."

"Your method of reassurance needs some work," he said. The tink of silver against fine china made his teeth grind as she stirred, and he wasn't sure why. The footage onscreen now was of Victoria touring the wreckage, crowds of somber neighborhood residents lining metal barricades put in place for the occasion. She looked very much in command of herself, and very alone. When they were married, she held his hand so tightly it hurt after they toured places reeling from violence or calamity. It meant so much to people to see their monarch at times like that, part of the peculiar magic of her position. But he was one of the few people to see the cost, the way she would shake afterwards. He had been the only person who could comfort her, tucking her into his side, distracting her with political gossip or bits and pieces about the children until she sagged against him instead of holding herself so perfectly, terribly straight. *No one to do that for her now*, that voice pointed out. Not cruelly. Simply stating facts.

"She's hardly her grandfather during the Blitz visiting people in the East End with their homes destroyed." Helena scraped butter over her toast. "Or do you think she's happy for the chance to visit a nightclub, no matter the circumstances?"

"Tell me you're not enjoying this, Helena," Malcolm said, gaze fixed on his ex-wife pressing hands with a weeping woman. "Tell me you aren't taking potshots at Victoria while Eddie was in a life and death situation not twelve hours ago."

"It's a nightclub fairly popular with gay young things, and her own son was caught up in it, no tear-stained visuals are going to keep that off peoples' minds," she told him, with the cool rationality that, once upon a time, had so intrigued him. "I'm doing my job."

"Drafting your next attack piece on my terrace isn't your job." He idly wondered what he was doing. He didn't want a fight. Fights were messy. "Although some might say it's a calling."

She relaxed at the joke, although he could tell she was wary. "All right, I'm sorry," she said, the words sounding peculiar coming out of her mouth. "That was tasteless, I admit. But it isn't going to look good for him, you must see that. Especially not with those pictures—"

Malcolm raised an eyebrow. Helena stopped talking. He found it almost arousing, the way she stared, as if she needed to reacquaint herself with him.

"It doesn't matter," she said, after a too-long pause. "I should get to the studio before they give my time slot to a shrill twenty-five-year-old with One Direction on speed dial. I'll be back in to say good-bye, of course, have to get dressed. Call a car for me, darling?"

Malcolm nodded after her, eyes narrowing once she was out of the room. Helena never got that flustered, and in all their years together had never explained what she was about to do.

It rose up in him suddenly that he was in the wrong place, that this breakfast room was a coward's prison, and that he belonged with his children. On the inside, hearing the reports as they came in, not waiting for news presenters to parrot filtered versions of the truth. He imagined sweeping all the breakfast things to the floor in one resounding crash. The trouble it would cause. That's what he liked best, wasn't it? Destroying things instead of taking his time.

Malcolm had to be smarter about it, this time around. So he waited until he heard the shower go on upstairs. He unlocked her mobile, left neglected on the sideboard next to the toast, and began digging.

12

Alex had a swing in her step as she walked down the Promenade in the Dorchester Hotel. She'd caught Daniel working late the night before, and they spent a few hours watching a silly movie and throwing popcorn at each other. Such a small thing to make even the hem of her white and blue flowered dress brushing her knees feel unreasonably delicious, but thinking about the way his eyes crinkled up when he laughed, she didn't care. She needed it, a week after a domestic terror attack involving her own brother. A week after Daniel hadn't abandoned her, that horrible night.

The hushed conversation and clink of china as the tables were set for High Tea washed over her. Mary had brought her and Gwen here when they were girls, and now Alex was seeing Gwen for the first time in seven years. Gwen had picked the location, so she must remember, too. Nerves settled in her stomach. There hadn't been a falling out. They had grown apart because of distance, after Gwen moved to America with her father, and because of life experience once Gwen's daughter was born and Alex went to university. Or at least, that's what Alex liked to tell herself. It was hard to maintain friendships that crossed the outer bounds of the "Kensington Bubble."

Alex heard news occasionally, because Gwen's mother, Joanna Leigh, was still the Queen's personal designer. Joanna and Victoria had been collaborating on her wardrobe since Victoria needed a wedding dress in the early 80's and took a chance on a woman her own age. Gwen had been brought along to the palace while she was still in nappies. Alex didn't have a single memory in which she didn't know Gwen. But after all this time, Alex worried she wouldn't recognize her, right up until the moment she did.

Gwen sat at one of the more secluded tables, laughing to herself at something on her phone. Her reddish-brown hair was tucked behind one ear. She wore a belted, A-line denim shirt dress that must have come straight from one of her mother's spring collections. Too casual for the cream-and-peach Dorchester, but Gwen's easy self-possession made her lightweight cotton outfit a joke at the tea room's expense. Her understated silver jewelry contrasted with the pearls and gold favored by the other women seated at their own tables, and next to her, the decorative palms brought to mind a tropical resort. A bracelet of multicolored plastic pony beads mingled comfortably with the stack of trendy bangles on her wrist.

She looked so pulled together and had clearly planned her outfit with such intent—a gentle declaration of war at the environment in which she found herself, that she seemed almost unapproachable. Alex froze, suddenly unsure. She felt as if she couldn't trust her motives or her desires. But she caught sight of herself in the mirror, and behind her, two members of her detail in plainclothes at a nearby table. She was a *princess*, and a bloody good one. She knew how to project poise in difficult situations. Hell, she *was* the difficult situation. Gwen glanced up, and smiled, holding a hand out as she stood up. Alex recognized some uncertainty in her face, too. It made her feel slightly better.

"It's so good to see you," Gwen said, pulling Alex into a tight hug. Her accent had flattened out after over a decade living in the States, but Alex could hear it coming back. Their hug went on longer than was strictly polite. They attracted a few quick, surreptitious glances from the other tea room guests before taking their seats, shielded behind a decorative column and a couple of potted palms. "Is Eddie all right?"

"He's shaken, got a bit of a cut on his face. I saw him right after."

"I'm so glad. They made it sound like a grenade went off in the middle of an orgy he was hosting, but then there was footage of him arriving at Downing Street with Arthur, and he looked fine. A little pale, maybe."

"That was his idea. He wanted to reassure everyone."

"It worked." A pause. "And Arthur's looking well."

"He's settling in. How's Maddy?"

"She's doing wonderfully."

Silence. Alex got the impression Gwen would rather be anywhere else. She shared it. Had they made a terrible mistake, coming here? Was it too late? Then Gwen spoke, all in a rush.

"Look, Alex, I have to get this off my chest. I feel horrible that we haven't talked for so long. That I couldn't be there for you. I want you to know, it wasn't anything you did. I—there was so much going on. It's the only excuse I have. I've been so nervous this week, thinking you probably hate me now, and don't want to see me."

Surprise and relief mixed in a way that was not entirely pleasant. "I didn't try hard enough, either. Or at all. We were… very far away, I suppose. And I didn't know what to do."

Gwen's bracelets knocked together as she reached over the table to grab Alex's hand. "I let you all down."

"Never," Alex said, fingers tightening around Gwen's. "You went off to America—and none of us *ever* blamed you for going with your dad—and then you had a *child*. You had other things to be thinking about. It's so hard to keep up even when you live together at Buckingham Palace, much less six thousand miles away."

"As long as you're sure," Gwen said, brow furrowed. "I don't want to pretend. I passionately don't want to do that." There was a kind of wistfulness in her voice that Alex understood all too well.

"No pretending," Alex said firmly. "I want to hear all about your life, and then I want to have lots of tea and ice cream with you and Maddy—where is your little clone, anyway?"

"Shadowing *Grandmère* for the morning," Gwen said, a sudden extra light in her hazel eyes. "Probably causing havoc. She insisted on dying her hair yesterday. I can only imagine what Mum's reaction was."

"Why did she do that?"

"It was a… well. You said you wanted news. Do you want news?"

"I did! I do!"

Gwen tapped on the handle of her teaspoon with a painted fingernail. "I told Maddy she could dye her hair because change deserves a change. We're moving to England."

Alex felt like she was getting an unexpected gift. "That's so exciting! I can't even imagine having you back in the country. But why now?"

"It's home," Gwen said, shrugging. "Mum finally convinced me to work for her, and Maddy… I don't know. California is lovely, but I never wanted to stay there forever. She's not really a rooted kid. She flits around activities, different friend groups. I don't feel guilty about turning her life upside down. Much."

"What does her dad think about it?" Alex knew nothing

about the college boyfriend Gwen accidentally got pregnant with. A restless, almost nervous expression flitted over Gwen's face.

"He's not in the picture any more."

"Are you joking?" Alex felt thunderous on her friend's behalf, which seemed like a normal, reasonable reaction. "Want me to have him killed? I'm reasonably sure I could make it happen."

"It's for the best. Honestly. We were too different to make it work. I don't blame him. She's happy. That's what matters."

"Of course, that's the main thing, but still. Does she ever ask about him?"

"Not as much any more. She's got her grandpa. Dad's thinking about returning to Cambridge. Although I think he'll have to stop calling it the Dark Side first."

"Have he and Brian Cox settled their feud?"

"It may be pistols at dawn, we'll have to see." Gwen's light tone didn't deter Alex from going back to the more intriguing topic.

"I never knew Maddy's father was out of the picture," Alex said carefully. "'Shrouded in mystery' is the best way of describing your mother's attitude towards the whole story."

Gwen sighed. "She's touchy about it." She rolled the stem of her water glass between her fingers. "The truth is, my mother doesn't know anything about Maddy's father, and resents it. Although what right she thinks she has—never mind. He was never *in* the picture. It seemed best at the time. A clean break. 'Are you in or not, choose now.' I have all the medical information I need for her. I didn't want to be fighting all the time. I'm sure that makes me the most selfish of mothers."

"No," Alex said right away. "I'm sure you had good reason. After all, he went, didn't he?" Gwen looked away, and Alex felt like a callous fool. "I don't much care for men who don't do right by their children," she said. "It goes against the grain."

"You sound like your brother," Gwen said, and then gave herself a tiny shake. "So things with Malcolm are about the same as always?"

"I can't stand him being with that woman, after everything. And we can't exactly socialize. Not that I would. Probably."

"He is your dad. It makes sense you'd take it hard."

"You know I appreciated you texting me," Alex said. "When things got really bad in the papers."

Gwen watched her like the years since they'd talked were a thick cloud of smoke between them. "It was the very least I could have done."

"I have all these good memories of him, I can hardly believe they were real. And, god, how did I get on to this? I'm sorry. It's been so long since I talked to someone who was there."

"We're at the mercy of the past. And—that's what friends are for."

"It will be fantastic to have you back home. And Maddy. I want to spoil her properly, and I'm sure the boys will, too."

"I'm not sure that's such a good idea." Gwen looked pained, as if she hadn't quite intended to speak, or to say that in particular.

Alex swallowed. "Obviously we'll respect your wishes, and I understand, I think, but you've been in it before. The press isn't as invasive as they used to be when it comes to children. So much goes on under the radar. And you're family."

"I need to think about what's best for my daughter."

"We're not so terrible, are we?"

"You know, when I was in college, my bikini slipped while I was at a friend's birthday party in Malibu. The pictures ended up in the tabloids because I was over eighteen, and they were calling me the Prince of Wales' girlfriend, and wrote it like I was sunbathing topless. I don't want to go back to that. And now I have to think about Maddy. All those rumors and making something out of nothing. It isn't right."

"I'm so sorry," Alex said. "I didn't know."

"It's not your fault! And honestly, it's not fair of me to barrel in here and say that I'm moving back, but by the way, I never want to see you again. I just live in fear of them getting to her."

"I understand. I do. I feel that way all the time. But know you'd be welcome. Arthur and Eddie, too. There's been a missing piece, since you went away. We'd protect your privacy. We know how to do that better, now."

Before Gwen could say anything more, she caught sight of someone behind Alex and relaxed into a brilliant smile. Alex turned to see a flourish of wild blue hair and a lighter blue sundress stalk up, couture Leigh scarf wound around her neck. She cozied up against Gwen, eyeing Alex.

"This is Alex. You met her when you were about two years old."

"You're really a princess?" Maddy asked, fist resting against her chin.

"I am," Alex said.

"So Mummy wasn't teasing me."

"Is that something she does a lot?"

"No, but my grandfather does, and I don't like being victimized," Maddy said offhandedly as she hopped up at the third place setting.

Alex couldn't help smiling. This girl knew how clever she was. "I understand that. But to prove my identity to you, what if I tell you all about being a princess?"

"Yes, please." Maddy tucked the sides of her dress under her and folded her arms on the table. Having her attention was like being caught in headlights. Her eyes were lighter and bluer than Gwen's hazel.

"I love your hair. I never would have been allowed to do something like that at your age."

Maddy grinned. "Mom said I could have any color I wanted if we moved here. And I can get a dog."

"I have a dog. Would you like to see pictures?"

"*Yes.*"

Alex pulled out her phone and, with a conspiratorial air, started showing Maddy pictures of Fenrir, her English Springer Spaniel. As Maddy exclaimed, Alex glanced at Gwen. She was watching them with a strange, bittersweet expression. But then it cleared, and the three of them launched into easy rapport. Alex and Gwen told Maddy stories about their shared childhoods, Maddy interrupting to ask question after question. Ice cream tea was served.

13

"**G**ood morning, Isaac." Eddie slid into the back seat of the town car. They hadn't been alone together since the night of the bombing. He tried to keep his nervous anticipation to himself.

The royal schedule did not stop in the wake of a domestic terror attack. It wouldn't dare. The perpetrators had been brought into custody, after all. Engagements were kept, obligations fulfilled, charitable functions and briefings attended. Victoria released a letter condemning the violence and offering her sympathy to all those affected. Eddie's own statement thanked the emergency responders and encouraged anyone experiencing post-traumatic stress symptoms to seek professional help. The wording heavily implied that he had already done so.

Isaac had been on administrative leave for the last week. It was procedure after a traumatic event. Eddie heard through Kimsey that there hadn't been a consensus on whether to treat him as a victim or an officer on the scene.

Eddie flinched when their eyes met in the rearview mirror.

Isaac wore his suit as usual, hair combed back, but his shuttered expression was unfamiliar. Eddie felt cold fear and hot shame slam together inside his head. Isaac was never supposed to know how much Eddie wanted him. They were never supposed to be afraid of each other.

In the beginning, Eddie hadn't been told much about Isaac's past. Only that being on Eddie's detail was a rest for Isaac. As far as nineteen-year-old Eddie was concerned, Isaac deserved the rest. Isaac deserved everything. Twenty-seven-year-old Eddie felt no differently. Letting his feelings for his bodyguard be known would have meant Isaac's dismissal, and Eddie didn't want that. He wanted Isaac near him all the time. So he promised himself years ago he would hide it. He stretched that promise to the limit, and finally broke it. And now Isaac knew. He stared at his hands, twisting his playing card suits ring on his thumb.

"I'm sorry." Isaac watched him in the rearview, anguish breaking through in jagged cracks in his composure and his rough voice.

The force of his words rocked Eddie to his core. "What?"

"I abused your trust." Isaac's hands at ten and two on the steering wheel, knuckles white. "In an emergency situation. I should have said no. I shouldn't be here right now. I didn't say anything during the debrief. I wanted to leave it up to you." It sounded rehearsed. Eddie didn't want to know what came next.

"Leave what up to me?"

"If I stay on. After what I did."

"What *we* did. Unless… unless you didn't want—" Eddie felt like he might throw up, incapable of finishing the sentence. Memories now essential to him threatened to burn up around the edges like film catching on a lit match.

"No, fuck's sake. I did. But it's not a question of wanting. I'm your bodyguard."

"Yes." There wasn't enough time for everything he wanted to say. There could never be enough time. The car had already idled in the courtyard for too long. Eddie pulled out his phone and scrolled through, as if he were double-checking something. It gave him something to do instead of vibrating apart in anger. "We were both there. We're grown men, and even though we might have made an objectively complex choice after a shocking event, we were there for each other, in that moment. I'm not a child." He looked up. "You don't have to protect me from myself. Or you. Ever."

Tension eased from Isaac's shoulders. Not all of it. But enough.

"Are you going to request a transfer?" Breathing was optional.

"No, sir." Isaac put the car into gear like he was locking something away. The side of his mouth quirked into a tiny grin like it had every time he drove, in Eddie's memory. Eddie turned his ring around his thumb again, tried to stop thinking about how it felt to kiss that mouth.

"'Sir?' We're alone. You promised to call me Eddie when we're alone."

"Only when I wasn't on duty. I'm on duty right now. Otherwise this would be kidnapping and car theft."

"You could be doing a favor for a friend. Anyway, you're not kidnapping me. I don't agree to it."

"One doesn't agree to be kidnapped. One doesn't have the opportunity. That's the point, innit?"

Eddie leaned his elbow on the lip of the car window and hid his smile in his fist. His heart felt like it was expanding too fast for his body, pressing against his ribs, and he had to shut his eyes against the urge to put his hand on Isaac's shoulder. Isaac wasn't leaving him. They were going to be okay.

∽

PART OF EDDIE'S MANDATE—ANY royal's, for that matter—was
to promote English brands and traditions. They all took it seriously, especially when it came to clothes. It wouldn't *do* to let all
that wardrobe money leave the Commonwealth economy.
Victoria had her own designer. Alex wore a rotating wardrobe
of Jenny Packham and Alexander McQueen couture for major
occasions, dipping into the catalogues of new designers and
off-the-rack collections for everyday appearances. Sophie wore
whatever she damn well pleased, but all her millinery was
British. Eddie and Arthur's wardrobes had a different impact.
Most people didn't understand the subtler language of feelings
and ideas conveyed by suits anymore. They felt the impact, but
weren't sure exactly why.

As boys, Arthur and Eddie went to their father's tailor, who
turned them into snappy dressers in miniature versions of
Malcolm's utterly correct yet tongue-in-cheek couture. As soon
as he was old enough, Arthur switched to their grandfather's
traditional, some might say stuffy, tailor. Eddie wondered if it
had been a conscious distancing from Malcolm, or identifying
more with his own legacy—the future king going to the former
king's tailor had maudlin, poetic symmetry. He had never
asked. Perhaps he could, now.

Eddie's own tailor had been in business for less than ten
years. Dandies & Cads focused on introducing people to the
pleasures of wearing bespoke, or near-bespoke suits, at prices
that weren't totally extortionate. He had met one of the owners
at a Liberty trunk show he attended with Alex during university, while picking out shirt fabrics, and took a chance. He
quickly became one of their most faithful customers. He was
surely their best known.

The shop was a repurposed Georgian townhouse located
on Savile Row, long considered by the fashionably wealthy to
be the only stretch of road in the world on which to have their

suits made. Peter Masters, the head tailor and someone Eddie considered a good friend, joined him as soon as he entered the large, airy upstairs parlor. Two other men were meeting with their tailors. Eddie noticed their eyes fall on him, widen in recognition, and skid away. One of the things that made him love this place was that the clientele didn't expect to see a prince in their midst, and he hardly ever asked for a private appointment. Peter led him to the full bar stretching along the back wall. Piles of fabric swatches and look books were already laid out for them. Such was the peculiar, magical bubble in which Eddie lived his life. He tried never to take it for granted.

Eddie settled onto a bar stool, swiveling around on it as an excuse to glance at his bodyguard. Isaac was doing his best impression of dull and imposing, his face composed into bland competence as he stood before the windows overlooking the street, hands clasped behind his back. His presence drew the gaze of the shop's other clients – it always did, and they invariably looked at Isaac far longer than they did at the prince. Eddie thought he could be posing for a portrait, with the morning sun streaming in and lighting him from one side. A loud, attention-seeking cackle from a man knotting a tie in a mirror across the room startled Eddie, interrupting his reverie. Peter's lips twitched. He mouthed *American* at Eddie, who ducked his head to hide his grin.

Peter busied himself with the fabrics and designs he'd chosen. A spare man in his late thirties, his hair a shock of light grey, he was as tall and lean as Eddie himself, which was one of the reasons Eddie trusted Peter to dress him. They exchanged pleasantries as Eddie flipped through the new look book and chose several fabrics he very much liked. They had skated close to the edge with his wardrobe in the past, Peter narrowing the cut of his trousers and jackets as much as he could. Now Eddie might as well go for something that much more fashionable and please himself. What were people going to do—speculate about his sexuality?

Still, he couldn't be flashy, or too trendy—couldn't indulge in the current fad for wild floral or geometric patterns on his suits, for example. He did sigh over two of the outfits Peter had drawn for fun. The first was tight trousers and a fitted jacket nipped in at the waist, covered in black-on-black embroidery that resolved into the Tube map. There was a black jacket that fell low on the hips, covered in an asymmetrical embroidery of a wild red orchid. His throat felt dry and tight as he realized, with a painful jolt in his stomach, that—relaxed standards or no—he might never wear something like it. Tears stung the corners of his eyes. An overreaction, certainly, but he had no control over himself today.

"What would you put him in?" he whispered to distract himself, nudging Peter and glancing meaningfully at Isaac. "If you could dress him in anything."

"Very little," Peter said, smirking at Eddie's huffy reaction. Trying to hide one's sexuality from one's tailor was a waste of time, and he never had. But his feelings for Isaac were a different story, out in the world.

"A suit, then. As if he were coming with me to something splashy and important. Where I might wear this." He tapped the orchid jacket. "Cannes, or a movie premiere. Or the BAFTAs."

"Doesn't he usually accompany you, your highness?"

"I don't mean as a bodyguard. So no black."

"No black," Peter repeated.

"I've seen him in enough of that for a lifetime." Eddie said, tracing the edge of a blue merino wool swatch. "In university he wore street clothes, but since then it's all dead matte suits and white shirts. Khaki trousers and a white polo if it's considered hot enough, which basically means we have to be in the Sahara during the dry season. I want him in something that catches the eye, pops against the background. I see him every day and he doesn't change. Maybe he gets—" *more beautiful, more maddening, the only one I want to see, god help me* "—older." Eddie avoided meeting Peter's eyes, afraid of what he might say.

"Charcoal," Peter said finally. "Or indigo. He'd look good in that, wouldn't he?"

"Like James Bond."

"He couldn't help it, if the tailoring was right. With the jacket taken in rather dramatically at the waist, really emphasize the shoulders." Peter sighed. "Gunmetal gray to make his eyes pop. A bit of silk in the blend."

"You've noticed his eyes?"

"He checks to make sure I won't try to assassinate you on a regular basis. It is hard not to, under those conditions."

"Right. Well. He's never looked at me like that," Eddie said, aware with a sinking feeling that if he wasn't obvious already, his petulance over not being seen as a threat gave the game away.

"I'm sure he's never looked at me the way he looks at you, either, sir." Peter's tone was gentle. Eddie swallowed. He ought to deflect. But it weighed on him, trying to deny his feelings when Peter knew every inch of his body in that academic, yet intimate way. They had had many quiet conversations over the years, and Eddie wasn't without knowledge of his own. Peter had been a stockbroker in his former life. He had lived with a younger man until the financial crash—an actor, who left him when he wasn't bringing in six figures a year any longer. The facts of their lives had a cost, and Eddie didn't want to add a lie to the bill.

Peter tapped the look book, saving them both. "Instead of making him your unsuspecting dress-up doll, let's talk about what you'll wear."

As they talked, Peter made notes on his tablet of fine white paper. He also dashed off a drawing that he tucked into Eddie's hand as he left the shop. It was a stylized fashion plate sketch of two men on the suggestion of a red carpet. One was definitely taller, the other broader, one with curls and the other with wavy black hair. They were standing so close together they looked like one figure. Eddie swallowed hard, and looked back toward the shop. Peter watched him from the window, and his eyes were kind. Eddie put the paper in the inside breast pocket of his blazer and raised his fingers in a mock salute as he got into the car.

With the unintentional carelessness that often accompanied relief, Eddie didn't think before he opened his mouth.

"We dressed you in there, you'll be happy to know I got you out of black," he said.

"You dressed me."

"A bit. Nothing outlandish, no plaid." He aimed a grin at Isaac in the rearview, but Isaac wasn't collecting. He looked almost angry. "What's wrong with that?"

"What's wrong? I'm your bodyguard. I'm supposed to be wallpaper. You don't think it's the least bit suspicious that you're suddenly paying so much attention to me?"

Eddie didn't think it would help to say that given how much Eddie talked about him generally, it probably didn't seem so sudden to anyone else.

"With Peter? He's not going to say anything, if that's what you're worried about. He's probably under an NDA, come to think."

"You still can't act like—"

"Like what? Playful? I can't enjoying talking with my tailor about what kind of suit he'd design someone who isn't me? We talk about dressing me all the time. What if I wanted a break?"

"Take it wi'someone else." The slurring and the furrow in his forehead struck fear into Eddie's heart. He had almost lost Isaac once today. Couldn't remember actually making him angry before. So he said the first thing that came to mind.

"We need to talk about it, then. Because I don't understand."

Eddie became positive, in the pause that followed, that Isaac wouldn't say anything else. He had visions of being left out in front of Kensington Palace like a piece of luggage, watching Isaac peel off in a squeal of burning tire and never speaking to him again. He was so busy smelling the hot rubber that it came as a shock when he heard Isaac say something in his most soothing professional tones.

"Isaac here, Curly wants to cut loose. No, we'll be fine."

Eddie was afraid, so soon after the bombing, that they were about to be reeled back in on some pretext. "Green zone only. Understood." Isaac tugged out his earpiece and threw it into the glove box. "You want to talk, fine. But I want to do it somewhere else. Not like this."

Beneath the anxiety at having hurt Isaac's feelings, Eddie felt a tiny thread of excitement. "Stay here," Isaac instructed, and left the car. He closed the door with quiet precision.

They used to do this often, get Eddie away for a few hours if there was nothing scheduled. Get fish and chips in a seaside town, be back in time for dinner. Once they got hopelessly lost near Dover, rolled the windows down, and sang Queen hits at the tops of their lungs until they bumped into the M20 purely by accident. Eddie thought at the time that Isaac had done it on purpose. Nothing like that had happened in years. His fantasies took a turn for an anonymous hotel room, or maybe Isaac's flat, where Isaac would make his displeasure with Eddie known. Slowly. Deliciously slowly.

Isaac came back fifteen minutes later with two large shopping bags from Abercrombie & Fitch. Eddie blinked away his distracted haze when Isaac slung one of them into his lap. "Change."

Eddie scrambled to get it done, the kick of Isaac giving him orders settling him. He might like that a little too much. In the bag he found cargo trousers a size too big, a soft, tight navy blue t-shirt, a large white button-down shirt made of heavy cotton he would swim in, a zip-up hoodie, and a beanie. An actual, honest-to-god beanie and a pair of...

"These are flip-flops."

"Very nice flip-flops."

"You're trying to make me look like a beach bum."

"A very well-dressed beach bum."

"Even so." But Eddie was already biting tags off. Isaac drove towards the center of the city. It felt like Isaac was trying to take him away, give both of them some room to breathe. If it took a spot of prince-stealing in order to do that, so be it. Practically in his job description. Eddie hoped Isaac was looking in the rearview as he pulled the t-shirt over his head. It was a bit of a struggle to get his trousers changed in the small space, but even more amusing to watch Isaac do the same in the front seat once he parked the car. Eddie pulled his new beanie down over his face for that. He thought he heard Isaac snort. Eddie transferred his black leather wallet, stamped with his family's crest, to one of the side pockets in his trousers. He rubbed over the worn stamp with his thumb.

Isaac got himself into a pair of dark wash jeans and tucked his white suit shirt into them, popping a few of the buttons over his white tank. Eddie could see a bit of his chest hair over the top of it. His mouth watered. Isaac did a sweep when they got out of the car. He put his hand in the small of Eddie's back as he led him into Hyde Park. They picked their way through and around all sorts—tourists, pairs of businessmen eating a quick lunch together, not talking much, some mothers sitting on blankets, watching their children play, older women sitting on benches, watching other people's children play.

Eddie loved being out this way with Isaac. He was proud

he got to walk next to someone so confident, so competent. His shining black shoes, the way he brushed his hair over to one side, he went from bodyguard to some kind of ultra-hip graphic designer type in seconds. And Eddie looked like a shift-less uni student.

The notion made his breath catch.

They found a spare bit of grassy bank after buying a couple of sandwiches at a mobile Pret stand, and Eddie reminded himself getting grass stains and dirt on these trousers was practically expected of him. The him he was in this moment, at any rate. Isaac leaned against a tree, pulling his shirttails out of his jeans, and Eddie lay on his back, gazing at the clouds.

"We've got some sunshine," he offered. Isaac tossed Eddie's sandwich at him. It landed on his stomach. "Do you want to talk or throw food at me?"

"Not sure," Isaac said. Then, after a minute, "You can't be dressing me with your tailor, your highness."

"Oh, no," Eddie said, sitting up and ripping into the sand-wich packaging. "We're not talking about that like this. No one's going to hurt me. No one's going to recognize me. Take your lunch hour, Isaac. With me. Here. While we have a conversation." Silence from behind him. Eddie looked back, finding Isaac staring at him through sunglasses. Then he pushed them up on his head. Seeing his eyes didn't help.

"Right. Look. This is…" Isaac cast around for the right word. "Compartmentalized. For me."

"I know that," Eddie said quietly. "And perhaps it's not the slickest thing in the world to discuss dressing you for Cannes right now."

Isaac snorted, pulling a knee up to his chest. "Why did you bring it up?"

"I wanted to think about you. What it would be like if you

were with me. As more-than." Eddie hugged his own knees, feeling about nine years old. "I know it's stupid."

A hand rested on his back after a moment. "Not stupid," Isaac said. "Impossible. This is something that happened once, Eddie."

"You mean it's over?" His voice came out a whisper.

"It was already over. It's always over." Isaac didn't mean to be cruel, Eddie knew, but it still felt like his heart was an orange in a juice press. "It has to be. What we're risking even sitting here like this—the scandal, your persona in the press…"

"Your career."

"Your reputation."

"Forget that, I'm a bloody prince, I could probably get away with murder as long as too many people didn't know about it. *Your* reputation."

A pause, and then, "My reputation," Isaac agreed.

"I'm not unaware of that," Eddie said.

"Never said you weren't aware, but there's too much tied up here to be coy about what it is. And what it isn't."

Eddie pushed himself up the bank so that he could sit with his legs crossed, hands folded in his lap as he watched Isaac's profile.

"Do you regret it?" The world went on around them, a little kid shrieked, there was the jingle of a dog's tags against its collar as it went by, and Eddie waited.

"No," Isaac said. Eddie could see how the admission cost him. He wanted to comfort him, wanted to stop feeling like the ultimate source of all problems in the lives of the people around him. "But you can't turn me into your boyfriend. And you can't treat me like I'm something to be dressed. I don't like it."

"I don't know why I think I need to, you do fine on your own," Eddie said, jokingly batting his eyelashes, but Isaac held fast to the point.

"Even if I were your boyfriend, it would be unacceptable to me. Especially then."

"Why?" Eddie didn't mean to sound so petulant, but he couldn't stop now that he was on a roll. "Why shouldn't I want you to come to Cannes? Why wouldn't we think about a suit or something? I did that with Stephen all the time."

"Stephen is the grandson of a duke, and I'm the bastard child of I-don't-even-know. I can't afford a bespoke suit, I can't afford to be the boyfriend of a prince royal, and I never, ever would want it to look like I've been *bought*."

"If you were my boyfriend... Look, if I worked in a coffee shop, if I weren't me, I would still bring you leftover pastries at the end of the day so you'd have something sweet, I'd still think of you, want to do things for you. It's the scale that's different to me, nothing more."

"Scale is incredibly important, Eddie." Isaac looked irritated and charmed all at the same time, so Eddie thought perhaps he took the emotional crux of his point even if he was still arguing with the premise. "Taking pastries from your barista boyfriend is different from taking tangible, expensive gifts from your very rich boyfriend."

"I don't see why it should be," Eddie said, obstinate. "Not if the feeling is the same."

"You know how important the look of things is. Better than anyone. You know it doesn't look good."

"I don't care what it looks like. You're the most loyal, caring person in my life, and you love movies, why shouldn't I want you to come with me? You'd be my date, photographed with me, designers would be falling all over themselves to dress you for nothing." Eddie wasn't sure how they'd segued to arguing like they were boyfriends in reality, but something about it made him feel pleased and warm all over, so he wasn't in any hurry to stop. Arguing about a hypothetical relationship felt much better than discussing how they didn't have a real one.

Isaac went blank, scanning the area. Eddie sighed. "I'm safe. I'm fine. No one's been hiding in the bushes for the last twenty-seven years with a rifle waiting for me to come feed the ducks."

"You don't know that for sure."

"Would you talk to me, please? You're upset. I don't know why, and I don't like that. *Please* explain." Eddie reached out and wrapped his fingers around Isaac's wrist.

Isaac stared at his hand like being touched was an alien concept. Then he sighed. "Never told you about my mother, have I?"

Eddie shook his head, taking a chance and moving closer over the grass. He could feel the heat of Isaac's body against his side. Isaac looked off across the man-made pond.

"My mother was a career party girl in the 80's. You should see the pictures. You probably *can* see the pictures, if you know where to look. She was gorgeous, a laugh, up for anything. She lived off her boyfriends. All very high tone. They'd give her gifts. Huge expensive things, clothes, furs, the lot. They bought her flats and sold them out from under her as fast when they were done, and it never seemed to faze her. She still rattles around the globe, taking from people who use her right back."

"How could that say anything about you?"

"If we were together, I'd be doing the same."

"Don't even think it. I don't want you to think it." Eddie's hand tightened, and Isaac flipped his wrist so he could hold Eddie's, too. "It would never be like that." He had never seen Isaac smile like that, all small and close, like he didn't know what to do with it, like no one had ever stood up for him so indignantly before. "Besides, I don't see your mum doing something so very wrong. If she'd been doing it with one man, she'd have been a pretty normal trophy wife, sounds like. So she plays the field. At least no one ever takes her for granted."

"They all take her for granted. Not her son, though," Isaac said. "How could I? She wasn't there."

"Is that why you grew up with your aunt?"

"Yeah. Lilli was too busy doing what she was doing."

Eddie rubbed Isaac's wrist. "I would never try to buy your affections. Or keep you with presents. Make you feel guilty."

"I know. That's why I reacted the way I did."

"It got me out anonymously in the sunshine wearing a shockingly comfortable new outfit, so perhaps you should over-react more often." Eddie stretched out, throwing his legs over Isaac's feet.

"That doesn't change you needing to be a touch less obvious, *Eddie*."

The emphasis on his name was clearly supposed to make Eddie feel sheepish. It made him want to squirm happily instead.

"I'll keep it together. Promise. If you do something for me."

"What?" With due sense of dread.

"Kiss me." Eddie propped an arm under his head and grinned at him without a trace of apology in his eyes. "Out here in the sun. Like you're my much-too-cool sugar daddy architect boyfriend and I'm your..." he thought of Peter and his quiet, all too knowing eyes, "...irritating brat of a grad student boyfriend who studies drama education and makes you beautiful dinners to make up for how I'll never be able to pay half the rent, but you love me anyway."

"Is that how it is? No room for improvisation?" Isaac was enjoying this, Eddie could tell, even though his voice stayed flat. "No room for kissing you like you're my beautiful, creative, free spirit of a boyfriend who hangs paper cranes and crystals in the windows and takes such good care of me and rubs my back when I come home late?"

Eddie's breath hitched. "This is starting to sound like a much better deal for you than for me, honestly—"

Instead of kissing him, Isaac stroked his cheek with the backs of his crooked fingers, pressed a thumb to his lips. Played along with the story Eddie made up for them. Want caught in Eddie's chest, hanging on for dear life, for more of this quiet resting in the sun. For the two of them, alone together. And he knew there was only one way to get as much more as he truly wanted.

14

"To what do I owe the pleasure?" Sophie asked, catching sight of Eddie in her vanity mirror after his soft knock at the door. "I'm not running late."

"Can't a fellow want a chat with his aunt?"

"If you squint at the family seal, it reads *Modus Ulteriori*." She gestured with a long-handled brush at the chaise in her dressing room. "So I doubt it."

A chandelier and wall sconces kept Sophie's dressing room bright and cheerful, even on late gray afternoons when the light coming through the windows was dim. In the adjoining walk-in closet, every gown or piece of clothing Sophie might reasonably leave the house in on official business was hung up in a clear plastic dress bag with a tag attached, noting the designer and last place it had been worn. The shelves and drawers devoted to the clothes she never wore in public held a mix of cozy sweaters, button-down shirts, jeans, yoga pants. Matched pajama sets, robes, and thick socks were there to grab at a moment's notice, but not the point of the room. Eddie made himself comfortable on the top of the low, free-standing, four-sided dresser that also served as table in the middle of everything. In some ways, she got off easy. Victoria's walk-in closets were an impenetrable forest, and her dressing room could double as a command center, if necessary, in case of a political coup. Most of her clothes were kept in climate-controlled attics; she called for specific items when she wanted them after figuring out her schedule, two weeks in advance at a time.

Sophie watched him perch between the portable black velvet tray (up from the vault) that contained her evening's jewelry and a selection of handbags. There was something of the marionette about how his limbs folded. He wore formal dress, as befitted the dinner in honor of Royal Ascot they were attending tonight. Sophie, widely considered the best horse-woman in the Kensington family, was major hostess at the yearly dinner, though Victoria attended, popping in to the cocktail reception beforehand. There was nothing like a crowd of royals to draw a crowd. Even better to see them in their natural habitat.

The highlight of the evening was a silent auction to benefit The Champion's Trust, an organization Eddie had founded in his teens and remained Patron of to this day. It provided medical care and board to horses who were retired from racing because of damage wrought by steroids and other, more hateful forms of animal abuse. The Trust was Eddie's idea, after it turned out his father had become mixed up in a race fixing ring. Sophie found it hard to believe that a sixteen-year-old thought to care about the horses, or that he had done it going on eleven years ago. Her nephew had been so much older than his years when she came back to London, during the divorce. He seemed wretched, hunted, passionately defending a ragged assortment of abused horses because his father had gone and he couldn't take care of his family.

"Something on your mind?" she asked. "We'll be together all night, you can talk my ear off as much as you like."

He winced, glanced away. She reminded herself to take her time, to let him come to the point when he was ready. Eddie would withdraw if he thought a person didn't genuinely care, if he was being a bother. "Not about this," was all he said.

Sophie applied herself to her eyebrows, filling them in with a pencil a shade lighter than her hair. "I miss the days of thick, swooping wings and turquoise eye shadow," she said. "Now it's all delicate nude shades and 'contouring,' as if the world is suddenly going to forget my fifty-two years' residence on the planet. 'Natural beauty' is an oxymoron in a culture that insists I shave under my arms."

Eddie attempted a smile. He put his hand in his pocket and removed a shilling piece, rolling it over his fingers in a steeple-chase flourish. The easy matinee idol move contrasted with his rounded shoulders and flat expression.

Her life had been placed permanently on hold years ago, lured from a cabana in the late evening Caribbean light by a phone call from an unfinished version of this man. *I don't think Mum is well,* he'd told her. *I think she needs help and won't say.* Her normally self-contained nephew was asking without asking, sounding more vulnerable than she ever heard him before. She told him she would be there, and got on a plane. Hadn't even thought about the consequences. She came back to distraught children, strangers she had only seen at Christmases and Trooping the Colour, when she could be bothered to come back for it. To be a friend to her sister, to muscle her own mother out of head-in-the-sand, stiff upper lip adherence.

I think she needs help and won't say echoed through her head as she watched Eddie. He played things so close, even in the family. More free with his security team than with his siblings.

"Marriage mart getting to you?" she asked.

"How'd you know?"

She pursed her lips and picked out a liquid eyeliner. "Your sister talks to me once in a while. I've been where you are. We didn't have dossiers in those days. Disapproval and guessing in the dark was good enough for us."

"It's like the beginning of old *Mission Impossible* episodes," he said. "Am I supposed to choose someone to date or assemble a crack team of intelligence operatives?"

"Imagine listening to a man you thought of as a kindly but forbidding uncle rattling off details of men's sexual histories to you whenever you so much as hinted at interest in them, lecturing you on the necessity of finding a suitable man."

Eddie's face lit up. "That does sound worse."

"Well, there you are," she said, silently congratulating herself on applying eyeliner without creating the impression of a rugby player trying to cut down on the glare.

"Was Rob one of their suitable candidates?"

"And let them win like that? I met him at a party. Liked the look of him, all upright and brooding. Didn't realize until the next morning that he was a Navy man. Practically threw him out on his ear." She rolled her eyes, rummaged through her top drawer, smiled at the memory.

"Why haven't you married him?"

"That's a rather personal question," she said, leaning towards the mirror to put on mascara. "We never wanted a fuss, I suppose."

"You're fueled by the consternation of tabloid journalists, Sophie," he pointed out. "I don't know how much I believe you."

"I've been hardened by exposure," she said. "Back then, I still thought it was fun to keep secrets from them, deny them what they wanted. Now, I take more pleasure in shoving their faces up against the glass. You might appear in public with a woman, but they'll never know why, or how serious it is."

"What if I want something—else?"

A frisson went down her spine at the bottomless roiling in his eyes in the mirror. Sophie didn't want her nephew to be at the mercy of his parents' mistakes, pieces of his heart forever being trampled underfoot. Part of her had wondered if this day would come. He and Stephen Everingham kept their relationship a secret for years before the threat of exposure—by Stephen's father, no less—forced them apart. But aside from that, and what she assumed had been healthy experimentation in university and discreet liaisons thereafter, Eddie seemed content to play the charmer with women. She wondered how much playing really went into it.

Sophie put her brush down with a click of bracelets on the marble top of her dressing table.

"I adore you, truly. You're the son I never had. But are you out of your mind? We have to stay politically neutral."

"Who I am is not a political statement," he bit out, but it lacked conviction.

"You are a Kensington. Try and avoid it."

"Look, it's not like I haven't thought about the consequences. I could do so much good."

"But who you are *isn't* a political statement." She forced herself to breathe normally as she ran down a list of reasonable arguments at high speed. "You'll give every bigoted clergyman and politician a face and a voice straight out of the royal family, painting a target on your back, your mother's back, Alex and Arthur's, and the experience for whomever you drag along on this quixotic odyssey would be traumatic, to put it mildly."

"Maybe this matters more than the public's reaction. Maybe it's time to say enough, I'm tired of hiding."

"And maybe it isn't! You can't possibly be thinking of doing this yourself. Who is it? Is he on you to come out the way Stephen was? Are you sure he's not in someone's pay—"

"For god's sake, I'm not being blackmailed. It's someone I trust with my life."

"That's a short list," she said. "It's Isaac Cole and then the rest of us. What does he think about *this* latest—"

The sudden lack of blood in Eddie's face stopped her short.

"Eddie. Edward, no. He's been on your security detail since you were practically a child. Think about how it looks."

"What about how it feels?"

The silence was glacial.

"Think about how it looks," she repeated. "Is *he* pressuring you into something?"

"Of course he fucking isn't, Sophie. He's *Isaac*. He doesn't know I'm thinking about this at all. Doesn't know the half of it. I needed to think it out. That's why I came to you."

She made herself swing around on her upholstered stool and risk being without the barrier of the mirror. The thought of Eddie willingly courting the avalanche of scandal and judgment that had almost destroyed them all a decade ago upset her more than she wanted to admit. Her, Sophie, the fearless one. On an intellectual level she understood it was unfair to expect him never to be out in public, and that there would always be reasons not to do it. But she had a fear. A fear of the same deluge that engulfed them all when Malcolm left the Palace in the dead of night. When news of the divorce became public. When her older brother, Eddie's namesake, went down in the freezing Atlantic one stormy day.

Judging from the way Eddie remained still as they watched each other, he had some notion of what she was thinking. Sophie didn't know how to make him understand. But she owed it to all of them to try.

"Do you want to know the real reason Rob and I aren't married?"

Eddie nodded warily.

"When I met him, he was on indefinite leave from the Navy pending review after three men died under his command. It happened during a night mission. The investigation found the radio was at fault, that the call about adverse conditions came in and wasn't received because of negligent maintenance. It was a flimsy defense. I know, because I asked someone for it."

She met his shocked look with pointed determination.

"I was a reckless, untried ninny. I thought it was a travesty of justice, that this good, upstanding officer might never command on board a vessel again because of a *radio*. So I put in a call." She moved the clasp of her bracelet around her wrist. "The truth is, Rob dropped the radio in the water and because it was supposed to be waterproof, he didn't check when he fished it back out. Then the call came in, and he didn't receive it. There were other radios he could have used. But he didn't check.

"He was so angry with me for interfering, for interceding on his behalf as if he needed the help, as if he couldn't take the consequences like a grown man and an officer. I hadn't given a thought to what it would look like, what it would *be* if I succeeded. Of course, once I did intercede, there was no coming back from it."

"He can't forgive you for that?"

"Oh, he forgave me. But he said he never wanted to risk it being brought up if he ever became my husband. They would dig and dig and find it. As it is, everyone is too confused by me and has too must respect for him."

"But he's one of the most decorated peace-time officers in his generation," Eddie said.

"Well, of course. Wouldn't you be the most careful person in the world after something like that?" She shuddered. "It was a mistake. It was an accident, on a mission going pear-shaped by the minute. He got through it. He says not a day goes by when he doesn't think of those men, and what he cost them. To this day he won't risk the story coming out. It would only cause pain to their families. So think about that."

Eddie stiffened. "What do you mean?"

"You know the sorts of things your Isaac used to do," she said mercilessly. "He wasn't helping little old ladies across the street. He was SAS. You know what they do."

"He was a linguist."

"A cold-blooded killer," she said.

"For his country," he countered. "On orders."

"Men like that are heroes when their names are blank stars on a memorial," Sophie told him. "Not paraded around in the spotlight in bespoke suits and Yves St. Laurent with one of the world's most eligible bachelors at his side. You'd do that to him? Drag his past into the light? He's not one of us. He's not from this world."

"He's been in it—"

"On the outside. He gets to leave. The tabloids don't bother him. They aren't allowed to, by *law*. Once he's no longer your bodyguard, that's over. There would be blood in the water, and if you tried to protect him it would be called undue influence. He, and you, would be under siege."

There was a knock at the door. "Time, ma'am," her assistant said, in a pleasant, posh voice. The same as everything around here.

"Thank you, Lucy," Sophie called. Her eyes never left Eddie's. "If you do this, you will be ruining his life."

She saw that he knew, no matter how much he might want to ignore it. Eddie's body language went even more taut, a bow ready to snap and send arrows she knew not where.

"I thought you might offer a little more support."

"You didn't come here for support. You came here so that I would talk you out of a disaster. You don't have a plan. You don't have anything beyond a wish for something easy. I am not without sympathy, but you have to see how unthinkable this is."

He bent his head forward, hands gripping the edge of her

dresser with white knuckles. She wanted to reach out, but she had never been that woman, and couldn't turn into her now. He would never accept it, and they had to go have dinner with several hundred people.

"The irony of having this conversation in a closet is crushing," Eddie said. The return of humor, even dark humor, was a relief without comfort.

Eddie slid off the polished wood and offered her his arm. The grinding, aching urge for defiance had left his face, pressed back and down, somewhere no one could find. She understood it very well, had since she was a child. But again, dinner. As he turned a smile on her, she wondered how many times he'd done that, shut off everything making him unhappy in order to get the job done.

Sophie suddenly imagined him as a butterfly struggling against the canvas back of a shadowbox, pinned alive, confused that his wings still worked when he couldn't seem to move.

15

The first day of Royal Ascot delivered superb weather for the races. Not too warm, and the only clouds in the sky were a pretty, fluffy white. No need to fear for the hats of the rich and mighty. Arthur and Victoria rode in the first carriage in the procession, Eddie and Alex in the second. Victoria wore a tailored, light green pencil dress, with a narrow belt in the same color and a matching cropped jacket with three-quarter sleeves. Her wide-brimmed hat was a paler green, trimmed simply in white ribbon. Alex fit right in with the fashion forward set in floaty yellow silk, wearing a modified men's boater at a jaunty angle.

When they were all together again in the Royal Enclosure, Arthur walked over to Eddie and adjusted the fall of his ascot. Caught by surprise, Eddie returned the favor. Malcolm used to be the one who did it for both of them. There was something comfortable about doing it for each other. Comforting. Brotherly, perish the thought. Sophie, who arrived later in the parade with Rob at her side, showed up grousing and demanded a drink.

Royal Ascot was one of those times they all missed

Malcolm, even if they never talked about it outright. It had been one of their favorite yearly outings. He loved horses. Victoria did, too, but she hadn't spent nearly as much time with the jockeys as Malcolm had. Thankfully so, as it turned out he'd been bribing them quite significantly over the years. But leaving that aside, Ascot was one of the times they acted most like a "normal" family. Even Victoria would relax a little, holding Alex's hand and talking to her about the horses. Arthur shadowed Malcolm. Eddie carried messages and placed bets. Once the races began, he'd collect Arthur and any friends he could find to see if they could sneak into places they weren't supposed to be. Those were the days, he thought, as he was absorbed by the need to prince in public.

Protocol prevented him from being approached first, but he was expected to start conversation with anyone who drifted near enough. Engage with people, flirt a bit, compliment the hats. That was the easy part. Royal Ascot was an excuse for the fanciest of everything a person might want from a garden party. A few days where the cream of society could pretend the world was always like this. Tickets to the Royal Enclosure were willed from one generation to the next. New blood had to be referred by someone who already had access, and security was intentionally unobtrusive.

Once the races started, he could fade into the foreground in the Royal Enclosure. But most of the people here hadn't seen him since the bombing, and they all felt entitled to their own personal moment of reassurance. Including, it seemed, someone Eddie didn't want to see at all.

Stephen Everingham, Lord Marbourne, leaned against a cocktail table. His body language suggested attentiveness to the man beside him, but he fixed his gaze on Eddie. Looking at Stephen was the attraction equivalent of staring directly into the sun, if a person liked that sort of thing. And Eddie had. Stephen would never be mistaken for anything but an aristocrat. Jawline like a Michelangelo angel, and as cold and hard when he chose. His self-effacing, personable manner came part and parcel with haughty, polite bewilderment that anyone he didn't care for might want his attention. He left his companion in the middle of a sentence, strolling towards Eddie as if it were still his right to do so.

In reality—that inconvenient place Stephen was occasionally forced to occupy—they hadn't spoken in two years. The last time Eddie saw him was at Fashion Week a few months ago, a glimpse of then-tousled blond hair and manic blue eyes, surrounded by models almost as tall as he was. The tabloids kept up with the prince's wild former "best friend," so Eddie didn't lack for information about his ex-lover. Longing for Stephen's strong, tapered fingers on his skin had been replaced with wanting defter, crooked ones.

The thought of Isaac didn't ground him now, as it so often had in the past. Since his conversation with Sophie last night it pulled at him, whispering in his ear that he was more selfish than ever. The strain of his hidden relationship with Stephen paled in comparison to what he would be asking Isaac to do. And Stephen was still coming at him with unexpected purpose.

Did he think after two years of silence Eddie could be wooed back by some sort of gesture? Or did he want a scene? A thrill rocked him, anxiety and anticipation born of long exposure to this one-man hurricane. He could out himself for good right here, a voice taunted inside his head. Drag Stephen in for a kiss, or slap him across the face, or any of a thousand other things princes *did not do*. Potentially torpedo his family's legacy and everything he had been working for over the last months. Or it could be torpedoed for him by Stephen's relentless quest to matter more than anything else in Eddie's life.

For a single, breathless moment, Eddie wanted to oblige him. The memory of the good—*very* good—times hung in front of him, star-flecked and shimmering. The fun. The whispered confessions. Flooring the gas pedal in one of Stephen's sports cars on the cliff roads along Monaco's shoreline in the middle of the night, feeling like a god trapped, however briefly, in mortal skin. Coming together again and again, in hotels and empty flats belonging to friends, thinking of themselves as saboteurs in the house of love, with the greatest of apologies to Anaïs Nin. But then, the limits of their relationship were defined in very public ways, and Stephen tired of it long before Eddie could afford to.

Crashing in now were the fights, the resentments and recriminations. The dark circles under his own eyes in a carousel of mirrors after nights of anguish. Stephen's constant refusal to act in a way that gave Eddie any cover, any flexibility. Forcing him to choose, over and over, finally asking Stephen to stay away from certain events in order to maintain the tenuous control over his image. Every time Eddie ran up against something he couldn't, didn't *want* to do in public, Stephen disappeared for days on end, partying hard, courting the paparazzi. It always sparked another fight, another breakup, another dance of self-conscious, soul-baring texts and pleading voicemails while Stephen posted pictures of himself in yet another beautiful, faraway place with beautiful, faraway people, begging and daring Eddie to join him with that haunted look in his eyes.

"You're looking very well, your royal highness," Stephen drawled. "Fresh air agree with you, out of the closet?"

"If you think having precious details of my personal life splashed all over against my will was *freeing*—" Eddie swallowed the rest of the rant down with an effort. Stephen could get him from zero to sixty faster than the cars Stephen loved to drive.

"I thought it would be better if you didn't have to do it alone." The cut-glass invitation of Stephen by his side was nearly more than Eddie could handle. It might be a sunny morning, but Stephen turned everything into the middle of the night. Eddie was instantly nauseated from exhaustion and afraid of what might happen next. If he turned him down, there was no knowing what could happen. In the past, it led to pills and benders that ended with Stephen waking up two days later and five thousand miles away. But Eddie reminded himself to slow down. Reminded himself that Stephen self-destructed with surgical precision, whether he could use Eddie as the scalpel or not. It took a long time to forgive himself for that. He hadn't forgiven Stephen.

"I'm not alone," he said, lifting his chin. "We can't do this. Not here. Not now. Not ever." Stephen tried to shrug it off with an arch toss of his head, but the regret and relief in his face told a different story. Eddie couldn't tell which one hurt more. "Go back to your boyfriend before he brains you with a champagne bottle." He slipped out into the main thoroughfare of the Royal Enclosure before Stephen could follow him. Or not follow him. He was halfway to saying the hell with his self-denying goals and trying to find Isaac when he saw someone he recognized.

Gwen Shelton stood alone. Clasping her purse in her hands, she went up on her toes, searching the crowd. There was something abandoned and yet resigned in her manner. He knew how she felt.

"Gwen!" He swept his dove gray top hat off and bowed low. Utterly nonplussed, she didn't do anything for half a beat, and then shook herself.

"Ed—your highness!" She went to curtsey, but he grabbed her hands and kept her upright.

"It's still Eddie, please. Even though you had the temerity to see Alex and not me." She seemed to shrink, and it occurred to him, too late, that Alex said Gwen felt very guilty over not talking to them all these years. "Not to worry, I always knew you secretly preferred her," he said. "We haven't seen each other since Arthur's investiture."

"Oh—yes. That's so unfortunately true. Do you hate me for missing your twenty-first birthday?" It sounded like a joke, but he knew it wasn't.

"Never, Gwen. You had a new baby. What would you have done, hang her on a hook?"

"I've tried, and she doesn't really drape."

"Truly. The best mother. And still the best friend anyone could ask for."

"You haven't been around me in ages."

"People don't change that much."

"Sometimes they do." She sounded wistful. He didn't like it. Whatever put that tone in her voice, he wanted it gone.

"Give it half an hour. We'll be up to our tricks again in no time. What do you think we should do? Get up on the roof of the Royal Enclosure? Try to sneak into the jockeys' dressing room?"

One corner of her mouth turned up. "We did get into some scrapes, didn't we?"

"We were mostly scrape," he said. His stomach gave a funny flip when she smiled, a fractious weight settling into place. "Although for real verisimilitude, we'll need to get Arthur involved against his will."

Gwen's expression flickered, but she recovered so fast he wasn't sure what he saw.

They had been the terrors of the nursery. Wherever she and Eddie went, there was sure to be something hidden or broken, or liberated, if it was an animal. Arthur followed along, half a step behind, a moment too late, two years older and immeasurably more burdened even as a little boy. As they grew, Gwen's boisterous unwillingness to admit to anything but the most aggressive optimism remained a good foil for Arthur's somber reflection. And then, during the royal divorce, her parents had split as well. Lawrence Shelton had taken the astrophysics department chair at Stanford when Gwen was sixteen, while Joanna stayed primarily in London. Transatlantic marriages, everyone tutted, as if that had been more than a symptom of the problem. As if, had they lived in closer proximity, they would have been better off. (According to Gwen, that was manifestly untrue. "Dad could live on Mars and they'd still be at each other's throats, only with a thirty-minute delay between everything they said.") Gwen had gone with her father to California.

"It's so good to see you," he said, tucking her hand into the crook of his arm. "And underneath such a stunning example of British millinery."

"Don't try it. This hat is like a swan in molt over a modern art installation. I tried to tell Mother, but she insisted." Gwen picked a bit of imaginary lint off his sleeve. "I'm very glad you're all right, Eddie. After what happened."

"Thank you. But none of that. This is a happy occasion, and anyone not looking cheerful will have to muck out the stables afterwards." He poked her in the side with one gloved finger. She gasped.

"And now we see the violence inherent in the system! Help, help, I'm being repressed," she squawked, as *sotto voce* as one could manage Monty Python references at Ascot. "It's good to be home. I swear, when I grabbed the right passport, I felt like everything was going well, for once."

"You know, Alex told me… If you want to avoid us, I will respect it. You couldn't have known I would run you to ground here."

Gwen watched the milling crowd for a moment before coming to some sort of internal decision. "I wasn't sure I wanted to join the circus again," she admitted. Eddie stiffened. "I know it's the worst, Eddie. I feel bad, because I know it's not like you have a choice about it. I didn't know if I could handle it. It was bad enough when we were kids. The minute I needed a bra there started to be rumors, you know?" She spoke very quickly, aware that they were standing in the middle of one of the most public events of the year. "It was unbearable then, and I can't help feeling things would only be worse now."

"I understand," he said, like an offering. Or an apology. "I don't blame you. It's not the most attractive proposition in the world."

"But then, well, with the coverage from the bombing, and what happened while you were in America, I told myself to stop being ridiculous," she finished. "As if being worried about a few pictures is an excuse for avoiding my friends. I'm a coward."

"You're not. You seem to have developed a sense of self-preservation, which is extremely worrying. But we can fix that. I'll make sure the image team keeps the tabloids off your back, right? Especially with Madeline involved. There are ways, obviously, we're not total prisoners. If you... if you want to be friends again." He didn't realize until he asked how much he wanted the answer to be yes.

"You know I do. You're a prince. And I'm a vulgar American now." She smiled. It was tentative, but it was a real smile, and he felt lighter all of a sudden.

"My favorite vulgar American. Absolute favorite. First class. Top notch. Come on, I'll take you to Mother and you can spit on her shoes or something. Isn't that one of your quaint American customs?"

"Only on Tuesdays, your royal highness. Her Majesty's penny loafers are safe."

Eddie snorted into his fist, and that was the picture the society pages ran the next day. The Prince, arm in arm with a woman he'd known forever, looking devilishly pleased.

There were also pictures taken from afar as Eddie presented Gwen to the Queen. And thus an idea was born in the minds of the popular press. A notion, merely. But an effective one.

"Gwendolyn, what a pleasure." Victoria kissed her on the cheek. "Your mother told me you would be here, and I hoped Eddie might track you down."

"You knew she was going to be here and didn't tell me?" Eddie put a hand over his heart, to his mother's arched eyebrow.

"I don't tell you everything," Victoria said. "It's policy."

"She told me." Arthur walked over, hands buried in his trouser pockets. He had an expression reminiscent of a smile pasted on. It warmed a few degrees when he tipped his hat to Gwen. "You came."

"I did," she said. Her hand tightened on Eddie's, like he was her lifeline. He welcomed it, even if he didn't understand why she was nervous about Arthur, of all people. Gwen's ability to mess with him had been second to none when they were children. In a world that had lately careened off several key axes, she was an anchor to a time before Stephen, before Isaac, before he exponentially complicated his life. Their physical boundaries had been more flexible than most people's, both of them much more tactile than anyone else in their respective families. Cuddling on the couch had been common long into their teens. Neither one of them let go now.

"How is your father?" Victoria asked.

"Dad's great. Still teaching, still making everyone rethink the foundations of the universe."

"I will never forgive his abandoning Cambridge and taking you with him," Victoria said. "I must say hello to a few hundred more people, but I'm sure the boys will be able to amuse you. Don't go too far, Gwendolyn."

She left in a waft of subtle perfume and conviction. The three grown-up children looked at each other, suddenly at a loss. Arthur's gaze caught on Eddie and Gwen's joined hands.

"How shall we cause a stir?" Eddie asked, moving Gwen's hand into the crook of his elbow in a smooth, practiced way.

"I should like to cause a stir," Arthur said wistfully. Carefully. Hopefully. "Grown out of that a bit."

"We could find the Prime Minister and knock his hat off," Eddie suggested. The Prime Minister was Stephen Everingham's father, and no love had ever been lost between them.

"They'd probably say the Prince of Wales showing such blatant political favoritism calls for the abolition of the monarchy," Arthur said. "Best not."

"Well, if Arthur can't play too, I think we should find a different game," Gwen said, a hint of her old assurance in the decisive way she nodded.

"Let's play 'avoid the parents,'" Eddie murmured.

"Oh my god," Gwen said, fingers tightening on Eddie's arm. "They're all together." Malcolm and Helena were talking to Gwen's mother, a tall, reedy blonde dressed in a daring black and white suit. Eddie noticed a chill coming from Malcolm. He kept his body turned away from Helena. Looking for someone else, perhaps. It seemed to be the theme of the day. Malcolm and Helena moved on after a moment, and Joanna turned to another frequent customer with a more genuine smile. Joanna and Helena were cordial, but in the wake of the divorce, Joanna never designed for her again.

"Mother looks like a work of art." Gwen fingered her own, vintage-inspired, 50's-style day dress with resignation.

"Come off it, Gwen. She looks like a traffic crossing." Arthur spoke low enough that no one else could overhear, but it was still a very unguarded thing for him to say. Both Eddie and Gwen stared at him as he went pink and coughed. "Does anyone know where Alex is?"

Gwen cleared her throat. "She took Maddy off me as soon as we arrived and I haven't seen them since. They've gone mad for each other. I'm not exactly worried, but if you see an extra-small jockey with blue hair racing in the third, let me know."

"Madeline's here?" Arthur looked around, as if Gwen might produce her daughter out of thin air.

"Alex is taking her responsibilities as adopted aunt very seriously," Eddie said. "She called me to ask if there were any horses up at the farm that might do for Maddy."

"Oh, god." Gwen pinched the bridge of her nose.

"Don't worry," Eddie said, with an unrepentant grin. "We'd stable it at Windsor, for weekends."

Gwen was about to fire back when Arthur said, "There they are," with such warmth that both Eddie and Gwen turned.

Alex and Maddy strolled through the crowd, small paper cups of shaved ice in their hands. Maddy was pointing and laughing as Alex leaned over to tell her something.

"Is that Alex's journalist with them?" Gwen asked. "She's mentioned him a few times."

"That's Daniel Black, yes," Arthur said. "Seems to be spending a lot of time at the family manse. Good man."

Eddie wondered why Arthur was talking like a reanimated Winston Churchill, but didn't have time to tease him about it.

"Cute man," Gwen agreed. "I should go rescue them from my dear daughter."

"I've been looking forward to meeting her," Arthur said.

Eddie saw hesitation in Gwen's eyes, but Maddy descended on them before she could say anything.

"Mum, Mom, we saw so many horses and apparently you can go to the stables, but Alex doesn't have time to take me and I really want to, please? Oh. Hello," she said, looking from Eddie to Arthur. The electric blue in her hair was fading to pastel, turning her eyes an otherworldly cornflower. "I've seen you in pictures."

"I've seen you in pictures, too," Arthur said. "Alex keeps showing them around."

"Will one of *you* take me to see the horses?"

"Maddy." Gwen was caught between quelling her and wanting to laugh.

"You're a bit of a mercenary, aren't you?" Eddie asked.

Maddy narrowed her eyes. "I don't know what that word means."

"It means," Arthur put in, "that you don't let opportunities pass you by."

She considered him, head tilted, making sure she wasn't being made fun of. "Then yes. I am a mercenary."

"Be a polite mercenary," Gwen said, fixing Maddy with a look.

"Will one of you take me to see the horses, *please*."

"If your Mum says yes," Arthur said, looking to Gwen hopefully. For a moment Eddie thought she would refuse, which didn't strike him as altogether fair. Arthur didn't have all that much experience with children, but he was responsible enough to lead a squadron of pilots into combat situations. With an appraising look, much like her daughter's, she nodded.

"Go for it. But Maddy, please, best behavior. If people want to talk to Arthur, absolutely no interrupting. Like when you're with Grandpa on campus."

"I *know*," Maddy said, and held her hand out to Arthur, like a challenge. He hesitated, and then took it. As they walked off, Arthur could be heard saying "All right, Madeline, do you know what a human shield is? Well, you're mine now…"

Gwen took a sharp breath.

"You okay?" Eddie asked.

"Yes, fine. She makes so many conquests. Every person she sees. I wish I had half her confidence."

"Where do you think she *got* it?"

"I hope she isn't pretending the way I was, most of the time."

"She's great, Gwen. Honestly. Come on, let's go look at horses, too."

EDDIE COULDN'T REMEMBER a nicer afternoon at the races since he was a child himself. He got Gwen talking about America. They had a proper catch-up, leaning against the rails and watching the horses parading around.

"Sometimes I feel like them," he said, jerking his chin at a high-strung two-year-old Arabian pulling at the bit and yanking his trainer around.

Gwen rubbed her knuckles against the back of his hand for a second. "I feel like a pace horse most of the time, there to keep other people calm."

"This is a very depressing conversation."

"It's deep, Eddie," she said. "Don't be scared." She watched one of the horses in the ring, a big bay, standing solid and relaxed next to the two-year-old, who looked about to shake out of his bridle. "There are worse things to be."

On impulse, he put his arm around her. She smiled up at him, and the conversation moved away to other things.

"You've changed," she told him, as they made their way back to the Royal Enclosure for the first race. He greeted the people who nodded to him, but didn't stop to talk. Gwen felt solid at his side. He didn't want to send her running by fulfilling his social obligations. In fact, he didn't want to fulfill his social obligations at all, so he made himself a promise to send her flowers and chocolates for letting him out of them.

"How have I done that?"

"I hesitate to say natural maturity, because we both know you have none of that. I don't want my hair to catch fire from lying."

"Is that what happens?"

"It's what my nanny told me," she said. She directed his attention to an outrageous hat going by on the head of a countess. She had a small smile on her face. He swung her around so that they were looking right at each other.

"What if I told you I'm asleep in a tower, locked behind glass and thorns?" He tried to make it sound lighthearted. He'd failed, if the way her forehead immediately creased was any indication.

"I'd say that we'd better find the extinguisher, because smoke is going to come from under your hat any second. You're not asleep. You're waiting for something." Gwen took him seriously, even when she teased him. He hadn't been imagining that quality in her, all these years apart.

"A princess?"

"A dragon slayer."

"You'd look good with a sword in your hand," he said. Her eyebrows lifted, and there was a second. An instant where he could have gone back on it and made it all right, a joke, blamed the outrageous fumblings of a disordered mind or something. But he could feel dozens of pairs of eyes on him. He felt rising panic, not wanting her to say the words growing like storm clouds behind her eyes, and his hand tightened on hers. He could see the instant she decided to believe him.

"It would have to be a very short sword," she said.

"We have an armory." He waved airily. "I'm sure we can find something. But only if you come back to Windsor for the reception. If you don't have plans, of course."

She looked pleased. "I don't know if I have a thing to wear."

"We'll probably spend most of the time under the stairs eating prawn cocktail as it is."

"I'll see if my mother has another outfit for me," she said. "As long as you're promising prawns."

Arthur and Maddy were deep in conversation at the railing in the Royal Enclosure when Eddie and Gwen arrived. Maddy stood on one of the rungs, Arthur's arm in front of her so she couldn't go toppling over. She hung on to it, going up on her toes. Gwen made a sharp little noise as Maddy looked up at Arthur, asking him a question.

"Apparently Arthur's good with kids," Eddie said. "You wouldn't know it, from how he copes with adults, but here we are."

"No, I mean, I never thought he wouldn't be. But it's incongruous," Gwen said. "And this hat is starting to pinch."

"Want some help?"

"I would love some," Gwen told him, and it sounded like she was talking about more than her hair.

VICTORIA COULD DESCRIBE a great deal of her job, if she were ever asked when her inclination was to be honest, as "dignified loitering." Ascot provided many marvelous opportunities for it. She stood by the ring, watching the horses go by. The trainers and the older teenagers leading the nervy thoroughbreds through their paces kept stealing looks at her. She made sure she smiled at each of them in turn. It came naturally after thirty years on the job. She had been talking to a few of the owners at the fence, but they drifted away after a discreet hand signal from Ainsley. Rob and Sophie were a few feet away, since it wouldn't do for her to be photographed alone on a cheerful social occasion like today. But they left her to her own thoughts. She needed to take a few moments at times like this.

The trouble was, her own thoughts weren't cooperating. She wanted to be thinking about the day, or the horses, or the rather sweet sight of Eddie and Arthur awkwardly reunited with Gwen. Or about Joanna's acerbic wit where ex-husbands were concerned. Victoria had caught sight of Malcolm a few times. Once with Helena, twice without. He looked well, although he moved in a bubble of cronies and never went near the jockeys now. She felt bad for him. He'd loved that part of things. Well, he wrecked that right enough, her own bitter streak reminded her. Race fixing was a crime when the punters did it. It was a massive, exploding scandal when the Prince Consort did it. No jockey went within fifty yards of him, even a decade on. Thank heavens she'd been above suspicion. Although she remembered a lovely note she'd received from the former jockey who broke the story, a Sidney Halley, who told her he would never have stood for her to be slandered. He had defended her innocence in court. Legally it was unnecessary, but it helped smooth out her role at the time.

This was the turn her thoughts took at Ascot now, and would, most likely, every year for the rest of her life. Time took the sting out of them, at least. Small mercies were the only sort she allowed herself. She watched a few horses go round the ring, liked the look of one and motioned his stable girl over. They spoke, and she gave the girl a gold sovereign. The stuttered thanks she got in return made her feel a quiet pang. The older ones tried to be aloof, but she was the equivalent of the fairy godmother in a story to them, and knew it. She enjoyed that extra swagger in their walk after her attention. The horse's trainer and she shared a look, nothing between them but the sweetness of watching teenagers feel proud of themselves.

Her eye caught on a man standing with him, on the other side of the ring, who grinned, too, she noticed. That in itself was unusual. She didn't notice men, as it would be akin to a celiac window shopping in a patisserie. Both useless and detrimental to her health.

He had his hands in the pockets of his morning suit. It was too big on him, which should have looked ridiculous. It *did* look ridiculous, but it also interested her. What sort of man went to Ascot in an ill-fitting suit? His top hat balanced precariously on tight, unruly curls, the barest hint of Buster Keaton about him. And his smile invited comparison to other old-time movie stars.

The especially handsome ones. He looked to be about her age, but the energy he had as he bounced on his toes, watching the horses come out of the stable, made him youthful. He looked curious. Exuberant. She hadn't been so enthusiastic about Ascot in far too many years, and not only because of Malcolm. Her life could be planned out, stretching out from event to event through the year, for the rest of her life. Without someone to lift the mood, or distract her…

That was one of the things that had sent her to her bed when Malcolm left. Even when their marriage had been terrible, he made her smile at public events. But now some strange man in an oversized suit made her smile, and she had no idea who he was. That might be progress. Of a sort.

16

After Ascot, Eddie threw himself into helping Arthur with preparations for the Innovation+Technology Summit. They found an unexpected ally in Gwen, who at long last agreed to come over for lunch at KP one afternoon and heard them talking about prospective trouble with a vendor. "I plan academic conferences professionally," she pointed out. "The experience does scale."

Arthur hired her on the spot. "She's like Hippolyta with a clipboard," he said some weeks later. Eddie's name appeared nowhere in the planning materials. He was the silent partner. As such, the day of the inaugural reception at the King Alexander Conference Centre in Westminster, he would not be missed if he arrived late.

Not that he had planned to be. Mikhail finally took Eddie up on his offer to call, and they spent over an hour chatting after Eddie's gym session. Mikhail told him about settling in at Galen's in Manchester, and Eddie didn't press him on what might be going on there. Mikhail asked after Isaac and Harris, told Eddie that the old picture of him and Galen showed up in the post. "No note or anything. Barely addressed, even." He asked after Eddie, tentatively insisting on hearing the "real answer." There were very few people in Eddie's life who did that. His descriptions of their neighbors had Eddie laughing when he looked at the clock and realized he was going to be late.

Isaac drove him to Westminster. Other than Eddie updating him on Mikhail, they hardly spoke. Eddie caught Isaac watching him in the rearview mirror more than once. Months ago, he would have made a joke, started a conversation. Now they each shifted away. Their private language of cocked eyebrows and crooked mouths still existed, but the awareness of how Isaac's body felt, how he tasted, the sound of his voice rough in Eddie's ears—it suffused everything when they were alone. To ignore it or banish it was a hopeless endeavor. Sophie's words echoed in his ears so loudly he couldn't think straight. *You will destroy him if you pursue this.* Isaac still had an encouraging smirk for him, but there was distance behind his eyes. Eddie couldn't push. Couldn't even ask. It was enough to be near him. It had to be.

Eddie shot his cuffs as he went in the VIP entrance. The seismic rumble of a full conference center surrounded him. There were over three thousand people here, luminaries from the tech, business, and education sectors all invited by the Prince of Wales to discuss making the UK a hub of technological innovation and investment. Of particular interest to the royal contingent was Arthur's Horizon Generation Foundation, which aimed to achieve full technical literacy in the UK by providing every British child of schooling age their own laptop computer with a full suite of creative and professional software designed to help them realize their dreams. Mention of this program was almost an afterthought in the conference materials, as if it had been around forever, instead of initiated in the last six months. One of the spells cast by royal involvement,

Eddie thought. By proximity, everything they supported was assumed to be as venerable an institution as they were.

He made his way to the reception hall and found Arthur finishing up a conversation with Benedict Seaton, the leader of the Labour Party.

"—it's been a pleasure, sir. Although I'm surprised a horde of concerned advisors hasn't descended on you for talking to me." Seaton had an easy manner and an excellent suit. His dark brown skin and artfully trimmed beard might send the bulk of England's political establishment running in terror of the future, but Eddie liked him, and liked Arthur talking to him. The demand that the Kensingtons remain aggressively politically neutral meant they had to operate in other ways.

"The Prince of Wales can occasionally be forgiven for having a natural interest in progress of the nation that is nominally going to be his responsibility someday," Arthur said. The two men shared a conspiratorial smile, shook hands, and parted ways. That boded well for the future. Eddie understood the Machiavellian turn to his thoughts, and didn't bother trying to redirect it. This was the circus. Arthur pulled out his phone, something the royal family never did in public. But in the current environment, it would look strange if he weren't holding a mobile.

"For shame, Arthur," Eddie said. "Checking Twitter at a time like this?"

"Of course. Nothing important going on here," Arthur told him. Something on his phone screen made him smile.

"Sexting?"

"It's Gwen, thank you so much," Arthur said. "She's texting me the beginnings of limericks."

"Why is she doing that?"

"Presumably she thinks it's amusing. Or it might be a cry for help. Her father is here."

"I thought he didn't come within six hundred miles of Joanna Leigh as per their divorce agreement."

"Don't be crass. Isn't it nice how he'll drag himself across an ocean for his daughter as long as she's doing something he finds interesting?"

"And my crassness is the issue."

"I think he came with Avi Forrest," Arthur said, ignoring him. "They're friends."

"The tech billionaire? This seems below his pay grade, somehow."

"I *am* the Prince of Wales."

"Oh, *are* you? And a very cute one, I'm sure."

"He's already given us a huge amount of consultation, I'll have you know. I sent him a handwritten note. Apparently those have an effect on people. And I think Gwen asked him over, as well. He's her godfather. How did we not know that?"

"We're a selfish people."

Gwen strolled over with her father in tow. He wore his suit like a cat wearing a set of antlers in a Christmas card.

"Arthur, Eddie, you remember my father?"

"Boys," Lawrence Shelton said, with a degree of ironic self-awareness that put Eddie at ease instead of putting his back up. Professor Shelton had never been comfortable in the rarefied atmosphere his wife moved in. He had an easier time with Arthur, Eddie, and Alex than he ever did with Victoria and Malcolm, filing them under "Gwen's friends" and ignoring any other considerations.

"Professor Shelton, it's a real pleasure to see you again," Arthur said.

"Yes, thank you for not interfering with the release of our fair Gwendolyn back into her natural habitat," Eddie chimed in.

"Prolonged exposure to the North American continent doesn't seem to have done either of us any permanent damage." Professor Shelton spoke gravely, in the way of all men with at least one grandchild and a sense of humor.

"I recommend a course of vaccination immediately. *Great British Bake Off*, *Doctor Who*, and *Poirot* marathons soon as she can. To make sure she pulls through."

Shelton laughed, pleased to be talking with him the way they used to. He had made Eddie the straight man for his jokes from childhood, drawing him out with more complex wordplay as Eddie got older. Eddie had wanted to impress him more than anything. Now he felt a kind of basic acceptance that almost made him tear up. He changed the subject at once.

"I'm surprised Avi Forrest is here. Was that your influence?"

"We've been friends since MIT," Shelton said. Discussing the tech giant seemed to relax him, as if being one of the most famous living scientific minds in his own right wasn't enough. "Not quite roommates, but we lived in the same building. Bexley. The land the administration forgot."

"I would love it if you introduced me later tonight," Eddie said, trying to forestall the storm of college reminiscence gathering on the horizon. "You're coming to the dinner reception at Kensington Palace later, aren't you? The tech stuff is Arthur's bailiwick, but I do enjoy collecting conversations with famous people." Shelton gave him a suspicious look, and all but rolled his eyes and snorted at Eddie's discounting his own intelligence.

"I'll see what I can do," Shelton told him, and then asked Arthur a technical question about funding and grants.

Gwen pulled Eddie over to the side right in front of a catering table, and he snared a few prawns after all. It was becoming a tradition again. He offered her one. She took it on autopilot, regarding him with thoughtful concern.

"Why do you downplay your capabilities so much? My father knows better."

"Protective coloration."

"What do you have to hide from?"

"Gwen, if it gets out that I have a brain in my head, the consequences for the nation could be drastic." He clasped her hand to his chest—prawn included. "Say you won't tell. Lives might depend on it."

She gave him a withering look. "All right, you win. I am undone in the face of your wit, be as flaky as you like in social situations."

Eddie sketched a bow and grinned at her. This was safe, making Gwen Shelton laugh in a room full of important people who thought he was merely fluff.

"It's easier to meet their low expectations than to attempt changing their minds," he said.

"Your image team is working on that now."

"Yes, turning me from notorious party boy to devoted lovesick swain."

"Arthur told me about your file. A *long-term* file. A *serious* file." She grinned at him. "Folder upon folder of eligible, unobjectionable women for you to choose from."

"It's not that funny," he grumbled. "I mean, it would be funny if I weren't the one who's supposed to choose. What if I want all of them? What if I want a harem?"

"I think you'd have to move to the 11th century to really sell the idea," she said. "I know it's a problem, but you're rich. You'll figure it out. And anyway, it's not as though you're auditioning women to be the next Queen of England. Surely Arthur has it a bit harder than you do."

"The stakes are certainly higher. Thank god we've left dynastic marriages behind. They end in very interesting assortments of facial features." He mock-shuddered. "Can you imagine reintroducing the Hapsburg jaw to an unsuspecting populace? He wouldn't be able to live with himself."

She snorted, louder than she meant to, and looked around

quickly to make sure no one had heard. "You don't have overlapping women in your folders, do you? That would be so awkward, if you both settled on the same one."

"My brother and I share many things. I don't think we could share a wife," he said, tapping his chin. "Despite, I'm sure, what you can find in dark corners on the internet."

"Oh, please don't," she said, hand flying to her mouth. Then she smirked against her fingers. "I should help you choose somebody."

"What?"

"Later tonight, after everything. I want to see. I think I ought to, as I am your friend, and I'll be stuck making small talk with whomever you choose for the rest of my life. I should get input. And Arthur. We'll have a party. Sort. Things like that. I'm very good at this, you should trust me."

Eddie didn't know how he found himself agreeing to it, but it sounded like the most fun on offer in the whole dismal situation. He wondered how hard it would be to get his hands on a fresh bottle of scotch between now and then. Maybe one of the bartenders would take pity on him.

"I think that's a brilliant idea. But right now, let's go say hello to my mum. If I have to put up with your parents…"

VICTORIA STEPPED into the room in a cloud of perfume and a tailored gray trouser suit. She usually dressed in color in order to be easily noticed, but today she wanted to make it clear that this was Arthur's show. A Japanese silk scarf printed with cherry blossoms, and her understated antique pin, commissioned by Prince Albert for Victoria I at the Great Exposition in 1851, were nods to the international cooperation on display in this particular venture, and to the history of Britain's contributions to innovation. Her silk shirt, a few shades paler than peach, clung to her, and her hair, blond fading to gray, was rolled into something that managed to be soft and severe all at the same time. She didn't check her reflection. A queen never did. She saw Arthur deep in conversation with a few high-profile guests. It made her heart ache. Arthur had not been born to do as he pleased, but she had made sure he got to, for as long as she could. To see him engaged in this part of his role did her good.

And then there was Eddie, making Gwendolyn Shelton laugh over by the food. He played the lovable, harmless scamp in public, a Wodehouse prince. Victoria could never bring herself to ask how much of his behavior was an act. He had never done anything that truly embarrassed her, and on solemn or official occasions he could be relied on to respond with genuine compassion.

But he misbehaved occasionally, from the time he was about nine years old. After that State Dinner he crashed in his pajamas. Never badly, only in public, and it took her a shamefully long time to figure out the correlation. If there was tension between her and Malcolm, if there had been fighting or tears between the siblings before they left, if Mary wasn't feeling well, he could be counted on to do *something*. Initially she put it down to justifiable acting out, but the flashes of calculation on his face forced her to accept that he did it to distract, to deflect, to take the attention off the rest of his family. Perhaps especially his brother, or his father. *Or his mother,* and wasn't that a horrible thought?

He didn't cling to her as a child. He stayed on the edges, always seemed to be slipping off somewhere. Arthur had been her baby, the first time she'd said no, *this* is more important than being the future queen. Alex, sunny and outgoing, was easy to mother. She had loved Eddie from the minute she held him, with the fierce, uncomplicated love she had for all her children, but he'd been like quicksilver as he got older. She could never get him to stay still long enough to get to know him, and if she were being brutally honest with herself—and why she should be now, here, of all places—she hadn't made the time for it. Then after the divorce, and university—she pushed those thoughts away. Good enough to see him happy now, gesturing wildly as he told Gwen a story. She wondered if there was a duck pond in this convention center, and if so, how long it would take them to find it and fall in.

The summit director was making introductions and she responded automatically while castigating herself for parenting failures great and small. One learned over time how to be present in the moment, and how to strongly give that impression when one did not have a choice. Smile politely. Make eye contact. Allow the other person to be the one to pull away. Going through the motions of availability often did the whole job in a pinch.

"Come here often?" American accent. She smiled politely despite the irreverent opening, made eye contact, and only then realized that this latest introduction was to one of the most powerful and well-known private individuals in the tech world. He also happened to be the handsome man she had noticed at Ascot. She hadn't recognized him in that ill-fitting suit and top hat. His clothes fit beautifully now. And his smile was even wider. Some organ in her chest turned over abruptly. She didn't need Ainsley to whisper relevant facts in her ear for this one.

"Mr. Forrest," she said, holding out her hand. He took her fingertips gently, as he had undoubtedly been briefed to do. She felt put out, suddenly, that he'd known they would be speaking before she did. Though of course, she did know she would be talking to Avi Forrest, but how dare Avi Forrest be this particular man? *Pull it together, Vic, you aren't making any sense.* His hand was warm, and there were calluses on his fingertips. Up close, she saw gray at his temples and a hairline working on a truly impressive widow's peak under the curls, but he looked in fantastic condition for a man who had to be in his early fifties at least. She had the idea they were of an age. She recalled something about him being a cyclist, fielding his own team for the Tour de France on the condition that he could train with them whenever he found it convenient. That wasn't exactly a relevant fact, but she knew it all the same. There didn't seem to be an ounce of excess fat on him. Well, perhaps around his cozy-looking middle... *Victoria, get hold of yourself, what is the matter with you?* "How are you enjoying the conference?"

"I'm very impressed with Prince Arthur's dedication to the cause," he said, letting go of her hand. He didn't sound like he was from the West Coast. His voice sounded like New York City, clipped and fast. She loved New York City. "And with how few representatives of the military are here. I've been at a lot of these and hosted a few of my own. Usually the first day or two is 'how can we better humanity' for the press, and then the brass moves in and the rest of the week is all 'how can we blow each other up.' In the nicest possible way."

"Arthur feels quite strongly, as do we all, that the United Kingdom's military technological innovation is in good order. This summit is meant to be about education, diversity, and cooperation."

"And I'm saying I appreciate that," he said. One corner of his mouth went up in a smile that, frankly, she was going to have outlawed the second she got back to her desk. "He's doing a good thing. It's one of the reasons I flew over."

"Having someone of your caliber here in person does add to the proceedings. How fortunate that you were able to take the time." There was absolutely no hint of sarcasm in her voice. None at all. She was very good at this. The best— though she was horrified at herself for slipping into impolite behavior. Because it *was* very good of him. Because he was an influential, important man complimenting an event she felt strongly about, never mind that he was admiring something one of her children had done.

The other side of his mouth went up, and she realized that he knew she'd spoken without thinking. She kept her breathing even. Her expression didn't flicker. His got brighter. "It looks like you've got some other people to say hello to, your majesty. I won't keep you."

It was the same speech she'd heard every day throughout her life, the polite letting-off-the-hook people were told to give her so that she would not have to dismiss anyone. And now, after thirty-five years and thousands—thousands!—of interactions ending in the exact same way, her back went up. She wanted to tell him, icily, that she was the *queen*, and that he would stand there and talk to her as long as she pleased, about anything she wanted, and that she was not here for *him* to dismiss *her*. She felt very strongly that this was the correct course of action and was about to open her mouth and say so when her sanity made a mad dash for control and strangled her brainstem until an appropriate smile flattened her lips out.

"It has been a pleasure," she said, offering her hand again. He took it, watching her face with such single-minded intensity that she felt weak in the knees. *If this is how he looks at computers, no wonder they do incredible things for him. Victoria!*

"It's all mine," he said. This time, when he smiled, it was truly amused, but not at her expense. More like they'd both been told a joke, and he got it, and she hadn't figured it out yet. It was a smile that said she would figure it out sooner or later, and then they'd have a laugh. She hated him. She walked off hating him. Her hand was tingling where he ran his thumb over her knuckles, very lightly, as he let go. What could he have possibly meant by doing such a thing, she asked herself, as she moved through other, much less interesting conversations.

Smile politely. Make eye contact. Continue thinking about Avi Forrest's motives. And his grin.

"Having a good time?" she asked Arthur as soon as she had been presented to everyone in the room on her list, sidling up to him as surreptitiously as the Queen of England could. "It's a hit. I'm so proud of you."

He went the slightest bit red. "I'm a thirty-one-year-old man, your approval should not mean so much to me. But thanks, Mum."

"I'm also your sovereign. Generally it's a good idea to have me pleased with you."

"I'm thinking about abolishing the monarchy as soon as I ascend the throne."

"Do what you like, dear, I'll be dead. But do keep in mind, they'll want you to give back the palaces and a lot of the jewelry. Think of all those tiaras."

"I don't wear tiaras."

"And isn't that a shame? They're gorgeous and great fun. Well, some of them. Some of them are frightfully heavy." She had the sudden urge to reach out and tuck some of his hair behind his ear. She hadn't done that in years, and couldn't possibly do it now. But she could murmur quietly, "Now be a good son and take me over to Lawrence Shelton. I should say hello to him and Gwen."

"He's talking to Avi Forrest right now, do you want to interrupt? They're speaking solely in numbers at this point."

"I would be delighted to interrupt. That poor girl looks as though she's about to drop dead of boredom. Your brother has abandoned her."

That got Arthur moving and looking around for Eddie, who was in conversation with a couple of businesspeople. As they passed, it turned out that they were talking about horses. Of course they were. It concerned her, sometimes, how Eddie could find the racing crowd in any group of people. Brought up unpleasant associations. But perhaps it had been long enough now. He ought to be able to love what he loved without being measured against a useless, pernicious parent. Either of them. Although she had her uses, if it came to that. Such as interrupting men without repercussion. She did enjoy that one.

"Gwendolyn, what secrets of the universe are you suffering through having explained to you now?"

"Your majesty!" Gwen curtsied, only slightly wobbly this time. She must have been practicing since Ascot. Victoria pressed her hand.

"I forbid the pair of you to go on speaking in tongues," she said, giving Shelton and Forrest an arch look. Shelton blinked, not quite sure what to do with her smooth, calibrated displeasure. "You were invited, you don't need to prove you deserve to be here."

"Do you ever feel the need to prove it?" Forrest asked, and all his attention was on her again, drat the man. *As if you didn't come over here in the first place for exactly that reason, you bloody teenager.*

"Never," she said. He nodded, as if she'd said something profound, a glint in his eye.

"Neither do I," he said. She found she liked sharing a lie with this man. Arthur, bless him, gently guided the Sheltons into another conversation, leaving her and Forrest facing off over a high-top cocktail table. "Would you like a drink, your majesty?"

"I would," she said. "Gin and tonic, please."

"A classy drink for a classy queen," he told her as he walked away.

When she was seven years old, a rather nervous man from the protocol office named Cecil Asquith was put in charge of teaching her how to respond to any social situation "with due sense of both gravitas and perspective." She wondered how he would advise her now.

"I'm trying to decide if I can get away with having you thrown in a dungeon," she said, once Avi returned to her side.

"It depends on what you wanted to do with me there," he said, considering it. "And why."

She was taken aback by his frank acceptance of her premise, and by the undeniably sexual turn. That made her feel out of her depth, and she rebelled against it.

"Because you're impertinent," she told him. He laughed into his drink. Snickered, in fact.

"I'm too old to be impertinent, and you're too young to tell me I am."

"I'm the queen. I'm ageless. And you look like a little boy when you smile like that."

"I get that a lot. Time Magazine says my sense of childlike wonder is part of my staggering success."

"And of course you believe them."

"It's revelatory. I never knew so much about myself before."

"Don't let it go to your head."

"Too late." They sipped their drinks in companionable silence. Then he shocked her to the tips of her high heeled shoes with an incongruously personal statement. "They're in awe of me for doing, not being. It's different for you."

"Quite," she said, letting a very real chill into her voice. "As if I never *do* anything. How could I possibly? With hundreds of public appearances for charitable causes and international goodwill a year, millions of pounds raised and donated, on public display at times of great upheaval, often great personal upheaval. I have no time to *do* anything."

"More impertinence from the upstart American tech wunderkind," he said wryly. She risked a glance at him, expecting sheepishness. Victoria did not count on there being real embarrassed pain and an apology in his eyes. *Good.*

"Are you still calling yourself a wunderkind? You're old enough to be a grandfather."

"A palpable hit, your majesty. But I would need children who got started early, for that. And don't get me wrong, they probably would have. A complete lack of parental supervision, statistically, breeds grandchildren."

Victoria laughed, keeping it very quiet. "Not once you had sufficient staff to keep them in line."

"The damage would have been done," he said.

"Is that why you never had a family?" She knew that about him too, for some reason. More relevance. *Honestly, Victoria.*

"No one wants to come second to computer chips and operating systems that don't even exist yet," he said. The hum of the reception continued around them, but it felt like they had come unmoored from their surroundings. "I wouldn't do that to another person."

"So you've been alone all these years?"

"In some ways that matter. Most ways don't."

"It's different for me," she said, not sure why she suddenly found herself confiding in a strange man in the middle of a cocktail reception. Queens did not do that, and Victoria didn't think of herself as the sort of person to do it even if she hadn't been one. And yet— "I had my children, and my sister. And my former husband, of course. As long as that lasted."

"You were married for a good long while. Almost twenty years, right? That's a good run for a marriage."

"A good run? They're supposed to last forever."

"And isn't that unfair? Anything else lasts twenty-one years and it's a conversation piece at parties. A car, a vacuum cleaner, a cat? It's a legend. Most things now aren't even supposed to last that long. But a marriage goes sour after two decades and it's some big shock to the system. It's harder to keep a relationship going than the average car over any length of time."

"How did you know how long I'd been married?"

"You're a visible person."

"You don't seem like the type who keeps track."

He grinned and shrugged. "You've caught me. I'm a closet Anglophile, tea and biscuits and a shrine of you in the guest room. God, don't look so terrified, I'm joking. I remember when you got married because I was using a clip of the coverage of your wedding to test some graphics software in the early 80's. I remember when you got divorced because I saw a picture of you in the paper and thought, 'Hey, I know her from somewhere.' I thought maybe we went to college together, until my best friend's wife brought it up in context."

"I simply have no idea what to say to any of that," Victoria admitted, taking a sip of her drink. "And I'm a trained diplomat."

"I'm sure that, when faced with another trained diplomat, you are a master of your craft. I'm an anti-diplomat. I met the president of the United States about ten years ago and the first thing I told him was that I voted for the other guy."

"You did it on purpose."

"Well, they were infringing on several patents of mine at the time."

"Aren't they allowed to do that?"

"Sure. Doesn't mean I can't be," that outlawable grin was back, "impertinent."

"You know how to behave," she said, tapping the rim of her glass. "You choose not to when it suits you."

"I usually have a reason," he told her. "Sometimes, you're right, the reason is that it suits me not to."

"It makes you unpredictable," she said. "Not to be trusted."

"I don't trust people who aren't at least a little unpredictable," he shot back, shifting his body a little bit toward her and a little bit away from the rest of the room. She noticed it the way another person might feel a sudden breeze. "Someone who invariably does what you expect has an agenda. If they go off half-cocked, if they screw up, if they miss the mark, if they go too far, that's how you know something's going on under the surface. Even if they don't understand what it is."

"That philosophy sounds very familiar," she said, suspicious and intrigued. "Where did you get it?"

"Jane Austen."

Victoria smiled at him, and for the first time in an extremely long time, she put heat into it. Approval, as something other than a queen. In return, his brown eyes got warmer. They were having a conversation. It might have become flirtatious. She might be in a position to do something about it. She might need a cold shower.

"Will you excuse me?" she said, and he blinked those warm eyes at her, like he was surprised she was leaving, like she had thrown her drink in his face, ice and all. Like he was disappointed to be left by her.

She made her way to Gunny, whose brows didn't twitch at all—bless her—as the Queen told her what she wanted. Gunny raised her comm to her mouth and breathed a few instructions into it, and then nodded. "Room 2316, ma'am, to the right and down the hall. If you're sure."

"Thank you." Victoria tried to maintain her composure. "Give me two minutes, then, if you please." He'd been watching, she thought. But he had no idea what she was on about as she left the room. It gave her a thrill. She didn't have thrills very often.

Room 2316 was a conference room, but not one of those dreary ones with the accordion dividers in case they wanted to make the room bigger or smaller. No, this one was crypt-like, the rumble and noise of the reception gone once the door shut. The lights were off, the projector on. A collection of bright logos swirled on the screen on the far wall. She leaned back against the table, hands gripping the wooden top on either side of her hips. The pattern in the carpet swam in front of her as she wondered what the hell she was doing.

Avi's arched, curious eyebrow when Gunny motioned him through the door and shut it near-silently after him destroyed her usual sense of both gravitas and perspective in any social situation.

"I waste more time in rooms like this. Not exactly a dungeon," he said, looking around, shoving his hands into his pockets. "But definitely a torture chamber." He spoke lightly. She didn't speak at all, staring at the tips of her shoes and the swirling carpet beyond them.

"Don't you find," and his voice was much closer now, "that time passes so much more slowly in rooms like this? I should get Shelton to look into it, because it might be that all the time that flies when you're having fun is actually trapped in conference rooms."

"What an interesting idea." She said it for something to do with the air in her lungs, the heat of the projector on the side of her face so intense it might incinerate her. His feet came into her field of vision. He stopped right in front of her, face in shadow when she looked up.

"Why am I here?"

"I don't know," she whispered. "It appears my grand plan had one major flaw in it."

"What's that?"

"I can't explain my plan. I did have one. But several key elements seem to have eluded me."

"You want me to apply my boundless intellect, informed by my childlike sense of wonder, to the problem?"

Reality seemed to take a short vacation as they locked eyes. At least, she thought, it was quiet as it left.

"I think you wanted to be unpredictable for a couple of minutes, and you didn't want to do it alone."

Victoria nodded. Her throat was dry and her heart

pounded, and she felt far too warm in her suit jacket. He took his hands out of his pockets and very gently reached out, brushing his fingers over the backs of hers where she still held on to the table. She turned her hands over and grabbed his. It felt like their fingers were sparking.

"You should know," he said, "I don't pay attention to my own press. It's all bullshit. They're trying to sell tickets to a show that doesn't actually exist, and I need to feed the beast that *does* exist, all those people who work for me and depend on me for their livelihoods, the global marketplace I'm trying to shape because maybe I can do some good eventually, for someone, and it's an awesome, terrifying, disheartening responsibility for an arrogant, flippant kid from the suburbs who got beat up a lot. But I do have this brain in my head, and it's telling me there's only one reason you and I are in here right now. I don't know why now, and I don't know why me. And I hate to be that needy guy, but tell me this is at least a little bit about me."

She tightened her grip on him. "Of course it's about you. I haven't wanted—" She trailed off, horrified with herself now.

Avi's voice was so light, it almost disappeared entirely. "I don't know what's allowed here. Is there some kind of protocol?"

"Bloody hell, I hope not." She practically lunged. It was not queenly. It was not graceful. But it got her kissing him, and that had become all she cared about accomplishing in the last fifteen minutes. She wrapped one arm around his waist, still holding one of his hands. He let go with the other so that he could slide it to the small of her back, under her jacket, and the feel of his warm fingers pressing silk against skin made her want to throw her head back and scream.

His theory about conference rooms was wrong. Time flew. She was bent back over the table with her arms tight around him when Gunny knocked gently on the door. He kept kissing her throat. Her eyes were screwed shut against the light from the projector, and the world spun all around them at many times its normal observable speed. He hadn't touched her hair. He'd tried his best not to wrinkle her. She had not been as kind to him, though he looked so rumpled to begin with that she told herself she couldn't see a change. But she could, because she knew his glassy look was because she bit him hard under his ear, where the curls would hide the mark. His impeccably tailored suit jacket had long creases down the sides where she clutched at him. It could only be called fair play. Her heart wouldn't stop racing because he'd kissed her like their hearts were broken and this was the only way to heal them.

When Gunny knocked again, Victoria pushed against his chest. He went without a single complaint, without anything but a small groan that she knew she would be replaying at length for possibly the rest of time.

"I don't suppose I have to tell you that this must remain between us," she said, trying her best to sound authoritative though she didn't have her breath back. It spoiled the effect.

He raised an eyebrow. "I know, Vick."

Victoria wanted to go back to kissing him. Life was so much simpler then. A minute ago.

"Can I call you?" he asked.

She froze. A hundred different possibilities assaulted her at once, and she couldn't figure out which worst-case scenario to follow first. Could she... date? What would the consequences be? When would she have to acknowledge it? And trying to balance another high-profile life with her own felt instantly like a fool's game. Even now, for the last five minutes, she was ignoring her responsibilities. And what did she want, besides the mortifyingly obvious? Anything? What would that mean?

Avi must have seen the panic in her eyes, because he held up his hands. "It's okay. I understand. No pressure."

"The downside of being unpredictable," she said.

He shook his head and laughed at himself. "This part never gets easier."

"I wouldn't know." They were, at least for one more moment, united in wistfulness. He reached out and brushed a tendril of her hair back into her up-do.

"There. Perfect Queen."

"Thank you," she said.

"The only thing you have to thank me for is fixing your hair," he said, putting his hands back in his pockets. She went up on her toes and kissed him again, a quick brush at the corner of his mouth. And then she stepped back, made herself turn and go, memorizing him in the projector light throwing half of him into darkest, enticing shadow and the other half into bright, impossible relief.

17

"You can't date Cynthia Rhys-Withers." Gwen lay on her stomach on the thick carpet in Eddie's living room, ankles crossed behind her. She paged through Cynthia's file. "She's evil."

"You went to school with her ten years ago," Arthur said. "People change."

"Not that much." Gwen handed the file to Eddie, who flung it into the "No" pile. The three of them had retreated to Eddie's flat at KP after the official tech festivities were over for the evening, each liberating a bottle of wine from the caterers on their way. Arthur tucked himself into a corner of Eddie's sectional couch, while Eddie and Gwen sat on the floor for their very important meeting. All the dossiers of women Sir Thomas thought would be suitable for Eddie were spread around them in a matchmaking avalanche.

"This is disgusting," she said. "Spying on all these women without their consent."

"It's all publicly available information," Arthur said. "Mostly."

"University records aren't! Arrest records aren't! Their

family connections, their incomes, their international conflicts of interest? It's like living in a police state where the goal is matrimony. I read that dystopian YA novel, thank you." Gwen shuddered. "If I were in one of these I think I'd go out and set fire to national monuments to take myself out of the running."

"That would be an awful waste. You'd look so pretty in a tiara," Eddie told her. "And in those official portraits? You'd soar."

"I can wear a tiara whenever I want. You can buy them for thirty pounds in stores."

"Not ones that belonged to Victoria the First. At least I hope not. Has anyone checked recently, Wart?"

"Don't call me that."

"You don't think it's a joke of the proper Ex-caliber? Ow! Don't throw pillows at me, I'll call Isaac."

"I'll call Byers."

"My bodyguard can take your bodyguard." Eddie stuck his tongue out at Arthur and picked up another folder. "Come on, we have to get serious about this. I need a steady girlfriend, apparently it's important for monarchist sentiment and national morale."

Gwen made a noise reminiscent of a rusty hinge and dropped her forehead to the carpet. "Why does it matter? I don't understand the fascination with royalty in the first place. You're basically useless."

"Excuse me, we are not 'useless.' We prefer to say our role is 'largely ceremonial.'" Eddie attempted to sound haughty. "Sounds much better."

"As long as we have to be here, we should do what we can to deserve it, don't you think?" Arthur asked.

"Are you actually defending the monarchy? You're not drunk enough for that," Eddie said. "And I'm not drunk enough to listen while you do." Neither one of them moved to pour more wine. "Tonight is for bending to the inevitable and finding me a date. The woman of my glossy magazine spread dreams is in here somewhere. Our mission, should we choose to accept it, is to find her." He grabbed a few more files and flopped on the Aubusson next to Gwen. "It's like Michelangelo saying that David was there in the block of marble and he needed to set him free."

"We're not building her from scratch," Arthur pointed out. "And you can't marry Kerry," he said, squinting at one of the names on a file tab. "I think she's an illegitimate cousin. That would be awkward."

"It would make the guest list shorter," Gwen said.

"I'd like my children to have normal blood clotting factors," Eddie said, setting aside Christina Everingham's folder. Stephen's sister was not an option for oh so many reasons. "Hemophilia is so last century. We're trying to modernize. What about Henrietta Manfred? She's not too serious. Wouldn't have to worry about introducing her, she's already visible and so on. Used to some of the hype, come to think, with the show-jumping."

Gwen made a face. "There's such a thing as too little substance. Oh, god, I'm being infected by the snobbery. Help, somebody!"

"That's my bread and butter, Gwen darling," Eddie said, pouting. "I agree, though, I don't want to be outdone in foppishness by my own wife."

She rolled her eyes. "Hard to do with you."

"Very true. Although if they are interested in fashion, that would be a plus. I like it."

"Well, that's me out of the running," Gwen said. "Thank Christ."

"You like fashion," Arthur protested. "You know more about it than most people. It's your mother you don't like."

"Excuse you," she spat back. "I don't recall asking for your opinion."

"Eddie asked for opinions."

"On the women in his creepy folders, not *me*."

"Arthur, Gwen, please try to focus on what's important here. That would be me." Eddie looked as forlorn as he could with a dozen manila folders spread out in front of him. "I had no idea they researched so many options. Arthur's list is much shorter," he told Gwen, who raised her eyebrows.

"Arthur has a list, too?"

"Arthur can't find his list," Arthur said. "Maybe I lost it in the move."

"You've had one long enough to lose it?" Gwen asked, eyes wide.

"Oh, Arthur's had a list of these since he was *born*," Eddie said, grinning darkly. "There are *princesses* on Arthur's list."

"I thought you were joking," Gwen said, horrified.

"Oh, go do something embarrassing with a prize-winning vegetable," Arthur muttered. "Get thee to a wifery."

"Bastardizing Shakespeare will get you nowhere with me." Eddie bent his head again. "Julia Egmont?"

Gwen peered over his shoulder. "She's not going to take time out of her career, let me see—revolutionizing nanotechnology—to hold your hand."

"Then I'm stuck. Either I've known them my whole life and can't bear the thought of being stuck next to them at a cocktail reception, much less forever, or I'm hopelessly outclassed by them, or both. And that doesn't even cover how this isn't a PR stunt and I'll have to do at least a little convincing. They do get a choice."

"You've known me your whole life and you don't mind being stuck next to me at cocktail receptions," Gwen said. "Don't you want to be stuck with me for the rest of your life?"

"You know I do," he said, clutching her hand. From somewhere above them on the couch, Arthur made a sound. It was not a comfortable sound.

"Come on, then," she said, already up on one elbow, eyes lit and wild. A solution was presenting itself in his foggy and increasingly desperate mind and he waited, breathless, for what she'd say next. "Ed. Edward. What if I dated you?"

He blinked. "No. No, Gwen, I forbid it. It's forbidden. I know you too well."

"You don't!" she said, and then went red. "You don't know me too well, you know me the right amount of well." She sat up, pushing her hair behind her ears.

"But—"

Neither of them heard Arthur's breathy, cut-off objection. Eddie and Gwen stared at each other, hearts pounding, for equally questionable reasons. They both wanted a way out, and in that moment, it became each other.

Eddie felt more comfortable with her than any woman he had ever known. Arthur might have his concerns, but he didn't know what it was like. Gwen was smart, and had a great sense of humor, and already understood. It wouldn't be a disaster. The thought crossed his mind that he needed to talk to Isaac about this for more reasons than checking the idea against a source of sanity, but he was nearly lightheaded from even the suggestion of relief. She knew him—was the first person he ever told about being queer—and they'd been having a lot of fun together recently—but there was Maddy to consider, and—

"I don't know what I think," he said. "You were saying you haven't decided what you're going to do in England, and this puts you front and center of a media storm."

She winced like a handful of ice cubes had just been poured down her back. "Better me than anyone else," she said. "Maddy likes you. I like you. I don't want to deal with the speculation over whether I'm dating either one of you, which has *already started*, thank you so much. This way we can be coy, ask for privacy, make sure that Maddy is kept out of the spotlight. Use the Kensington machine for our own ends."

Arthur leaned forward into the bubble of their mutual madness.

"It isn't that simple," he said, sounding as if he was trying very hard to stay calm. "You'd be dating a Prince of England. There are expectations."

"Well, I don't have any expectations," Eddie said. "If I do this thing, I'd rather do it with someone I like. Someone I can talk to. We'll have a good time. I won't have to pretend that, at least. I don't want to pretend." *About this. The rest of it I can't help.*

"I know how you feel," she said, and then her eyes filled with tears. "Eddie, I don't want you to be alone. You hate it."

"I'm not alone when I'm with you," he told her, over-whelmed by feeling like there was some kind of *solution*. Feeling so lucky that his best friend was back.

"The bloody pair of you aren't alone." Arthur downed the rest of his drink. "Have you thought about what happens if the two of you really hit it off as far as the press is concerned? You'll have to break up sometime, unless…unless you'd be willing to marry each other because a stunt went over well with the general population."

"It wouldn't only be a stunt," Gwen said. Eddie was shocked at the fierceness in her tone on his behalf, and Arthur looked as stunned as Eddie felt. "I wouldn't marry him unless I *want* to marry him. And—you can't find someone the way normal people do when you're a prince. You of all people should know that."

"Oh, I do know it." Arthur's voice cracked. "I know that it's important to think about other people, and not only your own convenience. Not to put that kind of pressure on them."

"So why would it be all right for you to make that call but not Eddie? I'm offering, he didn't ask. You've told me before that you'll marry for all kinds of reasons that aren't love."

"It's different. I'm the Prince of Wales."

"This isn't binding, *Arthur*. It's a conversation about creative ways of solving an unjust, preposterous conundrum."

"Can you even *spell* 'preposterous conundrum' right now?"

"Look," Eddie broke in. "We don't have to decide anything."

Gwen suddenly went quiet, scratching at the rug with one painted fingernail. "You never know, maybe they would dig something up about me that disqualifies me right from the get-go, if I did have a folder."

"No," Arthur said. His voice was firm. "They wouldn't. There's nothing objectionable about you, Gwen."

She pinned him with a questioning smile. "You don't think so?"

"I think," Arthur said, looking vaguely ill, "I am going home."

Her face fell, but she nodded, tucking her hair behind her ear.

"Good night, Arthur," they answered in unison. He pulled the door closed behind him.

Eddie looped his arms around his knees.

"He's so quick to think the worst," Gwen said. She chewed her bottom lip. "As if it would be that bad, spending more time together in a public context."

"Perks of being British, we wouldn't even have to hold hands."

"It's been nice seeing you more, with the conference and everything," she said. "And it's not as if we actually have to put out a statement. We'll be seen together, and everyone can draw any conclusions they want."

"You know," he said, "it would help with things, having it be a friend." He reached for her hand, turning it over in his and tracing the lines in her palm with his fingertips. "I got so used to thinking of this as the enemy. But it wouldn't be, if it were you."

The room was too quiet now. He wanted to tell her about Isaac. About how empty and alone he felt since his conversation with Sophie, and how this was the first moment where his life seemed to have any life in it since he woke up the morning after the bombing. She ought to know. Gwen would never judge him. But she might pity him, and he couldn't bear that. Not right now.

"We'll figure it out," Gwen said.

"Why do you want to?" he asked.

"I hate the idea of you being alone in all of this," she said. "You were my best friend. I followed the press all those years, all those articles in checkout lines with your face on them. It was surreal, and so unfair. They never told the truth about the person I knew. Besides, I don't want to lose you to some high society grand dame in training."

He pulled her into a tight hug. She held him, too, gripping her own wrists behind his back, locking him against her.

"I don't want to push you into it," he said. "But I do like the thought."

"I think we'll do all right," she said, grin a little shaky, a little sly. "Think of all the trouble we can get into."

They both laughed, but it was more strained than it had been even a few minutes ago. He kissed the top of her head and her arm tightened around his middle.

"It's just playing pretend." The words sounded raw and difficult coming out of his mouth, spread too thin over the surface of reality. She rested her chin on his shoulder.

"This may not the best idea I've ever had," she told him.

"I'll make it all right."

In the quiet of his living room, he could think to himself that she belonged there. That they had been left to their own devices together at the end of a long night, and no one disapproved, and no one's trust was violated. No secrets necessary, and someone he loved in his arms. "Do you mind—?"

Gwen laughed on a short little breath. "I think we'd better."

Eddie bent his head and kissed her. It was awkward at first. They both giggled from the incongruity. Their ghosts ran down the hallways of Buckingham Palace in high-top trainers, the streamers on her princess peak hat becoming glittering lavender banners over her sweater and leggings. His jeans and green t-shirt made him the dragon. She chased him with a foam sword past the Louis Quinze and Chippendale furniture. The rattling he heard in his memories was of Ming porcelain.

It became a kiss to lose himself in. The giggling stopped, replaced by the tentative surprise of discovering that they wanted to keep making out on the floor like teenagers. They had when they were teenagers. Out of boredom, and on a few occasions when they were trying to figure Eddie's sexuality out, like it was something quantifiable if they tried hard enough.

His thoughts were so loud that he didn't hear the door open, and there was no way to hear those particular footsteps if their owner didn't want to be heard. Gwen yanked away, covering her mouth with her hand. "Excuse us," she said, blushing. "If that's—I mean—I'm not really used to this." The silence behind him meant only one thing.

Isaac stood at the threshold, not a toe out of line. The lamp on the sideboard threw his face into merciless shadow, trapping him in stillness, turning him to stone. The priceless antiques in Eddie's memories crashed down around his feet. Words shriveled in his dried-up mouth. Helplessness overwhelmed him. He wanted to reach out, explain, struggle up to his knees and beg. Isaac didn't even look angry. There was resignation in the set of his shoulders. Hurt in the tightness of his jaw. Understanding in the softness around his eyes. Eddie knew Gwen didn't see it. He was one of the few people who could. Eddie spent the last eight years learning every flicker, every twitch marring the careful, studied blankness of that face. Eddie's guardian angel, his defender, the man he loved and could never be with. So maybe it was better this way.

"You'll do fine, miss." Isaac's voice didn't rise above a murmur. "Have to get used to it, that's all."

"Um, thank you." Gwen laughed gently, uncomfortably. Perfectly. If it had been anyone else standing in the doorway.

Wrong, it was all wrong, Isaac shouldn't be talking like this, Eddie had to say something, anything—

But Isaac got there first. Taking care of Eddie until the last. Seeing the unshed tears in his eyes and the panic threatening to engulf him. "Good night, sir."

"G-good night, Isaac."

Isaac turned away, but paused. "There's nothing to it." While he could have been reassuring Gwen, Eddie knew the words were all for him. "This never happened."

The door shut. Such a small sound for how much it hurt. He knew this was the moment when he needed to go after him, break away from Gwen, from his life, and run. Grab Isaac and refuse to let him go, damn the consequences.

But he didn't. And in that moment he learned more about himself than he ever wanted to know. Eddie heard Gwen speaking through a fog that grew thicker with every step he imagined Isaac taking on his way.

ISAAC HAD no memory of getting home, only the sensation of the Tube moving under his feet. He found himself at Sandra's kitchen table. He heard the tinny jingle of her ankle bracelet. Sandra walked in and her hand flew to her throat.

"Bloody hell, Isaac!"

"I'm sorry."

She flicked the kettle on.

"You're sitting in my kitchen in the dark, staring into the center of the universe at two o'clock in the morning. What's wrong?"

"Why did you raise me?"

Sandra blinked at him, then sighed. "You won't be put off by protestations of my love for you this time?"

"I've had thirty years of that, and I believe it every time. But it doesn't explain everything."

"Love never does, does it?" The light inside the kettle lit her face from below, like she was about to tell a ghost story. "You know I was in law school when you were born. Lilli and I were hardly speaking. Her life was not something I wanted to hear about, particularly. I was quite the little miss back then. When our mother called me and said Lilli had given birth, I hadn't even known about the pregnancy.

"You were so small when you were born. You didn't cry. I was fascinated by you, how you were so watchful from the very beginning. And jealous too, maybe. Lilli had the lion's share of love from our parents. Now she had a child to love her, too. She loved you at first, but it didn't stick. She lost interest in the whole thing, bit by bit. One day I went to her apartment, this posh place in Mayfair. Some oil tycoon was putting her up there, or his son, or someone. She swore up and down he wasn't your father. You were there alone. Maybe you were a year old.

"She wasn't there. She'd left a helpless baby alone while she went to do who knows what. Probably get her hair done. Another child would be crying or screaming, or trying to get out of the crib, but not you. You were sitting there like you already knew what to expect and what not to hope for in this world. And believe me, I didn't know anything about babies. I wasn't supposed to, I had other things to do in my life than be a mother, or even a close aunt. I wanted to stand up in court for what was right. I wanted to fight for people. But then I saw you. This little child, watching me. In that moment you became the only person I wanted to fight for. I picked you up and left."

She stood next to him, and covered his fist with her hand.

"Lilli and I didn't decide together that you would be better off with me. I took you, and refused to give you back. You were mine. Perhaps that wasn't fair of me, perhaps I should have tried harder to make sure you saw her, maybe I should have tried to make her be a mother to you. I didn't want to share you. Once you realized I was the place you belonged, that I would come back when I left the room? It took you a few months, but the smile you gave me, whenever you saw me... You were *mine*."

Isaac crumpled in on himself, the string in his spine connecting him to the rest of his life cut through. "You changed your entire life, all your expectations of it, for me. Not even *me*. A tiny child, who could have been anyone. Why does someone do that? Why can some people do that, and others not?"

A hot mug appeared in front of him. He pressed each of his fingertips against the hot ceramic until they hurt, one by one.

"Isaac. You're my son." Sandra gripped his wrist, stopping his painful little game. "I didn't know this is who you would be when I became your mother. No one does. People change. What they need changes. And when that happens, you have choices."

Tears burned at the corners of his eyes. "We had sex." Saying it aloud, in his aunt's quiet kitchen in the dead of night, made it real. Made it shabby. "The night of the club bombing. It doesn't matter. It's not the kind of thing that *can* matter. And I understand he can't be with me—hell, he's too skittish to risk publicly being with a man at all, never mind damaged goods."

"Don't talk about yourself that way."

Isaac had to ignore her, had to finish what he'd started. "Found him kissing this woman. An old friend of the family. She's the one he's been photographed with, the past few weeks. She's a good choice for him. Funny. Makes him laugh. Has a sweet kid, Rivvie's age. I can't guard his beautiful little family. I don't belong anywhere near a beautiful little family."

"You may not be an acceptable partner in the eyes of the Daily Mail or the Kensington public relations machine, but that says nothing about *you*." Sandra took his chin in her hand like he was still in single digits. "There is *nothing* wrong with you." They both knew it was true and not true at the same time for someone with a body count as high as his.

In the weak light coming in the window, Sandra looked ageless to him. They had sat here together so many times throughout his childhood, his teen years, both of them up late and meeting, by designed accident, as if neither one of them could bear the burden of wanting company.

"I can't watch," he whispered. "His story only ends one way, and I can't watch."

"No shame in that. You shouldn't have to." Isaac felt the truth in her words as a weight being lifted from him. "And he bears responsibility here," Sandra went on. "Leaning on you the way he has. Falling into your arms. He knew the conse-quences, but he wanted to play pretend."

"I don't blame him."

"I do. You're not the only adult here. You shouldn't be handed more pain and more bad treatment than most people just because you know how to take it. That isn't how it works. You spent years of your life being battered for your country. You deserve better than to be someone's tawdry secret."

"But I would have been content with that. If it were only the two of us. I would have stayed with him forever." The words were ashes and acid in his mouth. And longing. Over the years Eddie had chipped away at the consummate professionalism that used to define him, even if it had masked rage that he didn't quite feel any more. That, too, had been taken from him by a sweet demon with curling hair and green eyes. He didn't know what to replace it with. He didn't know where to start.

A warm hand rested on his back. "He's not the only man you'll ever love."

He could argue with her. Wrap himself in the agony. He had built his life around loving Eddie, and now he had to knock it down and see if there was anything worth salvaging. The future was a yawning void in front of him. Empty of everything that mattered.

Sandra didn't flinch when, for the first time in his life, Isaac buried his face in her shoulder and cried.

18

Isaac Cole simply vanished from his post. The story, according to Kimsey, was that he'd walked into Gunny's office, put his resignation letter on the table, and left without giving her a chance to argue. Not that she would have. Once an officer wanted out, they were done. Security clearances withdrawn, all privileges wiped away. Contact with former colleagues was discouraged. Schedule adjustments were made.

Harris became Eddie's lead protection officer. Kimsey and Finnery were promoted. Ignoring his team's concern for him became Eddie's full-time occupation. He avoided Tonya when he went to the Centre. Only when Mikhail asked what was wrong during one of their occasional text conversations did he even think about answering truthfully. *Cole left my detail—missing him.* Mikhail made a point of texting him more after that. Being an object of pity stirred him to at least try to pull himself together. It was all his own fault, so he had to fix it.

Gwen and Arthur tried talking to him about Isaac's sudden departure, but he shut them down with light detachment, saying he thought Isaac deserved a change if he wanted one.

The excuse worked with Arthur because they were both Kensingtons, and it worked with Gwen because she didn't know any better.

The worst part was how life went on without missing a step, as if Isaac had never been there at all. As if Eddie had never known him, or loved him, or betrayed him. Everyone tiptoed around him as if he deserved to be heartbroken over his bodyguard of nearly a decade walking out without a word. Under normal circumstances, perhaps he would have felt abandoned.

Harris offered, in his quiet way, to listen if Eddie needed to talk. The stress he placed on the word *talk* suggested that Harris had his suspicions. Eddie didn't know what he could say without risking Isaac's reputation, and he was unwilling to do that. All Eddie wanted was to be better than the man who had let Isaac go without a word. And if he couldn't be better, to be different. He got his hair cut. Sitting in the stylist's chair, he imagined every fallen curl as a memory—sitting in a park, grins in rear-view mirrors, pressing hot and close in a shower, years of smiles and jokes and late-night conversation and *devotion*. Not only Isaac's devotion, either. Eddie wished he could chop off every unbidden thought of his own for the last eight years. Maybe if he had done that, Isaac would still be there. Maybe that would have been enough forever, if not for Eddie's selfishness.

Spending time with Gwen became a lifeline. Getting to laugh, to relax occasionally, to forget. Speculation reigned among the gossip columnists as to what they were really doing, those "old friends." They were photographed one day in the park with Maddy, whose hair was now neon pink. As those pictures had a child in them, they were repressed, but that didn't stop the articles about cozy outings. No official comment from the palace was forthcoming. Victoria gave tacit approval to Eddie and Gwen's entire enterprise by inviting Gwen and

Maddy to come up to Balmoral along with Joanna, who often spent time with the Queen during her holiday.

Victoria had retired to Balmoral for the late summer and early autumn, as the monarch and family had since the time of her namesake. Family vacations weren't quite what they used to be, not since Malcolm had decamped. But all the children descended on their mother when time permitted. Sophie, too, would arrive to put on the requisite tweeds, and lounge on the overstuffed couches. They did their best. It wouldn't do to buckle under. Not for the Kensingtons to flee their ancestral homes due to bad memories. No. It was their responsibility to remain. The memories were welcome to leave.

"If I come, everyone will take that as a declaration," Gwen said one afternoon, as she and Eddie waited in the car for Maddy to get out of a summer dance class before they all went for Chinese food and a movie. "Are you ready for that?" She had settled into her role as international woman of mystery. Eddie didn't think there was enough appreciation for her in the world.

"You're still a friend of the family, aren't you?"

"We've stretched that one about as far as we can." Gwen tapped her fingers on her knee. "I do like it up there. And you could finally follow through on teaching Maddy to ride."

"I'll put her on a horse myself."

At least Balmoral was a place Isaac hadn't gone much. Fewer ghosts to ignore, deep inside the cordon of security the protection detail could organize up there. Eddie didn't need a bodyguard in a fortress.

The flight there, alone except for Kimsey, gave him too much time to think and too much time to do an internet search for Isaac's name through the web browser on his phone. He popped up a few results down on a site dedicated to a famous boy band. Eddie clicked through.

Isaac appeared, impassive and bearded, working security

for five of the most adored young men in Britain. He was breathtaking, body loose in the tiny clips of video available. Speculation abounded about him on the fan blogs, fueled by gifs of the boy band's front man giving him sultry looks. Eddie had to close the page when he saw that. He should never have looked to begin with. He played Candy Crush on the plane until his battery ran down. He didn't plug his phone in.

Kimsey had brought a pile of architecture magazines for the flight, and they chatted about how she was going to decorate her new flat. She asked him how he had furnished his place, and he barely avoided saying "we" every other sentence, thinking about how he'd consulted Isaac over his design choices. That had been when he and Stephen were together. Stephen wanted all sorts of input, and Eddie went with Isaac's preferences every time, although he never told Stephen that.

So many of Stephen's complaints about Isaac made more sense, now that Eddie realized how bloody obvious his feelings must have been, even back then.

By the time they landed, he was tired and irritable, his phone lying useless in the bottom of his bag.

It was tea time when his car finally pulled up to Balmoral's main entrance. Eddie could feel the airplane between his skin and his clothes, and he wanted a shower before dinner. Arthur met him in the front hall. He'd arrived hours earlier, courtesy of his Eurofighter Typhoon and an air force that took pride in supporting their favorite royal mascot. Despite flying up on the same day, Arthur and Eddie didn't ever travel together. The first and second heirs to the throne weren't allowed to. Alex and Eddie were, but Alex was staying in London for a few more days. One of the little girls she visited at the Children's Hospital was doing poorly, and besides, Daniel Black hadn't been invited to Scotland.

"All right?" Arthur asked, in greeting. "Gwen called me. Said you were low."

Eddie thought he would probably resent their talking about him so much, if he had any energy for it these days. "Tired, that's all. Did she tell you she and Maddy are coming up?"

"Yes. Do you know what you're doing?"

"I'm having some friends up here for the holiday. Mother invited them, if anyone asks. Daughter and granddaughter of her dearest friend, remember? You can't deny the company is welcome."

"Mum would do anything if it put a smile on your face at the present time. Think of the consequences for five minutes."

"I do. Look, I don't have to explain myself to you. I thought you'd be happy about this, for Christ's sake."

"Of course I am," Arthur said. "It's fantastic when they're around, but—"

"But what?" Eddie buried the strong urge to rub his temples.

"Pardon me." Arthur didn't do sarcasm well, but he tried. "Far be it from me to suggest that you don't have everything completely in hand."

"What do you mean by that?"

"You're forever arranging things. *Strategizing.*" Arthur was trying for anger, but Eddie saw guilt most clearly. Guilt and self-righteousness, neither of which he understood. "You're going too far if you think some tabloid romance is going to make everything all right. It's not you and some woman after publicity involved this time. How far are you prepared to take this charade?"

"First of all, don't talk about *any* woman I've been involved with that way. And what if it isn't a charade? Is it so unbeliev-able that we might actually care for each other?"

"But—I thought—"

"You thought *what?* Arthur, you can't take off and ignore the rest of us when it happens to suit you. This is life on the ground. It's messy. It's complex. We are doing the best we can, each of us. So what exactly is it?" He gripped the leather strap of his carry-on so tightly he no longer could feel his fingers.

"I thought—that business with Stephen Everingham, and then all those women. I'd hate it if you and Gwen have some arrangement—"

Eddie rolled right over him.

"I am, in fact, not dooming either Gwen or myself to a life of enforced celibacy. Whatever you *thought*." Eddie stressed the word to see Arthur flinch. "If you have a problem with me, you should look around at everyone from Sir Anthony on down, because we have enough queers in service to hold our own Pride parade." Isaac's face flashed through his mind, stiffened his back as he faced down a man he had spent a lifetime making room for.

"I never, I didn't mean—it's not about that."

"So it's me in particular, is it? I know what's expected of me. I know what I expect of myself. I would never plan to be unfaithful to *anyone* I chose to spend my life with. Especially not Gwen."

Arthur reached out, and for one bizarre moment Eddie couldn't tell if his brother was going to hit him or hug him. Either would be equally unexpected, and both probably deserved. But Arthur took his bag off him, slinging it over his own chest.

"Let me take this upstairs." An apology, given. "They'll want to hear all about it, you know, if you do mean to… if you do want." He stopped talking then, like a clockwork soldier run down. Eddie nodded, although it was halting. An apology, accepted. Maybe he'd been wound too tight, Eddie thought, as they climbed the stairs to maunder down the ancient hallways. Gloomy landscapes and dead relations glowered at them the whole way.

"If you don't have to," Arthur said, when they were at the door of Eddie's room, "I wouldn't drag yourself—or anyone else—into something just to end up miserable." He spoke with repressed anguish.

Eddie regarded his brother, compassion for him fighting its way through the bone deep disappointment in what Arthur seemed to think of him.

"I am not our father. Don't believe everything you read about me in the press. Actually spending time with one's family is very instructive, but I suppose you wouldn't know much about that, after all."

Not many people could boast of being able to shut the door in the Prince of Wales' face. Eddie took advantage of the opportunity with relish. He went for his phone with trembling hands, wanting to talk to Isaac more than he wanted to breathe. But then he remembered he couldn't do that. His cell was out of battery and he'd used Isaac up. Maybe he *was* like his father. He knelt down by the side of the four-poster bed, looking for a power outlet. The dead battery he could fix. A few minutes later found him sitting on the wide, polished hard-wood floorboards, staring off into space, as if the way out of this tangle could be found in the twining vines of the William Morris wallpaper.

AT DINNER, the family discussed Gwen and Maddy's impending arrival. The mood was generally positive, and not merely because she'd be another person to play cards with, or because having a child to focus on lightened everyone's mood. The Kensingtons were far too canny for that.

"She's a good choice," Sophie said. "Sensible. Charming. You'd better put her in touch with a stylist. Although it's Gwen," she went on, thoughtfully. "She has access to her mother's army. Joanna won't let her daughter be seen looking anything but her best."

Privately, Eddie thought that was far more for Joanna's benefit than Gwen's.

"It is a sensible idea," Victoria said, in her usual quiet way, when they were all together in private. "She understands what it means to have a public position."

"And you always were thicker than thieves," Sophie said, smiling encouragingly at her nephew. "You've had more life to you since she came back." Her pleasure was genuine, but Eddie had seen the naked relief in her eyes when he told her that Isaac had left. She saw Gwen as a symptom of his recovery from a temporary illness. He hadn't forgiven her.

"Of course I approve of that," Victoria said, the slightest spike of irritation in her voice. "I'm not only thinking of the practicals."

"Could have fooled me," Sophie said, reaching forward and spearing another courgette on her fork. "You were already writing the headlines, I could see you over there."

"Let's not get ahead of ourselves," Victoria said. "Rather, let's not get ahead of Gwen and Eddie. There isn't any pressure," she told him. "I'm glad you're spending more time with her, and if this is the best way of making that happen, I'm all for it."

"Thanks, Mum," he said, hoping his smile got into range of his eyes.

Arthur gazed into his wine glass and said very little, though what he did manage to emit was supportive enough.

There had never been a whisper of homophobia from his family when Eddie told them he was bisexual. Still, it was terrifyingly clear that they had no idea how to cope with it should the worst happen and the world find out. *Should the worst happen.* Eddie understood the phrase in his marrow. The Queen of England simply could not have a bisexual son. It would not do. There had already been enough upheaval in the Kensington circus over the years. More scandal would be unthinkable, no matter what it was. No one ever sat him down and told him the world knowing his sexual orientation would qualify. No one had to.

So the photos would remain in circulation as a frustrating curiosity. A reminder that no matter what the public and the press thought they knew, the Kensingtons were in control. Always.

GWEN AND MADDY were smuggled to Balmoral from Edinburgh in a black car. "I know it's a lot of trouble for a little holiday," Victoria said, rising from the outdoor lunch table to greet them in her thick flannel shirt and riding breeches. "Please don't hesitate to ask for anything you might be missing."

"This is still the strangest part," Gwen said, as she gave Eddie a polite kiss on the cheek.

"What?"

"How weirdly normal you all are when you're away from London."

"We try," Eddie told her, gravely. Maddy, wandering ahead of them, suddenly shrieked.

"Horses!"

"Well, that's our afternoon." Gwen looked at him sideways, clearly wondering if he would balk at following the whims of a child so soon. He grinned at her.

"Let's go."

The horses were a motley combination, with some of the finest racing and jumping lines in England represented, as well as solid old draft horses from the surrounding farms. Even the older thoroughbreds had checkered pasts. Many of them had been mistreated as part of the race fixing scandal that tarnished Malcolm's reputation back in the early 2000s. His father hadn't known directly about any abuse, but that didn't matter to Eddie. He lobbied Sir Anthony and Victoria successfully at the time to buy the horses, most of them ruined for racing and with health problems of varying severity, and stable them at Balmoral, at personal expense. Eddie spent as much time with them as he could. Those horses were now in their late teens and early twenties, as well fed and happy as the best veterinary care could make them. Some of them still loved being ridden, so city kids were bused out and taught to ride when the royal family wasn't in residence. That meant there was no shortage of horses to choose from for Maddy.

On his way down, Eddie ran into Arthur on the stairs.

"Going for a ride?"

"Giving Maddy her first lesson. Do you want to join?"

The momentary wistfulness on Arthur's face gave way to uncomplicated pleasure. "I would love to."

Somehow it happened that Arthur was the one to hoist Maddy onto a horse for the first time. He put her in front of Eddie on a soft-hearted fellow named Butter for a walk around the paddock. He gave Gwen a leg up on her own mount—another sweetheart, since she hadn't ridden in over ten years—and headed for his horse.

All the Kensingtons could ride. A good seat was a must. Alex had briefly flirted with show-jumping in her teens, but they were all devotees of cross-country and racing. Gwen was a natural as a child and hadn't lost her seat, much to the shock of her daughter, who had never seen her on a horse before. Maddy peppered Eddie with questions and, when she finished with him, asked to be transferred to the back of Arthur's horse for more discussion. The four of them had a lovely afternoon. It felt simple to be tramping around Scotland together.

The next few weeks at Balmoral went like that. Alex finally arrived, walking on her own private cloud and blushing whenever someone mentioned Daniel Black's name. Everyone was on better behavior than usual because of Maddy. There were more riding lessons, stories to tell, old board games to dust off and play. A whole castle to explore. Maddy started venturing into secret passages and disused attics all by herself, turning up with cobwebs in her hair and occasional treasures in her hands —including a couple of marbles Eddie and Arthur had declared lost and gone forever when they weren't much older than she was now.

Eddie relaxed more than he felt he deserved, but when he wasn't alone, he could avoid thinking about Isaac. He felt as if he had drifted away from himself, and expected the feeling to go away when they all returned to London. It did not.

Time, tide, and the official engagements schedule waited for no one. The social calendar picked up when the Queen returned to Buckingham Palace. The Prince of Wales completed his move to Kensington Palace, earning it the nick-name "The Nursery" in the rags. Appearances were made at the right places. Eddie threw himself into work. Arthur continued strategizing the tech agenda, conferring remotely with Avi Forrest, who seemed very interested in providing expertise in the wake of the conference. Alex and Daniel Black continued their nightly swimming dates and the rest of them pretended not to know. Gwen found a beautiful flat in London and escaped from her mother's townhouse, to the delight of all involved. She enrolled Maddy at the same progressive day school Eddie had attended as a child. Eddie's new suits arrived from the tailor. He could hardly look at them. The drawing Peter had done for him that day was tucked into the frame of his dressing room mirror. Every morning he stared at the two men in the sketch, walking away from him.

In October, Eddie and Gwen went on their first official outing as a couple, a movie premiere at the Odeon in Leicester Square. At the reception with the cast afterwards, Gwen's delighted blush as she talked to Gavin Pemberton made Eddie smile. She suggested Gavin play him in a biopic, and Eddie argued he'd do much better for Arthur. They shimmered together, gracious and playful. He kept his hand at the small of her back whenever they stood beside each other. He could feel the excitement in the room, eyes sliding over him, hungry gazes pooling on the back of his bare neck. He held it together until he reflexively looked to the corner of the room, searching for Isaac. He didn't remember the rest of the night.

LONDON JOURNAL EMPLOYEES tended to go for after-work drinks at a pub across the street from the *Journal*'s original location. Office lore had it that when deciding where to locate the new, modernized building, Gilda drew a three-block radius around The Goose & Barrel on a map and told the real estate team to put it somewhere in there. A few years ago, the new generation of pub owners decided to rebrand the venerable, beer-soaked institution as The Plaid Goose. They hired a few bartenders who referred to themselves as mixologists to work alongside the old guard on weekends, to draw the sort of crowd that thought signature cocktails were cute instead of offensive. The pub's mascot was now a painted goose in a plaid waistcoat. Hating the change was a major topic of conversation among the regulars, who refused to stop calling it "the Barrel" in gloomy tones. But some things didn't change, even with the addition of a wine list. The dart board, and the large wall filled with pinned-up newspaper clips, for example. The first time a Journal reporter got a story put up on the wall by their colleagues was considered an occasion of note, especially since they then had to buy the next round.

Daniel only returned to the Barrel once his first article on the Queen Mother's papers was published. He worked hard on that initial piece, focused on her experiences in World War II, including the well-loved story of her marriage to the Prince of Wales—in a Tube Station bomb shelter—during the Blitz. When he walked in, all the *Journal* reporters stood up and gave him a round of applause as he stood awkwardly leaning on his cane. "Good to see you in print again," the bartender told him. Daniel came in a couple of times a week now. The anti-anxiety medication he had finally started taking as prescribed lulled most of his PTS-fueled agoraphobia into a dim undercurrent of a wish to be back in his flat. Or Mary's study. Or Alex's room. Between that and the painkillers for his hip, he couldn't have anything alcoholic, but that wasn't a problem for anyone. He talked shop with his friends, occasionally fended off teasing when his picture appeared in the society pages after he shadowed Alex on some charitable outing or other. It felt like being alive. Not as he used to understand it, but as he might come to.

Daniel sat at the bar with a pint glass of ginger ale and a copy of *Men Explain Things to Me,* tuning out the crowd while a thunderstorm blew through outside. Someone cleared his throat, too close, and Daniel startled.

"Terribly sorry," a light, smooth voice said to him. "Tonic water, if you don't mind," it said to the bartender. Then, to him again: "You're the reporter working in Buckingham Palace, aren't you."

Daniel turned his head. The man next to him leaned one elbow against the shining dark oak, legs crossed at the ankle. His dark gray suit was pristine, and a rain-spattered camel trench coat hung over his arm like he was a 1930's matinee idol getting ready to break into a song and dance routine.

"Malcolm Varre." The Duke of Edinburgh held out his hand. Daniel shook it purely by reflex as he waited for his brain to catch up to yet another new reality courtesy of the Kensington assignment. "I've been enjoying your pieces on the Queen Mother. May I have a word?"

Nodding at the bar stool beside him was about all Daniel

could manage. Varre moved with the easy grace of a man who spent his life navigating pubs, passing a folded banknote to the bartender with a flourish a professional magician might have envied. He used a straw to muddle the slice of lime in his tonic water, and then set it aside on a napkin. Aside from a few oblique, bitter references, Alex hadn't talked much about her father, nor had he run across many references to him in Mary's papers. He wondered if Mary had excised her disgraced son-in-law after the divorce. Or if, given the rumors of addiction and overindulgence that followed the duke around from the very beginning, Mary found it a valuable preventative measure not to record anything in the first place.

"To what do I owe the fact of your company?"

Varre smiled into his glass. There was no real amusement in the expression—more like grim satisfaction. "I have a story you might be interested in."

"What's the story?"

"Me."

THE NEXT MORNING, Sir Anthony received a courtesy call from the Programming Director at the BBC. The Duke of Edinburgh had requested a one-hour time slot for a live interview at eight o'clock that night. Daniel Black did not show up at the palace for work.

19

The Kensingtons gathered at seven fifty-six that evening in unspoken solidarity. The family sitting room in Buckingham Palace wasn't used very often, now that the children were grown. But the plaid couch and flowered loveseats still accommodated them all as though no time had passed since the years of giant bowls of popcorn and passionate arguments about what movie to watch of a rare free evening.

Victoria sat at one end of the long sofa, still dressed from a dinner engagement with the National Portrait Gallery's Board of Trustees during which no one had talked about their plans for the rest of the evening, because everyone knew they would be at home watching her ex-husband on national television. Sir Anthony occupied the wing chair beside her, frustration pouring off him. Since learning about the interview, he had tried to get in touch with the Duke or anyone who might be connected with him, to find Daniel Black, or put pressure on Gilda Trafford to shut the entire thing down, but had been stymied at every turn. Malcolm Varre had no staff. No friends in the know. Ascertaining that Helena Wallace was out of the country was only scant comfort, because he didn't know what it *meant*, and that alone was an indicator of how great his failure had been. Victoria touched his wrist, but he felt sure he did not deserve the kindness.

Alex sat next to her mother, sandwiched between Victoria and Sophie as if they could keep her in one piece. Knowing it was about to be Daniel, *her* Daniel, chatting with Malcolm made her want to claw her heart out and fling it at the screen. He had called her that morning and told her what he was about to do. They fought like the lovers they hadn't been. She accused him of opportunism, of lying to her, of being no better than any other so-called journalist who wanted to cut the Kensingtons to watch them bleed. He shouted back that he was a reporter, and this was a story, and she needed to trust him. *"Or did you like it better when I was dependent on you?"* He'd snarled it, and her breath caught remembering how much it hurt. *"When you could pretend I was helpless, the way you want everyone around you to be."* She told herself he was wrong. She wanted him to be wrong. Now, she clutched her cell phone. He had texted her—*I'm sorry*—a few minutes ago. The words hovered in a red haze behind her eyes.

Eddie tucked himself into the corner of the loveseat in front of the windows, staring at the screen without seeing it. He missed Isaac so much it hurt to breathe, and the ache only got worse when he noticed that Gunny had slipped into the room, silent support for Victoria. Gwen pressed against his side, holding his hand. She anchored him in space, as did Arthur, sitting on the floor below them, leaning against Gwen's legs. Arthur and Gwen had been doing their best to protect him over the last few months, comfort him through pain that was as all-consuming as it was difficult to articulate. Arthur and he shared a quick, pained glance.

No one spoke. What could they possibly say?

When the BBC logo swooped off the screen at eight on the

dot, Richard Cross, one of the network's most venerated television presenters, sat at his familiar desk. A touch of bemusement marred his customary urbanity.

"Good evening. Tonight, we interrupt our regular programming to bring you an unprecedented event. Earlier today the BBC was contacted by the Duke of Edinburgh, requesting time to air an interview taking place this evening in his London home. We spoke with the interviewer, Daniel Black of the *London Journal*. For the last six months, he has been documenting the late Queen Mother's archived papers, and has presented a selection of them for publication. This will be the first time the Duke has spoken publicly about his divorce and his family. We now take you to his home in Belgravia. Thank you."

Victoria's first thought was that she had not been inside her former mother-in-law's mansion in a very long time. She noted that they had set up for the interview in front of the dining room fireplace, one that had once warmed the Duke of Wellington. With the kind of chilling detachment that often presaged a nervous breakdown, she idly wondered what other notable personages might have graced that same room. *Oh yes,* she thought, *the Queen of England. Me.*

Two ornately carved armchairs, meant to be found at either end of a table set for thirty, faced each other, lit so that the rest of the room was left in shadow. The white marble mantelpiece floated eerily behind them against a backdrop of green flocked wallpaper like the doorway to another world. Resting on a small table between the chairs were two glasses and a large pitcher of water, a reminder that the BBC did not take commercial breaks. The scene was set, the tone established, calculated to send a frisson of anticipation through the hundreds of thousands—millions—tuning in at home.

Interviewer and subject entered the frame at the same time, before the audio was turned on. Daniel's ruddy hair was freshly cropped short. He wore a dark new suit, artfully fitted to draw attention away from his injuries. The television makeup accentuated his hungry, after-a-story eyes, making them seem like dangerous pools, where things that grabbed at ankles lived. But there was also the self-contained air of David Frost about him, a throwback to days gone by, when men were men and reporters made them nervous.

Malcolm wore his crisp, charcoal three-piece suit like a second skin. He did not so much sit down as descend into his chair. As the sound technicians checked the lapel microphones one final time, the crinkling at the corners of Malcolm's eyes as he thanked them made him look approachable and pleasant. But his demeanor subtly changed as he watched the reporter withdraw a short stack of index cards from inside his breast pocket. With all the precision of an assassin rolling a silencer onto his pistol, or a surgeon laying out his tools, Daniel placed them on the table. Malcolm gazed at the rectangles of card stock in distant fascination, as if realizing for the first time how high the stakes were, and how devastating the consequences might be.

Across the table, careful to not upset the water pitcher, the two men shook hands. Even before the audio clicked in, everyone watching grasped what they were being promised. They were about to see the public consensual disassembling of someone most of the viewing audience had hated for over a decade.

It wasn't often a man took to international broadcasting to be crucified while handing his executioner the nails. Malcolm discovered within himself the similar adrenaline-fueled calm of waiting to ski down a double black diamond slope. Ever since yesterday, when he had left his house in pursuit of this partic-

ular reporter, he had felt no fear, no indecision whatsoever. The
sheer novelty of the endeavor should have been enough to send
him screaming into the night, but he felt no urge to run.
Helena had begged him, *begged* him, to do one of these with
her after the divorce. "People should know your side," she had
insisted. And of course, by extension, her side. He refused her
every time, for which he was now grateful. It would have made
tonight inconceivable. This was not a well one could drink
from twice.

Black had gone over the arc of the interview with him
beforehand, though he refused to provide individual questions.
He didn't want anything about Malcolm's responses to look
rehearsed, which was an endearing piece of naiveté. As if
Malcolm hadn't been thinking over his responses to questions
like these for years. It felt like he'd been waiting for someone to
ask them his entire life. Although it was unlikely Daniel would
kick off with *When did you realize you were destined to be a tremendous
disappointment?*

There were no nerves to speak of as Daniel introduced
them both to the viewing audience in broad strokes. No real
discomfort with what he was about to do. The film crew had all
been polite, kind in their different ways, the way nurses might
treat a terminal patient. He sat in his father's dining chair,
about to shatter the remnants of his public image, and they all
knew it. But this felt like the culmination of a series of
disgraces he had been allowed to get away with all these years.
No doubt Helena was watching in a Swiss chalet with her
friends, preparing the excoriating takedown she had
doubtlessly been suppressing all these years in case of such a
rebellion on his part, readying it to run and re-run in every
publication that would print it, inflating every dry admission of
responsibility into searing guilt.

But this wasn't about Helena. Or Daniel. Or himself, even.

It was about the few people in the world he hoped weren't watching. He knew he hoped in vain.

ARTHUR WAS TAKEN ABACK by how still his father sat. Malcolm lived in his memory as fundamentally in motion. He would fidget with anything to hand—a pen, a knick-knack, rolling a two-shilling piece across his knuckles or tossing it in his hand when his fingers shook too much from the cocaine or the alcohol. But now his body was quiet, face drawn and older than Arthur remembered. The only movement about him was his index finger, slowly tapping the arm of his chair as he regarded Daniel Black. Like he was keeping time. Or counting down. One steady beat every three seconds. Arthur recognized that move. He did it himself, in the briefing room, waiting for orders. He wondered if it looked that considering, that inevitable, when he did it. Had he learned it from watching his father, or was it one of those accidents of genetic imperative, like twins separated at birth who dressed the same way on opposite sides of the world?

Alex couldn't look at Malcolm without missing him. She had been sheltered enough to accept the explanation that her father was sick and needed to get well again. Her betrayals came later, when she realized the depth of Malcolm's infidelity, that he was never truly coming home. He had made more of an effort with her, taking her on trips and out to the theatre, until she rejected him in a blaze of righteous fury when his relationship with Helena became public. Even knowing the whole story, she missed him. Listening to him talk made her want to cry. Photographs only went so far. The sound of someone's voice was harder to come by.

Eddie watched his father and wondered, with a hopeful lump in his throat that he was powerless to squash down.

Living through the wreckage of what Malcolm had done left him guarded and wary. But his loyalty to Malcolm never quite disappeared. Though he was angry at himself for it, his desire to believe in the man refused to die.

Victoria tensed when Daniel began to ask questions. Malcolm was a private man. *I want my thoughts to be a secret, especially to myself*, he told her, when they were starting out. At the time it had been a declaration of political intent as they tried to figure out how to be married when she was going to be the Queen, and he only ever a Prince at most. She once knew him better than anyone, and though she had lost him, the certainty that she understood him remained.

"CAN YOU DESCRIBE YOUR EARLY LIFE?"

"I was born a few miles from here. My father was an explorer, a prominent archaeologist and author. He died twenty years ago. My mother was an accomplished horse-woman and a brilliant hostess. I have a sister, who resides mainly in Monaco. My upbringing was scrupulously correct. I was not. As a boy, I split my time between this house and our estate in the country, where my mother now lives. And at school, of course."

"Did you do well academically?"

"I enjoyed reading. I found the process of learning tedious. By the time I got to university, I had refined my ability to do only as much work as was absolutely necessary."

"Were you popular?"

"I have been blessed with the ability to seem more interesting than I am."

"Including in your romantic life?"

"Especially then."

"When did your substance abuse begin?"

Malcolm's gaze didn't flicker. "I was still in school when I began drinking heavily. Once I left university, I became a habitual cocaine user and occasional LSD user."

"Was your drug use of concern to you at that time?"

"I partied in the glam rock scene during the late 70's. Everything was on hand, anyone could get whatever they wanted. By my companions' standards, I barely kept up."

"Did the Queen—the then-Princess of Wales, I should say —know about your drug use when she met you? There are pictures of the two of you at some of those parties."

"She had undoubtedly heard rumors, but I stopped using when she and I began seeing each other."

"Was it difficult?"

"Well, I could still drink. That has always been a socially acceptable method of handling stress, though it shouldn't be. I was on the arm of the future Queen of England, flashbulbs in my face, brought into the fold of the highest reaches of society with countless demands on my time and attention. That is its own kind of high, and it never has a comedown. Until it does."

"When did you start using drugs again?"

"I never stopped drinking. By the late nineties I had a glass in my hand at all times. I began using cocaine again around the turn of the century. I am aware that this is one of the worst-kept secrets in Britain, and that speculation about my erratic behavior was rampant even at the time. I was protected by Buckingham Palace for the sake of my now ex-wife and my children."

VICTORIA WONDERED, numbly, how the rest of the country was reacting. She hardly knew for herself, and couldn't bear to look at her children. This was Malcolm in his purest form, ripping the curtain back on the worst time in their lives as if it was his story and no one else's. She tried to churn up some anger, but failed. *Because it is his story*, a small voice said. *He is allowed to tell it any way he sees fit.*

~

"DID YOU KNOW YOU WERE AN ADDICT?" Daniel leaned forward in his seat the way he'd seen Gilda do so many times, with everyone from prime ministers to plagiarizing reporters. Malcolm shifted in his seat, crossing one leg over the other.

"No. We have an idea of what an addict is in our culture, a tragic and extreme view of untreated addiction's consequences that permits us all to lie to ourselves. As long as we are not in visible, abject thrall to our particular fixation, we believe we don't have a problem. We think of each individual substance as a separate problem, when in reality, our minds are the battle-ground." He pitched his voice higher and spoke faster to conjure frantic rationalization. "I was not *addicted* to anything; I needed to function, and I thought the drugs and the alcohol allowed me to function. Therefore, I didn't have a problem. I had everything *completely* under control."

Malcolm shook his head, lips twisting in a brief, sad expression. For the first time, he glanced away before he spoke again. "Addiction is a chronic condition, not some failure of moral fiber. It has nothing more to do with what sort of person you are any more than a prolonged bout of the flu. But that isn't our general attitude. The shame is intense, partially because we don't intervene early enough. You already have to be in a great deal of trouble before you understand you need help. I am the poster child for that.

"It didn't seem so bad to me, even though my staff and close protection detail had to watch me ruin myself on a daily basis. I had essentially stopped talking to my wife at all, lest she realize the state I was in. Most people don't recognize how much trouble they've gotten into until they are forced to examine their own behavior in a new light."

"When did you reach that point?"

"One night I was brought back to the palace quite late. Drunk, high, propped between two of my protection officers. It wasn't the first time, believe me. Victoria—pardon me—my former wife was away on a trip, or else my team would have delivered me here. That was their procedure, can you imagine? My behavior was so frequent and so predictable it required *procedure*. I was making a great deal of noise—falling into things, on a paranoid rant. I assaulted one of my protection officers. We rounded a corner, and one of my sons was standing in the hall, looking terrified. He used to wake up screaming from dreams about the palace being attacked, when he was a child. Men with guns dragging us from our beds, and so on. I must have sounded like his worst nightmare."

Malcolm slumped, undone by the picture he was present-ing. He continued in a hoarse voice, a poorly assembled collec-tion of limbs in a suit, held together only by determination.

"In my head he was a toddler. I thought he shouldn't be up. I wanted to get him back to bed. I thought that very clearly. I lurched toward him, and I still remember the fear in his eyes. My own son flinched back from me because I scared him. I tripped over myself and fell flat at his feet. The last memory I have before I blacked out is of his white sweat socks on the dark blue carpet they used to have—might still, I don't know—in the East Wing at Buckingham Palace. I'm not sure I've looked him in the eye since."

Breathing was unmanageable during the pause that followed. Daniel couldn't take his eyes off Malcolm, watching the tattered flag of the man's dignity slip to the floor.

~

ARTHUR HADN'T THOUGHT Malcolm remembered that night. He was dimly aware of the whole room looking at him and Eddie, because most of them didn't know this story, and Malcolm hadn't specified which son saw him rolling and raving in the dead of night. He could feel his mother's eyes on him, because she knew he had been sensitive to noise until he started flying fighter jets, and she knew why. Eddie had been there too, that night. He hadn't left his room the way Arthur did, but his door was open. He also saw Malcolm fall. Arthur could still hear Malcolm's mad accusations echoing through the hallway, could see him sprawled out. He had staggered home in bad shape before, but nothing like that night. For a moment, they'd thought Malcolm might be dead, until his team swept him up and away. Now, Eddie leaned over and hugged him. Arthur held on to his arms with his free hand. Gwen already held his other one.

MALCOLM HAD THOUGHT he was inured to his own story, but it occurred to him, faintly, that he had never said it out loud before. Every word, pried out one by one, left him full of holes. The cameras were impossible to ignore, but he found them comforting, for once. He wouldn't hide from them, and they would record him faithfully.

"And that incident convinced you to get the help you needed?" As far as Malcolm was concerned, Daniel had retreated to the far end of binoculars viewed the wrong way through.

"I woke up with my child's terror of me burned into the backs of my eyelids. I couldn't pretend any more. It all tends to fall down around one at once, at times like that. I asked a friend for help, and was whisked off to a very discreet, very exclusive rehabilitation facility in Scotland."

"A friend? You didn't confide in your wife?"

Malcolm sighed, gaze catching briefly on a piece of china on the mantel. Victoria had given it to his mother for Christmas, years ago. He didn't know why it remained on display. "I couldn't face her. She had already forgiven several infidelities, quashed a dozen scandals, including my unintentional involvement in a race fixing ring that led to animal abuse and will haunt me until the day I die. She put up with my deteriorating ability to manage the pressures of public life. I allowed myself to be convinced that it was better to go, pull myself together, and then see what might be done about my marriage. That last part never happened."

It FELT like someone had reached under Victoria's ribs and was twisting her heart in rhythm with Malcolm's carefully chosen words. They had never spoken about the crumbling of their marriage. From all angles it was presented and enacted as a *fait accompli*.

Victoria felt old resentment and sadness rising inside her. Control over the past always seemed to belong to other people. Malcolm hadn't revealed that one of the people who *convinced* him to go had been Sir Anthony. It had taken years for Anthony to confess that he was the one who pushed Malcolm to call Helena Wallace instead of her. Fed up with Malcolm's behavior, Anthony had wanted him out of the way and recovering fast, somewhere he wouldn't require Victoria's help. He hadn't correctly predicted the outcome, and looked at her now with quiet, apologetic sorrow. She shook her head.

"We all did what we thought was best," she whispered. But she couldn't take her eyes away from the screen.

"*I was trying to escape myself,*" Malcolm said, regaining a measure of calm, as if it were that simple. "*That is not an endeavor overburdened with success stories.*"

"Do you believe now that there was any way to save your marriage?"

Malcolm stared at his hands, at the place where a wedding ring had been. The tan lines around it had faded a long time ago, but he still imagined the flash of gold, now and again. He would not say that on television.

"Without interference, we might have found a way forward. I hope that would have been the case. As it was, she took the lion's share of the blame, because nature and the popular press abhor a vacuum, and she refused to publicly humiliate me while I was doing all I could to stay sober. And I was still the father of her children. She thought they should be spared from as much pain as we could manage. It still wasn't enough. They never chose this life. I did. And that is one of the reasons I asked if you would be willing to interview me. Because my children have done nothing but amaze me from the moment they were born. I should have protected them, but I left. They became the wreckage of my life instead of its highest achievement. We are not passengers in our lives. We are not meaningless, or expendable. To be treated as if we are is unforgivable, but to *behave* as if we are is a betrayal of our very souls."

"Have you ever told your children any of this?"

"I doubt they would have given me the chance."

"Have you ever hoped for a reconciliation?"

"Of course. I don't believe I deserve one, by my own actions, and I was never worthy of Victoria in the first place. But it remains a wistful undercurrent to my life, instead of something to pursue."

Eddie stared at his father as if Malcolm would turn to him. He raised his hand to his jaw as Malcolm did the same on the screen.

Gilda once told Daniel that every successful interview surprised the interviewer, in the end. He only understood that now. He demanded Malcolm's confidences. Receiving them took more of a toll than he had expected. This man, with all the wealth and privilege in the world, had smacked up against his demons and lost, over and over, until he'd won. There was some honor in that.

"Why talk about this now? Over ten years on, having achieved what you referred to as, 'polite, embittered *détente* on all sides' to me last night."

Malcolm rubbed his chin with his thumb. It was time for him to do what he had truly come for, to become, in fact, the man he wished to be. He settled back in his chair, rested his hands on the chair arms, and met Daniel's eyes with a steady gaze. His index finger tapped three times.

"Because, even at my remove, I can see the same forces that destroyed me brought to bear on my children. Especially Edward. His privacy was invaded in an unconscionable manner by people who ought to have known better. Who should have *chosen* better.

"Think about how many people saw those photographs *before* they were published. From the person who took them and sat on them all those years, then unearthed them and decided to sell, to the journalist who brokered them, to the many editors who would have looked at the story—as many editors do, when it is about the royal family—to the person who laid it out. At any point, someone could have said it was too much, too mean-spirited, too small, revealing harmless details of a man's life against his own wishes in this terrible way. But no one did, it seems. Not convincingly enough, at any rate.

"Now," he went on, "every article that is published about him and the lovely woman he's seeing begins by doubting, implicitly or explicitly, that their connection is real. Every piece about him in any capacity mentions it, sounds the call from the mountaintops that here—here!—is something interesting. Titillating, of course. Scandalous, surely. And at the expense of a man who has done nothing but bear the burdens his unusual life placed on him from the minute he was born, every day, with grace I envy, and could never truly manage. He has had to do that, without support from his father, for far too long. All my children have."

Malcolm leaned forward. "Arthur, Alexandra, Edward..." He lingered over the names like they were an incantation. "They are considered, legally, to be of public interest in the same way that political figures or celebrities are. The first time photographs of them were published, they were days old. They were aware, from a heartbreakingly tender age, that their behavior reflected back on their family, on the world stage. That is a crushing weight. I know, because I have felt it firsthand, and couldn't manage it. Consider this an open invitation to focus on the one person in all of this—me—who could have chosen to make things better for all of them, and did not. I regret that more than I will ever be able to say."

20

H elena Wallace landed at Heathrow and exited the plane on the tarmac. Her chauffeur shut the car door very gently after her, somberly attentive, as if someone had died. Of course—he had watched the interview last night, along with everyone else.

The first time Helena had considered how difficult it would be to stage a dramatic confrontation, she was twelve years old, sprawled on the ratty old chesterfield in the kitchen. An afternoon soap opera blared across the long, low room. Her mother liked to have something on in the background while she totted up how much money they'd made from tourists over the previous weekend. On the television, a woman wearing a strapless evening gown covered in beads and rhinestones stormed in. Wide bracelets flashed as she tossed a white fur stole onto a chaise and demanded answers from the man she loved.

"You'd have to get there," Helena remembered saying. "And have a way to leave, dressed like that. So it's pretty much only something you could do in London. Or if you had a car."

"A chauffeur would be ideal," Imogen replied. "Someone to open the door so you could made an entrance."

Helena had grown up in barely genteel poverty, rattling around the still habitable parts of a grand manor house going to ruin. Her parents tried to hide their winces as they led loud, bored weekenders and embarrassed neighbors through the old pile for a few shillings a head. They told stories about the history of the place, from Tudor times on up to parties her grandparents threw. Those were Helena's favorites. The famous authors and actors who came for the weekend and stayed for months, dancing until all hours, singing around the grand piano in the drawing room, jumping fully clothed into the swimming pool. Tales of exquisite meals, cases of champagne, marriages, affairs, gowns, they fed her hunger for glamor, for belonging. Every stick of furniture in the place sparked a flood of reminiscence from her grandmother, and Helena followed her around like a hopeful puppy. She didn't realize until she was a bit older that anything of real value had been sold years ago.

If her grandfather had been able to exchange his stories for credit in Monte Carlo, he would have sold them, too. The house he kept out of pride, the Wallace family currency, and because he never got an offer on it that matched his idea of its value. Imogen and Helena drove to towns fifty miles away to shop at secondhand stores at the beginning of every school year. Helena's writing earned her scholarships at the succession of exclusive girls' schools that were her birthright and, once, would have been paid for without a thought. She would have been a line item in a ledger instead of a problem. What luxury. She became funny, outgoing, nice to everyone, so that she would be invited to weekends at friends' homes. Their houses were so much like her own that she didn't act awkward, or impressed. But they had teams of gardeners and domestic staff to keep them beautiful. Helena was determined to learn how to behave around unquestioned wealth, how to eat an artichoke, how much jewelry was too much on a woman, assuming she ever had any of her own.

Unlike the rest of her family, Helena figured out that pride could be built on visible accomplishments instead of crumbling structures. Hers went up brick by brick. Bricks shaped like being a fearless reporter, wheedling information out of people with a bright smile and a disarming, interested expression. Brick: sending her parents enough money to fix the roof without resorting to renting out for weddings. Brick: seeing her name in print on an exposé that caused a recall election in the North Country. Brick: confidences from her best friend, the Queen. She had created her pride from scratch. It belonged to her alone. She deserved it.

Helena scrolled through her Twitter feed. The world of royal observers was exploding at the revelations of the night before. Theories abounded, everything from the Duke being under pressure from Buckingham Palace, to this being the prelude to a reunion with the Queen, to speculation that they had never truly divorced—*What does it mean?* they all wanted to know. *Nothing,* she thought, in a silent scream. *It can't mean anything.* But Helena knew the dangers of self-delusion. A few of the commentators were already discussing her absence and potential role in the theatre of the previous evening. The shame she thought was long buried, the shame of a crumbling house and forever being on the outside, reared up. She straightened her spine against it.

She wasn't wearing diamonds, her white fur stole was nowhere to be seen, but she had the driver and the car. The trip through the city, as she stewed in her private disappointments and public humiliation, wrapped around her like armor.

Journalists mobbed the Varre mansion.

"Around back, ma'am?" Glenn asked. Good old Glenn.

"No, let me out. Go 'round and wait for me, will you?"

Helena took a breath, brushed an errant lock of hair off her dark glasses, and got out of the car herself.

The barrage of flashes and questions cocooned her. Unlike so many similar times in her life, she took no pleasure from it.

"Did he tell you he was going to do it?"

"Did you know about the drug use, Helena?"

"Getting a bit old for all this scandal, aren't you?"

She found she couldn't pull her usual trick in these situations and refuse to accept that individual words had meaning.

Hastings, Malcolm's butler, opened the door for her with a sour glance at the press outside. It wasn't the first time. She did not give him her coat, and he did not greet her with more than a nod. So that was the way the wind blew.

Malcolm sat in his breakfast nook, tea and toast laid out, lit from behind by the overcast, late autumn morning. The bare gardens through the large bay window surrounded him like the background in an Impressionist painting. *Man with Morning Paper,* as painted by Berthe Morisot. Helena willed herself to no longer find him attractive. It didn't work. His faded beauty seemed sharpened to a fine edge, deadly as the night she first saw him, thirty-five years ago.

Helena had met him for the first time in her University days, when close friendship with the Princess of Wales made her a social catch in her own right—in Victoria's borrowed clothes, but no one knew that. His sister was part of the weekend house party set. She occasionally produced him, her mysterious older brother, like a magician wrangling an unreliable rabbit. Stories about him were legion. Malcolm partied with rock stars and actors. Malcolm wore leather trousers and glitter in his hair. Malcolm crashed his Jaguar into the bollards outside the Houses of Parliament one wild night, tossed the keys into the Thames, and walked away. She had never felt sympathy for the bollards until this moment.

The first time she saw him, mixing drinks for his sister's

friends, he cut a dashing figure among the overgrown children playing dress-up all around them. When he handed her a glass of champagne, she felt like a guest at one of her grandfather's parties. As if she might finally belong. He already had fine wrinkles around his luminous green eyes in his mid-twenties.

Every brilliant, cutting opening remark she might have made died in her throat as he looked up. The eyes were the same. The spark inside them—the spark she thought of as being hers alone—was gone.

"Good morning, Helena. Weren't you enjoying Switzerland?"

"You bastard."

"'Why, Malcolm,'" he said lightly. "'You look exhausted. That interview must have been so difficult for you, how are you?'"

She wanted to cry, so she laughed. "Don't be absurd. You expect sympathy, when you've made me a laughingstock?"

"I rather think I did that to myself."

"Liar." She stalked towards the table. "You've destroyed my reputation, called my journalistic integrity into question, made it clear you have no respect for me whatsoever…" The points she had rehearsed over and over on the flight from Zurich withered under the frost radiating from him. Malcolm picked up a fork and rocked its tines back and forth against the tabletop.

"Are you more upset that I took a story away from you, or that you didn't see it coming?"

"I begged you for years to tell your side, to defend yourself from the hounding, the constant speculation. We could have done it. It ought to have been me. Standing by you, all this time."

He tipped his head back, mouth tightening. "Spare me the litany of your sacrifices. You were exactly where you wanted to be *all this time*."

"Not nearly," she said. Some of the anger in his expression gave way to a weariness familiar and heartbreaking as he absorbed a palpable hit to an old wound. He was easy to injure, though he didn't look it. Easy to turn the tables on him, remind him that he had failed to come up to scratch in his marriage and in what came after. His insistence on never living together, never marrying, keeping up a civilized plausible deniability, was painful even as it suited her. He didn't want enough, feel enough, give enough—her refrain born of a possessive longing she could never shake. Malcolm was all she had ever minded Victoria having instead of her.

Helena first crossed paths with Victoria Kensington in a drama class at school. They were put together in a scene from *The Importance of Being Earnest*, all about jealousy and fascination between two women—girls, really—who had no choice but to compete. Helena quickly recognized how awkward and out of place Victoria felt, in character and out. That made Helena curious, and curiosity was the only thing that ever made her kind.

To be intimidated didn't occur to her, when she sat down next to Victoria in the caf with her own plate the next afternoon. As a matter of policy, Helena resented everyone who had more than she did, but Victoria had so *much* more that Helena didn't bother. The princess was so clearly interested in being friends with Helena—honest, intimate friends—that it would have turned anyone's head. Helena told her immediately that she had no money, no status, nothing except ambition. *"That's all right,"* Victoria said. *"I have everything but ambition. We can share."*

And share they did. Most of Victoria's clothes looked better on her, anyway, as both girls gleefully acknowledged, standing in front of the floor-length mirror in Victoria's dormitory. By the next term, they were roommates. Victoria's generosity had been careless, and they both enjoyed Helena taking advantage of it. Helena helped her learn to harness it when she became Princess of Wales. Helena helped her craft a new public image after her brother died, and snuck her out at night, when the pressure became too much. Victoria wrote to all the newspapers on Helena's behalf after Helena left university, requesting that they consider her for a job. They became inseparable in their free time.

Malcolm was the only thing they couldn't pass back and forth. Being his Girl Friday hadn't been enough for Helena, though she had tried, for everyone's sakes. She really did try. But everyone had their limits, didn't they?

"Why did you sell those pictures of Eddie?" Malcolm's conversational voice broke in on the hurricane inside her. She had expected their end, if there ever was an end between them, to be a matter of cold politeness on her part, not this burning, humiliating rage choking off her ability to defend herself, to think.

"Who told you that?"

"Eddie."

"And you believed him?"

"I didn't want to. I told myself it couldn't be true. So I checked your phone."

"You *what?*"

"Took it off the sideboard."

"It's locked," she said, only realizing too late that in trying to call his bluff, she essentially confirmed his accusation.

"I've been at your side since your first smartphone. I know your passcode. Has it been so long since you understood me as anything other than your pathetic creature? I thought there were lines you would not cross. I told myself you had a conscience. My *son*, Helena. You held him the day he was born, for god's sake!"

"How long have you known?" She sorted through her

memories of the last few weeks, thinking about when he could have been alone with her mobile—

"Since the bombing."

She stared at him, resisting belief with every fiber of her being. But he held her gaze simply, cool and direct. The man she had once wanted beyond reason. That want became a chasm inside her, because she knew how he looked at Victoria, and the way he looked at her was only a pale echo of that admiration and devotion. Never mind that she had seen him ruined in the effort to give Victoria what she needed. Helena wanted him to destroy himself for her. She wanted it so badly she hadn't realized it had happened. Only in him making the effort to resist her did she recognize that she had gotten what she wanted. And now it was gone.

"You waited until everything died down. Until you couldn't be accused of trying to capitalize on a tragedy. And you knew I'd be away. You did this to hobble *me?*" She tried to make it an accusation, but some childish part of her took over and turned it into a question. A self-indulgent thread of hope.

One graceful incline of his chin later, it snapped.

"I did my best, these last ten years," he said. "Shockingly, it worked. I was a good little disgrace. Stayed quiet, behaved myself, appeared on your arm and in your orbit. The very picture of the chastened man. Took every hit thrown at me. Legitimized you. Adored you. Protected you. All while embracing sobriety and atoning in public. And I found myself realizing, months ago, as the enormity of your actions really sank in, really penetrated my consciousness, how backwards I'd done the whole thing. I should have gone through it all for my children. For my *wife*. It never occurred to me that I could try. You and Anthony Pritchard made it so very easy for me to disappear."

She felt her heart constrict as if defending itself from a

blow, but he was still talking, not giving her a second to recover.

"I don't fault either of you. I was well in to several interlocking breakdowns by the time you spirited me away to rehab in the dead of night. And I am, as ever, truly, grateful to you for that." His hand twitched, as if he wanted to reach for her. "In spite of everything, before or since, I am grateful. But Helena, I shouldn't have made love to you the night I came back. I should have gone home. Crawled on my knees across the courtyard through broken glass in penance for the harm I caused on the off chance they would take me back. And you knew it. And you knew if you made it easy enough to be with you instead, I never would."

"I loved you." She couldn't keep the tremor out of her voice, no matter how hard she gripped the chair.

"We both know that was over a long time ago," he said. "If you loved me, you wouldn't have gone near my son. Come to think of it, you wouldn't have shown up here in the dead of night to see if you could fuck your dearest friend's mentally ill husband when he was at an intensely vulnerable and fragile stage of recovery in the first place, but I don't suppose you thought of it that way."

"You think blaming me will solve anything? You think baring your questionable excuse for a soul on national television will make up in any way for what you've done?"

"No. But we know how the game is played. If you go near them, any of them, it will look like the bitter revenge of a woman who couldn't keep her lapdog in line. Not to the general public, maybe, but certainly to anyone in the know. And you couldn't bear that. I don't mind. Casting me as the villain is overdone, in any case. You can't make a scandal out of what people already know." He turned the fork over in one hand. "I haven't blamed you for anything. I have accused you of manipulation, of selfishness, of utter and complete disregard for the feelings of the people around you. You haven't objected."

"You've seen me do worse."

"Not to my children."

"I should get my things," she said, gathering herself. She couldn't win. A retreat was all she had left.

"There isn't much," Malcolm said. "It confused me, when I was walking around the house yesterday, before the camera crew got here. Thinking about how long it's been, with so little to show for it. Some makeup. A few pair of shoes. Not even a picture. There ought to be more."

"How can there be more? You're a collection of suits with a heart cast aside somewhere. You don't allow anyone in, and you never did. Not someone who could appreciate you. You have no capacity for real passion."

"And yet, here I am. Causing such distress, at great personal cost to the people around me, all my life. You don't need to compose your column about this at the moment, do you? Let us at least be done honestly."

"Very well. Good-bye, Malcolm." Helena tilted her head at the exact angle she had learned from a woman on the telly when she was twelve. "And *fuck* you."

21

Rain. On the roof of the car, in sheets down the windows, muddling the sight of his father's house as Eddie stared at its black front door. The reporters had been conquered by the elements and by nightfall.

"Are you sure about this, sir?" Harris's hands were tight on the steering wheel. He had been on edge since they left KP.

"I'm afraid so." Eddie was in knots with how sure. He hadn't been in that house, hadn't spoken to his father alone in years. "This has to be done."

Harris didn't argue, not even about staying in the car.

Eddie felt like the only person left on earth as he walked across the dark, empty street. The door loomed, gleaming through the rain, ready to swallow him up. Cold water falling on his head and running down his neck was the only sensation grounding him in reality.

His left hand reached for the doorknob instead of the small brass knocker, a reflex that startled him. He was brought up short by the sight of his pristine nails and the rings he wore on his fingers. At one of them in particular, on his pinky finger, the one turned around so the flat side would bite at his palm if he made a fist. He twisted the signet ring, with its Varre family crest, so it faced upward. The door was unlocked when he tried it. He felt like a character in a fairy tale, sneaking into a mysterious castle.

The house belonged to his paternal grandmother, and had been in the family since Wellington's day. Most of the antiques and furniture he remembered were still here, but his father's ironically modern personal style now informed the whole instead of Grandmother Varre's stifling propriety. The Mondrian in the entranceway and an Ellsworth Kelly over the fireplace might have given her a stroke. Eddie continued on, wondering how far he would have to go.

Not far, as it turned out. Most of the house lights on the ground floor were dimmed. The thick carpeting on the stairs muffled the sound of his boots. With due sense of trepidation, he followed the triangular slice of light up the stairs to the first floor study, Grandfather Varre's retreat.

This was the room he, Arthur, and Alex were excused to after dinner as children. They hadn't been given the full run of the house. (As if, growing up in Buckingham Palace, they didn't know how to behave around precious antiques; another one of the endless barbs Grandmother liked to hurl at her royal daughter-in-law.) The room was too dark in sunlight, but electric light made it comfortable. Navy silk damask wallpaper contrasted abruptly with the ivory carpeting. The built-in mahogany bookcases were stuffed full of history books and fine bound editions of novels. In front of them was a confusion, a proliferation, of decades of Varre family knick-knacks. There was a desk, a large couch, wing chairs scattered about. A gaming console had been set up here—grudgingly—for the amusement of the grandchildren, though the real game was Grandfather Varre coming up and sending them on scavenger hunts for hidden things. They went on expeditions through the house to places they were not allowed, following his clues to the same Ancient Egyptian statuette of a lion every time.

Each successive generation of Varre packrats added something to the whole. Malcolm's contribution appeared to be a smattering of blown glass objets d'art Eddie did not recognize, strewn among Grandmother Varre's rococo shepherdesses. Eddie used to collect them from all over the room and play with them behind the couch, left to his own devices when Arthur chased him from in front of the Nintendo, telling him Alex needed a turn. Those evenings seemed interminable at the time, but now he remembered the quiet, well-mannered conversation and occasional bouts of laughter from the adults downstairs with desperate fondness. He missed his forbidding grandmother and his sardonic, distant grandfather, who only genuinely came alive while telling stories.

He saw all this before he let himself look at the man standing in front of the neat desk where his grandfather's research projects used to repose in pleasant mess, his back to the door.

"Come back to finish me off, have you?" the light tenor said, with an edge Eddie recognized from the inside out. Malcolm turned around. The baleful, intimate curve to his lips froze solid when he caught sight of his unexpected guest.

Eddie hadn't thought his first emotion on seeing his father would be overwhelming affection. The need for self-protection and the awareness of Malcolm's many misdeeds were both swept away, in this moment, and Malcolm was only his handsome, tired father. The man who drank the cocktails Eddie made when he was small, no matter how inexpertly developed or violently colored they were. (And didn't that give him a flash of guilt now.) The man who taught him to dance, to ride horses, to tell a Manet from a Renoir and enjoy knowing the difference.

He had never seen that man at a loss like this. With an

ounce less good breeding, Malcolm's jaw might have dropped. He made an aborted gesture with the hand holding his water glass, as if he wanted to bring it to his mouth and speak over the lip. Eddie knew that move, did it a dozen times a week, learned from watching the master. He knew what came next, too. A retreat behind humor, razor-sharp and impassable.

"I have absolutely no idea what to say," Malcolm said, after a moment. "A sad commentary on a man confronted with his own son, but perhaps not an unusual one even in the best of circumstances. I acknowledge wholeheartedly that these are not the best of circumstances. Drink?" He tilted his glass at Eddie, who nodded. "Take your coat off. This isn't the dark ages, the heat is on. Much to your grandmother's dismay, if she knew."

Malcolm's brisk hospitality carried him along. Eddie wasn't sure if his father meant the welcome sincerely, but the feeling of being cared for lodged in his chest. He shrugged out of his coat, laying it across the back of a chair by the door, its seat cushion upholstered to match the drapes. He felt vulnerable without it, although he had chosen this outfit with special care. Black skinny jeans tucked into heeled, pointed boots, white silk shirt partially tucked in front, rings on most of his fingers, a narrow scarf looped around his neck. He thought Malcolm deserved to see him as he would like to be. That he should know what he had been protecting.

Malcolm handed him a tumbler filled with something clear and bubbling, with a slice of lime floating in it.

After a sip, Eddie blinked. "There's no gin in this tonic."

"I wasn't lying about that yesterday. Or the reason why."

Words piled up and crashed inside him. The rain made small talk with the windows as son and father regarded each other. The creases around Malcolm's eyes and cheeks seemed on the verge of caving in and leaving him an old man before his time. He was going gray with more than a distinguished

silver at his temples, an allover fading. Eddie hadn't quite realized his father *could* age, and thought *Don't leave me,* suddenly,
with childish anguish. But that spell had been broken long ago.
He wondered what Malcolm saw in him.

"To what do I owe the pleasure? A reward for good behavior?" Malcolm seemed to regret the words as soon as they were
voiced. Eddie didn't give him a chance to take them back.

"I saw Helena came and went today. News was full of it."

Malcolm shrugged. Devil-may-care, but Eddie knew this
devil did care. "Helena flew back from Switzerland to leave me.
Why do people do such things? Don't come back. It gets the
message across."

"You'd know," Eddie said, fingers pressing hard into the
angled valleys of heavy glass.

"I shouldn't have said that. Did you come to have it out, at
this late date?" It seemed like an honest question, if an incred-
ulous one. "In that case, you could have written."

"I came to thank you."

Malcolm's expression was bewildered. "To thank me."

"For the interview."

"Why are you thanking me?"

"Why did you do it?"

Malcolm swirled the ice in his glass.

"Contrary to what you seem to think, I do have paternal
feelings, as well as a sense of fairness. Helena's behavior
towards you injured those feelings. Significantly."

"You didn't seem to care about fairness the last time you
made a snippy little comment about Mum in public." Eddie
was proud of how his voice didn't shake. "We do read the
society pages."

"Eddie—"

"Talk all you want about wishing you'd protected us. You
never tried. Your bloody girlfriend insinuated and prodded and
revealed and you did *nothing*."

"None of it stuck. None of it was more than petty gossip. You had Buckingham Palace behind you, what did you need me for?"

"You were our father! Did you think it wouldn't hurt us?"

"I'm still—I never—" Malcolm cut himself off with an audible snap of teeth. Eddie quailed inside, bracing for the inevitable, dismissive set-down. Instead: "Eddie, why are you here?"

It struck Eddie anew, how tired Malcolm looked. The tightness in his chest grew. He couldn't avoid it any more. He had words for his father, a torrent of them jammed up and filed away from a decade of disappointment and isolation from someone who had been able to make the sun move through the sky for him. He swallowed too much tonic water and the quinine burned. He welcomed the distraction.

"I don't know why you picked now to discover you cared. You had other opportunities. You're still an *ass*. Were you honestly an addict, or were you bored and spoiled? Couldn't even be satisfied with a bloody literal queen, needed to fuck your way through half the aristocracy before you started on the popular press, didn't you? Couldn't be bothered to be a grown-up for five consecutive minutes." He flung the half-full glass at the floor. It landed with a dull thud in the thick carpet.

"Good god," Malcolm breathed, and then downed the last of his own drink. He took aim with his glass and pitched it right at Eddie's. Direct hit. His shattered. Eddie's only cracked. "Figures," Malcolm said, rubbing a hand over his face. The corner of his mouth twitched. Eddie heard the deep breath his father took, but it still came a shock to him when Malcolm spoke without fight or recrimination.

"You didn't have to thank me, and you didn't have to come here to do it. I didn't do it for your approval, I know I'm beyond that. But you're welcome, all the same. And if there isn't anything else…"

Eddie had a lump in his throat as he turned to go, dismissed. He grabbed his coat, swallowing against the urge to cry when he looked back.

Malcolm had one arm crossed in front of his stomach, head bowed. His hair fell into his face. Eddie watched him, the platonic ideal of both the fallen idol and the condemned man waiting for the executioner at long last. Regret rushed up his throat like bile, out of his mouth before he could stop it.

"Dad, I'm so sorry."

Of everything he'd said, that hit Malcolm the hardest. He rocked on his heels, hand carding into his hair at the back and tightening as he watched the puddle of tonic water soak into the carpet.

"That slice of lime doesn't match the decor at all," he said. "Wrong color entirely."

The advantage to looking so like his father dawned on Eddie, the answer to a problem that had eluded him all his life. He could see in Malcolm's eyes how much he wanted to keep Eddie here, for even a few more minutes, because it matched how much Eddie wanted to stay.

Eddie might have laughed. It might have been a hoarse sob. He didn't know. In the search to look anywhere else, he caught sight of the old blue faience lion sitting on a bookshelf by the door.

"Did Grandfather lift this from Highclere Castle, or was that one of his less true stories?" Eddie asked, running his index finger down the side of the statuette.

"Larceny runs in the family," Malcolm told him. "That was the most chilling and accurate indictment of my character I've ever heard," he continued, slipping it in so easily Eddie almost didn't realize what he was talking about. "I wish you could add to the interview. It would be novel to see something true in the papers."

Eddie flinched.

"I don't make comments about your mother," Malcolm said. "Not in public. Not anywhere. And the drugs had to come out eventually. It's not your fault. Helena held it over my head. The untellable story. If I didn't tell it, she would have done it for me."

"That's horrifying."

"That's life," Malcolm countered. "You know it. Pretend it's a game of chess. We're pieces, and we're players, and we all have our own boards. Helena plays with a rules variant demanding if you see an opening to capture an opponent's piece, you have to take it, no matter what."

"How did you live like that?" Eddie asked.

"With extreme care. The dangerous people in this world are the ones who can think a few steps ahead, who understand consequences. The most dangerous people are the ones who understand how to manipulate the consequences for other people as well as themselves. You know that in a way no one else in that benighted family seems to."

"Are you saying you're proud of me?"

"Of course I'm proud of you. I'm proud of all my children. Especially when they're unlike me."

Eddie's hands tightened on his trench coat. He wanted to put it down, to take his boots off and sit on the fat upholstered couch with his feet tucked under him. Really talk to Malcolm. Watch him pace, drink in hand. Pretend they did this all the time.

"It isn't so much to ask for, is it, for a father who leads by something other than opposite example?" Eddie said.

"You wouldn't think."

"Do you even want to be forgiven?" Eddie surprised himself with the question, but Malcolm considered it, observing his son thoughtfully.

"Is there forgiveness for me?" There were gaps in Malcolm's banter. Eddie could see them in the way conversation with him shifted, no solid ground, always another question to deflect with. Places where Eddie could recognize the raw heart of a man who lived in the constant shadow of having so thoroughly disappointed the world. But more than the world. The people he was supposed to love more than anything. Or at the very least, if not love, at least refrain from hurting with such blithe regularity.

"Are you sorry?" Eddie turned it around on him.

Malcolm seemed taken aback. Offended, nearly. "What good does *that* do? What should I be sorry for?"

Eddie gaped at him. "Are you actually from another planet? Sorry for cheating on Mum like it was a contact sport. For the drugs. For the alternate weekend schedule. For essentially vanishing when it came down to choosing us or your harpy. Because you could have said it wasn't true, what she wrote about us. You could have said something, come out against it, or, oh, I don't know, *stopped fucking her*. Mum never bad-mouthed you. She kept Aunt Sophie from burning you in effigy in Hyde Park every evening at dusk. And you went from party to party, and the horses, and the race fixing, while we cowered and tried to make it all right between us, while Mum collapsed a little more every day. We heard about it all from our school friends before we saw the papers. Mum wouldn't let us see the tabs, wouldn't have them in the house. So Alex and I bought them, snuck them home so we could see your face. Do you know what it did to us to see our father like that? To me? To be identified instantly with you because I was your little clone. Did you care?" The voice of an old protocol instructor sounded in Eddie's head, reminding him that a gentlemen did not raise one's voice except when one's honor was at stake. There was one lesson learned.

Malcolm's head was tilted back, eyes fixed on the ceiling. Eddie could tell he was listening because of the nearly imperceptible wincing as the angry words rolled over him. "What did it do to you? Come on, don't be shy now."

"You were my hero. You had a long way to fall. You managed, in the end. But I didn't want to believe anything bad about you, even when it was right in front of my eyes." He tried for nonchalant. "Nothing more than a silly little boy missing his father. Prince trapped in a fairy tale with the castle's resident dragon slayer gone."

It was hard to talk around the lump in his throat, but he went on. He willed Malcolm to look him in the eye. Needed him to finally understand. "I thought you'd come back, ride up on a white horse. You even had a white horse. I had this fantasy you'd gallop through the reporters outside the palace and shout up for Mum, for all of us, and make it right. I thought you could make it right." It was a new experience, knowing every word Eddie said hurt his father. He had dismissed people, said cutting things in the heat of the moment, but never before had he wielded sincerity in front of him like a flaming sword. "I don't know if I can ever forgive you for killing my hero."

Malcolm made a pained, choked noise, shutting his eyes. Eddie wanted to. Every bit of this conversation was like dragging both of them across a bed of nails. But he felt like they were in this together now. Determined to see it through. Eddie to say it, and him to listen.

"I never would have expected you to be up on a pedestal forever. You're a person, you're allowed to have flaws, hell, but I wish... I wish I could have kept you a little longer," he said, feeling suddenly shy. "That we all could have. You were such a fucking bastard the instant you had the opportunity. Were we holding you back from your ultimate evolution into a complete idiot?"

That terrible sound again. The sheen of tears on Malcolm's cheeks was somehow frightening, like so much rain down the car window that it became impossible to make out anything beyond it, horrible and fascinating. He started to bring his hand up to cover his face, but gripped the fabric over his elbow instead. He was doing it on purpose, Eddie realized. Forcing himself to let Eddie see.

"I have often thought you were what kept me from becoming that worthless man for as long as I did," Malcolm said, at length, each breath through his nose an intentional decision. *Why now,* Eddie thought. *Why are you doing this now.* He wanted to leave, flee into the night, away from what he hadn't expected. It wasn't satisfying to see Malcolm laying himself bare, it was awful. *Stupid, stupid, in over your head.*

"You were the one I got up in the night for. I'm not even sure how that happened. We had all that staff, d'you know, I don't think I ever so much as changed a nappy for Arthur. But you hated sleeping. You'd lie there, awake, then stand there, when you learned to stand, so judgmental of us for keeping you penned in when you so clearly had things to do. I looked in on all of you at night, when we'd get back. Half the time I was probably on a bit of something, but I'd check and there you'd be. Awake. Looking at me with those accusing eyes. Like mine.

"I'm convinced Arthur held me in contempt from the day he was born. He was Victoria's. The instant heir. Her creature. I had no part in it besides the contribution of genetic material. Alex..." A shadow passed over his face. "Alex made it easy on me. She only wanted my attention. But you were my familiar. You were the one who had to be minded, but you could sit and listen for hours, copying me. My miniature partner in crime. You were the one who needed direction from me. My *son*." He wiped his cheek with the back of his hand all curled over itself, like a child's. "I knew how to look like a good father," Malcolm said. "I didn't know how to be one."

"Dad—"

"Don't feel sorry for me. You've been so consistent, don't

take after me now." Malcolm did look at Eddie then, grim twist to his mouth. "Look at you. We're all aged prematurely by our parents. My father had a mistress my whole life. They had two children together. He'd go there on the weekends, play house with his other family, watch his good son play in footie matches."

Eddie stared, another shot to already bruised ribs. "Did Grandmother know?"

Malcolm laughed. Hollow and bitter. "Of course she knew. I didn't, for years. And then it made so much sense. He called me by another name sometimes, and I didn't know why. I wasn't the good son, you see. Merely the legitimate one."

"You have a brother?"

"And a sister."

"Did you ever meet them?"

"I did. You did, too. At your grandfather's funeral. Do you remember me picking you up? You were eight."

Eddie did remember. All that black. So many umbrellas. "I knew I was much too old for it."

"I picked you up so I wouldn't have to shake his hand. We could have shared something, if we were born in another country to other parents. His life couldn't have been a picnic. But I supposed, as people in pain often do, that protecting myself was brave instead of cowardly, and I used my confused, upset son as a human shield." Malcolm winced. "It's not restricted to my children. I'm a bastard to everyone."

"God, Dad." Eddie couldn't quite laugh, but he managed a watery, staccato burst that might do in a pinch. Which this certainly was.

"I know. I know. After that—the drugs, your mother, every-thing got worse. I didn't have anything to hold on to. It didn't seem fair. And, I was just turned forty, obviously a disaster. So how much easier to… vanish." He sighed, looking lost. "Heart-felt as it might be, I can't bring myself to insult us both with an apology. It's paltry. It would imply that an apology *could* fix the unforgivable. That's not what you deserve. And after all this I still think I know about what you deserve, because I'm your father. Which is why I made myself a human shield for you yesterday evening. Thus the biological imperative makes fools of us all."

Eddie picked the lion up. Ran his fingers over its ears. "I shouldn't be comforted by hearing all that. I shouldn't confide."

"I've spoken quite enough. If you'd like a turn."

For a moment he wanted it. Saw himself settling in. And perhaps there would be time, now. Someday. "Not... not tonight." Malcolm's barely restrained hopefulness pulled at him. "I'm not forgiving you. But I am sorry about what you're about to go through. Sorry it was necessary."

Malcolm's smile cut a little deeper into one cheek. "At least I have the satisfaction of knowing I did it to myself." A chill spread through Eddie at how much sense that made inside his own head. But Malcolm was still talking. "I was protected for far too long by sleeping with the enemy. Helena and I... there was only one way for that to end. But it was in a good cause. My sins in exchange for your protection. I'm your father. It's what I am supposed to do. There is no hurt done to me in defense of you that can't be wiped away. At least, that's how it seems to me. Forgiven or not."

The urge to understand the truths that had created his life overwhelmed him, and Eddie couldn't help but ask:

"I know what you said in the interview. But... why did you choose her? Why did you leave us?" The words were soft, and Eddie thought he might be crying as he asked.

"How can I answer in a way that will satisfy you? The addiction, the infidelity—I was compromised in so many ways. But I was incapacitated by pride and desolation. Inclination, if you like. I am a vain man. And I failed. I was convinced—and with a wrenching feeling of relief—that there was only one way out. Only one way to do the right thing. Of course there were other ways. I refused to see them. The disease, you know. But once that was under control... I had already failed *so* completely. I couldn't see the way back. Couldn't see asking for forgiveness. Can't even do that now. My imagination failed me, and I failed the rest of you. Round and round we go."

"Do you really regret it?"

"Every day."

"Well, that's a start."

As THE CAR PULLED AWAY, Malcolm stood at the window, watching. Left alone, for the second time in a night. Leave and be left, he thought, was a punishing destiny to bring on oneself. Or one's children. *I had already failed so completely. I couldn't see the way back.* His own words echoed in his head.

Round and round we go.

22

Gwen and Maddy were guests at Sandringham over Christmas, a month and a half after the interview. Reports surfaced that one of the largest apartments in Kensington Palace was undergoing extensive renovation. But it wasn't until a Tuesday afternoon early in February that the Lord Chamberlain announced Eddie and Gwen's engagement from the Palace of St. James.

The happy couple walked in and stood in front of the great fireplace in the receiving room for a photocall. They faced a sea of cheering journalists and photographers held at bay by a red velvet rope. Gwen's dark plum, scoop neck gown set off the Kensington engagement ring glittering on her finger. Twelve small diamonds surrounded a brilliant central opal, set in 24-karat gold. It had been Eddie's grandmother's engagement ring. When Mary and Alexander were falling in love during World War II, Alexander went hunting for a ring in the odds and ends of his own grandmother's jewelry box, so that he wouldn't have to wait to propose. Later, Mary consulted Queen Hélène's diaries and discovered that Eddy commissioned the ring for her during their secret courtship in Paris in the 1880s.

Victoria had choked up when she put the box into Eddie's hands. "She loved it more than anything, said she didn't want to be buried with it," Victoria told him. They had been standing in Victoria's bedroom, the morning before Gwen and Maddy arrived for Christmas. "She wanted it to go on into the world."

Now, Gwen took his arm as they'd practiced, resting her hand where the ring could be very clearly seen. Eddie wore dark trousers, a white shirt, and a matching waistcoat. His pocket square and tie had hints of purple in the stripes to complement her dress. They smiled and smiled. Cameras rolled, and the constant tide of flashes got more intense when the floor was opened for questions. The BBC went first.

"Gwen, how does it feel to be marrying your very own Prince Charming?"

Gwen laughed, leaning into Eddie's side. "I'm marrying my best friend. What else could I ask for?"

Eddie smiled down at her, almost missing the next question.

"Eddie, you've given away your grandmother's ring! What's Arthur supposed to do when it's his turn?"

"Pistols at dawn, possibly. No, honestly, Arthur's been so supportive. He's already volunteered to patrol London airspace during the ceremony. Even offered to wear his dress uniform while he does it."

Gwen poked him in the side. The reporters laughed. The questions continued in an unstoppable, heady rush, all about when (April) and whether Malcolm would have a role (yes) and if Madeline was looking forward to moving into Kensington Palace (already trying to decide between a woodland fairy or pirate theme for her bedroom). One of the last was directed to Gwen, asking how she felt about what came next.

"We're excited, of course, but it's very intimidating going into wedding planning. I'm sure you lot will tell us if we get anything wrong, won't you?" The press laughed, as they were meant to. That she had already established a professional camaraderie with them boded very well.

ARTHUR TURNED off the live feed of the photocall and left his empty flat. A few minutes later he was walking through the public spaces in Kensington Palace, down the staircase his great-great-great-great-grandmother hadn't been allowed to descend alone when she was the heir to the English throne, a girl under others' control, doing her best to survive. This landing was where she'd seen Albert for the first time. Arthur looked a little bit like him. He took the stairs at a brisk pace for Victoria the First.

No tours had been scheduled for today, so he didn't have to worry about gawkers as he wandered the halls, feeling like a ghost in his faded t-shirt and jeans. There would be a throng of people outside by the time he left for the celebratory dinner Sophie was hosting at Clarence House tonight, and he was grateful to be avoiding the spotlight a little bit longer. *But at what cost?* That voice sounded a lot like Group Captain Miles.

Without giving it a second thought, Arthur slipped back to the private areas of the palace. Apartment 3 beckoned. He glanced at the large brass number, and remembered insisting on being hoisted up when he was small to trace it with chubby fingers. As he touched it now, the unlocked door swung open, and in he went.

The air smelled of fresh paint and plaster. The walls were bare, the guest furniture gone, rooms ready to accommodate the soon-to-be-married couple, the ready-made little family. He and Eddie had lived there with their parents before Grandfather had died, shaking their lives like a snow globe, changing everything.

Apartment 3 might be silent, anonymous, and uninhabited for now, but it lived in Arthur's memory as drenched in light, the stage set for boisterous games with his baby brother and colorful parties thrown by his beautiful young mother and father. He remembered Mary holding him on her hip and explaining how he was related to the faces immortalized in the cacophony of silver-framed photographs gracing the piano and decorating the walls. His grandparents often joined them for dinner and drinks. Arthur had been allowed to stay up on those nights—Victoria's parenting style had a traitorously modern air about it—and he remembered sitting under the dining room table, using Swarovski crystal figurines to trace stories of epic adventure in the paisleys and vines of the antique, hand-knotted Indian rugs.

He climbed the stairs to the third floor. The stairway took a sharp turn along a windowed landing and he sat down on the mauve carpet with a pattern of deep gold filigrees that persisted up here, despite at least half a century of heavy wear. Outside the window, leafless trees gave the gardens a tattered air around the edges.

Arthur, fighter pilot, techno-geek, future king, loved gardens. The ones outside Kensington Palace were his sanctuary, even though the most terrifying and formative event of his life occurred there.

He had been three on that particular summer day. Only just old enough to remember everything. A rare afternoon alone with Mummy, teatime waiting in a picnic hamper on one corner of a large checked blanket. They watched at the clouds together, pointing out shapes. She read to him from a picture book about a pig and pancakes, the suspense of the book forever linked to the feel of warm denim under his hands as he put creases in her long, tiered skirt. They'd gotten up to look at flowers, her telling him their names and letting him pet them. "Gently, gently," she told him. "How would you feel if someone came up and pulled on you?" He was agreeing that it wouldn't be very nice when his childhood ended.

There was a man yelling. Three loud popping noises. He didn't know what they were until years later when he watched an action movie for the first time and threw up at the sound of a gunshot. His mother's arms suddenly around him, dragging him up, too tight, he cried out because it hurt, and then the world was bouncing and moving much too fast. He stared at the man with the black stick in his hand racing at them. Arthur didn't know whether to cry or not. This had never happened before. Time went so slowly as he watched more men, men in the black trousers and black polo shirts who were forever at the edges of his days, converge on the man with the strange thing in his hand. Another pop, and that man tripped on the picnic basket where they'd been a moment ago and went flying through the air into a flower bed. *How would you feel*, Arthur thought to himself. He never picked a flower again.

Mummy didn't stop running until they were inside the house. She still held him, so tight he couldn't even squirm. She didn't loosen her grip or sit down, pacing back and forth in a hallway where there weren't any windows, clutching him, their protectors around them. Her hands shook when she stroked his hair, lips pressed to the side of his head as one of the men in black told her sharp words that Arthur didn't know—*Critical condition. Custody. Accomplice.* He only sniffled when he thought of the picnic basket all kicked in on the grass.

His father explained what happened to him as soon as he got there, prying him away from Victoria with an arm around each of them in order to do it. "There was a bad man who wanted to hurt Mummy, but she grabbed you and got out of there quick as a shot. She was a hero, and you were too. You did everything exactly right."

"What a good little soldier you were," was what he remembered Grandfather saying, when they were all at Buckingham

Palace for the night. Arthur wasn't so much allowed to stay up as Victoria refused to let him out of her sight, so he was tucked under a blanket on a sofa in his grandparents' living room. He could see his Mummy tucked into Daddy's side on another couch, still in her grass-stained skirt and loose white blouse from the morning. It made him feel a little better to know where she was. Grandfather, taller than everyone, went down on one knee so they were eye to eye. "Didn't cry once. Mummy's little soldier."

Arthur nodded. He reached out and closed his hand around his grandfather's family signet ring. It was a game they had. Arthur grabbed the ring, and Grandfather would cover Arthur's hand with his own. But tonight, his grandfather shocked him by taking off the ring and closing it in Arthur's tiny fist. "A medal for valor under fire, your royal highness."

That same ring was on his finger now, almost thirty years later. He always had it somewhere on his person, either on his hand when he was on the ground or on the chain of his dog tags when flying. He missed his grandfather, the King, the man who had taken time out of his busy schedule to bring his little grandson back into the garden after it became obvious a week or so after the attack that Arthur was avoiding the outdoors at all costs.

"You've got to make a home for yourself in the frightening places," Alexander told him, bent over so that he could hold Arthur's hand. "You have to face the scary things, even when you don't want to. That way they'll never hurt you." Arthur listened, and he went outside, and he made a home for himself in the seats of fighter planes that went quick as a shot and veered wildly, where the popping noises he associated with the scariest moment in his life were normal and aimed at him with a frequency hidden from the press and his own family. Where sometimes he caused them. Where sometimes he was the bad man with the trigger in his hand.

He liked to think his grandfather would be proud of him. Alexander made a lot of time in the last year of his life for his grandson, who loved nothing more than running around after him, signet ring bouncing heavily on a chain around his neck. Arthur wondered now if Alexander passed his ring on because he already knew he was dying.

Duty. Responsibility. The knowledge that sacrificing one's life for one's country might be necessary. Alexander had been as willing to make that choice as any soldier, and had fought to do his part in wartime. Arthur had, too.

Arthur could feel Kensington Palace lurking around him, affectionate and forbidding. His official residence had been Buckingham Palace during his military service. But now, because he couldn't be what he had been, what he had *wanted* to be, he was here again.

He wished he could call Group Captain Miles. The people he trusted, looked to, were going to die off one by one until it was only him left, with more and more responsibility, duty, and sacrifice than he knew how to handle. It was crushing. And for once, knowing his brother was announcing his engagement to the only woman Arthur ever thought about loving, he let it crush him right down to his knees. Having it happen on a third-story landing on a pleasant winter afternoon instead of somewhere dramatic like the center of Westminster Cathedral or the courtyard of Buckingham Palace in the pounding rain yet another example of the unbelievably prosaic quality of his extraordinary life.

Kings didn't kneel. They might take a knee for a woman, some chivalrous idea coming down the ages that no power on earth was greater than that of passionate, romantic devotion. A nice story. The mauve carpet pricking through his jeans reminded him too much of funerals, and he shifted so he was sitting on the landing, lying back and crossing his hands over his stomach. He felt hidden, almost like he was a kid again.

He heard the click of dress shoes coming through the house below him. Expecting it to be his private secretary, he didn't get up. Michael had seen him in much more compromising positions over time, after all. The person who climbed the stairs was the very last person he expected to see.

Eddie regarded him for a moment, and then shrugged, sitting down and lying back as well, so that they were nearly shoulder to shoulder, looking up at the decorative molding.

"Big day," Eddie offered, sounding less like a confident, charming prince, and more like a little brother not sure if he was wanted. Arthur knew Eddie wasn't wanted, but he couldn't think of how to dismiss him without it looking suspicious.

"Where's Gwen?"

"She's at my place. Wants a bit of a break before dinner. Isn't it fun having all the parents together?"

"You're sure she's all right? She's never been on the receiving end of a press conference before, and—"

"I didn't abandon her the minute the cameras were turned off," Eddie said, irritation bleeding through his voice. "Do you actually think I'd be callous to her?"

"You are putting her through this in the first place." In the back of Arthur's mind he knew this was a bad idea, a dangerous path to go down, but he was sometimes a bad man. "Not sure that's what anyone needs."

"How long are you going to keep this up?" Eddie's voice shook. Arthur could see his fingers clenched together, knuckles white. "We're engaged to be married, why are you treating me like I'm imprisoning her in a dungeon? She said *yes*. She didn't have to say yes."

"Because she chose you." Arthur spoke so softly he could barely hear himself, and hoped Eddie hadn't. But there was nothing wrong with his brother's hearing—nothing at all.

"What?" Eddie struggled up to his elbows. "What did you say?"

Arthur wanted to say it. Just once. One time. Then he could be all right. He shut his eyes. He wanted to enjoy it.

"I'm in love with her," he said. "I'm in love with her, and she chose you." The aching relief at finally speaking the words aloud rushed through him. He opened his eyes to find Eddie looking at him, stricken.

"Arthur, I didn't—why didn't you *say* anything? I wouldn't have… How long—? Why didn't you say anything to *her?*"

He shrugged miserably. The carpet ripped a hole in his t-shirt farther open. "Gwen never made a secret of hating the circus. Held it in contempt, practically. And then she was gone. How do you tell someone something like that across an ocean and a continent when you're both teenagers? I almost said something to her during school, during that party in Scotland she flew out for, but that was during the mess with Catriona."

At first he looked at the ceiling, out the window, anywhere but Eddie's face, washed out beneath the subtle makeup he'd worn for the cameras. He sat up so they could talk properly, crossing his legs, leaning his forearms on his knees. Eddie mirrored him immediately, trousers showing dust from the renovation on what was, impossibly, supposed to be his home in a few months. Eddie, fastidious, impeccably turned out Eddie, didn't seem to care. That, more than anything else, drove home to Arthur that this was important. It hadn't seemed so a few minutes ago, more like whining, if Arthur were honest. Eddie's single-minded attention convinced him otherwise. So he began to talk.

Arthur didn't know when he first started to like Catriona Lewis, an elegant blonde who won dressage contests on her father's horses and read Jane Austen novels because she liked the way it made her look. During their first conversation at university, her arch, friendly demeanor suggested that she knew he was the Prince of Wales, but had decided not to let it bother her. When he brought it up during their first date, her response to him was straight from *Pride & Prejudice*. "You are a gentleman, I am a gentleman's daughter. So far, we are equals." She immediately drew him out, laughing at his jokes and inviting confidences. It felt like he could trust her.

She was possessive of him around other girls. She wanted to be involved in his life. His name was Arthur Wales at university, a mere mister like most of his classmates, and his professors affected a studied nonchalance about the whole thing. It made him feel his skin was on too tight, like they were all playing pretend for his benefit at the same time as he was grateful to them. Catriona made everything go more smoothly so that he wouldn't have to, all the while being an excellent date in any circumstance. He almost invited her home any number of times, but something stopped him. At the party in Wales celebrating his investiture as Prince of it, when he saw Gwennie Shelton-Leigh for the first time in three years, he finally knew what.

"We kissed that night," he admitted, back in the present. "Gwen and I. Up on the battlements." The memory of sharp cold on the Welsh coast, his plaid flannel shirt no barrier at all after he insisted she take his navy blue jumper. Gwen hadn't objected that hard. She swam in it, the sleeves falling over her hands. The dyed turquoise stripe in her hair glowed in the moonlight. "I don't know what possessed me. Or her." He trailed off. "One thing led to another, and we kept choosing to keep going. My hands were shaking the whole time. I was twenty-four, and not all that inexperienced if it comes to that, but... I don't know. It was special.

"I told Catriona in the morning, wracked with guilt as I was, and she acted like it was nothing, told me she didn't mind, that she was a little surprised that it came up so soon and to please remember that she expected me to be discreet. Then she tried to give me a blowjob."

Eddie slapped his hands over his mouth to stop his sudden laugh, and Arthur shook his head in embarrassed recollection.

"I actually went with it for a minute. I couldn't think of what else to do, but then I asked her why on earth she wasn't upset, and she got this strange look on her face and said why should she be upset? Why should she care as long as I was loyal in public and didn't drag her through it like my father had my mother. She was so clinical. Sitting back on her knees with her hand on my—it was a farce. I told her it was over and you know, I still remember what came over her. Like she'd been rehearsing it. She actually had tears in her eyes as she told me she would still be there for me if I decided to grow up into a man rather than a spoiled prince, and then she sashayed out of the room. She even looked back at me all come-hither. I was too stunned to think, trousers and pants around my ankles and all."

He got lost in the long-buried humiliation and confusion. "I was so naive. She'd been building a power base with me at the center from the beginning. I was so grateful to be away from the circus, I forgot that I bring it with me wherever I go."

"For what it's worth," Eddie said, "I think you proved you were a grown man with that. A spoiled prince would have taken her at face value and gone with it. Why did you ever get back together with her?"

"Habit? Desperation? It didn't work any better the second or third time around. She married Henry Percy, you know, the viscount. I think she's doing all right for herself."

"So what was different about Gwen?" Eddie asked.

"Catriona pretended not to care about me being, well, you know," Arthur said, thinking it over as he spoke. "But of course she did. She could feel the crown on her head. Gwen truly didn't care. To her it was like another limb I was born with. It doesn't impact anything because it's who I am, she doesn't consider it when she talks to me."

"She grew up in it with us, a bit," Eddie agreed.

"Exactly. It has presence, but no weight. Except it has all the weight in the world, because she doesn't want it. Not for herself, not for Madeline. She'd rather have you, and that little margin of freedom. I don't blame her."

"Arthur, I had no idea," Eddie said urgently. "I would never have gone through with it, wouldn't have done *any* of it if I knew."

"Known what? She prefers you, anyway." Arthur tried not to sound bitter, but lost the battle. "She offered. Suggested it herself."

"I did sound pathetic that night, to be fair," Eddie said. They stared at each other, dazed, as if this conversation made any sense at this moment. Like small talk at a funeral, Arthur thought. He hated small talk at funerals.

"Pathetic is going around," Arthur said, almost grumbling.

"I'm so sorry," Eddie said, green eyes fixed on him with unnerving intensity. He looked like he might cry. Arthur leaned forward and awkwardly touched his knuckles to the back of Eddie's wrist.

"It's not your fault," he said. "You couldn't have known."

"I should have," Eddie insisted. "You're my brother. Bloody hell." He thrust his hands into his hair, blinking in muted surprise when it was shorter than he expected. Arthur was filled with a rush of affection for his brilliant little brother, who knew—sometimes literally, as a child—when to make a splash, when to draw attention away from his mother or his siblings at a bad moment. That was the reason, Arthur had to remind himself, that Eddie had done all of this in the first place. To keep the spotlight away from perceived flaws in Arthur. To make sure no one questioned Arthur's nonexistent dating history, Eddie squired women about town, letting Arthur be the lonely victim of heartbreak and disappointment, a look that never, as far as Britain's endless supply of teenagers was concerned, went out of style.

"This bloody life," Arthur said, resentment a stone in his stomach. He rubbed the back of his neck. "Please don't tell her."

"That's ridiculous," Eddie shot back immediately. "She has to know."

"Of course she doesn't. I don't want her walking around pitying me while married to you. That would be mortifying."

"I don't want you to be unhappy."

"It's too late for that," Arthur said. "I never would have dragged her into this life unless she was willing to be here. It turned out she was willing. Just… with you. That's all. I'm going to be king, you know, Edward. I can't have everything."

Eddie took Arthur's hand. There wasn't any more to say. His fingers brushed against their grandfather's ring.

23

Weeks later, Eddie stood in the Wedgwood showroom, flicking through an album of options for his formal dinnerware set on an iPad while he waited for Arthur and Gwen. His conversation with Arthur should have changed things, he thought. It *ought* to. He had the nagging sensation that the only person who could make that happen was him. But as a numb, paper-thin slice of a human being, he didn't know how to manage it.

He had tried to curtail Arthur's involvement in the planning, but it turned out Arthur was unbelievably stubborn, and wouldn't be put off by a little thing like being in love with the bride. Arthur had become Gwen's ally in the lead-up to the wedding, as Eddie gradually faded away. He could drag himself into the present for short bursts, but it exhausted him. Easier, then, to leave the decision-making to people who were more enthusiastic about it with each other than either were with him. Sophie made the occasional contemplative remark about wondering exactly how many of them were getting married, but he ignored her. She had done enough.

Public approval skyrocketed after the engagement

announcement. The country loved wedding planning, the monarchy—when they were putting on a show—and being able to ignore Eddie's queerness. According to certain royal commentators, even those who had been halfway supportive at the time, marrying a woman was clearly "proof" there had been no truth to those "ugly rumors" from last year. Give him a beautiful fiancée with the right combination of secondary sexual characteristics and a spectacle of a wedding, and evidently no scandal could touch him. It made him feel like screaming. He retreated further into himself, and they all had to make do.

Gwen walked in wearing a turtleneck sweater dress under a maroon Burberry lace trench coat. Her black tights had a subtle dusting of stars where they disappeared into her high gray boots, striking the perfect balance between elegance and whimsy that was quickly becoming her trademark. Eddie greeted her with an expression that might be a smile. At least he could still do that. She kissed his cheek.

"Arthur here yet?" she asked.

"On his way from a meeting," he said, helping her take off her coat. "Take a look, they've done up some beautiful ideas for us."

"How am I supposed to choose?" she asked.

"I don't know," Eddie said. "But we're getting service for a hundred and twenty, and the family still occasionally uses George the Fourth's china, so no pressure there."

When Arthur finally arrived, he joined Gwen at the iPad and Eddie took to wandering the shop. Watching them together made him feel a disturbing combination of guilt and rage. He hadn't told Gwen what Arthur said the day of their engagement. Arthur involved himself in as many wedding details as he could. He and Gwen had a dozen jokes and catchphrases that were opaque to Eddie, even though he knew he'd been in the room for the advent of most of them.

Eddie wanted to yell at them. He wanted to fix it, from somewhere down the deep hole he'd fallen into. But the sky was so very far away.

THE EVENING BEFORE THE WEDDING, he got a text from Tonya, asking him to drop by the Centre if he could. He stared blankly at his phone, wondering how she could think he would have a spare minute to breathe after the rehearsal (in Buckingham Palace, not Westminster) and the dinner. There were so many receptions, so many guests, places to be, things to keep up with, and as he ran through the litany of obligations, something inside him snapped. Five minutes later, he was walking out the door with instructions to his private secretary to make his excuses to his family.

As Harris drove through London, Eddie slumped in the passenger seat with his hand over his face.

"What's on your mind?" he asked, finally, tired of Harris stealing quick looks at him.

"Are you all right, sir?"

"Just tired, after all that," Eddie said. "Lots to do, even though honestly, I didn't have much to do with it. Nothing like Gwen or Arthur. They've been wonderful throughout all this mess. I'll be happy to have it all done with, so maybe we can settle in." He spoke like he was going down a checklist of acceptable feelings. There was vicious satisfaction in doing everything properly. What a good boy. Maybe Harris didn't believe him, but that wasn't what Harris got paid for.

When they arrived at the Centre, Tonya was there to greet him as usual. She reached for him as soon as she saw his face. Her grip anchored him, reminding him of everything he was supposed to be doing—and he held on tighter.

"I have a little surprise for you," she said. She pulled him down the corridor with both his hands in hers, like they were contra dancing in a BBC Austen adaptation. She pushed open the door to the common room, and a roomful of applause greeted him.

Such naked, unabashed approval beaming at him from several dozen different faces shocked him. He could hardly tell who he was looking at. Eddie recognized the slope of a nose on one, the dusting of piercings on another.

"Your kids wanted to give you a send-off," Tonya told him.

"My kids," Eddie repeated. The empty sensation where his heart was supposed to be gave way to something wider, lighter. There was Ellie, he'd helped get her rabbit back from an abusive boyfriend's place. Fergus, he'd gone with him back to the community pool where he'd been raped and sat there while Fergus swam lap after lap, like he could outpace history. Jessica, Priya, Ahmed, Hamish. And Mikhail, some color back in his cheeks. Galen stood next to him, arm around his waist. Mikhail leaned into it as if he belonged there. Some of them were people he'd counseled in his years volunteering at the Centre, but most were ones he'd gone on missions for. Harris cracked a rare smile, as affected as Eddie, and it made him think of Isaac. These were his victories, too. They belonged to him as much as Eddie. That was fine. Eddie belonged as much to Isaac as he did to himself. He knew that now.

They all crowded around, handed him a piece of sheet cake that might have been from the Sainsbury's down the road. It tasted better to him than the meringue tartlets served for dessert earlier tonight. He accepted their congratulations and listened to story after story about how things were better now. How he'd made such a difference. Smiling felt like less effort, but on the heels of that came the threat of tears. He wanted to remind them it had been Isaac, that Eddie himself was super-fluous, that Isaac was the one who *did* it all, made it possible for Eddie to be unafraid. He tried to bury it. Tried to keep the door shut on all those memories. He focused on enjoying watching so many people who were clearly happier now. Galen and Mikhail were speaking to Harris in low voices, Mikhail's face open and cheerful and downright conspiratorial.

Tonya had a small wrapped package for him. "For you and your lovely Gwen," she said, kissing his cheek. "You'll be all right," she told him. "If this is what you want to do, you'll be all right." *It's not*, he wanted to say. But he couldn't. It would mean too much to acknowledge this wasn't a fairy tale ending. Tonya knew, anyway.

"We'd like to take you out," Mikhail said, startling him. "It's all right with Harris, and you've already fucked off. Another while won't make a difference." It was easier to agree than to face going back to the palace.

They brought him on foot to the river walk beside the Thames, a few city blocks away from the Eye, chatting all the while. Eddie heard about their cat, their plans to start a tattoo shop, their idea to host family dinner with other queer uni students once a week. They arrived at a large trampoline. On either side of it were a couple of struts in a V shape. A harness and some thick bungee cords were attached to the top of each strut. A rough-faced man leaned against the trampoline with his arms folded. As soon as they walked up, he let loose with a barrage of Lithuanian at Mikhail, who fired back in kind. The man bent to untie his sneakers. The details of this operation were lost on Eddie until Mikhail turned back to him.

"D'you want to? It's our wedding present. You get in and jump, and Pavel yanks down on the cords so you go flying up. It's a good place to think." Mikhail looked suddenly bashful, like it might not be enough, and Eddie felt his mouth stretch into a real, grateful smile. He nodded. He didn't want to disappoint his friend.

So Eddie removed his shoes and his blazer. He unwound his scarf, and in the semi-darkness, he stepped onto the smooth, woven surface of the trampoline. The lights from the building behind him cast a golden glow. He strapped in facing the river. The Houses of Parliament and Big Ben loomed before him. He shivered.

At first, he got the timing wrong, and couldn't quite get the hang of when to use the extra power from Pavel throwing himself at the cords to shoot Eddie higher, and when to come down on his own two feet. But once he did—

Eddie flew.

On shouted instructions from Mikhail, he discovered tumbling in midair, using the energy to land harder on the trampoline, giving Pavel more force to propel him even higher.

He kept his eyes open at first, each time he leapt into the dark sky. The lights of London were the only stars he needed. The Eye turned gently on its pins, designed as it was to be continuous, unbroken as British history itself. Eddie was a notably significant, and yet a small part of that, all at the same time.

What was his duty here? Was it to his family, or himself? Were those two things different? He didn't want to trap Gwen and Arthur into a life of useless yearning, not when they so clearly wanted each other, when they had a *chance*. And if he was the only one who could see the way out, didn't he have a responsibility to them to take it? He didn't want to punish them all with another divorce, another cloud, more rubble to clear away.

Eddie had listened to the subtext and occasional outright bungling comments from professors and politicians. He knew that many of them preferred him to Arthur, as future king material. He showed the interest, stayed in the public eye, he could navigate the social world. He had the deft touch. And here he was, thinking seriously of touching off a disaster. A barrel of gunpowder. Treason and plot. A Prince of Wales could not foment the unthinkable. But Eddie could.

The charming second son, the spare, the last resort. That man could do quite a bit, indeed.

And maybe it would bring Eddie some kind of peace. To make himself the villain of the piece as assuredly as his father ever had, to be ruined. Call off an international event, look like a heartless, selfish wastrel? Once he was that sort of villain, he could do anything. And his siblings could, too. There was more at stake than his reputation. And what did anyone want from them, in the end, but a good show?

It wouldn't get him what he wanted, in his heart of hearts. Some doors were made to stay closed. The crash of a rogue wave in his memory, hands on his rib cage to pull him up from drowning, his arms around a slender flame of a dancer in a dark nightclub—

All motion stopped, and he opened his eyes to find Mikhail and Harris holding him up as Pavel undid the harness. "You're crying," Mikhail said, and Eddie wiped his cheeks with the backs of his hands. His legs were jelly from the adrenaline of flying, his heart racing from what he was about to do.

24

E leven o'clock was ringing out from all those blasted clocks when Harris delivered him back to Buckingham Palace. They were all staying there the night before the wedding, as it made heading to the cathedral easier in the morning. Eddie couldn't help wondering if the rumors about escape tunnels dug out during the First World War were true. Jenny met him right inside the East Wing entrance. "Good evening, sir. Ms. Shelton-Leigh has asked to see you. She is waiting in the Queen Mother's study. She seems… agitated. And determined."

"Is everything all right?"

"As far as I know." Underneath her polished veneer there was a hint of irritation that she had no information to give him. "She spent some time with her guests this evening, then went upstairs to read to Miss Madeline and put her to bed. Then she asked me to intercept you on your return. Shall I let her know you're back?"

"I'll do it," Eddie said. "But thank you. For everything. You've gotten us through all this madness beautifully."

"Chin up," she said warmly. "You haven't become Groomzilla. I should say you've done rather well, considering."

"That 'considering' contains a multitude of sins," he said.

"And happily. If that's all?" At his nod, she tucked her iPad beneath her arm and retreated to the administrative offices, leaving him alone in the hallway. He watched her go. Eddie felt lighter, more human than he had in a very long time. He appreciated the job they'd all done keeping him in one piece, and resolved that it wouldn't be necessary any longer. He had work to do.

The Queen Mother's study had been Daniel Black's base of operations for many months before the interview, but the room was still unmistakably Mary's domain. The first thing Eddie saw when he walked in was the little *Nonsense 10p Extra* needlepoint pillow, stitched decades ago by one of her sisters. Mary's papers and diaries might be corralled into better order than they had ever been while she was alive, but the room still felt like a refuge.

How many times had he come in here, grabbed a book off the shelf, and put his feet up on the striped pink Chesterfield? Too many to count. He would have given anything to do so now. But Gwen was waiting for him. The sight of her in comfortable clothes tore at his heart, his guilt made of thorns. Against the odds, she had made a place for herself here, and he was about to take it away.

Gwen turned when the door swung open, her hands wrapped up tight in the cuffs of her loose white sweater. He felt an instant of relief that he couldn't see Mary's engagement ring on her hand. He had to tell her, this wonderful woman whom he loved, that—

"I can't marry you."

For one head-spinning moment he thought he'd blurted it out without meaning to. But then he saw Gwen's face. Determined, he remembered Jenny saying. She looked determined. And like a mirror of his own anxiety and shame.

"I know this is the worst time," she went on. "I can't believe it's taken me this long, but my head's been such a mess. I thought I could make it work, but I wasn't sure—not until tonight, and then you weren't here... Don't hate me."

Eddie offered his arms as he crossed the room, and she only hesitated for a moment before sinking into him.

"I could never," he said. "I'm so sorry I wasn't here. I haven't been here in a long time. That's part of what I wanted to talk to you about, but—no, don't cry, it's all right, I swear it's all right." He knew, at least intellectually, that it was not "all right," that "all right" had flown out the window several hours beforehand—apparently in multiple directions. But that didn't matter as much as the haunted pain in Gwen's eyes. It drowned out his own.

"I'm so sorry," she said, into his shirt.

"Please, please don't say that." He held her tightly. An edge of regret scraped along his spine that they didn't want each other enough, that they couldn't find a way. "You don't have anything to apologize for."

"I do. If you knew... I never should have agreed to any of this. I never should have come back to England," she said. "I can't believe I thought I'd get away with it."

"Gwen, what are you talking about? Get away with what?"

"Sit down, okay? I can't do this with you looming over me."

He sat down on the enormous sofa after all. Gwen crossed her arms and paced.

"I was so angry when I left England," she said. "At my family, at my father for dragging me across the world, my mother for letting him. I wanted to disappear, and then that awful thing with the topless pictures happened, so everyone found out I was your friend. They were constantly trying to get close. I got out of the habit of trusting anyone.

"The only person I talked to was Arthur. He gave me access to his private email server, and we started writing back and forth. I think he's the one who made those paparazzi photos go away. But emails were all we had, and whatever pictures of him I saw in magazines, a few times a year. He didn't feel quite real. More like a digital guardian angel than anything else. I did like him, and for a long time I thought he liked me. But we never talked about it, and he was linked to all sorts of women in the press, and we never talked about that either, and when he and Catriona Lewis got serious about each other…

"Sometimes you make a mistake and it's just the one thing," she said. She brought one of her hands to her mouth, lowered it with decisive finality, lifted it again a few seconds later. Eddie remembered her bitten nails from when they were teenagers. Her manicure caught the light from the lamp on the side table next to Eddie. The purples and reds in the stained glass shade reflected off the neutral enamel. "Either you can fix it or you can't, there are consequences either way, and then it's pretty much over."

Eddie nodded warily.

"I didn't make that kind of mistake," Gwen said. "I *thought* I made one mistake, but it turned out to be a dozen different mistakes, and they've all been multiplying exponentially for years. So here we are, on the brink of an international social incident, and it's all my fault."

"Gwen." Eddie leaned forward. "What did you *do?*"

"Maddy is Arthur's daughter."

Once, while learning to surf, a wave took Eddie under. First, the rushing in his ears spread throughout his body. The endless terror of not being able to breathe seemed far away, as if it didn't apply to him. He only snapped into full awareness when the water dragged him against the sand, an exposed conch shell gashing him across the chest. He still had the scar. This felt similar, except worse.

Every memory he had of Gwen, Maddy, and Arthur together over the last year appeared all at once as he looked for clues, signs. In retrospect, they were everywhere, down to the tilt of Maddy's head when she had a question. That was Arthur's. As were her eyes. The shape of her face. If he thought about it, under the wild colors in her hair, she looked like a Kensington.

Not merely any Kensington, either. "Good god," he whispered. "She's the heir." The sensation of dangerous weightlessness returned as repercussions and consequences clamored for his attention. His life was suddenly a sheaf of papers gone flying.

Gwen covered her mouth with one hand. Too late, he thought, dimly. No taking it back now.

"Who else knows?" he asked. His mind raced towards any number of inevitable catastrophes. Here was a scandal. More than a scandal. The next heir to the throne spirited away before birth and raised in a foreign country, kept secret from her family, from everyone? He got all the way to the constitutional crisis and a public outcry that would swallow them, before he could drag his eyes up. She had almost gone through with marrying him, when she *knew*, all along—

"Only you know."

Eddie's frantic calculations ground to a halt. She had carried it by herself. His heart ached, watching Gwen brace against whatever he might say next. She looked exhausted and defiant—and relieved. He knew how that felt, the release of finally *saying*. Of no longer being alone.

"It happened at his investiture, didn't it?"

She winced. "I thought we weren't that obvious."

"He did tell me something about it." Eddie neglected to mention how recently that had been. "And I can count."

Gwen covered her eyes with one hand. "I don't know if I should laugh or cry or what," she said. "I've never done this before."

He had to keep himself away from thinking about the ramifications, focusing on her as she told the real story of her daughter's conception for the first time.

"I was horrified at myself," she said, rubbing the sleeve of her sweater between her fingertips. "I flung myself back on a plane to California. He had a girlfriend, for God's sake. I told myself that girls must throw themselves at him all the time, I wasn't special, he wanted to celebrate his investiture and I was handy—"

"Gwen! Arthur would *never*—"

"You know how fucking cruel we can be to ourselves. And then when I found out I was pregnant... I didn't want what would happen next if I told the truth."

"Mother isn't Elizabeth of Russia," Eddie said, stung on behalf of his family. "No one would have taken her away from you."

Gwen gave him a dark look. "They would have seriously thought about it. Or what, marry me off to Arthur? That's a good look, forced to be the Queen of England as some kind of consequence for failed birth control. Who would believe it was an accident? How could I let him wonder, even for a second, if I'd done it on purpose? I couldn't do that to either of us, but I wanted to keep the pregnancy. It was all inevitable, after that." She settled onto the couch next to him and wrapped her arms around her knees. "My baby. My secret. It belonged to me. And, you know, the United Kingdom and the Commonwealth, potentially."

Eddie tipped his head against the back of the sofa. "Still

trying to get my head around that, if I'm honest. Christ, Gwen."

"Believe me. I know. When it turned out Maddy was a girl, I breathed a sigh of relief for a few years, but then Parliament went and declared that gender would be immaterial when determining succession. A victory for gender equality and a nightmare for me. I walked around in shock for days. And in shock because I was in shock, how was this my life?"

"It's a frequent plaintive cry from the East Wing," he said.

"I could have said something then, or any time. I know that. I kept thinking it would be fine. Arthur would marry someone else, have children, and I would have this secret all my life. But he kept not doing that. And Maddy was this happy, brilliant, wonderful child and I loved her, and I didn't want anything to change for her. There was always a good reason to keep lying. I got so far away from where revealing it felt like a possibility."

"I'm so sorry you didn't feel like you could come to me, to any of us. That you had to carry such a burden alone."

Gwen rubbed her eye with the hem of her sleeve. "I told myself I couldn't hide on the other side of the world forever, that it would be all right if I came back." she said. "I didn't mean to get involved with all of you again. I wanted to stay away. I was terrified someone would notice how much she looks like all of you, but it hasn't happened."

"The hair dye was a good choice," he said.

"Do you hate me?"

"Of course I don't," Eddie said, pressing his palms into his eyes. "I don't know *what* to make of you right now. Did you ever think maybe we wouldn't be complete ogres about it?"

"Once you're on the outside of this place, it is very hard to see yourself getting back in," Gwen told him. "And you know better than anyone what it's like to have a secret that keeps getting farther away from being told. You're willing to sacrifice all our lives to protect your family's image. I'm protecting my *daughter*."

"My family's image *is* my family," he said. It was a reflex, the last shout of a wrong man. "But it isn't. Tonight I realized I couldn't go through with it either." He took her hand before she could get it all the way up to her mouth. "We should never have gone into this. I was scared, and lonely, and heartbroken."

"But—why?" Gwen tilted her head. "When your body-guard left… was it him?"

Eddie laughed. A broken, joyless little sound at best.

"He joined my detail when I went to university. I was a teenager and, well, you've seen him. But that's not…" She had bared her soul and her secrets. She deserved honesty from him. "In my second year I was assaulted by someone I had been seeing."

"Oh, Eddie."

He couldn't look at her.

"It happened during a party. We snuck upstairs, and he pushed for more than we'd been doing, said… it doesn't matter. He went much further than I wanted. When I struggled, he hit me. Isaac tracked me down in time to… hear me protest. He slammed in, ripped my attacker off, and got me out. I was so shocked. Cored out. I can hardly tell you. I remember being taken to Windsor, given a physical exam. I didn't come out of my room for days. I couldn't face anyone emotionally. And logistically, I couldn't be seen in public until the bruises healed." Gwen gasped—he heard it, but he couldn't bear to stop now he'd started. "I refused to be without Isaac the entire time.

"They tried to separate us, but that didn't last long. I screamed when I woke up without him. He was the only safe place. The only one I trusted. We spent a week never out of arm's length, me in his arms more often than not. He told me things about his own past, helped me sort myself out. And, of course, I started seeing Tonya because of all that. That's why I decided to do work with survivors. Because most people don't have an Isaac.

"It bound us together. Not in a healthy way, perhaps, but I'm not sure we ever could have let go of each other, after. I was gone over him well before that. I don't know what it was, for him. Or if it was, for him."

Gwen put her hand on his. "I'm so sorry."

He did meet her eyes then, forcing himself to accept the sympathy. "Things got out of hand between us after the night-club bombing, but we decided that nothing could ever happen. That was right before I went after you."

"Oh, god, he walked in on us that night—is that why he left?"

"Probably. I don't blame him." Eddie tangled their fingers together, hesitantly. "Please forgive me, Gwen. I was looking for a way out. I didn't mean to hurt you. Or him."

She nodded. "What were you going to say, if I hadn't spoken first?"

Eddie sighed.

"I was out having an existentialist crisis earlier, real cliché night-before-the-wedding-behavior, but it suddenly looked so tawdry to me. So mean. I love you in every way that matters, except the one that would make marriage a good idea. And on this scale? I would be saying something about myself. The wrong thing. I'm in love with a man, but that's hardly the point. I intended to come out, someday. If not come out officially, then *be* out and let everyone draw their own conclusions. After those photos were leaked, I couldn't bear that. It felt like letting the enemy win. But, look, that doesn't matter in the long run. No one is going to care why I did it, or how, or when. We're all going to die eventually, why not be happy as we can now? But if I marry you, I cut myself—*both* of us—off from the possibility of future happiness. I would be surrendering to an unkind world, and dragging you down with me."

"Eddie, come on. You didn't hold a gun to my head." She scooted forward, hooking her legs over his lap and curling up against his side. The awkwardness of the last six months was pushed aside. In this moment, they needed to be friends again. Friends like they had always been, before expediency made them wonder if it wasn't something more. "We were both looking for the simple versions of our lives. Trying to live in the alternate universe where you're not in love with your ex-body-guard and I didn't have the Prince of Wales' secret baby. And even though this is a huge mess and there are millions upon millions of people looking forward to a wedding tomorrow morning that can't happen... right now, I feel better than I have in months. That has to be worth something."

"I think," Eddie said, taking her left hand and stroking a fingertip over her engagement ring, "that it's worth everything. What made you decide to tell me?"

"Maddy," Gwen laughed a little. "Like most of the times in my life when I come to definite conclusions. The two of us and Alex were checking over our outfits and jewelry for tomorrow, and Alex put the tiara I'm going to wear on Maddy. Playing dress-up, but with priceless historical artifacts, you know. So there she is, dancing around with Kensington jewels on, comfortable looking like a princess. Then there was a knock at the door."

She looked up, and the sadness in her eyes was like a punch to the chest. "It was Arthur. He said he wanted to check on us all before the big day. She barreled right into his legs to hug him, and it broke my heart.

"I told myself this was the best thing for her, being in her family without the structure or the responsibility of being directly in line for the throne. I told myself it was better for Arthur, not to stick him with a family he never asked for, or planned for. But I ended up in exactly the situation I wanted to avoid. I started thinking, what would it do to all of us if I came clean later and said no, wait, my daughter is the real heir? What would it do to her, and Arthur, and you, and whoever he ends up with, and their children? I can't keep pretending to be above all of this. I know what this life's done to your family over the years. How can I keep adding to that? I want her to have her family for real, and to know Arthur *as* her father. You've seen them together. They deserve that. I deserve it. Growing up, all I wanted was for my family to *look* right. But now? Whatever ridiculous shape my family is, I deserve to have it be honest."

"Gwen, I could marry you for saying all that." He put his arm around her. "But as it turns out, that would make me step-father to my niece, and I'm not sure how the Lord Chamberlain's office would draw that out on the family tree. Ow, don't hit me."

"You deserve it." She rested her head on his shoulder. Eddie felt more whole than he had in months. Years. But the decor downstairs came back to him, and his arm tightened around Gwen as she stiffened against his side. "Eddie... What do we do now?"

It felt like another rogue wave. Eddie couldn't help but remember coughing on his knees in the wet sand all those years ago. Strong arms had pulled him up, then. Scarred hands, crooked fingers. But that was a sense of loss for another time. He had more important things to do right now. Like panic. Panic was definitely first on the list.

25

E ddie got up to pace, the soles of his shoes slipping on the fine nap of the carpet like his socked feet had on the surface of the trampoline. He was still up in the air, and he knew it. One hand deep in a pocket, the other gripping the hair at the back of his head. *Focus. Assess the situation.*

"All right. What's our situation? What's our major problem right now?"

"I think it's the wedding in Westminster Abbey with one thousand, eight hundred, forty-three guests and international television coverage scheduled for tomorrow," Gwen said.

"Fucking hell, I want to lie down. Goodwill towards the family at an all-time high, that's an advantage though, isn't it?"

"Not if there isn't a marriage." Gwen shook her hands out. "I will not bite my nails. I will not."

Eddie stopped short. "You and I have been media darlings for months with Arthur." He rounded on her. "Do you love him?"

"Do I *what?*"

"We don't have time for a stirring rendition of *Fiddler on the Roof*. Are you in love with him?"

"How do I answer that question? He's Arthur. He's the father of my child. I don't know what he's thinking half the time, and I'm pretty sure I know him better than anyone."

"I'm pretty sure you do, too," Eddie said. "And you need to tell him about Maddy. And—think about it, you were already getting married tomorrow. What does one little tiny change in groom matter?"

"You have to be fucking kidding me. Didn't I *just* say I wanted things to be honest? Walking from one sham marriage into another—"

"We have one chance to fix this." Eddie dropped to one knee in front of her, putting his hands on her knees. "There's no going back from what we do tomorrow. Forget the past. Forget everything leading up to this moment that made you think you can't have what you want. Imagine you can. What does that look like? If it's shaped like my brother, even in silhouette, that changes everything."

GWEN SHUT her eyes while he spoke, clenching her hands into fists, manicured fingernails digging into her palms. Disappointments and joys blossomed in a kaleidoscope of memories pointed at this moment. This person she was right now. Unable to stay out of the Kensington orbit, even when she had the choice and all the reasons in the world to avoid them. Huddling in a supply closet eating ice cream cones with Arthur during a garden party in high summer. Sitting in their party clothes in the den, playing a racing game a few years later, too close together on the couch. The first time she knew she wanted to kiss him. All the times he materialized at her side during social functions, the stares and comments she could feel at her back, because she was the one the Prince of Wales came to get. The thrill of being on the inside, and the knowledge that somehow, some way, she'd pay for it. Deciding in the same moment she didn't care. When she couldn't bear it any more, running away to America after they made love and he tried to tell her he loved her. Taking him with her as best she could, anyway. The way he was with Maddy. The way he was with her, now. That hot feeling when he grinned at her over wedding planning, and the treacherous thread inside her, tugging, *what if... I wish...*

"This is absurd."

"I promise you, it isn't." Eddie watched her with such earnestness, she almost believed him.

"I had his baby, hid her for eight years, and then almost married his brother. How is he supposed to... how can we..." The thought of telling Arthur all that made her want a quick rescue.

"You have to talk to him tonight," Eddie said. The cant of his head and the urgency in his voice made her draw back.

"What aren't you telling me?"

"It's not my secret," Eddie told her. "It can't—I can't... oh, fuck." He regarded the molded plaster ceiling as if it might have answers he lacked. "He's been in love with you for years. He didn't want you to know. Remember when we were looking through those potential bride profiles, and he wouldn't show us his? You were in it. That was why." Now he really seemed worried. Given how her face must look, Gwen wasn't at all surprised.

"Excuse me?" The kaleidoscope inside her twisted, narrowed, until it was all shadows and a red, pulsing dot of light inside her mind. She stood up the way she had been taught in her recent bout of protocol classes—with care, grace, and attention to detail.

"What are you going to do?" Eddie asked.

"I don't know," she said, feeling very far away from herself. "But I might kill him. And then I'm going to very seriously consider killing you. How many secrets can a human body contain, Eddie? Aren't you full?"

He might have said something else, but she barely heard him. She left the room in a fog. Her feet made no noise in their shearling slippers. In some ways the palace felt like a boutique hotel, even in the family quarters. Lights on in the corridors no matter what time it was, footmen at the press of a button, 24-hour room service. She passed the suite of rooms she and Maddy were staying in tonight, before their move to Kensington Palace, to the apartment she had painstakingly redecorated with Eddie in the run-up to the wedding. And with Arthur. Constant Arthur, lurking at the edges of her life, never putting himself forward, but forever there.

She redid her ponytail as she walked, the familiar action enough to stop the endless spinning in her head. Nothing felt real. The adrenaline rush of telling her secret hadn't abated at all. And what did Eddie mean by *Arthur was always in love with her*.

It didn't take long to arrive at Arthur's old rooms. The little removable placard in its holder beside the door—*HRH Prince of Wales*—taunted her. She thought of Maddy, and her heart, and used the side of her fist to pound on the solid hardwood. It made a very satisfying noise, shaking in its frame. She wanted to do that to the man behind it, too.

He answered it himself, an edge of childhood fear banked in his icy eyes. That turned to confusion when he saw her.

"Gwen."

"Don't *Gwen* me," she said, pushing past him. Dark green walls and looming wooden cabinetry threw the edges of his sitting room into shadow in the low light. The room reminded her of a hotel suite, now that all his personal items were in boxes in his new flat at Kensington Palace. His new flat just down the hall from hers, come to think of it. The only item out of place was an untouched drink on the table beside his chair.

A black dress uniform hung on a clotheshorse, ready for tomorrow, crisp and pressed. Just waiting for Arthur to step into it and give it life, even though it looked like a funereal shadow at the moment.

Arthur, in a tight white undershirt, still in his suit trousers from the rehearsal dinner, was the only item that did not quite belong. He was barefoot, for one thing, despite the chill of the place. His hair stood on end in thick straw-colored peaks, some of it damp, as if he had recently shoved his head under a tap.

"What's wrong?" Arthur asked, closing the door gently, walking towards her, concern taking over everything. "Did Eddie do something? Are you all right? Is it Maddy?"

"It's all of that, you unbelievably selfish, cowardly jerk," she said. "How could you not tell me?"

"Tell you *what*?"

"That you're in love with me."

"I'm going to kill him." Arthur said. "Is he trying to get out of this at the last minute?"

"We both are. And I have dibs," she said. She couldn't remember ever feeling this pure weaponizing of all the fear she carried inside her.

"All my life," she began, and her voice cracked. She looked from the carpet—a louder geometric pattern here than in Mary's study, probably some designer's idea of masculinity becoming a prince—to Arthur's face, stormy and shocked. She took a deep breath.

"All my life, I've been afraid. Of being left, lied to, moved around for the convenience of other people like a piece of antique furniture nobody wants but they can't quite get rid of it, either. I've been afraid of it because those things happened until I was old enough to say I wouldn't tolerate it any more.

"I was a box to check for my mother. Item, daughter, one, to be cared for by others. To my father, I wasn't as interesting as the cosmos. The mysteries of the universe or a kid asking why the sky is blue? But I was there. I existed, and I was theirs. I was sure of that, and I didn't understand why they were so uninterested in me. It's why I arrange my life so that I can be with Maddy so much. Because she's mine, and she should never wonder about that.

"So to learn that the person I trusted most in the world hid something from me? Even under these circumstances. You could have said, Arthur. You could have said something."

"The last time I tried to talk about my feelings for you, you ran back to the other side of the world."

"I was twenty. Don't try to tell me you've gained exactly zero perspective on that night in the last eight years. I know you better than that."

"Then you know why I didn't say anything. You weren't interested in this life at all, then you appear after so many years and suddenly you and Eddie were embarking on some kind of high-wire act in the public eye, what was I supposed to do? Stand up and loudly proclaim that, no, I wanted you instead? Claim my rights as the elder brother and heir? I think not," he bit out.

"There has been a lot of time in which to have a different kind of conversation about it," she said, controlling her desire to howl. "Rather than let us run roughshod over you, like your feelings didn't matter, like you're some kind of untouchable monolith. How could you keep that from me?"

"Oh, I would tread very carefully about me keeping information from you, Gwendolyn."

Those words opened a trapdoor beneath her, but she couldn't seem to fall. "You knew."

His eyes lit up. He covered his mouth with one hand, some deep tension drifting out of him. "She is, isn't she?"

Gwen shook her head like the action could make all of this go away. "You didn't know for sure."

"I hoped. When Mum showed us pictures, or I caught your

posts sometimes. She looks like… like me, at least a little, and when her hair started growing in…" He pointed at his hair and shrugged. He was glowing, and of everything, that made Gwen feel the worst.

"How long have you 'thought?'"

"Since she was two or three. And once I got to know her? God, she's amazing, Gwen. I wanted her to be mine."

Gwen made a strangled, hurt noise. "Why didn't you ever *say* anything?"

"You seemed happy. I couldn't risk our tenuous peace by barreling into your life with what might well have been inaccurate, bizarre accusations, demanding blood tests like an unhinged conspiracy theorist. And what then? Ask you to bring her back when you were happy where you were and with what you were doing? Ignore the power imbalance between us? I'm the goddamned Prince of Wales."

"You know what, Arthur? Fuck you. *Fuck you* for thinking I would buckle under to what you want, now or then, without a fight. I wouldn't if you were going to be High Emperor of the Universe, never mind the ceremonial figurehead of a nation that spent money going to war over the Falkland Islands!"

"I have *always* maintained that was a stupid thing to do!"

"You know what else is a stupid thing to do? Acting like you avoided us for years out of concern for exerting undue influence because of your lofty social stature, your most royal of highnesses!"

"I avoided *you?* That's a laugh. You didn't speak to me for years after that night. I had to learn about your baby—*our* baby—from a note buried in a memo from my mother's private secretary to mine, with an action item that said 'Send gift? Circle if yes.' I hadn't even known you were pregnant."

"Well, I know you did that," Gwen said. "I got a stuffed unicorn in the mail with one of those impersonal form congratulations notes on your stationery."

"I picked out the unicorn myself," Arthur said, crossing his arms protectively. "But I didn't know what to write. I didn't want to accuse you."

He dropped into a chair, forearms on his thighs, head in his hand. "I didn't want to pressure you into a relationship you obviously didn't want. I was twenty-four. I didn't know what to do. To ask anyone for advice would have been a gross violation of your privacy, and courted consequences I didn't want to risk. I do have a responsibility not to throw my weight around," he said, apologetic. "Sometimes things happen when I do that."

"I was scared you'd think I did it on purpose," Gwen said, in a rush. "That people would say it. You told me how careful you had to be, I thought you'd never believe me."

"So tell me," Arthur said. His voice low, he looked defeated, sitting on the edge of the side chair. "Let me prove it to you."

Gwen took a deep, hitching breath. "I got pregnant. It was an accident. Maddy's your daughter."

A relieved smile spread over his face, reaching his eyes for the first time in so long. "I believe you."

She wiped away tears she couldn't help with the cuffs of her sweater.

"Are you going to tell her?" Arthur asked. He sounded so tentative, it broke her heart. "I know it might make things more complicated, but I would... even if it's only as her uncle, I'd like to be involved. As much as you'll let me. She's your daughter. And after tomorrow, Eddie's, I suppose." He sounded as if it pained him to get the words out. "It's only fair for him to have my future. Look at everything I'm getting." His eyes flicked around the dark room, and the emptiness in them made her feel cold.

She suddenly saw the two of them as two points of bright-ness in the vast sleeping palace, so close they were almost a single star. A hundred feet away, their sleeping daughter, connected to each of them by a line of light. Hers was wide, strong enough to walk on, a beacon. His was a thread, taut and fragile, spun thin over distance. In her silence, he tensed, as if she were about to break it. But she knew, in that moment, that she would never.

"We're—" her voice cracked, and she had to remember how to breathe, "not getting married tomorrow. Eddie and me. At all. We can't, either of us. We're not—we don't feel it."

Whatever she was about to say next collapsed when she saw the look on his face. He watched her with so much intensity, she almost didn't recognize him, his intrinsic awkwardness nowhere in evidence.

"What *are* you going to do?" he asked. Everything in the room seemed to be watching them, like it was all enchanted. She imagined his dress uniform leaning forward. The air was a solid and didn't exist, all at the same time.

"Well… Everyone's been invited. The catering's in. The weather's supposed to be excellent. It would be a shame to disappoint. To waste such a beautiful day. You and I planned it," she said, feeling hopeful for the first time in months. "You were right there with me. Were you picking what you wanted, too? Did you know how much I…" She trailed off.

"Gwen—" He didn't move a muscle, holding so still, as if she might vanish. "Kiss me."

He straightened in his chair as she walked towards him.

The sweetness came after. At first, she kissed him like there was something left to prove. Until her hands tightened in his hair and he made a noise as much of surprise as longing.

It hurt her, that sound. The wasted time inside it. The thousand rejections they'd given each other when all they wanted was this. She took his mouth with intent, giddy with finally being able to touch him like she wanted.

"Do you really want—?" Arthur asked, confusing her for a

half a second, because *yes, of course I want*— "The scrutiny, the society, the expectations—it's all horrible. Nothing compared to marrying him." *Oh.*

"I'm not marrying him," Gwen said, as if that solved anything. When she leaned in again, he pulled back. But he also slid his hands under her sweater, resting them on her hips.

"I'm serious," he said. "If you aren't sure…it's the rest of your life. Maddy's life. You can still get out. I'll protect you from the worst of it. From all of it. You can go."

Gwen cupped his face in her hands, the light stubble under her palms convincing her this was actually happening. At twenty-four he had been handsome in the raw way passably attractive men at that age can't help. Now he was defined, solid in the Kensington jaw and Varre cheekbones. A face made for a portrait in three-quarters profile, done in oils. The inevitable thought crossed her mind—he was going to be a king someday. That was what he'd grown into, flying fighter planes while she snuck glances at him in drugstore checkout lines. She committed the difference to memory.

"I'll protect you from the worst of it, too," she said. "Us against the world. Spending the last few months with you, watching you and Maddy together, it was like seeing the shadow of everything I ever wanted, and now I'm stepping into the sun. We'll make it up as we go along."

He inhaled, sliding his arms around her waist. "I'd settle for a life near you."

"You don't have to. Look, we have a chance. There's a whole wedding tomorrow, one that we basically planned together. Come on, Arthur," she said, raising an eyebrow. "You think it won't be fun?"

"Confounding the press core and infuriating the world," he said flatly. "We'll be accused of fraud. You of the worst sort of gold-digging. Me of being a dupe. We'll be drawn and quartered, hung out to dry, and roasted."

"Live a little." Her femme fatale purr turned into a shriek as he stood, hauling her legs around his waist.

"There might be a siege." He walked towards the bed. "That's what you're signing on for, Gwendolyn. Besiegement at the palace gates."

"Let them," she said. "I know a pilot. He'll get us out of here."

"They'll have public opinion." Arthur set her down on the edge of the bed, searching her face as she nodded. There was no point in hiding her apprehension, but it paled in comparison to everything else she felt. The dawning light in his eyes made her think he began to understand.

"I'll have you."

A sharp knock a few minutes later brought them back to reality, and they reluctantly broke apart. Arthur answered the door.

"Eddie told me to come get you—and Gwen—and bring you to Mum's study in fifteen minutes," Alex told him. She caught sight of Gwen, redoing her ponytail at the end of Arthur's old bed. "Wouldn't it be priceless if someone told me what's going on?"

26

A thin slice of light cut across the hall carpet beneath Victoria's study door. Even on the night before one of her children got married, the red dispatch boxes demanded her attention. Eddie hesitated. He could not remember, past the age of about nine years old, ever coming to his mother's study without an appointment. Part of him felt worse for interrupting her than for the hurricane he was about to unleash on them all. His phone buzzed with a text from Alex. *Got them. Heading down in 15.* He'd gone to find Alex right after Gwen stormed out, telling her the rough outline of what he was thinking and asking for her help. She had agreed so quickly that he wondered what kind of a pack of reckless sociopaths they all were.

He hoped Gwen and Arthur had admitted how they felt and decided to go along with his wild plan. But he couldn't wait for them—and, in any case, he felt he should do this part alone. He raised his fist, and thought he heard Victoria's rare, soft laugh, dying out as he knocked.

There was an unusually laden pause before Victoria called out, "Come in."

His sense that the last six hours were an exceptionally vivid dream was reinforced by the sight of his father, ensconced in an armchair by the fireplace.

Malcolm looked sheepish and Victoria like she had been caught at something. Neither reaction filled him with confidence. Malcolm had his suit jacket off, but was otherwise altogether buttoned up, as he'd been for the rehearsal dinner earlier that evening. Victoria had changed into a pair of dark blue pajama trousers with silhouettes of crystal chandeliers on them, a Christmas gift from Alex, topped with a fluffy tartan robe. Her slippers were shearling. She seemed vulnerable with only remnants of makeup on and her hair taken down.

Eddie put his hands in his pockets, and gave them both a flat look.

"I *do* hope I'm not interrupting anything," he said, sarcasm his only shield against whatever this was. Victoria bristled at the challenge, and for a second he thought she was going to say something without thinking, but Malcolm smoothly broke in.

"I merely stopped by to catch up," he said.

"I'm surprised the protection team let you within fifty yards."

"As am I." Malcolm smiled at him. Eddie found himself smiling in return.

Victoria watched their interaction with deep suspicion, and other feelings no one could have named, but her demeanor creased into real concern at the fact that Eddie was standing in front of her. "What's wrong? Why are you here?"

"There's some news. About an old friend of the family."

Victoria's eyes widened. So did Malcolm's. *News about an old friend of the family* was one of the code phrases the Kensingtons and their staff used to indicate the importance of speaking in private, as soon as possible.

"Well, that's my cue." Malcolm stood up.

"No, it's all right. You'd better stay." His father's presence comforted Eddie on a subterranean level, even as it seemed to go against the key founding principles of the universe. Gravity would be going next.

"What's happening?" Victoria asked, all business now.

"The short version is that I'm not getting married tomorrow, and I'd like to discuss how we want to manage it as a family. Just us, before we get Anthony or Sir Thomas and Portia or anyone in."

He had never seen his mother gape before. Malcolm retreated to the butler's pantry next door and came back with a fresh drink for Victoria. He made sure their fingers did not touch as he handed it to her. He had a glass for Eddie, too. "Tonic water, lime, plenty of ice," Malcolm told him, the same as he had poured Eddie the night after the interview. Malcolm picked up his own glass and clinked it against Eddie's.

Victoria threw back a swallow of her drink and coughed. "There's no alcohol in this," she said accusingly. "I desperately hoped there would be."

"Wits about you, Victoria," said Malcolm. Fondly. Eddie took an aggressive sip of his tonic.

Mother and son finally focused on each other. He felt like he might break. Victoria gripped her glass, knuckles white.

"No wedding?" She sounded confused, nearly forlorn. "Eddie, why—why on earth? I thought you were…settled." She sagged, bracing one hand on the surface of her desk, staring at him like she had never seen him before. It tore at him. He wondered if anyone had a thick skin for upsetting their mothers, deep down. He did not.

"I'm not," he said. "I'm the furthest thing from that. I'm so sorry, Mum."

"No," she said harshly. She cleared her throat. "No need to apologize. Ever." She put her glass down and straightened up. It looked for a moment like she might hug him, but she rounded her desk instead, sitting down behind it with practiced elegance. Mum become Queen. "Who am I summoning?"

"All of them."

SOPHIE ARRIVED FIRST, coming abruptly to a halt in her monogrammed men's pajamas. "What is *he* doing here?"

Malcolm regarded her with muted challenge. Eddie would have found their interaction funny, if he weren't on the verge of falling apart.

"Malcolm is not the enemy tonight, Sophie," Victoria told her sister. Malcolm retreated to the fireplace, and leaned on the mantel with his back to the wall. He made himself unobtrusive, as murmured conversation could be heard in the hall.

"I am," Eddie said.

Gwen's father entered next, book still in hand, reading glasses pushed up to the top of his head. Her mother followed, taking in the scene and sharing a quizzical look with Sophie as the women took over one of the couches. Sir Anthony slipped in, not a hair out of place despite the late hour. Gunny took up her accustomed, unobtrusive place off to one side, expression neutral as always. Looks can, as they say, be deceiving.

Eddie raised his eyebrows at his mother, who regarded him levelly in return. The power she wielded with the touch of a few buttons on her phone took him by surprise. He wondered what else she could accomplish so easily, and hoped he would never have to find out. The drumbeat of anxiety underlying his every thought slowed to a faint roll. He had begun to feel less ragged as he assessed the options before him.

Victoria sat quietly, so still that she might have been waiting for the signal to begin recording an address to the nation. This was the image—Queen at work—that had become iconic in the years since the divorce. And now she stood up.

"Your meeting, Edward," Victoria said, relocating to her favorite wing chair.

He braced himself against the front edge of Victoria's desk, realizing how the action was so like her, after all.

Courage came in imagining Isaac standing at the periphery, immovable, watching him like Eddie was the only person in the room. Someday, he swore to himself, he would explain all this to Isaac, properly. Isaac, who deserved it more than anyone, even though he knew it already.

"All of you know some of this story. None of you knows all of it." Eddie took a drink of his tonic water, the ice cubes bumping his teeth as he drained the glass.

"I have never only, even primarily, been attracted to the opposite sex. It didn't bother me, but it seemed to bother the rest of the world very much. Children understand how this works much sooner than most adults think. By the time I was old enough for it to matter in practical terms, I felt strongly inclined to keep it to myself. I won't tell you that social pressure played no part in this decision, because of course it did. I was encouraged to maintain my privacy by many of the people in this room. They were convinced the level of scrutiny we experience would be prohibitive to my well-being if certain information became public." He caught his mother's stricken face and Sir Anthony's regretful stare. Eddie sighed.

"I don't believe you were wrong to advise me as you did. To insist, even, when I was still so young. I never wanted to hide. It became a habit anyway. We all know how that is." He chanced a look at Malcolm, whose expression was unreadable. "Relationships with people I loved withered and died under the necessity of deniability. The women I spent time with made my life so much better—bearable, honestly—at my loneliest. And, of course, there was Isaac Cole."

The door opening interrupted him, giving him an opportunity to get control of the lump in his throat. Alex, looking about fit to explode, pushed Arthur and Gwen in front of her. The two of them moved as if gravity really had taken the night off and couldn't touch them, their joy shouting to him across the room. They weren't touching, but they might as well have been dancing. If jealousy stabbed at him, so soon after saying Isaac's name, that was how it had to be.

"Isaac was everything to me," he said, inviting the newcomers into the story. They arrayed themselves in front of the door. Alex's eyes went wide when she realized what he was talking about. "He risked his career and his good name for me. I wouldn't even risk a few headlines. I don't think I understood what caving under that pressure did to me." A slight motion across the room caught his eye—Sophie pressing her hand to her mouth. He shrugged. "This is the life we know. This is how we've survived. The trade-offs are built in, and we usually don't question them. What's the point? Well. Sometimes there is a point."

Gwen walked over to him and tucked an arm around his waist. He rested his cheek on her hair for a moment, savoring the closeness. But he had to keep going.

"Gwen and I can't get married tomorrow," he said. "She is a brilliant, kind, vital force. To be the focus of her generosity and her great capacity for love is as overwhelming as it is beautiful. I have never loved a friend more, or been more grateful for the gift of that love in return." Gwen covered her mouth with her free hand. Her engagement ring was gone. He didn't know what to read in to that.

"We wanted to create a family that could last. We believed we might have built a foundation for that. And maybe we could have, in a universe in which we aren't deeply and irrevocably in love with other people." Gwen went up on her toes to kiss his cheek.

"I have never been prouder to be your friend," she whispered. He hugged her tightly to his side.

"And you've come to this conclusion—" Joanna Leigh checked her watch, her customarily modulated tones not in evidence. "Eleven hours before the ceremony is scheduled to begin."

"Ten hours and fifty minutes," Lawrence put in.

"Thank you, Laurie," she shot back at her ex-husband. "That is unimaginably helpful."

"Just being precise."

"Perhaps if I were permitted to finish a thought before my arithmetic is fact-checked, oh internationally regarded physicist—"

"Mum, Dad," Gwen interrupted.

"And *Gwen*," her mother changed course mid-stream. "I know your stock-in-trade is reckless decisions, but have you thought about what this is going to do to Maddy? To your life? You'll be notorious."

"You can't throw Maddy's existence in my face in the same breath you use her as a club, Mother, you have to pick one or the other," Gwen said.

"I'm not sure she does," Arthur offered. He looked at Eddie with a question and an apology in his eyes. Eddie lifted his chin and stepped back, letting go of Gwen for good.

"There are implications," Sir Anthony said, in his brutally calm way. "It isn't a full state occasion, as Eddie is not in direct line to the throne. But the city is filled with guests who will have to be notified. The gifts, the souvenirs being sold by various interests, and, of course, the press will want their due. Are you prepared to publicly confirm certain facts in order to absorb some of the backlash, your royal highness?" There was a respectful light in his eye, a strong echo of his reaction when a much younger Eddie made the case for having a queer body-guard on his protection team.

"I am, if it comes to that."

"It will." Sir Anthony's expression was dark. "I lived with a man for thirty years before our country allowed us to marry, and his mother still refuses to have the man who 'corrupted' her son in her house. I have protected your interests as best I could without sugar-coating the consequences, and I won't start now.

"Your status won't save you. You've abused it to the fullest, led them a merry dance and dropped them flat. Involved one of your oldest friends and her daughter—a child, Edward—in your queer little games, and after all that didn't even give them the wedding pictures they wanted." He spoke in a mild monotone, but every shred of him projected sheer agony. Eddie thought he understood. That kind of exposure would have been Sir Anthony's worst nightmare when he was younger, and it happening now would mean that he had failed in his duty. "They'll eat you alive."

"Then I'll be eaten. I'll do interviews. I'll go into seclusion. I'll be caught on a gay beach in France. However it goes," Eddie said. "I've been waiting for the other shoe to drop for so long I didn't realize I was the one holding it. This is my life. All our lives."

"You'll bring down the monarchy," Sophie said.

"It's not treason," Gwen snapped. "It's bisexuality."

"The people who will mind the most don't even know what that *is*."

"So let them learn," Alex said, raising her voice. "This isn't some freak show. He's not even in the direct line of succession."

"That's easy for you to say," Joanna hissed, up and pacing now, the layered hems of her silk robe fluttering about her. "You're going to come out of this without a scratch. What about Gwen? She'll be run out of the country."

"Again," Arthur said, in what was very clearly his Prince of Wales voice, "I'm not sure it will come to that."

Arthur couldn't shake the sense that he was taking Eddie's cover away in a war zone. A good pilot would never do that to his wingman. But Eddie nodded, encouraging him to go on. And looking at Gwen was like flying, the same giddiness Arthur felt every time he was in the air, knowing he could go anywhere and do anything a sharp contrast to the awareness that he wore his life loosely, in service to something else.

A ripple went through the room as he strode forward. It turned into a collective gasp when he went down on one knee and reached for her hand.

"I was nine years old the first time I thought about proposing to you. You were going to America for the summer to visit your grandmother. I wanted you to stay, and I thought marrying you was as good a way of making that happen as anything else. My feelings are much deeper and my motivation farther reaching than it was twenty years ago, but the result is the same." He reached into his pocket and pulled out her engagement ring. He had asked for it back on the way here, wanting to do the thing properly.

"I have been in love with you all my life," Arthur said. "Stay with me?"

Her smile was the moment at the highest point of the climb, when gravity fell away. "Yes."

Then came the inevitable dive.

"When did *this* become a good idea?" Joanna demanded.

"About twenty minutes ago," Gwen volleyed back.

Alex broke in. "Haven't you seen how they look at each other? If this makes them happiest, it's our responsibility to see it through." She glared at Joanna. "Whatever the *implications* are."

"It's up to Her Majesty," Sir Anthony said. "As Prince

Arthur is in direct line to the throne, he must secure the permission of his liege in order to marry."

No one said a word.

"I know it's a lot to take in," Eddie said. He leaned back against their mother's desk, arms folded. "But we have an opportunity to get ahead of the story. If Arthur and Gwen use the wedding tomorrow."

"It's hardly the family car," Sophie said. "You can't just take it out for a spin to see if you like it."

"Everyone wants a love story," Eddie told her. "Let's give them one."

Sir Anthony tapped his fingers on the arm of his chair, looking at Eddie as if the prince were an overeager and not too clever assistant. "Point. The marriage of the Prince of Wales is a state occasion. This wedding is not. To go through with it makes it look like the family is dodging its responsibilities to the country."

"Technically, a state occasion isn't mandatory for anyone who isn't a sitting monarch," Eddie said. Everyone stared at him. "What? I read the briefing books. This is a chance to show off at extreme expense. The festivities tomorrow definitely count."

"The guest list is inadequate for the wedding of the future King of England," Sir Anthony bit off. "Too many family friends, not enough political leaders or commonwealth dignitaries. It reminds the world that you are private individuals with great personal wealth instead of heads of state."

"Arthur isn't King yet, and if he wants to get married in the back of his favorite pub he is technically allowed to."

"There are consequences to every one of these decisions," Sir Anthony said. "Especially as they set the stage for however you explain what is, at best, melodramatic behavior. I'm not sure how you're going to do that, by the way."

"Come off it, melodrama is why they keep us around. Pageantry, tradition, and gossip."

"It considerably weakens the monarchy—"

"Fuck the monarchy," Queen Victoria said. All heads turned to her. "They can't have it both ways. I know you're only thinking of us, Anthony. Of course there are risks. But I'm not going to forbid Arthur to marry Gwen, as if that would help. And I think calling off the wedding would be worse than going through with it in a somewhat... modified fashion. We've weathered storms before. At least we can put some happy faces on this one. If you're sure," she said, looking at Arthur and Gwen, and then Eddie. "All of you. This isn't something to be... it can go horribly wrong."

Malcolm snorted. Victoria shot him a look, and he subsided.

"I'm sure," Gwen said, and Arthur wanted to put his arms around her. So he did. After a second she sank back against him, and he felt the sky open up as if he were leveling out.

"We've talked about it," Gwen continued, her hands wrapping around his forearms where they were crossed over her stomach. "The pressure, the exposure. The effects on Maddy. I know we can figure it all out," she said, focusing on Victoria.

"I have all the confidence in the world in you," Victoria said, and came over to them, holding her hands out. Gwen and Arthur each took one. There was a slight tremor in Victoria's grip, but Arthur did not remark upon it. "I want you to be happy," she said to him, and he swallowed against a rush of emotion. "Gwen, I truly meant it when I said I could not wish for a better daughter-in-law. I think the two of you should get some sleep. In the morning, we will carry on. Let me worry about how. And that *is* a royal command."

She looked around at the assembled company, lingering on Joanna, Sophie, and Sir Anthony. "I know there will be challenges tomorrow. But we'll be able to face them better on a good night's rest."

They all knew a dismissal when they heard one. Joanna left, shaking her head in disbelief. Lawrence hung back for a moment, but a silent exchange between him and Gwen with eyebrows and a head tilt had him following his ex-wife. Arthur made a mental note to ask her what that was about. He realized, with dawning amazement, that he could.

Alex was vibrating with curiosity. "How did this happen? I need the whole story. Do it in charades, I don't care."

"I'll tell you," Gwen offered. "I need to check on Maddy, anyway." She looked up at Arthur with a mischievous grin. "You can help me stay away from your brother. It's bad luck, you know. Before the wedding."

Arthur wanted to pick Gwen up and go right back to his bedroom, but Alex grabbed her first and practically shoved her out of the room. Alex called a series of goodnights, including the last "Good night, Mum! And—Dad, I guess." She hovered for a second in the doorway, before crossing the room in several long, determined strides and throwing her arms around Malcolm's neck. He hugged her fiercely, with the abandon of a man who didn't know if he was to have another chance.

"Don't be too hard on your journalist," he murmured. She pulled back, jaw clenching, but Gwen poked her head back in, and Alex left in search of the story.

In the commotion, Eddie slipped out of the room through the butler's pantry. Arthur saw the flash of his crisp white shirt as he left.

"Victoria," Sophie said. "Vick, how can you think of *allowing* this? Of abetting it? We'll be drawn and quartered." Arthur had never heard that panicked note in her voice.

"I know, Soph." Victoria held her hand out, and Sophie warily took it. "I know. What else can I do? All our lives it was drummed into us to stay out of the spotlight, and of course it didn't *work*. We were already there. And then I did the same thing to my own children." The sisters stared at each other. "We were taught to be loyal to an ideal instead of each other. If my legacy is realizing that's not enough anymore, so be it."

Sophie opened her mouth to argue, but then exhaustion took her over. "You're thinking of Edward."

"Yes. Edward."

Arthur realized, after a moment of confusion, that they were talking about a man he had only seen in photographs.

"Mum and Dad tried." Victoria's voice shook. "They paid journalists off, they pulled strings, they begged him to be *discreet*. It killed him, in the end. You and I both know that, even if there's no way to prove it. I can't do that to my son for another moment. It's been far too long already. There has to be another way."

Sophie finally nodded, pulling away to compose herself.

Arthur could see that Victoria was concerned about Sophie, but he watched her push it away and get to work. She went to her desk and motioned Sir Anthony and Gunny over to join her. They were deep in hushed conversation in seconds. Arthur was struck anew by the sheer amount of organizational power wielded by that triumvirate. And by its limits. Working with almost limitless resources, and yet maneuvering inside rigid restrictions, Victoria needed help. She could share her burdens with Gunny and Sir Anthony, with the Lord Chamberlain and her veritable army of protocol officers and assistants—but she could never put them down. A monarch was only permitted to do that in private, and there, Victoria had been alone for years. Not even her children could change that. And Arthur had been skating on that edge—of never having someone to advise *him*, the person, and not the idea, until a few minutes ago. Until Gwen.

He looked at Malcolm, who was paying attention to Victoria, with a different air of admiration. It gave Arthur a chill.

Malcolm noticed Arthur watching him and strolled over, braced for impact but unwilling to let the moment pass.

"Holding up?" Malcolm asked conversationally, as if they spoke all the time. "Big day tomorrow."

"Is your superpower the concentrated ability to ignore what's going on around you? That would make sense."

Malcolm ignored the dig. "Gwen is splendid for you," he said. "Makes you laugh, I think. Always did."

"She does."

"That's an important quality in a partner," Malcolm told him. "Her job is to feel when you cannot, to be the heart of the country and commonwealth, while you are its soul."

"How can you be talking like this?" Arthur asked. "I'm one wrong inhale away from a breakdown, and you're philosophizing about god knows what."

"I know what it means to support a head of state. Look at your mother," Malcolm said. "Pulling things together at midnight so her children can turn the world on its ear by tomorrow lunch. She could command an army, but this is her emergency. Despite the dire predictions Sir Anthony is honorbound to make, she forges ahead to do the right thing. She's staggered under the weight of her circumstances so many times. She has nowhere to fall, so she stays up." Arthur was shocked by the warmth in his voice. "I will never be free of how badly I treated her."

"I've never heard you talk like this," Arthur said.

"I loved your mother, as bad a job as I did of it. And I will love you, and be impressed by you, no matter what."

"Thank you," Arthur said. "I don't... I don't know what to say."

"Think fast or lose your chance," Malcolm said. "Sophie clearly has murder on her mind."

Hearing her name, Sophie rounded on him, but she was

distracted by Sir Anthony and Gunny bowing to Victoria and leaving the room.

"Well," Victoria said, ambling up to them with her hands in her pockets as if this weren't the strangest night of their lives, "the patents and heraldry have to be redrawn, but I'm not waking anyone up for that. Arthur, don't sign *anything* tomorrow except the marriage license. Anthony is off to scare up a blank one so we're ready with that, at least. He might have to fill it in on an actual typewriter. Eddie's dukedom will have to be put on hold for now. I'm not giving it to you."

"I already have Cornwall," Arthur pointed out. "It's huge and makes far too much money."

"It's the spirit of the thing," Victoria said. "If I don't discipline my wayward children by denying them grandly outsized archaic titles, how will they learn?"

Arthur smiled a little, but he could see the tension in her face as she went on.

"It all has to be post facto now, so we have a bit of time. Gunny is making the arrangements for extra security in the morning."

"You don't think there'll be an actual riot, do you?" Sophie asked.

Victoria shrugged. "I don't know. But I'd prefer a civilized circus if we can manage it."

"Give Eddie my dukedom," Malcolm said. "You should have taken it away in the divorce in the first place."

"I can't go around stripping people of titles and land because they make me angry. It's not democratic. Besides, if I took yours for bad behavior, I'd have to take everybody's."

"That would be the democratic choice."

Watching his parents banter was the last straw. "Mum, is this all right? Really?"

Victoria smiled wryly. "I don't quite believe it, but I can't come up with a reason for saying no that doesn't make everyone miserable. This might very well make everyone miserable, but at least it will be in service of how you feel, rather than a lie."

He had no idea what to say to that. "Thank you." That would have to do. Her smile brightened, and even though he was a thirty-two-year-old former combat pilot, it reassured him.

"Get some sleep," Victoria told him. "You're about to get more attention than you've ever had in your life, and that's saying a tremendous amount."

Arthur pressed one hand against his stomach, as if that could fight off the rising nausea.

"It will be all right." The sound of Malcolm's voice was jarring, offering comfort where none should be allowed. Arthur betrayed himself by searching out his father's eyes. He could only offer Malcolm a short nod. He accepted a kiss on his cheek from Victoria, a hug from Sophie, and walked out of the room, stunned. He might be able to sleep after all.

"AND THEN THERE WERE THREE," Malcolm said. Victoria tried not to let the old familiarity of his tone affect her.

"Does that mean we get to kill you next?" Sophie crossed her arms. "I've seen the play, I think you're up for drowning."

Malcolm held up his hands in mute surrender and retreated to the tall windows.

"Please, Sophie. Malcolm's been halfway helpful this evening. And I cannot play referee between the two of you on top of everything else that's gone on tonight." There was a ringing in her head that kept getting louder as she replayed the last hour. "I couldn't have done anything differently."

Sophie hesitated, then sagged. "What were you going to do, forbid it? Clap them in irons and march them to the altar under armed guard? That would make a nice spread for the front page of the Mail."

"Perish the thought," Victoria said, relieved that her sister was coming around. "It's late. I'm sure Rob's waiting for your call."

"I don't want to leave you alone with him," Sophie whispered.

"For pity's sake." Whatever Sophie saw in Victoria's eyes, it must have convinced her, at least temporarily, that Victoria was not about to make it a double wedding in the morning. She settled for ignoring Malcolm as she left the room.

"Is it a bad time to abdicate?" Victoria joined Malcolm where he stood at the windows, hands firmly in the pockets of her robe. They both looked out into the pitch dark as if it were the most fascinating view.

"That would be upstaging the bride," Malcolm said. "Brave thing she's doing, sticking her head in the lion's mouth."

"I don't envy her that."

She caught the corner of his mouth turn up. "Oh, it's not so bad. They'll have each other."

"Were we ever that happy?" She didn't mean to ask the question so bluntly.

"I am sorry to inform you that we probably were. I recall feeling that happy, at least." Beguiling warmth suffused his voice, and Victoria risked a glance at his profile. The gray at his temples and scattered through his hair was a match for the fine lines at the corners of her eyes and the deeper ones around her mouth. And yet, in the window they were glossed, years of mistakes smoothed away. As if what might have been had happened, after all.

Catching each other's eyes in the glass, for one suspended moment, there was nothing between them. Their mutual understanding hadn't been dimmed by betrayal and anger. She felt as if she could reach out, take hold of the edge of all that time, and rip it away. Had they ever been as beautiful as their reflections looked right now? His fingers brushed her cheek, and she turned. They were close enough to touch the past the way it might have been.

She covered his hand with her own, pressing it to her face. "You were so dear to me," she said. He ducked his head, more boyish than a man of sixty had a right to be. When he looked up, tears glinted in his eyes, and he gave her the tiniest shake of his head, returning her hand to her side.

"I survived you once, Victoria. I'm not sure I could do it again."

Victoria stepped away from his warmth, clearing her throat, trying to right the universe. "I should check on Eddie. I have a feeling that's what a good mother would do. Will you be all right?"

"Don't worry, love. If it is the only thing I do for the rest of my life, I will be all right."

27

E ddie sat in bed in his childhood room. The only illumination came from the laptop balanced on his legs. Most of his actual childhood had been put in storage, but his framed set of original trilogy *Star Wars* posters remained on the walls, and a few of his more impressive LEGO builds were still displayed on the built-ins. Sitting up late in this bed reminded him of the time before Isaac, the years when he felt so much more alone.

The problem with world-changing, life-defining moments was how they were followed by long stretches of extreme banality during which he had to face everything he would rather continue avoiding. That meant thinking about tomorrow while he brushed his teeth and changed into gray fleece-lined pajama trousers and a faded sweatshirt he had nicked from Isaac in university. That meant thinking about Isaac, while he scrolled through his anonymous Instagram account and wondered how he was supposed to sleep.

He double-clicked a folder buried on his hard drive with the path name *Documents > Old Hobbies > Cake decorating > Rosettes*.

Photographic evidence of Isaac at Eddie's side—two steps behind or a few feet away—was easy to come by. But over the years, and usually by accident, a handful of pictures had made their way to Eddie that revealed something deeper. At the time, Eddie told himself it was proof of their friendship. Now, the images made his breath catch and his eyes sting.

The earliest one was taken by an enterprising yearbook photographer at Cambridge, in the quad at Eddie's college. Isaac was allowed to stick close and smile then, as one of the "undercover" members of his detail. While Eddie barely looked old enough to be at university, Isaac's black hair falling over his face made him seem nearly as young, even though he had been in his late twenties at the time. They were laughing. It was a good picture, the kind a friend might take.

Another one a few years later, Isaac in full military gear as Eddie toured a refugee camp in the Middle East. Eddie wasn't looking directly at him, but his body canted towards him, the back of his hand touching Isaac's forearm above the semi-automatic rifle in Isaac's hands. Eddie, about to say something, Isaac, tilting his head to listen though his attention was directed outwards, in a strangely intimate moment captured by an official pool photographer.

The third was the worst of all. Alex took it two years ago while they were on holiday for her twenty-first birthday, on an anonymous luxury charter yacht in the Caribbean. Eddie had been climbing the rope ladder after going for a swim off the side. Isaac leaned over to give him a hand up. Eddie remembered the sunlight sparkling on the water, how it felt to be pulled near to Isaac's warmth after coming out of the ocean. Isaac had been dressed casually for once in a black t-shirt and black-and-yellow board shorts, wraparound sunglasses hiding his eyes. But there could be no hiding his smile, lopsided and fierce. No preventing Eddie's own, bright enough to power a city block. Alex caught them in that moment, hands clasped tightly as Isaac dragged him up.

It hurt to see the two men in that picture, finally recognizing how gone for each other they had been. Eddie didn't know if he would be able to feel that wildly delighted ever again. If he'd ever want to. *Pain au chocolat* tasted better in Paris. Isaac couldn't be replaced.

He dimmed his laptop screen when there was a soft knock at his door. "Come in." He didn't know who he had been expecting—Arthur, probably—but when he saw his mother, guilt crawled up his throat.

"May I?"

Eddie nodded, putting his computer to the side. He turned the bedside light on and moved to get out from under the covers, but she held out a hand to stop him.

"Please, I came to see how you were."

"I'm all right," he said, trying out a smile. It didn't go well, but he persevered as she sat on the edge of his bed, looking as nervous as he felt. He shifted over to give her more room.

"We did this so rarely, you and I," she said. "I used to read to you and Arthur, before Alex was born. You listened so attentively. Never minded that I read Arthur's books, even when they were too complicated for you. Do you remember?"

Eddie pulled his legs up. If he thought back far enough, he did remember flashes of content curiosity. The warm and safe feeling of listening to his Mum, falling asleep no matter how hard he tried to stay up. He couldn't bear to tell her.

"Maybe a little. Nanny Jean did most of the reading to me, I think."

"And thank Christ for Nanny Jean," Victoria said, a hitch in her voice. "She was so good with you. So much better than... Well, it was all my own fault, wasn't it? I employed a crack battalion of dedicated childcare professionals, surely I could have asked any of them how to be better to my own son. But you didn't seem to need me. You never got angry, never complained even though…" She finally met his eyes, and the bottom dropped out of his stomach. She was so sad, and searching, and he wanted to put his arms around her. Wanted to pitch forward and cry into her arms, the way he never had once in his life. "You've had so much more to hide. I had my head firmly in the sand. Worse, I was content that way."

"Mother…"

"Do you remember the night you walked into the State Dinner with the Americans?"

He nodded.

"I had no idea what to do. I was frozen solid. So many things didn't come easy to me about being a mother *or* a monarch, and Malcolm was so quick to take care of them, and I needed that, I suppose, but I wished even in the moment that I had been the one to haul you into *my* lap. I was amazed by your audacity, coming down to see what all the fuss was about, strolling into the ballroom in your Spider-Man pajamas, for pity's sake. You reached out and poked at the First Lady of the United States' earring, and she laughed. Everyone melted for you. You were fearless."

Victoria took a deep breath. "And I worry, a bit, that some of your fearlessness slipped away because you were trying to protect *me*. That shouldn't be the direction it goes in. I should protect you. It is my responsibility and my joy to protect my children. Even when they do such a good job of acting like they don't need it that I believe them.

"You know," she went on, looking up at the ceiling and biting the inside of her cheek, "When your father left, I was so sure you were angry with me. I thought you'd want to live with him. Not Arthur or Alex, but you—I was sure. I could never allow it, so even before things got so bad, I think I pulled away too much, waiting for when I would have to break your heart. I never meant for you to get so far away that you couldn't tell me anything."

Eddie hated seeing his mother on the verge of tears. In her pajamas yet, after she had barely flinched before signing on to his French farce. But he couldn't find the words to comfort her, and he didn't want to lie. "I thought you couldn't stand the sight of me, back then. I thought I was too much like Malcolm for you to love me."

Victoria gasped as if he'd struck her. "Eddie—"

"But it started before that. Arthur and Alex see you as Mum. I can never quite shake you being the *Queen*. I couldn't get past it. You had more important things to do, and I was taken care of. I suppose you and I felt similarly." He watched her cringe at the plaster. "They never had a problem demanding your attention. I never even wanted to ask. I just wanted you to think I was all right. That I was worth...loving."

"You *were*, Eddie, that's what I'm trying to tell you. You were, and you are, always worth loving. And I do."

Eddie couldn't help the short, hiccuping sob that bubbled out of him. She cried, too, holding one hand to her mouth. They couldn't seem to navigate getting closer, but she took his hand, linking their fingers. They held on tight until the tears passed.

Victoria stroked her thumb across his knuckles. "When I was a teenager, some rag wrote a piece about how I had 'mannish hands.' When you were a teenager, the tabs said you were 'dainty.' I wanted to buy the paper and have all the reporters exiled to the Arctic to do pieces on penguins."

"Penguins live in the Antarctic," he said inanely. He looked at their joined hands. His were much bigger, but there was something similar about them, in the way their fingers hardly tapered at the ends.

"You see, that's the kind of thing that needs to be investigated by accredited journalists," she said, with a watery smile. "I should have made more room for you. As you were. As you *are*. Without thinking it was necessary to shove it off in the corner all the time. I never wanted you to think you'd have to break your own heart for me. I should have questioned your getting engaged to Gwen."

"You were pleased about it at the time, if I recall correctly."

"That was because I thought you were making a decision that would make both of you *happy*."

"Are you telling me there wasn't any pleasure at the morale booster?" He waited. A slow flush bloomed on her cheekbones. "You can't. We're political animals, Mother, you and I. We know the score, and we knew an openly queer prince was not in the playbook."

"I only wanted to protect you from going through it alone."

"And what about when I was with Stephen? I don't recall you okaying a photo-op then."

"I was supposed to put the weight of the Kensington press team behind your relationship with that attention-seeking little fiend? He made my skin crawl, Edward. Him, and his father lurking in the background, hurling abuse at him on the one hand and milking your 'friendship' for all it was worth with me on the other. Yes, I was very excited to give *that* connection official legitimacy."

Eddie blinked at her. "Why didn't you ever say any of that to me?"

"I didn't want to alienate you." Victoria seemed to collapse inward. "Were you ever going to tell me about your feelings for Isaac Cole?"

"Not if I could help it," Eddie admitted. "I didn't want there to be a question about his professionalism. Especially once that was a valid concern."

He had seen her express sympathy in photographs and on film. It was jarring to see it in person, directed at him. "It's much better this way, Mum. She should be with Arthur, for so many reasons. Not the least of which is she actually loves him. And Isaac... he doesn't belong in all this. He'd despise it. I wouldn't ask him to do it."

"Shouldn't that be his choice?" Victoria asked. "There are some advantages," she went on. "The food is excellent. And there's all that money." The rare flash of sarcasm was gone as soon as it came. She looked around the room and sighed. "If he loved you, he would be willing to put up with it. Gwen was, and she's not in love with you."

"She's been my friend my whole life."

"And Cole hasn't?"

"It was his *job*," he said bitterly. "A job he had to leave because of me."

"I seem to be running at an information deficit," Victoria said, a dry note to the words that made Eddie think Gunny was about to get the grilling of her life from her boss. "But it was clear how much he cared for you."

"It's over. I took him for granted, and I never told him how I really felt, and I paid. It can't be made up for now," he said. "I'm a grown man. I can make my own decisions, and I have. I can't go through with this, so I'm not going to."

"You don't have to take it all on yourself," she said. "First of all, your brother and your very recently affianced have responsibility here, too, and I think you should let them take it. And second, I'm the bloody Queen of England. I can make things happen."

They actually smiled at each other.

"I want you to stay above the fray, Mum. It has the advantage of accurately reflecting reality, and I can't hide behind your skirts for this."

"If you're sure. But remember, my skirts are very wide." She lifted her hand, glancing at him for permission before combing his hair with her fingers, tucking a stray lock behind his ear.

"I always liked your long hair," she told him. "I like this, too."

Of everything tonight, that was what made him start to cry again. This time, she reached out and hugged him. It was awkward. They got the hang of it. Eventually, he slid down under the covers, a victim of his own depression and adrenaline crash. She rubbed his back in slow circles until he fell asleep. Like a proper mother would, she thought.

Victoria tucked him in when she left, moving the computer to the bedside table. Her thumb brushed the trackpad, and the screen lit up on the last photo he'd been looking at. One of Isaac pulling him up into the sunshine, a grin on Eddie's face.

Had she ever seen that look in his eyes? She shoved her hands into the pockets of her robe as she'd seen him do a thousand times, the way he'd learned from his father, perhaps even from her. She felt the way it forced her back to curve, a veneer of false comfort over the singing desire in her body to hide. She walked back to her room like that, passing official portraits of family members, alone in their frames. Never smiling. A very personal kind of state-sponsored propaganda. She thought of Malcolm, alone in his guest room, and she thought of her unending loneliness and the last time she'd felt it lift, even for a moment.

Then she took her mobile from her night table and texted Gunny. She didn't need much. A phone number. Some information. An address.

28

T hree black cars rolled through London just before dawn, skirting the barricades and crowds already gathering on the route between Buckingham Palace and Westminster Cathedral. Some enthusiasts had waited all night.

In the center car, Victoria stared out the window, hands clenched in her lap as mansions and tourist attractions gave way to neighborhoods that felt lived in, worked in. It wasn't a long drive, but six miles was a magic trick in a big city like hers. Stray a bit from one's own territory and every block told a new, unfamiliar story.

The cars pulled to a halt, in unison, in front of the last row house on a street that had seen worse days and had its pride. An attitude of triumph despite the odds suffused every recently painted railing and tended front walk. Though whether the triumph was over austerity or gentrification would be hard to say.

～

INSIDE THAT HOUSE, a small girl lay in a nest of blankets on the floor, watching a movie after a night sleeping off a fever, while her grandmother had a few minutes to herself. Rivvie heard the sound of cars, and, like any good investigator, climbed the back of the couch to see who it might be at this time of the morning.

≈

SANDRA FINISHED MEDITATING in the sunroom off the kitchen. The day promised to be warm, so she kept the doors open to the scrap of back garden left after Yossi extended the house. The sun was coming up, birds were singing, and she shivered her way through some mindfulness. She needed it, today. Poor Isaac. Bloody royalty. Sandra never cared one way or another about the Kensingtons, although her sister was forever going on about something she'd read about this one or that one when they were young, criticizing the princesses' style, sighing over the Prince of Wales. She had a sobbing fit the day he died, in 1974. Her mother, too, occasionally picked up a glossy magazine to flick through while her nails dried. It was theatre to them.

All entertainment has a price, she thought. A bitter one, this time. She'd let him sleep. It seemed kindest. He would be assaulted with images and clips of the royal wedding for the rest of his life. He didn't need to be awake for the deed. The church bells ringing all over the city would probably see to that once the whole thing was over.

If the elephant masquerading as a small child currently rampaging down the hallway didn't startle him up first. Rivvie slammed into the kitchen, all wild eyes, cutting off Sandra's protest.

"Granny, the *Queen*."

"I said we're only watching as long as you're quiet about it, didn't I? I don't care if the Queen's on."

"No, Gran. The Queen's *outside*."

Rivvie wasn't a lying child. A brisk knock echoed through the house.

"Go upstairs. Don't wake your uncle."

Rivvie nodded and scrambled up the stairs, although Sandra could tell she was lingering on the landing as Sandra opened the front door.

The Queen of England. Dressed for a morning at home in gray slacks and a blue silk blouse, hands clasped in front of her, as if standing on a stranger's doorstep at dawn were one of the duties she ordinarily performed. An air of mild discomfort hovered near her without touching her. Sandra supposed it wouldn't dare. Beside her, she saw a long-suffering, highly skeptical woman about their age, trying her best to look impassive. More men and women in black suits were in position by the cars.

"You'd better come in, then," she said, pulling the door wide and turning on her heel.

With Victoria Kensington standing in her kitchen, Sandra put the kettle on and got her favorite mugs out, large handmade ones with paisley details and a light green finish.

"Do sit down," she said, in her plummiest, most refined lilt. Victoria didn't look surprised, but Sandra rather thought she wouldn't. She had a contrary urge to reach for the workaday, ubiquitous Barry's Tea because it ought to be good enough for Her Majesty, but that was pettiness. The loose leaf Fortnum & Mason Royal Blend that she used every morning would do. When Victoria saw the tin, the irony didn't escape her.

"I use that all the time." Victoria made the valiant effort to smile, to connect, to prove she was in on the joke. Instead, she looked as if she knew how very out of place she was, arriving unannounced in a stranger's real life.

Sandra wondered what she made of the cheerful Moroccan tile, the well-worn appliances, the cabinets decorated with the artistic output of several enthusiastic children and one truly talented one. Prints of art made by famously talented adults on the walls, postcards, an oversized calendar all filled in. Yesterday, today, and tomorrow suspiciously blank except for one word: *Isaac*. Victoria lingered on the name. A shadow crossed her face. So she knew something about it, Sandra thought, and wondered if that made her like Victoria more or less. Victoria's gaze landed on Sandra's customary early morning Batman teapot.

"Doesn't fit, does it? It was a gift from Isaac and his stepbrother. They went in on it with their pocket money. Probably the first time they ever decided to do something together that didn't involve black eyes," Sandra said. "I thought they'd bring the house down with them when they were children." *You only have one chance with me*, she thought, staring at her unexpected guest with unwavering intensity. *Don't fuck it up.*

"Mine used to run," Victoria said. Haltingly, as if she wasn't sure how to behave. Sandra felt like they were suspended in a bubble outside of time. The first line of a picture book she read to Rivvie in the mornings floated through her head. *When the sun rose, my friend came to visit me.* But they weren't friends. Not at all. Victoria had a personal stake in this conversation, even if Sandra didn't know what it was yet. "They didn't fight. They ran. Everywhere. I envied them, and I told them to slow down."

Sandra nodded. The fragile détente between them was bound to break eventually. But they both wanted to keep that from happening for as long as possible.

Victoria sat down in Sandra's usual seat, facing the sun room. Sandra settled in across from her, tracing circles on her mug as they waited for their tea to brew.

"Your skirt is beautiful," Victoria said. "I used to dress like that. Once upon a time."

"I used to dress like you. I was a law student. *Quite* correct. All twinsets and pencil skirts."

"What changed?"

"I discovered a world that didn't care so much what I wore."

Victoria stared out the window. The neighbor's wash was hanging next door, left out all night. "I discovered the whole world cared desperately what I wore."

"You became Queen of England. I became queen of this street. It's a matter of operating on different scales."

Victoria accepted the fact and the tea with a graceful nod. They glanced at the wall clock at the same moment, and each woman straightened. Somewhere, in the deep recesses of her memory, Sandra heard a gavel, bringing a meeting to order.

"I assume you're here about my son," Sandra said, over the rim of her mug.

Victoria's brow furrowed. She was about to open her mouth when Sandra cut her off.

"I don't care what his file says, or what's on his birth certificate, never mind he didn't enter the world through my own personal body. He's my son. I couldn't love him any more than I do and, while he is a grown man who has done unspeakable things to other women's children, I am his mother. I won't see him hurt if I can prevent it. If that means throwing you out of my house on your ear, your majesty, I will."

Victoria looked taken aback, but she rallied. "You're right. This is about your son. Isaac." She rolled the contours of his name in her mouth as if she had never tasted it before. "Please believe me, I'm not here to compound any pain he must be feeling. He has been treated with shabbiness I never would have expected from one of my children. And I cannot help but feel it was my fault." She raised her eyes, filled with apology, to Sandra's. "Would you allow me to start at the beginning?"

Sandra settled back in her chair and crossed her legs, toasting her unlikely guest. When Victoria spoke, it sounded unrehearsed, her tone wondering at her own daring.

"Understand, the lives we lead, the world we inhabit—I'm only a few miles away from where I was born in one direction and where I'll be buried in another, but I might as well be on the North Pole, or the moon. And it's only because of poor dynastic planning and tragic, senseless death that *I* am a queen at all.

"There is no good reason for me to bear what I do, and yet, I carry on, because some ideas are bigger than any one person, and we have a duty to do as much good as we can in the time that we have, with the resources available to us. The money, the organizational power, we do what we can with it, while staying carefully 'apolitical,' as if there is such a thing. There are only a handful of people alive who know what it takes to walk that tightrope, and I'm related to most of them. I was an antique from the second I was born. And so were my children.

"The pressure is staggering." She rubbed at her bare left ring finger. "Like having a woolly mammoth on your chest. The unimaginable wealth, the social influence, the weight of a thousand years of history… we call it 'soft power,' but the divine right of kings is long gone as a defensible philosophy. We're making nice to the revolutionaries, putting off the inevitable storming of the palace gates, giving them what they want in exchange for existence. What they want is usually us. Everyone deals with it in their own way. Arthur buried himself in military service. Alex resisted it until the press turned on her, and when my mother died, Alex threw herself into continuing Mary's philanthropy and baiting journalists. And Edward…"

Victoria took a deep breath.

"He was such an understanding child," she said. "Not

sympathetic, that's not quite what I mean. Arthur was the sensitive one. Edward discerned. He calculated. He understood what was expected and what was necessary a little too well, a little too soon. I know now. I was so clear with my children that they shouldn't be selfish, that they shouldn't put themselves first. I didn't expect he would take it so thoroughly to heart," she said, and now there was a wobble under the words.

"We all fuck up our children," Sandra said. "You aren't the first mother to do it, God knows you won't be the last. You're not special, Victoria."

The woman across from her jolted at her own name, like she wasn't sure who it belonged to.

"Do you know," Victoria said, "I've been shot at multiple times, once when I was pregnant and sitting in a garden with my three-year-old. Not some freak accident. A man with a gun genuinely wanted to kill us, specifically. The fences at Buckingham and Kensington are jumped dozens of times a year, our homes broken into, occasionally former members of staff sell pictures to the papers. We're followed in the dead of night. But the most horrible part is reading the threats against my children. The worst kind of threats, stomach-churning, never-sleep-again stuff. They don't know about most of it, and they won't if I can help it. I'm not the first mother to fuck up my children, I've just done it under much more opulent, dangerous circumstances than most."

Victoria spoke with such bitterness that Sandra hardly recognized her from the yearly Christmas Address and the newspaper photographs. "When Eddie told me he was bisexual, it terrified me. The exposure of it. How difficult it would be for him, because of who we are. I didn't allow any talk of him coming out publicly. I wasn't thinking of him, I know that now. I was thinking of all the horrid people in the world and the things they say. I felt I had given them so much already.

They took it without asking. My marriage. My brother's memory. I couldn't think about giving them my *child*.

"My private secretary floated it as an option at one time, when Eddie was out of university and seeing a man who was, on paper, very suitable. I don't even remember my reaction. I think I shrieked. I clung to the idea that Eddie would fall in love with a nice girl."

Sandra found herself nodding, more sympathetically than she intended. "Isaac never gave me the chance," she said. "He came home with a black eye, and when I asked what this one was for, he said his flaming homosexuality. He enunciated very clearly."

"How did you react?"

"I think I told him flaming homosexuals needed to learn how to dodge and got him an ice pack," she said. "I didn't know what to do, and he generally responded best to sarcasm. We didn't learn sincerity until... well. Until he went to work for your son."

Sandra found she had to make Victoria understand, too.

"He was like stone, before." Sandra told her. "Not cold. Cold would have been something. He was impenetrable, even to me. When he was little, he would wake me up and tell me he had a bad dream, but he never talked about it. He wouldn't cry. He'd get in bed with me, curl up against my back, and lie still until he fell asleep again." The memory tugged at her roughly. "It was like that with everything. Nothing seemed to scare him. Everything made him angry. It wasn't a surprise when he went into the SAS. Something for him to do with all that rage? I was almost glad for it. But when he came home, started following your son around..." She picked at the edge of a placemat. "It's the only reason I let you into the house."

Victoria traced one of the paisleys on her mug. "Edward—Eddie, the nickname was his father's invention—he was so happy when Cole joined his team. No shortage of gay men around him, god knows, but Cole was different. A light came on. At first, I thought it was all excitement to be going away to university. Being free, getting to live a more normal sort of life for a teenager. If you can call attending university with a press gag order and a twenty-person protection detail 'more normal.' Edward looked for him in a crowd, didn't like to be without him for more than a day or two, but that wasn't unusual. I've had the same bodyguard for over thirty years. When it was brought to my attention that he was well and truly smitten with his bodyguard, Cole had already rescued him from something terrible. One of the worst things a mother can imagine. What could I do about it? Separate them on some pretext? It would have hurt him so much. At that point he was a grown man, and Cole's behavior was above reproach. Even if they did go on tremendously unwise revenge missions for some of the people Eddie met doing charity work. God knows I wanted to put a stop to that."

Sandra shook her head. "Hard to enforce a bedtime when they have their own security forces?"

"You laugh," Victoria said darkly. "Though one of us should." She turned her gaze out the window again. "I was relieved when Cole left. I thought it meant Edward finally didn't need him any longer. That he'd healed. My own child walking around like a ghost with a smile painted on, suddenly wanting to marry a woman he'd known since he was a child and never showed the slightest bit of romantic inclination toward, and my first reaction was *thank God that's sorted out.*" She rubbed her temple with one immaculately manicured hand.

Sandra snorted. "I was thrilled when Isaac left. After a while I thought that job was him avoiding life, far too in love with a man who would never acknowledge him. I don't want him exposed, either. You people are toxic. It's nothing personal," she added, realizing how cold it sounded.

"I appreciate the thought, but it's not as if I can argue,"

Victoria said. "We're not a terribly nice crowd, historically. Shabby, as I said. Cold. The throne catches people in its orbit and makes them pay. You take it on as armor after a while. You have to. For a long time I didn't think so. I tried to do it differently. But that…" Her thumb returned to her left ring finger. "Doesn't always work."

"Demonstrably. He's a mess, that boy of yours."

"He's had a very hard time," Victoria said stiffly. She wanted to protect her child too, Sandra thought.

"I understand," Sandra said. "While your boy was being coddled through every feeling he ever had, mine was ripping himself into pieces for his country. For his *queen*. So perhaps don't talk to me about hard times."

Victoria didn't rise to the bait. She sipped her tea. "I respect that."

"Thank you."

They both relaxed. Sandra looked at the clock again. So did Victoria.

"Something must have changed. You're in my kitchen."

"Edward isn't getting married today."

"Bloody hell."

"I can't begin to tell you how much."

"What about the woman—Gwen?"

"They both decided not to go through with it. She's marrying Arthur instead."

Sandra glanced at the clock. "I can see why you're in my kitchen. I'd want to hide out, too."

"The fact is," Victoria said, "Eddie's done everything his role ever asked of him, and more that wasn't. And the last thing he was looking at, the night before a wedding that I should *never* have allowed, was a picture of him and Isaac. They looked so real together. The way two people who love each other ought to be. That's why I'm here. He's about to create a storm the likes of which we haven't seen in decades.

Some of my gloomier advisors think it might bring down the monarchy entirely. I want to give him the chance at not doing it alone. Both of them."

Sandra looked around her kitchen, remembering the first time Yossi brought her here to this house he found for them, when they were new together and utterly mismatched. No money, no community, a pack of kids who couldn't stand each other, nothing but righteous fire in their hearts and the conviction that *here* was real life. Or would be, if they worked hard at it.

"Well," she said, after a pause. "I'm not going to be the one to wake him." She went to the kitchen door and opened it. Rivvie practically fell into the room.

ISAAC WOKE up when the door to his childhood bedroom clicked open. Omer, the best brother a man could ask for, had gotten him massively drunk last night, kept him from killing a man down the pub, then got him up the stairs into his old room on the third floor and into bed. Boxes of books lined the walls, beneath his old Bowie and Green Day posters. The blinds were yanked up with enthusiasm that should have brought the whole apparatus down, but his bad luck held. Now there was sunshine shellacked to the outsides of his eyelids.

He opened one eye. Rivvie stood next to his bed, holding her favorite stuffed rabbit. Her other hand was a fist on her waist, miniature Sandra read in head tilt and arch expression. Who said nature trumped nurture? He raised an eyebrow, looking pointedly from the rabbit to her face. She pursed her lips.

"What time is it?"

"It's past seven. In the morning," she told him with relish.

"Gran says you're sad, and so we should be nice to you. And make sure you haven't *died of drink*."

"Aren't you a little young to be doing her dirty work?" He scooted over.

"It's a living," she said, hopping up. The mattress tilted, falling away from him at all angles. He groaned into the pillow. When he looked up, niece and rabbit were still there. Both had an accusatory glint in their eyes.

He struggled up, sitting back against the wall. 7am. He rubbed his face, fingers catching on rough stubble. Over the past nine months, Isaac trained himself to stop thinking about Eddie's schedule and likely mood. It was much harder to break the habit than it had been to create it. He could feel all the ground he had gained slipping out from under him like fine sand today, and he gave in to what he couldn't help in the first place.

Eddie would be awake by now, if he managed any sleep at all last night. Showered, shaved. Jenny would be with him, walking him through the day. Probably confiscated his cell phone already. Was Eddie full of energy, every inch the excited prince in love, ready to start this new chapter in his life? Or was he pacing, anxiety-ridden and sharp, raw and alone for as long as he could be before he had to go face the world?

Rivvie patted his arm. She tucked something soft, furry, and acrylic into the hinge of his elbow. He felt utterly pathetic. When the eight-year-old thought applying stuffed animals to the problem would help, the situation was dire.

"You're very sad, aren't you."

He thought about denying it. Thought about how good it would feel to pretend he had some control of himself. Then he nodded.

"Is it because of the W-E-D-D-I-N-G?"

"Did Sandra tell you not to talk about it?" Even as he asked the question, he realized she must have. Today's events were the most anticipated in the world right now. The fact that his family was the only one not talking it to death in the last few weeks couldn't be some trick of fate.

"She said you had a broken heart," she said. "So I brought you Bun." Accepting how much of an honor this was, he cuddled Bun to his chest. Its floppy ears, lined with bright floral fabric, fell over his hands. Eddie would love it. Probably make up a story about it in minutes. He wished he'd ever brought Eddie to meet Rivvie. They would have loved each other. Eddie had offered, every time Isaac mentioned her in conversation. But no. Too good for it. Didn't want favors. Such a small thing to regret so much now.

"Are you in love with the woman who's going to be princess? Is that why you quit right after he fell in love with her?"

Save him from professional soldiers and perceptive children. "Worse," he said, petting the stuffed rabbit.

"What could be worse?"

"I'm in love with the Prince," he told her. It felt good to say it, like a necessary relieving of pressure. The ache still resided in his chest, but it didn't hurt so badly.

He could almost hear the cartoon sound effect as she blinked, eyes going wide. No one had ever specifically told the little cousins anything about Isaac's sexuality, as far as he knew. Maybe he should have prepared the ground for it better. As it was, Rivvie had such a look of concentration on her face as she assimilated the new information that she looked furious. He waited for the verdict. He had never really cared what anyone thought of his sexuality before, except Sandra and Yossi.

When the reaction came, it was emphatic. "That's *tragic*," Rivvie said. "So why aren't you marrying him? Men can get married now."

All the reasons why not—*because the monarchy, because he doesn't know, because the world is not so kind as you think, because...*

"Come on." She slid off the bed and held her hand out. He tried to hand her Bun, but she shook her head, impatient with him. "If you haven't died I'm supposed to bring you."

His heart, without mortification, flew upwards. "Why?"

"I don't know," Rivvie said. "But the Queen's here, and there's a woman like you in the house. With a gun," she added.

A dozen scenarios ran through his head and quickened his heart rate.

The brain-wiping confusion only intensified when he looked into the hall and saw Gunny standing at the foot of the stairs. She looked from his ratty pajama bottoms to his face and shook her head. He told Rivvie to wait outside while he pulled on a pair of dark jeans instead.

Rivvie dragged him past his old boss and into the kitchen. Where the Queen of England was indeed sitting with Sandra at the table, cup of tea in front of her.

The stuffed rabbit was still in his free hand.

"Please, don't bow," Victoria said. "I don't think it's the time."

Nearly half a life spent training to be surprised by nothing, and he couldn't do more than gape like a child. Which wasn't fair to the child in the room, some still-occupied chamber of his mind informed him. Rivvie was doing all right. Better than him; she seemed to be breathing. "Are you actually the Queen?" she asked, at the same time as he blurted out, "Is Eddie all right?"

"I am," Victoria said, smiling at Rivvie. It was the fairy godmother smile she used on children all over the world, concentrated for one small girl. "And he is," she told Isaac, her lips thinning in appreciation of some private joke.

He looked at Sandra, in the dark gray activewear t-shirt and tiered, embroidered skirt she meditated in. Her arms were crossed, one hand raised to prop her chin up. It had never occurred to him before how much the two women resembled each other, in a fair English Rose kind of way. She raised an eyebrow, and he took reassurance from her calm. It didn't matter how old he got or how much training he had, he thought. If Sandra didn't think there was anything to worry about, he knew in his gut it was all going to be fine.

"We should leave them alone," Sandra told Rivvie, getting up in a swirl of skirt and long hair.

Rivvie's principles did not generally allow her to leave a place where interesting things were happening, but royalty took precedence.

"She looks like Princess Elsa grew up," Rivvie remarked to Sandra as they left the kitchen.

Isaac and Victoria watched each other. They might as well have been squaring off in a wrestling ring, for all their unease.

"That's the highest compliment Rivvie can give," Isaac offered into the silence.

"I'm flattered, I promise. I'm sure she's as extraordinary as your aunt."

"Ma'am. I'm hardly dressed and holding a toy rabbit, I'd rather not listen to you condescend about my family. I probably deserve it. They definitely do not. With all due respect."

Victoria looked taken aback. "I didn't mean to—I'm sorry." The way she held his gaze, braced and unflinching, indicated she was apologizing for much more than some poorly chosen words. Isaac regarded her warily. "I couldn't quite believe it when she opened the door. She sighed and told me to come in. I was sat down right here in a minute flat. I'm not sure how to feel about it."

"That's Sandra. She has that effect on people."

"She loves you."

"That's the only thing I ever knew for sure."

The question of why she was here of all places, of all *days*, itched, burrowing under his skin in unpleasant stings of confusion, anticipation, dismay. Victoria was so remote even in her own environment that she seemed made of wax in Sandra's kitchen.

"Why did you leave Edward's detail?"

Isaac crossed his arms. This was the first time the Queen had ever seen him off duty, and his feelings about the woman and her personal choices aside, she was still his monarch, and had been his ultimate superior, at least in name, for his entire professional career until nine months ago. Various responses glittered through his mind like koi in a dark pond—*This is quite a time for an exit interview, Because I'm a traditionalist and didn't want to fuck him without a ring on my finger, I didn't realize you cared*—

"I couldn't watch him climb into a coffin and pull the lid on," was what he settled on. It came out more harshly than he intended, and Victoria went pale under her makeup. "I didn't mean... He built tiny bridges from one day to the next, ma'am. For duty. For you. For Top Gun and Sugar Bowl—" he snorted at himself for the reflexive use of code names. "But mostly for you. Because it was the right thing. And then it was the wrong thing, but he didn't stop. I was there with him."

Victoria shocked him by nodding. "You've spent more time with him than I have, by quite a margin."

Isaac hadn't known that acknowledgment would mean so much to him. "Please believe me," he said, searching for the gap in his own armor that might make her understand. "Nothing happened until the bombing. I never would have—"

She raised a hand, cutting him off, no censure or disbelief in the gesture. "I don't need to hear that," she said. "Your loyalty, your care for my son, that wasn't in question for a single moment in my mind. Ever."

"Even when—?"

"Isaac," she said. The use of his given name startled him out of his self-loathing. "Of course not. It was clear that you were more devoted to him than life."

"It's part of the job."

"Rarely the way you were doing it. Do you know how many reports I got, from Gunny, from Sir Anthony, from the image team, from anyone you could think of, about the two of you, since the day you joined his detail?"

He could feel his face arranging itself into something horrible, and she shook her head. "You were professional at all times. Edward wasn't."

A memory of Eddie the way he had been flickered through Isaac's mind, all fluffy curling hair and impossibly sunny smiles tucked away in long-sleeved polo shirts and khaki slacks. The image morphed into jeans and tight band t-shirts with loose plaid shirts open over them, bracelets up his wrists, in college, and the smile in his mind took on a terrible shadow. One that, when he looked at Victoria again, was reflected on her own face.

"After what occurred at university, separating him from you would have been cruel. Punishment, when he needed care. When he needed *you*. I know you don't think much of how I handled things over the years," she said, and even if he wanted to contradict her out of politeness, which he did not, she didn't give him the chance. "And I won't explain myself to you more than to say that at every point I did what I thought was ultimately in the best interests of everyone involved."

The Eddie in Isaac's head skipped a few iterations, landing on the version from the pre-wedding coverage. Short-haired, wearing a collared shirt and a waistcoat, beaming vacantly from magazine covers and press photos. Sleeves rolled up to reveal forearms showing time in the gym. A recent development, because aside from the year following the attack in college, not even Isaac had been able to tempt him into a weights regimen. Somehow, Eddie had turned himself—or been turned—into an ultra-masculine dandy with a razor-edged smile.

"And now?" he asked, not backing down an inch.

"Do you love him?"

The question wasn't unexpected. A lifetime of training in lightning-fast assimilation of new data and an innate talent for analysis indicated this was where she'd been going the whole time. And it wasn't even the first time he'd been asked that morning. As freeing as confessing it to Rivvie had been, to tell Victoria felt like throwing her a rope tied at the other end to his own middle. During a hurricane.

Victoria couldn't escape being the Queen of England, even sitting in Sandra's kitchen, one hand around one of her hostess's favorite mugs. It was in her bones. Even while trying her hardest to be, somehow, just a woman of the size and shape she was, instead of the embodiment of a monolithic idea that had survived on this island for a thousand years. She always had an ulterior motive, the longest view in mind. She wasn't asking him how he felt about her son out of curiosity.

He took a breath and called Eddie to mind. Eddie in his faded pajama bottoms and old t-shirts, loose-limbed and relaxed, sitting on his kitchen counter, telling a story. Eddie comforting someone who needed it. Looking for the good in the world, always up to learn something new. Buying Isaac different pastries until he picked a favorite, because Eddie thought a person should have one. Everything about him, because Isaac had fallen for all of it.

"I do love him," Isaac said, and had to close his eyes. Nothing felt real. The world was twirling off its axis again. "I do." When he could look at her again, Victoria's mouth had hardened into a determined line. "I left his detail because I love him. Without each other, we have half a chance at some kind of life, maybe. Being with him every day? Not a chance."

Sudden warmth was not the reaction he expected. He hadn't felt the full force of it directed at him since the morning he was introduced to her after being hired.

"I would be most grateful if you accompanied me to the

wedding today," she said. "He is about to do something very brave and very foolish. He ought to have someone who is only there for him."

"Is this your way of punishing me, ma'am? Because it would be very effective."

Victoria straightened in her chair, tilting her head up and to the side, and he had to hand it to her. He was a hardened killer, and she could still made him shiver.

"Ma'am—"

"A *very* brave and *very* foolish thing. Gwen and Arthur are going to be married this afternoon. Eddie is throwing himself to the wolves for them. For himself. And, I think, for you. But he doesn't believe he deserves you any longer. I am asking you to escort me to the wedding and perhaps give him the option of happiness. You both should have it."

Oh, Eddie. A tendril of hope shot out of his heart and wrapped around his throat. He stared Victoria down, searching for the lie, the evasion, the angle.

It wasn't very often that a queen left her face open. She didn't flinch from his examination. Victoria let him see the pain, the uncertainty, and the conviction. The fear for Eddie's happiness, if not his safety. He heard a dim echo of Sandra in this room with him fifteen years ago, asking *is this really what you want?* the night before he left for basic training. He saw it in Victoria's eyes. The steadiness showing him that Eddie's answer was the same as his had been. This was really what he wanted.

"Does he know you're here?" That last piece of him scrambling for independence, to belong to no one and nothing, hoped he did. Hoping he could refuse on the grounds of Eddie's cowardice. But Victoria seemed taken aback, effectively ending his objections on matters of principle.

"Of course not," she said, sounding insulted on her son's behalf at the very notion.

Every muscle in his body screamed for him to go with her, his crooked fingers cramping from the tension. He looked down, trying to force them to open, and saw, as if from a distance, that he was clutching Rivvie's rabbit so tightly one of the flowered ears was in danger of coming loose. He relaxed his hand and rubbed his thumb over the bunny's nose instead.

"He might not want to see me," he said, his voice quiet and small. "I left him."

"Isaac." Sandra walked back into the kitchen, arms crossed. "You have a chance. You're allowed to take it."

He looked between the two women.

Joy and apprehension raced each other through his veins. Something beat at the inside of his chest, his belly, up into his throat. Hope. Instead of wings, it had sledgehammers.

"What do you want me to do?" he asked. "Stand up in Westminster Cathedral and object? Throw myself at his feet and beg him to take me instead?"

"I don't think that will be necessary," Victoria said, looking at him with shrewd cornflower eyes. "We have to get back."

"Right now?"

"You were willing to die for my son. Will you live for him?"

Isaac's back straightened. He didn't have to ask himself if he wanted to be at the eye of the storm with Eddie. It would mean being with Eddie. He already knew.

Through a haze, he heard Victoria and Sandra murmuring in an undertone. Then the Queen was gone.

Rivvie broke the spell, running in and demanding to know what was going on. He hauled her up and handed her the rabbit back. Sandra wiped away a tear with the side of her hand.

"I think I'm going," he said, rubbing the back of his neck, swallowing against a wave of nausea he hadn't even experienced the first time he did a HALO drop from the belly of a cargo plane over the Kazakh mountains.

"I think you are, too." Sandra pulled him in, cradling the back of his head like he was smaller than Rivvie. He held her tight.

"What if he doesn't want me?" he asked, the fear of not being good enough, being wrong, never fitting, overpowering him.

"You're not that lucky," Sandra told him, pulling his head down so that she could kiss his cheek. "I put your dress uniform in the car. This is your *life*, Isaac. Go have an adventure."

29

"Invasions have been carried out with less planning. I mean it, Eddie. I have personally been part of actual invasions that involved less attention to detail than getting the lot of us to Westminster on time."

"Ah, but did their secondary colors coordinate as well?" Eddie watched Arthur pace, check his reflection, pace again. "You're going to put holes in the carpet. Mary loved this carpet."

Arthur stopped. He tried to put his hands in his pockets, but the trousers of his dress uniform only had one, put there specially so that, as best man, he had a place for Gwen's wedding ring. He shook his hands out. "She would have loved this nonsense, wouldn't she?"

"Grandfather too, I think. They liked farces best."

A soft knock at the door distracted them. Peter Masters came in, holding two garment bags with the Dandies & Cads logo on them. The tape measure around his neck was an unusual accessory for his pristine morning suit. Last-minute outfit switching had necessitated an emergency call to Eddie's tailor in the wee hours.

"Good morning, sirs." Peter hung up and unzipped the bags. They each held a different uniform for a colonel in the Irish Guards. For Arthur, the bright red mounted officer's uniform with full complement of gold braid and buttons, the blue riband and star of the Order of the Garter, and Arthur's own campaign medals and RAF wings. For Eddie, a more somber black dress uniform coat that he already had on hand. The overlapping black ribbons and maroon sash emphasized his height. The gold braid draped off one shoulder and the heavily embroidered black collar and deep cuffs made him look, frankly, somewhat dangerous. Relatively, at any rate.

They shrugged the coats on to check the fit. "Peter, you're a wizard." Eddie rolled his shoulders. "What about yours, Arthur?"

"I had no idea we were so close in size." Arthur's valet, MacGregor, and one of Peter's assistants got all the ribbons and buttons situated on the breast of his uniform.

"Pardon my brother," Eddie said. "He's on his way to a nervous breakdown." He adjusted the fall of his cross-belt.

"And you?" Peter fussed over Eddie himself, making sure the hems of the uniform tunic lay evenly, searching for stray threads like his job was in bomb disposal. He was in on the secret. The number of people who knew had ballooned to about twenty by 5:30am for logistical purposes.

"I'm…" Eddie swallowed. "I feel fine, and then light-headed, and then fine again. Sort of numb, maybe? But also like I could fly if I had to. Much better than yesterday. So that's something."

"What are your plans, post ceremony?"

"Arthur and Gwen will lay the groundwork, talk about how in love they were and what fools they were, how amazing it was of me not to stand in the way at the last moment. I'll appear in public looking a bit down, but ultimately cheered up by the happy couple and my lovely niece. Then I'll come out officially

in a couple of months. Don't know how yet. There are possibilities. I haven't ruled out dancing on a bar while singing Cole
Porter." Eddie felt a smile—a real one, for this man who did so
much for him—pulling at his mouth. "I'm terrified."

"If you'll pardon the presumption, I am very happy for
you." Peter straightened, and regarded him with an artist's eye.
"And if I may say—you look better than ever."

"Thank you. I still have that drawing you did last year. Of
the two men at Cannes. I think I'd like to order that suit after
all."

"It would be an honor." Peter cleared his throat. "Now give
us a turn. Both of you."

Eddie and Arthur stood side by side. "We'll do, I think,"
Arthur said.

Another knock at the door. This time it was Malcolm,
looking every inch the proud father at the wedding. He wore
the black and gold uniform of the Blues and Royals, in which
he still technically held the rank of colonel. Ceremonially
representing a household regiment sent the message that he
supported his family above all. The fact that he had been asked
to participate had shocked most royal observers, but the
Communications Office was not commenting at this time.

"Well, aren't we a packet of toy soldiers?" His smile at
them was honest and sly. "Time to go."

Gwen woke up at 7:30am to Maddy and Alex jumping into
bed with her. The shock kept her nerves from hitting until she
was alone in the shower. Surreal to be lathering up and realize
that in a few hours, she would be married to the Prince of
Wales. Only slightly less surreal than knowing at the end of
those same few hours, she would be married to *Arthur*.

After her shower, Gwen pulled on a white satin dressing

gown and went to meet her team. Her hair was dried and styled back off her face in a soft updo at the nape of her neck that wouldn't interfere with her veil or need fiddling with. Makeup was next. Her manicure had survived the previous night intact, which felt like a miracle under the circumstances. Everyone withdrew afterwards to give her a few minutes to herself before her mother arrived with The Gown. She drank a strawberry smoothie, but that was all she could imagine keeping down.

Victoria walked in. "Don't get up," Victoria said. "It's your wedding day."

"I'm not sure I could stand if I tried."

"I know. I thought they were going to have to carry me down the aisle." She brought a black velvet box out from behind her back. "I wanted to give you something."

Gwen opened the box. A pair of tiaras winked up at her, one nested within the other. Delicate gold filigree scrollwork contained clusters of diamonds surrounding gleaming opals. One was sized for an adult, and the other for a child.

"My father and brother had these commissioned for my mother when I was born. To match her engagement ring, of course. We never wore them. Sophie came along and he had the Cartier diamond trio set made. But I have always felt rather sentimental about these. My mother wasn't supposed to have me, you know. Her doctors said it was too dangerous, but Mary carried on. She adored you, and she would have adored Madeline. Father and Edward, too. I think they all would have wanted you to have these. Mum's motto is inside both of them. *For courage, and for love.* I think it suits you both. My gift to you."

"I don't—I don't know what to say. Is it too late to change my hair?"

"You're about to be marry the Prince of Wales and become a Duchess, Gwendolyn. You can do whatever you like." Victoria knelt down in her slacks next to Gwen's chair. "I would be delighted if you and Maddy wore these today. After all, it's not only you becoming a princess. And it's not every day I become a grandmother."

Gwen took a deep breath. "You became a grandmother some years ago."

"I know. It's all right." Victoria shook her head at Gwen's horrified expression. "We'll get it sorted out. We're not the warmest of families, but I believe we could be. If you help us. Give us a chance."

"I will."

"Well, then." Her eyes bright, Victoria brushed at imaginary dust on the legs of her trousers. "I think your mother and her flock of assistants are here to get you into your dress, and I should get changed. I'll see you later."

Gwen's hair stylist returned to sew the tiara into her hair, the last thing to happen before her gown went on.

The dress had two layers, the acres of train held in place by the top layer of sheer silk. Underneath, delicate allover cream-on-cream embroidery on a streamlined princess silhouette held it all together. It was plain, almost severe, except for the buttons that began at her throat, dipped under her right arm and down the center back of the dress, only to curve again around the skirt.

"I think this might be the best thing I've ever made," Joanna said. The slight tremble in her voice pulled Gwen right out of her thoughts. "And I designed a wedding dress for a queen, you know."

"It's a beautiful dress," Gwen said, smoothing her hand down it. "The button detail is incredible, modernizes it—"

"I don't only mean the dress." Joanna stroked the swoop of Gwen's auburn hair. "My lovely daughter."

"Mother—"

"This isn't the time, of course. We both have too much eye makeup on. But I wanted you to know."

Know *what?* Gwen wanted to ask. Mothers were supposed to be comforting at moments like these, not wildly confusing. Obviously, ten minutes before Gwen's wedding to a prince was the perfect time for Joanna to have an emotional crisis. Nothing else was going on.

"I love you, Mum," Gwen offered, guessing that might be the right thing to say. Joanna pulled away, brushing at her sleeves and sniffing loudly, before heading to the sideboard where a light breakfast had been set out. Well, that was one excessively overwrought person beset with unrealistic expectations down for the day. Nineteen hundred to go.

Alex came into the room, holding the skirts of her dress out to the side to shield Maddy from Gwen. Everyone on the far side of the room started cooing.

"Do you want to see the real star of this show, fresh from the hairdresser's?"

"Of course I do." Her voice caught in her throat.

Alex made a big show of whisking her dress away from Maddy, and Gwen gasped. It wasn't at all feigned. Maddy's tea-length white party dress had the same embroidery as Gwen's, and matching buttons all around the hem. Her hair had been dyed back to something like its original color a few weeks ago, for the wedding, and Gwen felt a warm glow pushing back against the terror.

She motioned Maddy over and showed her the tiara. Maddy bit her lip.

"Do you want to wear it? You'll have to be very careful," Gwen told her. Maddy gave her a wide-eyed, utterly feigned look.

"*Really?*"

"Oh, my god, you sarcastic little baggage, come here." Gwen and Maddy maneuvered carefully into a hug, along with their dresses. "Are you scared?"

"No. Well. There's going to be a lot of people."

"I know, sweetheart. I'm scared, too. But we're doing this together, right? And you know you can't disappoint me?"

"Right." Maddy grinned at her. "I can't disappoint you."

"Not ever. You're my star."

While the hair stylist redid Maddy's hair around the smaller version of the tiara, Gwen walked to the open window. She needed some air. She needed to jump and make a run for it into Hyde Park. Become a nun. She was marrying Arthur. *Marrying Arthur.*

When she turned back, Alex was kneeling next to Maddy's chair, making her laugh. Joanna fixed her own makeup in the mirror, talking to Victoria, who had slipped back into the room in a pale blue day dress, adjusting her delicate swoop of a hat. Sophie lounged on the sofa in a smart, expertly tailored morning suit, apparently unconcerned, texting someone. Oddly enough, this was her family. Some of it, anyway.

"Maddy and I need a minute," she said. When they were out in the hall, she thought longingly of pelting down the corridor and away. But she had too much gown on for that. And she was marrying Arthur. The father of her child. Her child, who was currently looking at her, waiting to hear what she had to say.

"Okay, kiddo. Things are going to go a little differently today than we planned…"

THEN IT WAS TIME. They all got word that Arthur and Eddie were off, the first in the parade of royals leaving from Buckingham Palace. Once they were gone, the bridal party went down to the courtyard to get into their cars, all leaving at precisely timed intervals. Victoria got into her own car, accompanied by a man in ceremonial dress blues, with the distinctive beret marking him as a member of the Special Air Service. He flashed her a smile, and Gwen thought she recognized him. But he was gone too quickly for her to be sure.

Her father helped her into the Rolls-Royce and got in the other side. Her hands shook around her bouquet. She could hear the crowd roaring outside the windows—actually roaring —for her. She knew she ought to be waving, but she couldn't seem to move. The wedding couldn't start until she arrived. All the dignitaries and the prime ministers, and representatives of nearly all the royal families left in the world, all the cousins and faces to keep straight and—

"So here's the thing about stars," Lawrence said. Gwen stared at him, disbelieving. It was her wedding day, she was getting married in *minutes* to a *prince*, on *international television*, she didn't have time for one of his—she made herself stop, because this was her father. The man who'd sat with her every time she was sick, every time she cried over a boy or a girl or a bad grade or a disappointment, the one with her in the hospital the night Maddy was born.

"Okay, Dad."

"The iron in our planet—and our bodies—came from a star that exploded billions of years ago. We'll never know which star it was, but we're alive because of it. I knew that intellectually, it's one of those things you know and it amazes you and maybe you make an inspirational graphic out of it and put it up on social media and a million people share it. But I never *understood* it until I held you for the first time." He reached out and tapped her chest right over her collarbone. "And that feeling never went away, kiddo. It never has. I've named about a dozen stars after you, and you shine brighter than all of them."

"That's a physical impossibility," she choked out.

"I don't care." He adjusted her bouquet so the fall of roses was off-center. "Asymmetry is more attractive," he told her.

"How is this real?" she asked him.

"It's real because you make it real. You're my star." He readjusted the fall of her veil, too. She wouldn't change it. Not for anything. "Let's go."

Isaac stepped out of the State Limousine in front of Westminster, and gave the Queen of England a hand out of the car. He walked beside her, half a pace behind and to the left, as the Archbishop of Canterbury greeted her and escorted her down the crimson carpet, past all the wedding guests, to their seats. Walking into Buckingham Palace earlier this morning felt like jumping off a cliff. But that was nothing compared to this. His crash course in protocol for the day had come from the Queen and Sir Anthony. Mostly, he had to stay at her side and say nothing. This suited him.

"Oh, you do clean up beautifully. How are you holding up?" Sophie asked, as soon as he took his seat beside her, behind the Queen. The game of musical chairs that ended with him sitting there had Malcolm in the first row, next to his ex-wife.

"Ma'am, I am fifteen seconds away from a complete nervous breakdown."

"You'll fit right in. Did Vick tell you about your dukedom yet?"

"My what?"

"Think of it as a battlefield promotion," said the Queen. "Now come on, it's starting. Let's try and keep it together for the next hour and a quarter, shall we?"

When all the guests were settled and the bride was poised for arrival, the sign was given. The music swelled. Eddie and

Arthur walked out to take their positions at the front of the Abbey. Neither one of them would look particularly happy on the video, Eddie thought. Or maybe they were both smiling like they had no idea what was going on, also a distinct possibility. The last thing Arthur told him before they set out was, "I'm going to faint, and I can't tell if it's because I'm happy or because I'm terrified," and Eddie couldn't agree more.

As they rounded the turn and saw their family, Arthur inhaled sharply in surprise. Eddie's brain refused to process the scene before him. A man in dress blues sat next to his mother, completely still, his gaze fixed only on Eddie. The stillness called to him, as did his dark hair, smoothed back for the occasion. And when he and Eddie made eye contact, the stillness broke, and half the man's mouth curved up into a smile.

Eddie's feet kept moving, taking him past his mother, who had tears in her eyes as she watched both her sons, and past Isaac, who had just remade the world.

Eddie and Arthur switched places as they walked up the stairs to the altar, and the whole Abbey seemed to take a collective breath. Eddie was officially no longer the groom.

GWEN COULDN'T FEEL her feet. Or her face. Or her hands. Her train dragged against the carpet, a very effective anti-fleeing device for the bride. The fact that she hadn't fallen over or dropped her bouquet was the only evidence she had that her limbs remained in working order. Her face already hurt from smiling, but she was not inclined to stop. The world was a slow-motion blur until the moment she saw Arthur, and everything came into focus, all at once. And maybe that's what being in love is, she thought. Arthur turned to watch her, but his eyes kept flicking to Maddy and Alex, who walked a few steps behind her train, holding hands. He didn't look away until

Gwen stood next to him. Eddie leaned around him to grin at her, and she couldn't help laughing.

The music changed. Nineteen hundred people sang the first hymn with questioning disbelief in their collective voice. The Archbishop of Canterbury gave Arthur and Gwen—and his Sovereign—one last, intent look, and then:

"I was informed earlier this morning, by Prince Edward, that with full hearts and the greatest humility, and with unending gratitude for the support of their family and friends, Prince Edward and Miss Shelton-Leigh have concluded that they are not suited to the holy bonds of matrimony. For which the main reason must be the ultimate happiness of Miss Shelton-Leigh and Arthur, Prince of Wales, who stand before me now. I have spoken to all three of them, and am proud and delighted as ever I have been to say—Dearly Beloved…"

WHEN THE SERVICE ENDED, the newlyweds and family retreated to sign the registers. Knowing that pandemonium waited for them when they reappeared, everyone lingered over their signatures. Arthur felt a tug on his sleeve. He looked down to find Maddy watching him carefully.

"Mum says you're my father, and that she was sorry she lied about today, and that she lied about you being my real father, because she says you are."

Arthur couldn't do much more than nod.

"Mum told me my father was an enchanted prince when I was little. I didn't believe her." She watched him like he had the answers. Like he could make it all right. He wanted to.

Arthur knelt on the flagstones, trying to figure out how to explain, aware he had an audience and that time was running short.

"I know you're probably confused, and maybe a little angry

that we didn't tell you." She nodded. "Listen. Your Mum was right. I was an enchanted prince. I was asleep. You and your mum woke me up. And I promise you can ask us all the questions you want later, but we have to go back out there and ride in the open carriage and smile at everyone now, so please answer me one very important question. Is it all right with you if I'm your father?"

Maddy looked a little shy. "I wanted you to be," she told him, like it was a secret. Arthur thought his heart would burst. "When I met you the first time. I wanted you to be my father."

"So we're a family now?" Arthur asked, straightening up, holding one hand out to Gwen and the other to Maddy. "It's very important that you agree. We can't be one unless you say."

Maddy smiled, and it was like the sun coming out. "Yes. But you can't keep things from me any more. It isn't okay."

"We won't." Gwen bent and hugged Maddy tight, disregarding the fall of her gown.

They processed back into the church in a slightly different configuration. Arthur had picked Maddy up in his arms, and Gwen tucked her hand in the crook of his elbow, and that's how the Prince and new Princess of Wales left Westminster. The crowds outside went wild.

AFTER THE NEWLYWEDS processed out of the chapel, Victoria left the Abbey walking beside the Archbishop, smiling benignly, as if nothing had surprised her today or ever could. Eddie could swear Avi Forrest winked at Victoria as she passed, and Eddie thought he should make a note to ask her about that later. Then he thought perhaps he didn't want to know. Any one of the myriad options was too complicated to think about and promised an instant headache. The original plan had been for Eddie to leave the Abbey escorting Alex, but Malcolm took his daughter's arm for the journey outside.

Eddie was surprised to see Daniel Black, braced on a cane, next to his editor-in-chief. Malcolm and he shared a brief, friendly nod as they went by. There was a dark, hopeful look on Daniel's face as he watched Alex, and her smile froze on her face when she saw him. She flipped him off behind her back, very subtly, as she went by. They were still being recorded, after all. But Daniel bit his lip and grinned, and Alex's step had a lightness to it that Eddie recognized.

Sophie and Rob were firmly arm in arm, and that left Eddie to walk beside Isaac. He couldn't stop staring at Isaac, aware of all the cameras, afraid one might catch him, realizing that perhaps it wouldn't be the worst thing. Standing next to him made Eddie feel like crying. He nearly did when he was ushered into Victoria's open carriage with Alex, and Isaac stepped away.

"Smile, dear," Victoria murmured. "Don't look stricken. He's riding back in the car with your father. You'll see him again in a few minutes."

"Mum, how—?"

"*In a few minutes.*"

The crowd's cheering was all the more powerful for containing a distinct note of bewilderment, though the news must be all over the internet by now. Eddie's heart pounded too loudly for him to hear a thing.

As soon as the carriage pulled out of sight in the courtyard at Buckingham Palace, Victoria took his hands.

"Listen," she said. "He came for you. It's up to you now. If I could give you more time, I would. Believe me, all right? I asked him if he'd come today, and he said yes. I *know* you had plans of martyring yourself to the sound future of this family, but if there is one thing I have learned in my life, it is that all of this is bigger than we are. Bigger than any one person, and it will crush you bodily if you let it, and everyone you love. So if you have a chance at happiness, at being *known*, and loved, then you take it and you hang on as long as you can. You understand me? You take it when it's offered."

THE BALCONY APPEARANCE was noisy as ever, thousands of people in the square below yelling their approval, congratulations, confusion, whatever it was. Eddie stood off to one side with Isaac, who appeared at his side again as soon as his car arrived at Buckingham Palace, and simply wouldn't be moved.

A couple of the people who had been notified of the wedding's change in personnel that morning were higher-ups in the RAF. As it was now Arthur, their undisputed favorite son, getting married, the flyover of Buckingham Palace was much more involved, to the tune of an extra fighter group doing barrel rolls along with the traditional complement of planes. Eddie pressed his hand to the small of Isaac's back when the modern fighter jets thundered overhead, and Isaac startled for a split second, but relaxed into the touch. He looked up at Eddie, grateful and somehow unsure. Eddie wanted to kiss him right there. He held off on it, focusing instead on how Arthur and Gwen looked together with their daughter. Isaac leaned his shoulder against Eddie's. Just slightly, but it meant everything.

Arthur hoisted Maddy up in his arms for the flyover, pointing the planes out to her. After that, everyone but Gwen and Arthur retreated. The roar of the crowd swelled when they kissed.

Afterwards, everyone gathered in the White Drawing Room. That hadn't been in the schedule, but they all needed a chance to get their stories straight before luncheon.

"We need to decide on what we're going to do," Victoria

said. "And we need to decide on it now. I am usually of the opinion that we need to tread lightly, but I'm in a bit of a mood today."

"I'll say," Malcolm said, sitting on the bench in front of the gilded piano that had belonged to Victoria I. "You're positively anarchic."

"All right," Alex said. She leaned against the mantel, took off one of her shoes and brandished it first at one parent, then the other. "That's enough. I don't know what's got into either of you, but I want it to stop, right now."

"Well, that's us told." Malcolm swept his daughter a little bow from the waist.

"I think we should tell the truth," Gwen said.

"You are new here, aren't you," Arthur said, but the sarcasm didn't come through. He couldn't stop beaming at her.

Eddie tugged on his lower lip with his thumb and forefinger. "We've got our plan for the next few weeks sorted out. It's today that's the problem, isn't it? I can go downstairs, make an announcement. Take the heat."

"Absolutely not," Victoria spoke up. "You will not be 'taking the heat.' There will be no heat. If anyone so much as lights a match in your vicinity, I believe I have a standing army on call."

Before he could say anything, she stood up and pressed a button on the telephone nearest her. Sir Anthony came in, followed by the Archbishop of Canterbury and a number of people Eddie only recognized from pictures on Isaac's phone. Rafael Harris came in as well, dressed in a morning suit. Beside Eddie, Isaac froze.

"We have an unprecedented opportunity to give the press an extra kick while they're reeling," Victoria said. "All of this is coming through the palace, through my office. And what we are going to say is that Her Majesty Queen Victoria II is delighted to announce the marriage of her son, Prince Edward of Wales, to Captain Isaac Cole, a highly decorated former member of her armed forces. The ceremony was conducted in Buckingham Palace, with family and a few close friends in attendance, the same day as Prince Arthur's marriage to Gwendolyn Shelton. After the ceremony, also performed by the Archbishop of Canterbury, the happy couple departed before the reception so as not to overshadow the festivities. Photographs and a statement will be forthcoming as soon as they return from their honeymoon. If this is what you want. We can do it right now."

Eddie stared at her. His mouth worked, but no sound came out. She was fearsome. He looked at Isaac, who had the kind of resigned expression on his face a good soldier might if his commanding officer informed him that, due to a clerical error, the camp had to be moved several feet to the left.

"Mum, can… Might we have a minute?" Eddie asked.

"Yes, but don't be long. We have guests."

Eddie took Isaac's hand and dragged him next door. His earlier comment to Arthur about wearing a hole in the carpet taunted him. Fuck the carpet. They had to have another one somewhere, right? Some warehouse of Buckingham Palace-applicable carpets, waiting for their moment to be brought out, when the last one couldn't be fixed any more. Like royalty. Eddie felt like he couldn't be fixed any more, either.

Isaac wasn't talking. The sight of him made Eddie aware of the gaping void that he'd lived with for so many months. As if all the light and all the warmth that Eddie knew how to feel was contained in Isaac, and Eddie borrowed a little at a time.

"You came back."

"Hard not to, when your sovereign shows up on your doorstep at six in the morning and asks you."

"I didn't ask her to, I would *never*—"

"I know."

Eddie knew that Isaac was waiting for him to decide. Isaac

never treated him like a sure thing. Never assumed he was welcome. Isaac didn't have to choose this, the hardest option. Every concern still existed, every contingency against them remained, even now that Isaac had been introduced to the world on Victoria's arm. Some part of Eddie wanted Isaac to make the next move, wanted to be absolved of that much more responsibility. But this was his life, and the man in front of him was the one he loved, and he finally, *finally* had them both in one place.

"You once told me," Eddie said, casting back many years to a conversation before dawn on the bank of a lake in Scotland, "you'd been fighting your whole life. It didn't matter what you were doing, or where. Existing meant constant battle. I never, ever wanted you to think you had to fight to be loved by me. My love was yours—*I* was yours—from the beginning, and I will never forgive myself for making you doubt it."

Isaac took a step nearer. Eddie held up his hands. "Please. Let me say this. Because you're here, and I never thought you would be here again. I don't deserve it. I should have gone after you. I never should have kissed Gwen without talking to you. I should have come out years ago, and taken the hits. I didn't know. But I knew I wanted you. You're all I've wanted since I was eighteen years old."

Isaac's hands were on him. Only his hands, in white cotton gloves, thumbing under his eyes to stop the tears falling. That touch was enough to make Eddie's knees threaten to buckle, even so. "You don't have to—I forgave you for breaking my heart the day I met you. I knew you were going to, that I wouldn't be able to help it. I only have a heart because of you. It's always been yours."

"I don't want you to fight any more," Eddie said. "I want to make things easier for you, that's all I ever, ever wanted. If it's easier for you not to do this I'll understand."

"I went to a royal wedding with your mother, Eddie. I think I've shown my commitment to the cause."

Eddie made a sound. It might have been a laugh. "You did. You have. But what if this is a disaster? What if we can't survive it? What if—"

"I'll go anywhere for you if you believe it. But you have to believe it. You have to see it, because I don't. I don't see the way forward, and I never have. But you? You can imagine it, if you let yourself. And I trust you. I don't know how to walk next to you, instead of behind you. But I'm willing to try. I have to try. I can't walk out on my heart again. You'll have to tell me to go, this time."

"*Never.* You're everything to me. I want to go everywhere we've ever been together again, so I can hold your hand while we're there. Take you home with me every night. Try to make you understand in any way you'll let me. So I can pay attention to you the way you deserve, every minute, instead of hiding it and worrying about goddamned photographers and what people might think. I want them to think exactly what I do— that you're the best, most loyal, fiercest person I have ever known. That you're the only person I can imagine spending the rest of my life with."

Pain in Isaac's face, gouging deep lines on either side of his mouth. "That's not all I am. Not all I've done."

"There is no one else I would rather have with me. And I'll tell you that every morning, if it helps convince you."

Isaac stared at him for a long, long moment. Eddie's entire life was in that moment, trapped in glass, ready to shatter. And then— "I think that's a small price to pay for waking up with you every morning."

The last of the lights came back on in Eddie's heart. He unbuttoned his gloves, tugged them off. Then he did the same to Isaac, fitting their bare hands together. "I can hardly think our way out of this day, much less the rest of our lives. All I *can* imagine with you is forever."

"So imagine forever," Isaac told him. "I have time." He pulled Eddie in. They kissed with the reeling awareness that it wasn't illicit, or fueled by guilt and terror. For the first time, they didn't have to worry about getting caught. They got caught anyway.

There was a brisk rap at the door.

"I love you," Eddie whispered, smiling against Isaac's mouth.

"And I love you."

Sir Anthony poked his head in. "Good, you're still dressed. Her Majesty has left it up to you, Captain, to decide if you would like to join the family. She strongly hopes that you will."

Eddie swallowed. "Mum's one hundred percent behind this, isn't she?"

"I believe that is an understatement. Come along, children."

Eddie didn't let go of Isaac's hand as they walked back to the drawing room. When they entered, it was to find Victoria and Sandra deep in conversation. Isaac's uncle and Arthur were discussing engines, and a little carbon copy of Isaac who had to be his niece was now playing tag with Maddy. Avi Forrest had wandered in, and stood by the piano with Malcolm. The two of them looked for all the world like they were about to break into a rousing chorus of "Well, Did You Evah?"

Isaac brought Eddie over to meet his family.

"Sandra, this is Prince Edward. Eddie, this is the woman who raised me." Sandra looked him up and down, and Eddie hadn't felt so examined in years. She was worse than the popular press and his university lecturers all rolled into one. But she smiled when she saw their linked hands, and nothing could bother him at this moment, anyway.

"You'll be good to my boy?"

"As good as he'll let me."

Isaac flushed along his cheekbones, as if he couldn't handle more than two people wanting good things for him. Eddie held on to him tighter. The tension in Isaac was still there, but a little more of it left when Rafael Harris walked up with Isaac's step-brother.

"You're going to need more than one best man to see you through this, Cole," Harris said.

"That'd... be all right."

Not to be outdone, Arthur, Gwen, and Alex all insisted on standing up for Eddie.

Eddie and Isaac were married by the Archbishop of Canterbury with their family and friends looking on. They promised to love, honor, and keep one another. The rings, hastily retrieved by Alex from Eddie's overnight bag, were both his. As he slid the one he chose for Isaac—with its card suit cutouts—onto his finger, Isaac murmured, "I'm a gambling man, after all." Eddie got so flustered he had to be reminded twice of his next line.

A STRING QUARTET PLAYED VIVALDI. Eddie heard it as he and Isaac snuck out of Buckingham Palace in hastily donned street clothes. Avi Forrest's private plane was waiting at Heathrow to take them to his yacht, currently anchored in the Mediterranean.

"You saved me," Eddie told Isaac, settling against him in the back of the unmarked car. "I didn't want to go to all those parties today. Or, you know, to the rest of my life, without you."

Isaac wrapped an arm around him. Eddie thought his heart might break apart without that steady pressure. "You saved me first."

Eddie reached up, sliding his fingers into Isaac's hair. Closed his eyes as they went around a curve, pressed his lips against the pulse in Isaac's throat. Finally home. Whatever came next, as long as they could hold each other, he wasn't afraid. "I'll save you always."

POSTSCRIPT

I hope you've enjoyed *The Spare*. Visit my website to subscribe to my newsletter and be the first to know about everything Kensington, as well as my upcoming projects and releases!

If you'd like to help *The Spare* get more exposure in these algorithmically weighted times, leaving a review on a retail site is a good way to do that, but telling your friends (if you think they'll like it!) is the best thing you can do.

Read on for a bit of chat about how I created the alternate history and some very sentimental acknowledgments.

Thank you so much for reading.

—Miranda

AHISTORICAL NOTE

The Spare is, technically, alternate history. I wanted to be careful not to change too much, otherwise I would write an entirely different kind of book.

I found the branch point I needed in Prince Albert Victor, Duke of Clarence and Avondale, Edward VII's eldest son, who died in an influenza epidemic in early 1892. His family nickname was Eddy. Rumors surrounding the real-life Eddy's sexual orientation and escapades were used as weapons against him and his family throughout his life, especially in the wake of a police raid in 1889 that targeted a brothel catering to, and staffed by, men. While Eddy hadn't been at the brothel, and was never named by anyone who worked there, rumors that he was involved persisted in his social circle and throughout history.

About his sexuality, as with so many historical figures, there is no way to know. It is clear from his personal papers that Eddy had very strong feelings for a number of women throughout his life. In 1890, he and Princess Hélène of Orleans desperately wanted to marry, but they couldn't finagle permission from both Queen Victoria and Helene's father. As gently as I could, I let him live, and let them marry in 1891.

If anyone is curious, he ascended the throne on Edward VII's death in 1910, and was a steady presence through constitutional crisis and World War I until his own death in the 1918 influenza epidemic.

I have relied on the inexorable grind of the twentieth century to do its grim work and carry history along no matter who resides at Buckingham and Windsor. I left the decline of the constitutional power of the monarchy intact, even without Edward VIII and his abdication. In my world, Eddy and Helene's oldest son, Victor I, was more militantly anti-fascist and martial towards Germany in the 1930s, and Neville Chamberlain's government sought to limit the monarch's constitutional power in order to prevent the King from committing England to anything they thought would be disastrous, and to force the monarchy into a more politically neutral role. When the government changed, Victor and Churchill got along very well.

There are very few differences between the world of *The Spare* and our own besides the change in the main line of the Royal Family, and this is by design. There are a few technical differences in the various Acts of Succession, including one very decorously put through during WWII because of the Prince of Wales's wartime courtship with the woman who later became his wife, that children of royal blood who are conceived before their parents are married are still eligible to inherit the throne.

In more modern news, the skeleton of *The Spare* was finalized before Brexit ever came to a vote, and I decided to let that be. I had to edit out most of the parliamentary politics that existed in earlier drafts due to length considerations. While Brexit may still happen in the world of *The Spare*, it has not yet come to a vote or a serious public campaign.

There is a great deal of information available about the way the real royal family's life works, but it's all necessarily specific to how the Windsors have chosen to articulate and organize their power since the end of World War II, and especially since Elizabeth II ascended the throne.

Because so many of the decisions that the Windsors made were based in their own personalities and preferences, I gave the imaginary Kensingtons similar free rein (or reign, if you will) in ordering their own lives for the last one hundred-plus years. Staffing, organizational structure, scheduling, finances, I did some cursory research and then made the rest up. I was striving for plausible inaccuracy.

Nowhere is that more true than in how royal security actually works. I had no interest in getting it exactly right. It just had to be, in broad strokes, believable. I am making no claims to procedure. Nor, to my knowledge, is there a secret staircase in the Royal Opera House.

ACKNOWLEDGMENTS

This book would not exist without Dr. Elaine Savory, who told me very sternly ten years ago that I would have to stop sympathizing with the emotional problems of British aristocrats if I was ever to truly understand Jane Austen. I did try. But I was not, as you can see, completely successful.

For invaluable support, enthusiasm, and help with the tailoring, Luke Reynolds deserves all the hand-knit sweaters. Any errors or misplaced buttons are mine. Sarah Rees Brennan read the original draft of the first seventeen thousand words and did not advise that I immediately hurl my laptop into the sea, for which I am eternally grateful. Kaila Stolar gave feedback on a later, much longer draft, she's a hero. Brina Starler has been endlessly enthusiastic and supportive. Jaida Jones yelled with me about the vicissitudes of fate and publishing, and at me every time one of the characters was upset. (There was a lot of yelling.) Cat Sebastian was encouraging and kind at precisely the right moments, and introduced me to Bran Cedio of Crowglass Design, who is responsible for the amazing cover. Rose Lerner and Olivia Dade were generous with advice as I embarked on publishing this book myself, and I am so grateful for their help. All my love.

To all the friends who fielded middle-of-the-night emails and frantic messages about what goes on in the middle of a book anyway, about writer anxiety and insecurity and plot problems, thank you. You know who you are. To all the writers on Twitter who have been free with information, help, cheerleading, and liberal use of the heart emoji, we are all in this together and I appreciate you so much.

This book would not exist without my parents. My incredible, ever-supportive parents, Judy Ruderman and Robert Dubner, who have championed me in every possible way for my entire life. My mother brought her incredible editing skills to this novel through countless conversations about structure and theme, and three full line edits on different drafts. My father has been a constant source of morale throughout this entire process, and has never stopped believing that writing is the best thing I can be doing with my time. This book is for both of you, and it's only the beginning.

This book took almost five years to appear in the world, from the first day I sat in the Argo Tea on 26th Street and 7th Avenue and banged out a 1600-word outline in an hour and ten minutes, to the day I pressed "Publish" across several major ebook platforms and sent it out officially. That's also about as long as I've been with my partner. Ellis Amity Light, you are everything to me. If not for you, I wouldn't know enough about love to write an entire book about it.

And to you, dear reader, who has come this far. Thank you.

ABOUT THE AUTHOR

Miranda Dubner is a writer, textile artist, and freelance editor. She lives in the Hudson Valley with her family. *The Spare* is her first book. (More accurately, *The Spare* is the first book that she's letting anyone else see.)

Visit mirandadubner.com to be kept updated on further Kensington adventures, and on Miranda's upcoming work.

twitter.com/writingmiranda

instagram.com/writingmiranda